BOOKS BY JOHN O'HARA

Appointment in Samarra
The Doctor's Son and Other Stories
Butterfield 8
Hope of Heaven
Files on Parade
Pal Joey
Pipe Night
Hellbox
A Rage to Live
The Farmers Hotel
Sweet and Sour
Ten North Frederick
A Family Party
Selected Short Stories
From the Terrace
Ourselves to Know

Sermons and Soda-Water: Three Novellas
The Girl on the Baggage Truck
Imagine Kissing Pete
We're Friends Again

Five Plays
The Farmers Hotel
The Searching Sun
The Champagne Pony
Veronique
The Way It Was

Assembly
The Big Laugh
The Cape Cod Lighter

BOOKS BY JOHN O'HARA

Appointment in Samarra
The Doctor's Son and Other Stories
Butterfield 8
Hope of Heaven
Files on Parade
Pal Joey
Pipe Night
Hellbox
A Rage to Live
The Farmers Hotel
Sweet and Sour
Ten North Frederick
A Family Party
Selected Short Stories
From the Terrace
Ourselves to Know

Sermons and Soda-Water: A Trilogy
    The Girl on the Baggage Truck
    Imagine Kissing Pete
    We're Friends Again

Five Plays:
    The Farmers Hotel
    The Searching Sun
    The Champagne Pool
    Veronique
    The Way It Was

Assembly
The Big Laugh
The Cape Cod Lighter

The Cape Cod Lighter

JOHN O'HARA

THE CAPE COD LIGHTER

RANDOM HOUSE · NEW YORK

FOREWORD

The modern attacks on the novel as a moribund art form have spread out a little to take in all fiction, and they are more interesting for their vehemence than for the literary accomplishments of the people who insist that fiction is passé. Shortly after Ernest Hemingway died, a man whom I shall call Monk Lovechild declared that Hemingway and all other first-class writers of fiction might just as well abandon creative writing and turn to journalism. Mr. Lovechild almost made it appear that Hemingway shared his view. It was a very tricky performance on the part of Love-child; the only trouble was that Hemingway was on record, about five years before his death, with an antipodally opposite statement to the effect that fiction writers ought to *stay out of journalism*. There was nothing equivocal about Hemingway's statement; you could not mistake his intent. But after he was dead his characteristically forthright opinion was completely ignored, or rejected, by Mr. Lovechild. Abraham Lincoln, of course, is on record with a speech which can be quoted to support the thesis that he was not opposed to slavery. That's one of those things that come back to embarrass the memory of the great, like certain well-intentioned remarks made by Woodrow Wilson and Franklin D. Roosevelt and Herbert Hoover. In this case, however, Hemingway said one thing, and Mr. Lovechild pretended that Hemingway had said something else. It so happens that on a previous occasion Mr. Lovechild had taken out of its context something *I* had said, and used it to hold me up to scorn, so I was familiar with the Lovechild technique. Mr. Lovechild, who I hardly need say is a journalist, not a fiction writer, once described a stroll he took on a main thoroughfare of a Western city. He told of looking at a certain building while on this walk, and the only trouble *there* was that you can't see that building from that street. I suppose Mr. Lovechild would call himself a creative journalist, which still does not excuse his tin ear when he is reporting dialog.

Why bother so much about a man for whom I have no respect? Well, for two reasons: Mr. Lovechild has a good job on an important publication, and a lot of readers assume that what he says must be true; and, in spite of his proclaimed aversion to fiction, he has used a personal relationship directly to influence the awarding of a major literary prize for a novel that did not deserve it. Without proof, I nevertheless have not the slightest doubt that this fellow Lovechild has written novels that were no good, and it is people like him that have been attacking the novel and, more recently, all fiction.

I don't think anyone would deny at this late date that the most consistently abusive criticism of fiction books appears in the newsmagazines. Week after week, year after year, the resentfully anonymous reviewers on these publications behave like little bullies, insulting men and women of talent and discouraging men and women of promise. But who are these reviewers, and what's the matter with them? Well, here I have special knowledge. I have worked on *Time* and *Newsweek*, and inevitably through the years I have picked up information about the background of their book department personnel. Invariably they majored in English in college, wrote for their college literary publications, and "tried to write" after graduation. In junior year they say, in a tone of surly apprehension, "I think I'll try to write." And so they send their little pieces to *The New Yorker* and, second time around, to the literary magazines; and when they are defeated by what they call the *New Yorker* formula, they try the novel. In the Thirties they wrote their own versions of *Appointment in Samarra;* in the Fifties their successors had a try at *The Catcher in the Rye;* and now, I guess, the successors of the successors are busy with the writings of John Updike. Fortunately for me, *Appointment in Samarra* had already been published; fortunately for J. D. Salinger, he had published *The Catcher in the Rye;* unfortunately for those young men who thought the novel looked so easy, they had to take those jobs on the newsmagazines.

If they didn't go to work for *Time* or *Newsweek,* they got jobs on *The New Yorker* or in publishing houses, or they became teachers. In other words, it might be said that there is a pool of unsuccessful writers of fiction who are all too readily available for occasional book reviews. With their background it is not surprising that there is so much spiteful condescension in the pieces they write for the Sunday supplements. (I never see the little magazines so I don't know what the hell goes on there, but I can guess.)

But now they have a Cause. The exciting word is getting around that not only the novel, but all fiction, must go. Not go-go-go; just go. Mind you, there are a few favorites who can still get under the wire. Certain crude efforts of certain novelists, short story writers, and poets, which could not be put aside without politico-social repercussions, will get the nod. But the exceptions are being made for writers who in general have pretty much the same stories to tell, and they would not in any event have done much to support the cause of creative writing. The writers for whom the exceptions are being made will shortly be found in that pool I mentioned earlier.

It is not seismologically disturbing to find, among the New Enemies of Fiction, a man whom I shall call Tootsie

Washburn. (You'd be amazed to learn how easy it is to make up these names.) Years ago, in my drinking days, Tootsie became a patron of a saloon that had been a favorite of mine long before Tootsie had been given a job in the lowest form of critical enterprise, namely, radio and television reviewing. Night after night Tootsie would engage me in conversation about the novel; the novel in general, and the novel that he in particular was writing. That was about seventeen years ago, and Tootsie's novel has yet to be published. He *may* have put it aside to work on the play he announced for production two or three years ago but that so far has not been produced. He may have decided to withdraw his *play* in order to better his chances of getting a certain drama critic's job, but he didn't get that either. He seems to be having more success in making a play for the Elsa Maxwell set, which is exactly where he belongs, but he still finds time to devote himself to the Cause of the N. E. of F. Thirty-two years ago *I* wrote a radio column under the byline Franey Delaney, although I didn't own a radio; but that didn't keep me from admiring successful novelists, playwrights, and short story writers. I suppose it's true that if you really admire creative writers you're much more tolerant of their success, and in spite of all his early humility and compliments, Tootsie Washburn never quite convinced me that he was a sincere fan. Of course I could be wrong there.

In my extremely impressionable youth, when I read everything from *Miss Minerva and William Green Hill* to *Memories of the Kaiser's Court,* I came upon a squelcher that I remember without being able to recall where I saw it. A noble lady, putting some jerk in his place, said: "Your insolence can never hope to reach the height of my disdain." It became so popular in our crowd that all one of us had to do was say, "Your insolence—" and the others would finish the quotation, in chorus. When you are eighteen a crusher like that comes in handy. I bring that up now because some of my friends, and others, wonder why I bother to reply to my critics. Well, as a rule I don't. Apart from the enormous work that would be involved in replying to all of them, it is usually a wasted effort. But I am neither a noble lady nor a noble anything, in spite of the O'Hara claims to royal Irish blood, and I haven't got the dignity to carry off a crusher like "Your insolence, etc." Fighting back at critics, like fighting cops, is a losing proposition from the start and I know it. I knew it on the two or three occasions when I tangled with law enforcement. But I have a long record of defeats of one sort or another, and so I cannot, even in my mellowing late fifties, resist speaking up every two or three years. It seems to me that if we novelists and short story writers and playwrights don't speak up, we deserve to lose out to the unimaginative. If we chicken out in dignified silence we don't even have the fun of making the dullards' victory just a little harder to come by. My own position is a curiously enviable one, and I make no boast of bravery, since I probably have taken more abuse than any of my contemporaries and all I can get is more of the same. Nor is it good enough to say that we fiction people ought to let our work speak for itself, without stooping to literary brawls.

Foreword

What happened to all those pious protests against conformism and the climate of fear?

Come on, you fiction writers and fiction readers. Up our Cause! Have some fun—and don't think this hasn't been.

JOHN O'HARA

Princeton, New Jersey
Spring 1962

CONTENTS

The Cape Cod Lighter

The Cape Cod Lighter

APPEARANCES

Howard Ambrie stopped the car at the porte-cochere to let his wife out, then proceeded to the garage. The M-G was already there, the left-hand door was open, and the overhead lamp was burning, indicating that their daughter was home. Ambrie put the sedan in its customary place, snapped out the light, rang down the door, and walked slowly toward the house. He stopped midway and looked at the sky. The moon was high and plain, the stars were abundant.

In the kitchen his wife had poured him a glass of milk, which rested on the table with a piece of sponge cake. "I'll be able to play tomorrow after all," said Howard Ambrie. "There's hardly a cloud in the sky."

"Oh, then you've thought it over," said Lois Ambrie.

"Thought what over?"

"Jack Hill's funeral. You're not going."

"Was I thinking it over?"

"You said at dinner that you hadn't decided whether to go or not," said Lois Ambrie.

"That was only because I knew the McIvers planned to go."

"I don't understand your reasoning," she said.

"Well, then I'll explain it to you. Peter and Cathy *want* to go to the funeral. I don't. No reason why I should. But

I didn't want to inflict my *not* wanting to go on their *wanting* to go. Impose, I guess, would be a better word. Influence them. Or for that matter, take away their pleasure in going to the service. I said I hadn't made up my mind, and so there was no discussion about it. If I'd said I definitely wasn't going, or if I'd definitely said I wasn't going, they would have wanted to know why."

"What would you have told them?"

"What would I have told them? I'd have told them that I'd much rather play golf tomorrow."

"Well, that would have started a discussion, all right," she said.

"I know it would," he said. "And I know what the discussion would have been. Wasn't Jack Hill one of my best friends? Couldn't I play golf after the service? And so forth. But I disposed of all that by simply saying I hadn't made up my mind."

"You disposed of it as far as the McIvers were concerned, but will you tell *me* why you're not going?"

"I don't mind telling you. In the first place, I've never considered Jack Hill one of my best friends. He wasn't. He was a lifelong acquaintance, a contemporary, our families were always friends, or friendly. And if you wanted to stretch a point, we were related. All of which you know. But in a town this size, at least until just before the War, damn near everybody is related in some way or other."

"Yes, and damn near everybody will be at that funeral tomorrow," she said. "Therefore your absence will be noticed."

"Maybe it will. I thought of that. But the fact is, I never liked Jack and he never liked me. If the circumstances were reversed, I'm sure he'd be playing golf tomorrow. There won't be many more days we can play this year. I noticed driving by this afternoon, they've taken the pins out of the cups, and I wouldn't be surprised if they filled in the holes. The golf shop is boarded up for the winter. In fact, Charley closed up a week ago and went to Florida. I hope there's enough hot water for a shower. I hate to come in after playing golf in this weather and find no hot water."

"You're playing in the morning," she said.

"Playing in the morning. We're meeting at ten o'clock, playing eighteen holes. Having something to eat. Probably the usual club sandwiches. And then playing bridge. I'll be home around five, I should think."

"Who are you playing with?"

"Same three I play with every Saturday, and they won't be missed at Jack's funeral."

"No, they certainly won't be. None of Jack's old friends, and none of your old friends, either, not in that foursome."

"Lois, you talk as though the whole of Suffolk County were going to be at the church tomorrow, checking to see who stayed away. Are *you* going to the funeral?"

"Yes, I'm going. Or I was. I don't know whether I want to go without you."

"Oh, hell, call up somebody and go with *them*."

"No, if you're not going, I won't. That would make your not going so much more noticeable. 'Where's Howard?' 'Playing golf.' "

"Listen, I'm not going, so don't try to persuade me."

"I think you ought to go," she said.

"No."

"I'll make one more try. I'm *asking* you to go," she said.

"And my answer is I think you're being God damn unreasonable about this. Jack Hill and I have known each other over fifty years, we were thrown together by age and financial circumstances. His family and my family had about the same amount of dough. But when we got older and could choose our friends, he never chose me and I never chose him. We were never enemies, but maybe if we had been we'd have found out why we didn't like each other. Then maybe we could have been friends. But we never had any serious quarrel. We never had a God damn thing."

"He was an usher at our wedding."

"I *knew* you'd bring that up. That was twenty-five years ago, and I had to have him and he had to have me because our parents were friends. It was one of those automatic things in a small town. I couldn't ask one of the clammers, and he couldn't ask one of the potato farmers, but that's *all* it was. And since you bring that up, about being ushers, Celia didn't ask me to be a pallbearer or whatever the hell she's having. Celia has more sense about this than you have."

"There aren't going to be any pallbearers, and you know it."

"All right, I do know it. And she's very sensible, Celia."

"I'm asking you again, Howard, please. Put off your golf till after lunch, and go to this funeral with me. It isn't much to ask."

"Why do you care so much whether I go or not?"

"Because I don't want Celia knowing that you stayed away."

"Oh, Christ. All right. Although why you care what Celia knows or doesn't know—you and Celia were never that good friends."

"But you will go?"

"Yes, I said I would, and I will. But you certainly screwed up my weekend."

(6)

"You can play in the afternoon and Sunday."

"Father O'Sullivan can't play Saturday afternoon, he has to hear confessions, and he can't play Sunday at all. And Joe Bushmill is going skeet-shooting this Sunday. It's not only my schedule you loused up."

"I'm sorry about that, Howard, but I do appreciate it."

"Oh, sure. You have no idea how you complicate things. We had to get a fourth for bridge, because O'Sullivan has to be in church at three o'clock. And now they'll have to get someone to take my place at golf *and* bridge."

"I'll do something for you sometime."

"Why didn't you make your big pitch before tonight?"

"Because I took for granted that you'd be going to the funeral. I just took it for granted."

"I suppose the same way that people took for granted that Jack Hill was a friend of mine. Well, he wasn't. I'm going to bed. Oh, Amy's home. The M-G's in the garage."

"I know. Goodnight, dear."

"Goodnight," he said. He bent down and kissed her cheek.

Light showed on the floor beneath Amy's bedroom door, and he knocked gently. "Amy? You awake?" he said softly.

"Father? Come in."

She was sitting up in bed, and when he entered she took off her reading glasses. "Hi," she said.

"What are you reading?" he said.

"Detective story. Who won?"

"Oh, your mother and I took them. We always do, at their house, and they usually win when they come here." He sat on the chaise-longue. "As Mr. McCaffery says, what kind of a day's it been today?"

"Fridays are always easier than other days. The children seem to behave better on Friday. That is, their behavior is better, probably because they're in a better mood. Their schoolwork isn't as good, but you can't have everything."

"Do you like teaching?"

"Not very much, but I like the children."

"Well, it's nice having you home for a year."

"Thank you, Father. It's nice being home."

"Is it?" he said.

"Have a cigarette?" She held up a package.

"No thanks. You didn't answer my question."

"I know I didn't. Yes, it's nice being home."

"But that's as far as you'll commit yourself?" he said.

"That's as far as I want to commit myself."

"You mean you don't want to think more deeply than that?"

"Yes, I guess that's what I mean. I'm comfortable here, I have my job, my car to run around in, and I had no idea we had so many detective stories. This one was copyrighted 1924."

"There are some older than that, early Mary Roberts Rinehart," he said. "Believe I will have one of your cigarettes." He caught the pack she tossed him and lit a cigarette. "Are you making any plans for next year?"

"Not exactly. I may get married again. I may not."

"This time you ought to have children right away."

"It wouldn't be so good if I had a child now, would it?"

"It might have kept you together, Amy, a child. We had you the first year, your mother and I."

"Father, you're practically implying that if you hadn't had me—"

"I know what I'm implying," he said. "And I know you're no fool. You know it's often been touch and go with your mother and I. You've seen that."

"I guess it is with everybody. But a child wouldn't have kept Dave and me together. Nothing would."

"Well, what really separated you?"

"Well, it wasn't his fault. I fell in love with someone else."

"The man you're thinking of marrying?"

"No."

"The man you're thinking of marrying is that doctor in Greenport?"

"Yes."

"But the man you left Dave for was someone else?"

"Yes."

"And what's happened to him? He's gone out of your life?"

She looked at him sharply. "Yes."

"Why? Was he married?"

"Yes."

"Where did you know him? At Cornell?"

"No, Father. And don't ask me any more questions, please. You voluntarily said you wouldn't ask me any questions, you promised that when I came home after my divorce."

"I did, but with the understanding that when you were ready to tell us, you would. It isn't just idle curiosity, Amy. Your mother and I have a right to know those things, if only to keep you from making the same mistakes all over again."

"I won't make that mistake over again. And I'm not ready to tell you what happened to me with Dave."

"As far as I know, Dave was a hell of a nice boy."

"He was, and is, but I wasn't a hell of a nice girl. No father likes to face that fact about his daughter, but there it is."

"You're not a tart, you're not a chippy."

"No. But that's not all there is besides virgins, Father."

"Oh, I know that."

"Well, when does a girl get to be a tart in your estimation? Is it a question of how many men she sleeps with?"

"It most certainly is, yes."

"How many?"

"Yes, I walked into that one, didn't I? Well, a girl who sleeps with more than two men before she gets married, she's on her way. I can see a girl having an affair the first time she thinks she's in love. And then the second time, when she's more apt to be really in love. But the next time she'd better be damned sure, or she's going to be a pushover for everybody."

"Well—that's more or less my record. The second time was also the man I left Dave for."

"Oh, you had an affair and married Dave and continued to have this other affair?"

"Yes."

"What's going to prevent your having an affair with this same guy after you marry your doctor? . . . You had an affair with a married man before you married Dave. He sounds like a real son of a bitch."

"I guess maybe he was, although I didn't think so. I guess he was, though."

"You're not still seeing him?"

"No. I did after I divorced Dave, but not after I began dating the doctor."

"You're—to use an old-fashioned word—faithful to the doctor?"

"Oh, you're so smart, Father. You've tricked me into admitting I'm having an affair with the doctor. The answer is yes."

"Hell, I knew you were probably having an affair with the doctor. I'm no fool, either, you know. Well, it's been a very interesting conversation between father and daughter.

It's a good thing I'm not *my* father, or you'd be—well, you wouldn't be here."

"No, but we wouldn't have had this conversation, either."

"You have a point. Goodnight, dear." He kissed her cheek and she squeezed his hand. "There *is* that," he said. "We wouldn't have had this conversation. Goodnight again."

"Goodnight, Father," she said.

The girl sat in her bed, holding her glasses loosely with her right hand, her book with her left, both hands lying on the pink comforter. Her mother came in. "What was that all about?" said Lois Ambrie.

"Our conversation? Oh, mostly about Dave and me."

"He didn't say anything about Jack Hill?"

"No."

"I'll be glad when Jack is buried and out of the way."

"I know," said Amy.

"Your father is getting closer to the truth, Amy."

"I guess he is."

"I had a very difficult time persuading him to go to the funeral tomorrow."

"Why did you bother?"

"Appearances. 'Why didn't Howard Ambrie go to Jack Hill's funeral?' They'd be talking about that for a month, and somebody'd be sure to say something to Celia. And then Celia'd start asking herself questions."

"I wonder. I think Mrs. Hill stopped asking questions a long time ago. She should have. I wasn't the only one he played around with."

"You can be so casual about it. 'Played around with.' And you haven't shown the slightest feeling about him, his dying."

"I didn't show any because I haven't got any. Other

than relief. I'm not grief-stricken that he died, Mother. As long as he was alive I was afraid to marry Joe. Now I think I can marry Joe and settle down in Greenport and be what I always wanted to be. But not while Jack was alive. That's the effect he had on me."

"He was no good," said Lois Ambrie. "Strange how your father knew that without knowing why."

"I know why," said Amy. "Jack was the kind of man that husbands are naturally suspicious of. Father was afraid Jack would make a play for you. Instead he made a play for me, but Father never gave that a thought."

"I suppose so. And in your father's eyes it would be just as bad for me to cover up for you as it would have been for me to have had an affair with Jack. I'll be glad when he's out of the way. Really glad when you can marry Joe."

"Did you go over and call on Mrs. Hill?"

"I went over this afternoon, but she wasn't seeing anyone. Fortunately."

"She *is* grief-stricken?"

"I don't think it's that. No, I don't think it's that. As you said a moment ago, Celia probably stopped asking questions a long time ago. I'd put it another way. That she's known for years about Jack. Now she doesn't want to see anybody because whatever she's feeling, she doesn't want anybody to see *her*. Grief, or relief. Maybe she doesn't even know yet what she feels. Fear, maybe. Whatever he was, she stuck with him all those years, and suddenly he's gone and she's fifty-two or -three. I don't know what's in Celia's mind, but I'm glad I'm not her. Did you see Joe tonight?"

"Yes, I had dinner with him. We had dinner at his sister's house in Southold. Spaghetti. She's a very good cook."

oner, and he was usually the murderer. If they did not he right man it was because the guilty party had had to hop a coal train and get out of town. The only outrs who were tolerated in the Gravel Hole were Father glielmo, the pastor, and Dr. Malloy, who spoke Italian, t even Dr. Malloy carried a gun. Other outsiders who had siness in the Gravel Hole would have to wait on the steps the Bucket of Blood, and sometimes that was as far as hey got.

That was the original Bucket of Blood, and to give the name to Jay's place was rather unfair, although not entirely so. Jay's offered whiskey, beer, and, in the winter, a place to come in out of the cold. You could not get a sandwich at Jay's; the only edibles were bowls of salted peanuts on the bar and on the tables in the two back rooms. Jay had an alarm clock on the back bar and on the wall a large Pennsylvania Railroad calendar, showing a passenger train coming out of the Horseshoe Curve. Otherwise the saloon was devoid of decoration; there was no name on the windows, not even a ladies' entrance sign on the side door.

The neighborhood was as rough as any in town except the Gravel Hole. Within two blocks were four whorehouses, all owned by the same unmarried couple but differing in price and clientele and in the youth and beauty and cleanliness of the staff. The tracks of the Reading Railway ran parallel with the street, behind a fence which was broken by gates opening for spurs of track that led into warehouses and lumber yards. There were two blacksmith shops and half a dozen garages in the neighborhood, an old factory that was used as a drop by the beer mob, and such small businesses as a welder's shop, the shop of a man who repaired band instruments, a tinsmith's, a plumber's, and the headquarters of other artisans who had to make a lot of noise by day and

"That will be quite something, an Ambrie marrying an Italian boy. Will you have to turn Catholic?"

"I will if he wants me to. If it means that much to him. I'm not sure it does, but it would probably make a difference to his family."

"Can he marry a divorced woman? I have no idea what the Catholic church says on that."

"We haven't discussed it, so I don't know either."

"Your father's great friends with the new Catholic priest, O'Sullivan. They play golf and bridge together every Saturday."

"So I gather. When the time comes, whatever they say I'll do."

"It would be quite a feather in their cap, an Ambrie turning Catholic."

"They may not see it that way. I understand they can be very tough about some things."

"Well, I suppose it's their turn. Goodness knows I still can't get used to the idea of having one in the White House. Can I get you a glass of milk or anything?"

"No thanks, Mother."

"Then I guess I'll be off to bed."

"Mother?"

"What?"

"I'm sorry I caused you and Father so much trouble. You especially. All those lies you had to tell."

"Oh, that's all right. It's over now. And it was really harder on your father. He never knew why he didn't like that man."

"And *you* couldn't tell him, *could* you, Mother?"

"What?"

"Oh, Mother."

Lois Ambrie looked at her daughter. "Is that another

detective story you're reading? You mustn't get carried away, Amy." She smiled. "Goodnight, dear," she said, and closed the door.

THE BUCKET
OF BLOOD

The place had several nicknames before J
it more or less permanently became Jay's. O
known as the Bucket of Blood, a name that d
cause it was not really all that tough, and bec
ready was another Bucket of Blood in another
that deserved that name. The original, genuine
Blood was in one of the Italian sections of town, a
hood known as the Gravel Hole, that was entirely p
by the families of day laborers who worked on th
gangs for the railroads. They were miserably poor, s
by the Italian grocers and fruiterers and barbers and
blers, and so feared by the town police that they ign
everything that went on in the Gravel Hole. "Let them se
it among themselves," was the attitude. When there was
Black Hand War, which would break out every two or thre
years, and word of a homicide would leak out of the Grave
Hole, the town police would notify the State Constabulary,
who were good cops and among whom were men who spoke
Italian, some of whom were themselves Italian. The staties
would put on civilian clothes and drive to the Bucket of
Blood, which was the first building at the north end of the
Gravel Hole and considered to be the deadline for outsiders.
In a couple of hours the staties would usually come out with

went home quietly at night. No one had any legitimate business in Jay's neighborhood after seven in the evening, and the municipality spent very little money in lighting up the area. When darkness came the visitors to the neighborhood were there to drink or hire a woman, or both, and if they could have paid for better whiskey or better women, they would have been some place else. Nevertheless Jay managed to keep out of serious trouble.

He began by letting it be quickly known that he gave good value. He would explain how he cut his booze to anyone who asked, and he made a point of calling it booze in the aggregate and an individual drink he called a steam. Alcohol, caramel, and water were the principal ingredients of his booze, and he charged twenty-five cents for a shot in a two-ounce glass that he filled to the brim. He drank it himself out of the same bottle he poured for the customers, and he drank moderately but steadily all night long. "The party I get my white from, my alcohol, he knows I drink it myself," he often said. "If he wants me to stay in business, he gotta give me good stuff." The house bought generously; if two men were drinking together, the house bought every third round; if there were six at a table in the back room, the house bought the seventh drink. Nearly everyone could establish credit after a third or fourth visit to Jay's, and he would carry a heavy drinker even though he knew the customer had exhausted his credit elsewhere. But he made no effort to hide his preference for booze drinkers over the customers who drank beer. "I can't help it if the beer comes to me with ether in it. That's the way it comes. I'd have to charge a man a half a check for a good glass of beer, supposing I could get it in the first place. I bet you if you went to every joint in town right now, this minute, you wouldn't be able to find a barrel of real beer. Maybe the Elks. I understand they get delivery, but you have to be an Elk or with an Elk. I'm talking about where an ordinary fellow can go in and order a glass of beer, pay ten, fifteen cents for it. What they do at the breweries, they make good beer, then they take the alcohol out of it to stay out of trouble with the law. Then they get word that it's okay to make a shipment, and they quick needle it with ether. So a man comes in my place and drinks ten or fifteen beers and he's putting away a lot of ether. Bad for the disposition. I get more trouble out of my beer drinkers than I do out of my booze drinkers. They get sleepy and they try to stay awake and all they get is disagreeable. I'll tell you something else. Nine times out of ten a man don't know the difference between near beer and good beer. Nine times out of ten. If they want the taste of beer, they ought to drink Bevo. If they want a belt out of it, they ought to drink a boilermaker. I don't make a nickel out of my beer drinkers, but I have to accommodate them. Most of them don't have no place else to go, and I can't be so choosy."

Jay was *formal* with his beer trade. He gave them no cause for complaint; he was polite to them, and he would listen, hear them out, when they tried to hold him with conversation; but when he bought them a beer he would not drink with them, and when they tried to buy him a beer he would say, "That's all right," or "No thanks, it bloats me." But he would drink steam after steam with his booze customers, and he was such a little man to have that capacity. He was in his middle thirties, but already the upper half of his thin little face was shaded blue and his eyes were teary. He would lift a shot glass, take a breath, knock back the liquor, stare straight ahead as it went down, take another breath, and plunge the glass in the rinsing tank. He never said so, but he wanted and needed every drink. He seemed grateful for the company of booze drinkers, and he was; he had a personal superstition against taking a drink by himself. He respected solitary drinking in others; that was how some men preferred to drink. But he knew that he was in control of his own drinking only so long as he could make a rule about it and stick to it. The booze was there, gallons of it, and one little nip more or less would not do him any harm, but if it meant breaking his rule it could be, would be, the sign that he had lost control, and no one had ever seen him in that condition. Well, no one in this town.

Jay's last name, Detweiler, was fairly common in the town. There was a Detweiler a butcher in the west end of town; Detweiler Brothers had a furniture store and undertaking parlor on the main drag, out of the high-rent district; Clara Detweiler taught French in the public high school; Billy Detweiler had had half a season at third base with Reading, in the International League, before breaking his leg; Isaac Detweiler was janitor and night watchman of the Citizens Bank, a former fifer with the Spanish-American War Veterans Fife & Drum Corps. There had been Detweilers in the town for seventy-five years, and they had paid their bills and minded their own business, attended the Lutheran or the Reformed church, and they were respected. Jay had no idea of their existence when he arrived in town, nor had he had any intention of getting off the train. He was on his way to a county fair sixty miles away to join a carnival show in the fall of 1919, when he was stricken with acute appendicitis. The conductor put him off the train at the first town that had a hospital, having wired ahead to have an ambulance meet the train. The appendix ruptured while Jay was riding to the hospital and he nearly died of peritonitis. It was inferred from papers in his pockets that he was some connection of the local Detweiler family, and he became temporarily the beneficiary of all those years of respectability. He was in the surgical ward for three weeks, a free patient, and by the time he was able to convince the hospital people that he was not a Detweiler of Gibbsville and that the eighteen dollars in his pocket was all the money he had in the world, he had also made a good impression with his courage and appreciation for everything that was done for him.

"What are you going to do when you get out of here? You're going to have to wear a belt for six months, maybe a year," said the doctor.

"A belt? What kind of a belt?"

"A surgical belt. You won't be able to do any heavy work. Not that you have been, judging by your muscles."

"No, I always stayed away from that, if I could."

"But you spent a lot of time outdoors."

"I sure did, Doc. I sure did."

"What *do* you do?"

Jay smiled. "Well, I didn't exactly lie to you, but I didn't exactly tell you the truth either. I told you I was a salesman. Well, I sell, but I don't sell carpet sweepers or kitchen cabinets. I'm a pitchman."

"A pitchman. Oh, yes, I've heard of that. With a side show, a carnival."

"That's correct, sir."

"Three-card monte and that sort of thing?"

"Well—if necessary."

"Hasn't been very profitable for you. You didn't have very much money on you when you were admitted."

"I was on my way to Bloomsburg, to the Fair. I had a job waiting for me with a friend of mine, but he don't know where I am. But I'll get in touch with him. He has an address in New York City."

"How old are you, Detweiler?"

"I'm just turned thirty."

"Just turned thirty. Why don't you turn honest? You seem like an intelligent fellow, and I guess you have to be sharp-witted to make a living in your profession, if I can call it that."

"And quick on your feet."

"I'll bet. You're quick with the booze, too, aren't you?"

"It's a weakness of mine."

"Yes, and I know what the other one is, too."

"How could you tell that? I'm clean as a whistle."

"The tattooing."

"Oh, Norma. Christ, that was in Muncie, Indiana, a long time ago. I'll bet she weighs a ton by now. Undying love. Well, she got J. D. tattooed on her rump. Not very big, about a half an inch high. She wanted it, I didn't ask her. But she couldn't have it too big. She done the dance of the seven veils and she had to cover up my brand with makeup, working. Norma. I was twenty years of age and I guess if she leveled with me she was thirty. The first real woman I ever had. Gave me up for a knife thrower, Captain Jack Montague. Johnny Muntz was the real handle, but I let him be Jack Montague, he was awful handy with them shivs."

"You're going to need some money. What do you plan to do?"

"I'm going to pay back this hospital. And you."

"You don't owe me anything. I'm on surgical duty. But you're expected to pay the hospital for medicines. Your belt."

"That I intend to. I'll work here, an orderly, till I'm off the nut. Of course what I could do, you give me a deck of cards and let me go upstairs where the rich patients are."

"Wouldn't *that* be nice?"

"No, I wouldn't do that here. You people here saved my life. Just give me a cot to sleep on and my scoff, my three meals a day, and I'll work as long as they say till I'm in the clear. Meantime I can get in touch with my buddy through *Billboard* and maybe he has something lined up. I can put the arm on him for a little walking-around money, *if* he answers my letter."

"You can't be an orderly. Too much lifting, and a lot of things you'd have to learn. But maybe you could run an elevator, something of that sort."

"It's a funny thing. I want to get out of here, but all the same I got a feeling for this place. I was ready to cash in, wasn't I?"

"Yes, you were."

"I come to in the ambulance, heard that bell ringing and I got it through my head, that nurse, never seen me before, nobody ever seen me before, but they're doing all they can for me. Then I guess the thing popped, huh? And the next I remember I was in a bed with clean sheets. Thirsty! God, I was thirsty. For water, not booze. Water. And I hurt good . . . That conductor, *he* was a nice fellow. *He* went to a lot of trouble. You know, Doc, I had him pegged for a mark. I only had eighteen bucks in my kick, and we don't generally take a risk with railroad conductors, but this guy I was gonna make a pitch. And then what'd he do? He saved my life."

"Well, young fellow, think about it."

"I do."

"Because it's something to think about. These were all people that you call marks. Easy marks, I guess that means. But one after another they helped save your life. You should have seen the pus in your belly. So do think about it, Detweiler, and stop being a wisenheimer."

Jay, seated in a white enameled iron chair, ran the elevator, worked off his debt to the hospital and made himself agreeable to the staff and patients. They were sorry to see him leave, but he had located the crap game that is to be found in every town the size of Gibbsville. In his cakeeater clothes, now not fitting him too well, he was obviously neither a cop nor a muscle man, and he was admitted to the game. He quickly identified the professionals in the game, and he bet their way; right when they bet right, wrong when they bet wrong. He was not interested in handling the dice himself and he passed up his turn; but he nursed his $10 case money until he had won $100, and then quietly departed. He was followed into the alley, and he knew it. He suddenly stopped and turned. "Get any closer and I'll rip your gut," he said.

"I ain't after your dough. I want to talk with you."

"You can talk standing in front of the restrunt, around the corner."

"All right, I'll meet you there."

The stranger, whom Jay recognized from the crap table, led the way to the Greek's all-night restaurant, which lighted up the sidewalk. He offered Jay a cigarette, which Jay declined.

"I oughtn't to smoke either. I just got out of the hospital, too."

"I don't remember you," said Jay.

"I be surprised if you did. You want to make a couple dollars?"

"Always do, but first who *are* you?"

"My name is Bartlett. Red Bartlett. I live here in town."

"Doing what?"

"Well, this and that."

(*23*)

"Like time? You done a little time, I know that much."

"Yeah, I been in the cooler. Nothing big. Breaking and entering. Assault and battery. I guess you done a couple of bits yourself."

"Uh-huh. I was hung for murder, and I did twenty years for holding up a stagecoach. What do you want, fellow?"

"I seen the way you were playing them dice. You look to me like a fellow was trying to get enough to leave town."

"And you got a proposition that me and you go in it together, we cut it up, and I leave town."

"You're pretty cute," said Bartlett.

"I'm cuter than that. They don't pin it on you, but they pin it on me because I blow town. Mister, I just as soon they didn't see me talking to you, anybody as dumb as you are."

"Six or seven hundred dollars, your end. Five, anyway."

"Listen, God damn you, I wanted to blow this town tomorrow, and now I can't. A thick-headed son of a bitch like you, you're gonna go ahead with this, whatever it is, and now I gotta stay. I gotta stay, and I gotta be able to account for every minute. You son of a bitch, I wish I never saw you. Goodnight, mister." Jay entered the restaurant and sat at the counter, drinking coffee and eating the bland filler of custard pie, until daylight. He went to his rooming house, carefully reminding the landlady of the time in case questions should be asked later. The precaution was unnecessary: at four o'clock in the morning Bartlett had already been shot and killed while resisting arrest during the burglary of Detweiler Brothers furniture store–undertaking parlor. It was a Saturday night, the beginning of the month, when instalment payments were due, and there was more than $4,000 in the strongbox to be banked on Monday morning. Bartlett had once worked as a helper on Detweilers' delivery van, and even then had been fired for clumsiness.

Jay went back to the crap game that afternoon and watched it for a while without playing. It was a different game. The night before it had been professionals and working men with the gambling itch; today it was high school kids, the easiest kind of marks but the worst kind of trouble makers, who rightly suspected each other of using the tees, the miss-outs and plain ordinary loaded dice. Bad news. The house collected a nickel a pass, and the professionals stayed out of the game, waiting while one or two of the kids became big winners and cleaned out the small bankrolls, Mom's money from the sugar bowl. The professionals sat against the wall, staring at the caps of their shoes until they heard a kid say, "I'm shooting five dollars. Five dollars open here." The professionals jumped down from their high wire chairs; the men had been separated from the boys.

Soon the game resembled that of the night before, with the appearance of the winners from the night before and the losers who had promoted new bankrolls.

"Two to one no six," said a man.

"He sixes," said Jay, and he was back in the game. It was a long evening, less profitable than the previous one, but when at last he was $50 ahead on the night, he quit. Once again he was followed into the alley, this time by two men who immediately took him by the arms. They were two of the men he had identified as professionals. "Where we going?" said Jay.

"Up the street."

"Where up the street?"

One man laughed. "They call it the Bucket of Blood."

"And what happens there?" said Jay.

"We have a couple of shots," said the man.

"Out of a gun, or a bottle?" said Jay.

"Oh, a bottle. Why did you say a gun?"

"My little joke," said Jay.

"Maybe we'll throw you in front of a train, but we don't carry a gun."

Immediately Jay broke loose. "Well, I carry this," he said. He backed away, and they could see his knife, which he held as though he were shaking hands with it. "One of you gets it for sure, right up the gut," he said.

"Cut it out, Detweiler. We got business to talk."

"Like throwing me in front of a train. Lousy bastards."

"That was kidding. We both got guns, if we'd of wanted to knock you off."

"And I'm a cop," said the less talkative of the men.

"A cop?"

"You should of known that."

"A town cop?"

"A town cop. Put away that sticker and we go have a drink. Go on back to the dice game and ask anybody if I'm not a cop. Chapman, my name is."

"What kind of cops do they have in this town?" said Jay. "You *are* a cop. I can tell it now, but I didn't before."

"You're a sick man, Detweiler," said Chapman. "The two of us could make a run for it and I could shoot you as quick as I gave it to Bartlett."

"You gave it to Bartlett?" said Jay.

"Yeah."

"Who's this other fellow?" said Jay.

"Me? You heard them say my name. Dave Bangs."

"I know both your names, but what do *you* do, Bangs?"

"I hustle a buck," said Bangs.

"This town is wider open than I thought," said Jay.

"This town ain't wide open, only a couple streets," said Chapman. "You satisfied now, or do we run and shoot?"

"I'll say one thing about this town. It got the coldest-blooded cop I ever run up against. All right, buy me a drink."

The whiskey was so bad that Jay was almost afraid to finish his drink even after he had diluted it with water. "My first since I got out of the hospital," he said.

"The beer's even worse," said Chapman. "I'll send you around a couple of pints of drug-store rye tomorrow."

"Make it the first thing in the morning," said Jay. "Tomorrow's get-away day for me."

"Well, maybe. Listen to us first," said Chapman.

"Listening," said Jay.

"I owe you a favor, Detweiler. When I seen you talking to Bartlett I figured he was ready for something. What, I didn't know, but it was pretty near time he needed money."

"Where were you when I was talking to Bartlett?"

"Across the street. I follied you out in the alley. I seen you pull the toc-jabber on him, too. You know how to use that thing, don't you?"

"Now that I'm talking to a cop I gotta watch what I say."

"All right," said Chapman.

"This here guy's the smartest detective on the force," said Bangs.

"Out of how many?" said Jay.

"Two," said Chapman. "But last night didn't take much brains. You gave Bartlett a no, and all I had to do was hang on to him. I no sooner saw which way he was headed than I knew where he was going to."

"Tell me some more about how smart you are, Chapman. How did you know I wouldn't go in with Bartlett?"

"Well, I heard you call him a son of a bitch. Your voice carries, for a little fellow. Secondly, why should a smart little guy like you go in with a dumbhead like Bartlett? What was the percentage for you?"

"Yeah. He said my take would be five or six hundred. I understand there was close to five thousand dollars at the furniture store. He was a muttonhead, all right."

"He sure was. I went to school with him till fifth grade, he never got no further. They had him in Glen Mills for a couple years—"

"What's Glen Mills?"

"Reformatory. He come out of there worse than he went in. Strong as an ox, but used to beat up his old lady, a scrubwoman over at the Pennsy station. Kids with paper routes. A hooker down the street, she had him arrested for a. and b. He broke into a couple stores and we sent him up on one. He was what you call a habitual criminal, and if he ever had a hundred dollars in his pocket, I doubt it. Maybe a hundred, but I'll bet he never had two."

"Never two," said Bangs.

"No, I don't think he did either," said Chapman. "He said to me, the time I put the collar on him, he said, 'I'm gonna excape outa here. Excape. And I'm gonna come down and kick your brains out.' You know what? The warden told me Bartlett was a model prisoner, so model that he *liked* it up on the hill, and I wanta tell you something. Our county jail ain't one of your model prisons. They got rats up there the size of a fox terrier. I was up there one day and I seen a rat this big right on top of the warden's desk. I shot it. The warden was sore as hell, but I don't want to be in the room with a rat that big."

"And Bartlett was even bigger," said Jay.

"Yeah, Red was bigger. But not as smart. How smart are you, Detweiler?"

"Ah, now comes the pitch," said Jay. "Well, I been known to have two hundred dollars in my pocket. Maybe three. Maybe four. But there's a lot of guys smarter than me. Maybe if I was a little smarter I would have been a detective."

"Uh-huh. It's gonna take a week or ten days, but we'll find out how smart you were."

"What's the capital of Michigan?" said Jay.

"Michigan? Detroit, I guess. Why?"

"Illinois?"

"Well, I know it ain't Chicago," said Chapman. "Springfield? Why?"

"The capital of Michigan is Lansing, and you're right about Springfield. That's where the records are kept, and that's what you want to do, isn't it? Find out if they have a sheet on me? They have. But why should I save you the trouble? That's what they pay them clerks for."

"Illinois we know about. You did a year and a day in Joliet, assault with deadly weapon or something like that. We got an answer from Illinois. That was where your sharpie suit came from, Illinois. Some little town. The hospital reported you to us. New York State you're in the clear. Pennsylvania you're in the clear. You had eighteen bucks on you when you went in the hospital, and you were headed for the Bloomsburg Fair. I could run you in now and fingerprint you if I wanted to."

"But you won't, because you want something."

"Yep. You know who owns that crap game, and the joint we were playing in?"

"Well, I thought it was Jerry, the house man. But you ask me the question like that, who does own it? You? You and Bangs?"

"I and Bangs, we both got our fifty percent," said Chapman.

"Nice," said Jay.

"Yeah, but it's all I get. I don't take another nickel. I don't get to collect from the hookers. The saloons. The ordinance violations. Carnivals. Circuses. Taxi companies. Fortune tellers. All the other poolrooms in town. If you started another dice room in town, I'd close you up inside of fifteen minutes. But if you wanted to open up a saloon you'd have to see someone else."

"Well, that's the way it should be. Nobody gets too greedy. And the mayor and them, I guess they cut themselves in on your take," said Jay.

"That's none of your business, Detweiler."

"Right, it isn't," said Jay. "Well, wuddia got in mind for me?"

"We're looking for a man to take Jerry's job, and we gotta have one right away. Jerry got consumption and they're sending him to the sanitarium. The way I see it, winter's coming. That's your worst time of the year, but it's our best. When it's cold weather we got fellows waiting for tables to shoot pool, eleven o'clock in the morning to midnight. We make good money off the pool tables. But the big money, naturally that's the dice room. Payday at the mines. Payday out at the steel mill. And you know who's good for a bundle every week?"

"No."

"These traveling orchestras. Every week beginning October to April they get a famous jazz orchestra, famous ones that make Victrola records, one right after the other. They all like to shoot dice."

"And what you don't get, the hookshops do. I know them traveling orchestras," said Jay. "Do you handle muggles?"

"Them marijuana cigarettes? No, that's handled by a

fortune teller and one of the hack drivers. Or there's a doctor on Lantenengo Street, if you got the right send-in. Nose candy. The needle. That's pretty quiet around here. Not much call for it except the hookers."

"And Jerry."

"Yeah, Jerry. Cocaine."

"And Dave, here," said Jay.

"Not me," said Dave.

"Have it your own way," said Jay.

"How about you?" said Chapman.

"Not so far, but there's no telling. Is that why you're giving Jerry the boot?"

"Partly. But he has consumption, too," said Chapman.

"He looks it. In other words, he was stealing too much."

"A little too much, yeah. You don't mind a little, but Jerry all of a sudden began stealing ten-fifteen dollars a day."

"A broad," said Jay. "Most likely some broad he was paying for her dope."

"What makes you think I took it?" said Dave.

"Yeah, we're back to that," said Jay. "Well, I guess I knew over a hundred men and women that took it."

"Were you ever wrong?" said Chapman.

"I been wrong."

"And you could be lying, too. I mean about you not taking it," said Chapman.

"I could be lying, but I'm not. It'll come to that, maybe, but my weakness is the booze. That I admit. Even this lousy rat-gut, now I started, I want another. What's the job, and what does it pay?"

"Fifty a week. You're house man. The pool tables, we got a kid racking up and shooting for the house. The dice game, you don't handle the dice. That is, you don't play. You collect on every pass, and a guy craps out, you say who gets the dice. And you keep the game honest."

"How honest?"

"Well, the dice have to hit the board on every roll or it's no dice."

"That's not what I meant."

"I know what you meant. There's two guys you never take the dice away from."

"Dave is one," said Jay. "And a fellow named Sol Green."

"That's correct. Anybody else you get suspicious, you change the dice. But not Dave, and not Sol."

"What if there's trouble? A chump starts a fight?"

"Usually it's an out-of-town guy that starts a fight. If I ain't there, Dave and a couple our friends can handle it. I don't want you pulling that toe-jabber unless the guy goes for you. But the way we handle a squawker, the first thing we do is get him out in the alley. Stop the game, and get that guy out in the alley."

"What about them kids?"

"There's a kid named Lefty Permento, they're all scared of him. We give him ten bucks a week and he shoots pool for free. An ugly bastard, but he sure likes to fight."

"Fifty dollars a week," said Jay. "Should I have a talk with Jerry and see how much I can steal?"

"Don't steal too much. Remember, this is all I got except my hundred and twenty a month from the police department. And it's *all* Dave got."

"And I'm there all day and all night," said Dave.

"Yeah, what are *my* hours?" said Jay.

"You come on at six o'clock. Very seldom you're there after ha' past one, two o'clock in the morning. Saturday and

Sunday afternoon, you come on around one. You get Mondays off."

"Who does the bookkeeping?"

"We do, in our head. The Greek owns the building, we pay the rent in cash. Everything is cash. Electricity. Everything. Dave pays that stuff."

"Well, we'll give it a try," said Jay. "Say, I want to ask you—why do they call this place the Bucket of Blood?"

"Search me," said Chapman. "They got a place the other end of town, down in Little Italy. They call it the Bucket of Blood, too, but there they got reason to. This joint, I don't see how he keeps going."

"Who's the owner?"

"The fellow tending bar, Matt Hostetter. He's on his last legs, too. And yet when I was a kid this place did business. My old man and all the guys from the car shops and the freight yards used to come in here. Why? You want to buy it?"

"You never can tell."

"Just don't buy it with our money," said Chapman.

"*Some* of your money," said Jay.

He ran an orderly game for Chapman and Bangs. The dice players made him prove that he knew what he was doing and what they were doing. He could be witheringly sarcastic, but generally he was good-natured and he talked continually. "The man's shooting twelve dollahs, five covered, seven dollahs open, now two dollahs open. Fi' dollahs he's right coming out, fi' dollahs he's wrong. Shoot the dice, and his point is eight. Eight's the point and it's two to one it eights for fi' dollahs and five to two no eight the hard way. And—crap it is. The dice go to Mulligan. Mulligan, your dice. The man shoots two dollahs and he's covered, and you watch Mulligan run that deuce up to sixteen thousand dol-

(33)

lahs. Well, not this time, Mulligan, a pair of beady little eyes. But Mulligan's a dead game sport and it's two dollahs open. Two dollahs. He's wrong for five dollahs, five dollahs he's wrong coming out and—*no dice!* The money *got* to be on the table, not in the air. No ghost bets here, gentlemen. The money *got* to be on the table. That's better. All right, Mulligan, roll them."

Beginning with his first night, he held out five dollars that was due the house and on big nights he got away with ten. He ran a faster, more efficient game than Jerry had run, and he stole a great deal less. All winter he made between eighty and a hundred dollars a week; he paid his room rent punctually, subsisted largely on eggs, and kept a pint of fair whiskey always within reach. And he saved his money. When warm weather came and with it a slackening off of business, he persuaded Chapman and Bangs to close the dice game for a month except for the big paydays, and he and Chapman would make tours of the amusement parks. During intermission and after the dance was over they would get a crap game going among the touring musicians and the concessionaires, and Chapman was delighted to discover that he had not lost a nickel by closing down the indoor game. On this deal Jay and Chapman went halves, and Bangs was not in it at all. Jay encountered some old carnival acquaintances among the concessionaires, and he could always get a carnie friend to act as a shillaber. The shill would win a little money and make a noise about it, and the musicians and concessionaires and the roustabouts would be ready to be taken. It was seldom necessary to sneak in the educated dice more than two or three times during a game, but it had to be done at precisely the right moment and under the suspicious eyes of the concessionaires. The smarter men among the concessionaires could tell when Jay and Chapman *ought* to throw in the educated dice, and they would drop out of the game temporarily, but even with this knowledge the concessionaires were never sure enough of their suspicions to risk a challenge. And most of them knew that Chapman was a cop, carrying a gun, and that Jay had done time out West for cutting up a fellow with a knife. At the end of the summer layoff, Jay had saved up nearly six thousand dollars.

"The parks all close Labor Day," said Chapman, one night when they were driving back to town.

"Yeah, nothing lasts forever," said Jay.

"You must have a pretty good little bundle."

"Pretty."

"Dave wants to get a new man," said Chapman.

"I'd be sore too, if I was Dave, but we didn't need him. He would have been a li'bility. Clumsy. If he'd of been with us I'd of spent all summer waiting for him to throw out three dice."

"He wouldn't throw out three dice. He's too good for that. But you're right, he's getting clumsy."

"Chappie?"

"What?"

"Have you got a new man?"

"Well, we talked to a fellow down at the shore. Bangs knew him before. I just as soon get rid of Bangs and go partners with you, but Bangs has the money and you don't. I don't either, you know. I ain't finished paying for my house and my wife's old lady has to have an operation."

"That's all right. A year ago this time I was almost dead. Now I'm alive and a little ahead. If I bought Matt Hostetter's would I get any help from you?"

"As long as you don't open up a dice game. And as long as you don't mean you want any money from me."

"Just a good word with the right people. Hostetter wants five thousand dollars. He's crazy, but if I offer him thirty-five hundred I think he'll sell."

"I could make him sell. Not me, but Schmidt. All I do is I say to Schmidt, put Hostetter out of business and put a real go-getter in there. You'd be better for Schmidt than old Matt is. Matt's on his last legs."

"I wouldn't want to muscle him out. That wouldn't be good for business."

"You'd be doing him a favor. You understand, though, you have to get your goods where Schmidt says."

"I'd have to talk to Schmidt about that. Hostetter's been taking anything they send him. It's a wonder they don't go blind, drinking the stuff he sells."

"Well, you work that out with Schmidt. I wish you and me could go in together, but right now Bangs has the bankroll. Why do you want to run a broken-down joint like Hostetter's?"

"I tell you why, Chappie. From Hostetter's the only way you can go is up. I'm in business for about as little money as it's possible. And the main reason, I got a place of my own. No partners, my own boss."

"Yeah, I wish I didn't have so many partners. I got Dave, I got the mayor, I got the chief of police, I got my wife, my wife's old lady, my two kids, a couple broads always asking for stocking money. Maybe you think I got it good, but if you want to know the truth of the matter, I'm in hock to Dave for over four thousand. I owe on this car, and it's two years old. My house ain't paid for. Where does it all go? I don't live high, but if I had to live on my hundred-and-twenty cop's pay, I couldn't do it. My wife says to me, quit. Quit running the dice game, she says. Where would she be if I quit? And her old lady with a private room in the hospital? Don't be surprised if one of these days I come around and put the arm on you."

"Wait till I get on my own two feet, though."

"You'll be all right. I got a feeling. I just got a feeling. Jay, I'm gonna let you off at the Greek's. I got a date with a broad. You don't have that trouble, do you? I never seen you with a broad. What do you do when you want to get your ashes hauled? Not that it's any my business."

"Sophie."

"Sophie? The waitress Sophie? At the Greek's?"

"Uh-huh."

"She's kind of big for you, ain't she?"

"You mean I'm kind of small for her? I always liked big broads, and *I* don't have to *feed* her."

"Sophie, huh? Well, wuddia know. You know who else is there, don't you?"

"Sure. Dave."

"Just so you know. He could get her fired from the Greek's, and he would in a minute. He don't like you, Jay."

"That's a pleasure. *I* don't like *him,* and I got a word of advice for you, Chappie. That's a fellow that carries his own deck. We all carry our own deck—you do, I do, we all do. But Dave is the kind of a guy, he lets you think he's Big Hearted Joe. Like you owe him that four thousand dollars. Yeah, but whose four thousand dollars? I guarantee you, that was never money he had his hands on. I'm willing to lay the odds it was money you held out on him and told him. Am I right?"

"Yeah, but I don't think you're guessing."

"That's all I am, is guessing. Nobody had to tell me that about Dave. If you ask Dave for the *loan* of a thousand dollars, watch him try to wriggle out of it. He wouldn't like to part with money once he has it."

"You're a hundred percent right. I held out on him, once for fifteen hundred, the other time for three thousand. I told him I had the money and I was ready to give it to him but would it be all right if I held on to it. So you're right, he never had the money in his hands."

"Yeah, I met all kinds, including a lot of Daves. If you ever get the chance to get rid of him, do it. Not that you'd do a favor for me, but a favor to yourself. Well, goodnight, Chappie."

"I'll talk to Schmidt. Goodnight, Jay."

During the first week of his ownership Jay had Matt Hostetter back of the bar with him. "The new owner," Matt would say, serving a customer. At the end of the week Jay handed Matt five ten-dollar bills. "That's for the good will, Matt. Now so long, and don't ever come in here again. It's my joint, and I don't even want you for a customer."

"No hard feelings, young fellow. You treated me all right," said Hostetter. Matt went home, sat in a rocking chair, and in three months died of an embolism. Jay was among the mourners at the service in the Lutheran church and among the contributors when the hat was passed by the undertaker. Jay held a folded five-dollar bill between thumb and forefinger, suspended over the hat, and before he dropped it he said: "Three months ago he had enough to bury him."

"I guess he did, yeah. Don't know where it all went to," said the undertaker.

"Wild women, probably," said Jay.

"Oh, no. He was too old for that." The man was deeply shocked, but he took the money.

Schmidt, the cop who exercised authority over the lower-grade speakeasies, was surprisingly tractable when Jay announced he wanted to change alcohol dealers. "I'm for it," he said. "They were palming off some terrible stuff on old Matt. If somebody went blind, it'd sooner or later come back to me and it'd be my rap. You go ahead and get your alcohol where you want to. But beer, beer you have to stick with the same people. That's over my head, *I* take *my* orders on who supplies beer. And you take your orders from me. If I see you putting in some other beer, I'll come down here and close your place. That's my orders, Detweiler, so no trouble, you understand?"

"Sure," said Jay.

There was a noticeable improvement in the class of people coming in. The old customers stayed, but now the place began to attract the low-salaried white collar men who could not do without their booze; the artisans who had to have cheap whiskey; the pensioners who had nothing much left in life but the conversations and long silences they could share with other pensioners. The word had got around that Jay Detweiler served the cheapest decent drink in town. Among the new customers were a few men who were fearful of patronizing Matt Hostetter's old place, which they had always heard to be a dive for cutthroats in a neighborhood that was occupied by the most lawless element in town. But when they went to Jay's on a trial visit they found it to be not nearly so bad as they expected. The badly dressed, unshaven derelicts were there, but the place itself, though bare of beautifying features, was scrubbed clean and smelt clean; in among the beer and whiskey smells was the smell of strong soap, and the smell of disinfectant in the toilet was almost overpowering, but reassuring. The new owner, Detweiler, appeared to be rather young to be the proprietor of such a place, and he was certainly not equipped by nature to handle a fracas. He was frail and polite, and though he had a blackjack hanging on the back bar in plain sight, he seemed too agreeable as well as too fragile to be effective if trouble broke out. He wore a collar and tie and a waistcoat in which he kept fountain pen, pencils, pocket comb and a notebook. His customers were not aware that Jay had changed his style of dressing; he no longer wore his cake-eater suit, with its low-cut vest, or a string tie or striped silken shirt with a tiny, too-tight collar. He could easily be taken for a ticket seller in a railway station, standing behind his bar and dispensing his goods. After a while the timid ones enjoyed the cheap thrill of patronizing a place that was nicknamed the Bucket of Blood but that was hardly more disorderly than any hose company on a Saturday night.

The new proprietor was there every day but Sunday, from nine o'clock in the morning till one or two the next morning. On Sundays he would not open up until dark, and his customers had to do the best they could to get through the day without booze. The rest of the time Jay was at his place of business from opening to closing. At lunch time and at supper time he would have his food brought in from the Greek's by a waiter known as Loving Cup because of the size of his ears. Jay would put the tray on one end of the bar and eat the food standing up. He never licked the platter clean; he ate only because he knew how important it was for a drinking man to get some food in him.

At the end of his first year his pocket notebook showed him that he had recovered nearly half his investment. His bookkeeping was simplicity itself: it had cost him just under five thousand dollars to get going; twelve months later, after paying all his bills, including the payments to Schmidt, he had about two thousand dollars in cash, and he owned the business to boot. He refused to complicate the bookkeeping; the first year had been a gamble. He had put five thousand dollars into a game, and he came out of that game with two thousand cash, a business, and his living expenses for a year all taken care of. He had never worked so steadily and so hard in all his life, and he had never enjoyed himself so much. He was strongly tempted to give a party on the first anniversary, but decided against it; instead, he waited until midnight and then announced that thereafter until closing, all drinks would be on the house. He gave no reason except, "I just happen to feel big-hearted tonight." His custom of buying free drinks was so well established that his explanation was accepted without curiosity.

It amused him to think back over his first year and to realize that in all that time he had lived in an area that was roughly four blocks by three—squares, the town people called them. He had never so much as taken a stroll two blocks to the north, two blocks to the south of the Greek's, one block to the east of his rooming house, or one block to the west of his doctor's office. He read the town papers thoroughly and he knew what was going on, but he had not had time to look around. The area in which he had confined himself was not much larger than the area to which he had once been confined by the State of Illinois—with the great difference that when he was in the pen he had not been free to wander. Twice in his lifetime—once by a judge's sentence and the other by his own preference—he had stayed put for a year.

He had run away from his uncle's farm at fourteen, and since that time he had wandered up and down and across every state east of the Dakotas, north of Tennessee, west of Massachusetts, and south of the Canadian border. He had stayed out of the South, where the small town cops and sheriffs were said to be mean; and he had stayed out of the West because of the distances between towns. Up and down, back and forth, with circuses, carnivals, medicine shows, Chautauquas, Tom shows, and working the county fairs alone or with a companion. He had put cardboard in his shoes and newspapers under his shirt to keep warm; ridden in the caboose with a too friendly brakeman and had two teeth knocked out by a special cop on the Nickel Plate; slept in a van with a dog and pony act, and driven his own Cole Eight after a highly successful week at the Columbus State Fair. He had seen all the awful things that can occur in a circus train wreck; and he had felt the dull, sickening hatred of a "committee" in a town in southern Indiana, where a man from a previous carnival had raped a little girl. He had comforted a tent-show girl whose six-hundred-dollar boa constrictor was shot by a drunken miner in Kentucky. He had been taken for his only aeroplane ride by an Army lieutenant in Rantoul, Illinois, whom he had taught the O'Leary belt trick. He had got crabs at a fraternity house in southern Illinois and gonorrhea from a corset demonstrator in Fort Wayne. He had run twenty dollars up to sixteen thousand in a crap game in Louisville on the eve of Derby Day and was about to drag his winnings when a friend almost imperceptibly shook his head, and Jay took the motion as a signal to make one more throw. But the friend was only being bothered by an insect on the back of his neck, and the dice came up a deuce and an ace. And now, after about twenty years of knocking around, he owned his own business in a town he had never heard of two years ago.

Jay had often pondered the mysterious ways of fate. Throughout his life accident and coincidence and luck had governed his actions with the unpredictability of a pair of honest dice. To some extent you could figure the percentages; they were known. It was easier to make an eight than a nine, harder to make a five than a six. You could shake the dice noisily in your fist—a pair of honest dice—and if you were very good you could improve your percentage by little tricks, like holding one die in the grip of your little finger. But in his study of the behavior of dice he had often given them an honest shake and an honest roll, and still come up with some strange sequences. Once he had rolled fourteen (or fifteen?) four-three sevens in a row, without manipulating the dice during the shake or the roll. And he had seen experts, using his dice, roll out numerical sequences in arithmetical order from two to twelve and downward from twelve to two. You could improve your chances legitimately or semi-legitimately. But you could not always explain accident and coincidence and luck; you just had to believe in it because it was there.

If he had not been put off that train, he would have died. But he *had* been put off the train, in a strange town that was full of people who had the same last name as his own. In all his wanderings he had never met another Detweiler, and in this town there were thirty or forty of them. He still had not met any of his namesakes; he was sure they would not like to claim kinship with him. And he knew so little about his parents that he would not be able to establish—or deny—any connection with the local Detweilers. He had no recollection whatever of his father and almost none of his mother. He had been raised by her brother, always with the reminder that he was another mouth to feed, with no credit for doing a man's work from the time he was able to lift a pitchfork, and to take a man's beating before that. His uncle was named Ben Russell, and he had always called him Mr. Russell, not Uncle Ben. He had never called Ben's wife aunt. She was, if possible, harder to get along with than Ben. Even now Jay hated to see a counterman cut into a fresh pie; it reminded him of the hundreds of times Mrs. Russell had sliced a pie into six wedges for the six Russells and nothing for Jay.

Now he could cut the pie the way he wanted it—all six wedges for Jay Detweiler. Unlike Chapman, the detective, he did not consider himself in reluctant partnership with people who were essential to his business, and, also unlike Chapman, he did not regard as partners the people who were essential to his pleasures or who were dependent on him for a living. He paid a scrubwoman to keep his place clean, he paid room rent to Sadie Tupper, graft to Sergeant Schmidt, so much to the beer mob, so much to the alcohol mob. He took what he needed out of his own till, and he gave Sophie George ten dollars every Sunday.

The first sign of discontentment in his new way of living was the discovery, on awakening one Sunday morning, that he had no desire to go to Sophie's room and spend the day with her. He had desire, but not for Sophie, and in a little while he was knocking on the door of the second best of the whorehouses. It was eleven o'clock in the morning, and the door was opened by the bouncer, a booze customer of Jay's, a man known as Sport. "The girls are all asleep," said Sport. "If that's what you came for." He was in a pair of pants pulled over a union suit and his hair was uncombed. "Come in, have a cup of coffee."

"Thanks," said Jay. "When do they start getting up?"

"Well, those with their regulars, they'll be getting up any time now. A couple the girls got Sunday regulars. You ever been here?"

"No."

"I thought you weren't. I didn't remember seeing you. I wasn't sure. You want cream and sugar? I make good coffee and I like it good and sweet. They say it spoils the taste, but I say it gives a different taste. My coffee you can drink black, and it's good that way, or you can put cream and sugar in it and it's just as good, only different. All the girls here say my coffee spoils it for them when they go to a restrunt."

"It has a nice aroma," said Jay.

"That's the tip-off. If it don't have a nice aroma, it ain't gonna have a good taste. You might as well start a new batch."

"I don't want to wake up any of the girls. Ain't any of them up yet? They all asleep?"

"I'll call upstairs," said Sport. He went to the hall. "Hey, anybody up?"

"Who is it?" a woman's voice replied.

"A friend of mine," said Sport.

"I'll be down," said the woman.

"That's a girl named Jenny," said Sport. "She come here from Fort Penn a month or so ago. Good-lookin' broad. She'd pass for respectable—if you didn't look too close. She don't dress like a hooker, is what I mean. Age, maybe thirty, maybe a little younger, a little older."

The woman, wrapped in a kimono, appeared. "I smelt that coffee and it woke me up. Hello, mister."

"Hello, Jenny," said Jay.

"You want me to take him on? Can I have a cup of coffee first?"

"Well, what do you think, Jay?" said Sport.

"Fine, fine," said Jay.

"A friend of yours?" said Jenny.

"Great pal of mine," said Sport.

"As soon as I have a cup of coffee, all right?" said Jenny.

"Sure, sure," said Jay. "There's no rush."

"Sport, you're gonna have to get the doctor for Beulah. She got a pain in her stomach and the sweats."

"That sounds to me like appendicitis. I had that," said Jay.

"Can she die from it?" said Sport.

"She sure as hell can," said Jay.

"I'll say she can. I had it too. I was operated four years ago," said Jenny. "I nearly died from it."

"So did I," said Jay. "Did yours rupture?"

"I thought only men got ruptures," said Jenny.

"That kind, but appendicitis can rupture," said Jay.

"They didn't tell me anything about that," said Jenny. "I just remember I had the gripes so bad, and the sweats. Did you have to wear a belt after? I had to wear a belt and I was out of work for over two months. Went back to work too soon anyway, the doctor told me. I got a thing they call adhesions, and had to be operated again. So you better get the doctor for Beulah, Sport."

"I will. I'll call him up on the phone," said Sport.

"And don't take all day about it, or you'll wheel her out of here to the undertaker's," said Jenny.

"Keep your shirt on," said Sport.

"If she keeps her shirt on I get a reduction," said Jay.

"You're a kidder, mister," said Jenny. "Anyway, I don't have a shirt. Well, any time you're ready, I am."

Jay became a Sunday regular of Jenny's, and she became a customer of his, as much, she told him, for the conversation as for the booze. He had never encouraged Sophie George to visit his saloon, and strictly speaking he had not extended a more than casual invitation to Jenny; but he was pleased with Jenny's visits. The other women among his customers were not much different from the men; drinkers in skirts, nothing to look at, and only too well aware that they had to stay out of trouble or be barred. Jenny was welcome—so long as she too behaved herself, and didn't come in too often. That she liked Jay personally was obvious to him.

Once in a while she would drop in of an afternoon, alone or with another girl, and take only a soft drink—a "temperance," she called it. She had been shopping for a bottle of perfume, a hat, a new kimono, and she felt like chatting before going to work. "It does a person good to get a breath of fresh air," she would say. Some of the girls in her house never left the place except to go to Dr. Traff's for their weekly examinations. "Which is a laugh, the inspection he gives you," said Jenny. "But if you don't go once a week, Sport won't let you work. He's under orders, just the same as the rest of us. Oh, I guess it's some protection, for a while. Sooner or later you're going to run into hard luck, but it's the same in your business. Sooner or later you're liable to get a bad shipment and they'll all go falling out of here with the blind staggers."

"It ain't the same thing, Jenny," said Jay. "I get a report on every shipment before I mix a batch of booze. Don't forget, I drink more of this than anybody."

"Yeah, and I don't see how you do it and stay on your feet."

"I don't let it get control over me."

"It will, though," she said.

"Yeah, the odds are it will, some day," said Jay.

He liked her friendly interest in him, and it was only old-time caution and not anything she said that put him on his guard with her. It was a long time coming, half a year or more, but he was ready when she made her pitch. "I want to get out of working in a house," she said, one afternoon.

"How do you mean? You'd have a hard time working

independent. You couldn't rent a room, the cops'd make it tough for you. This is a small town, Jenny."

"I know. I was thinking if you and me, the two of us lived together."

"Married, you mean?"

"Well, either way. But I could make seventy-five to a hundred a week here."

"Hustling?"

"How else? And the two of us could stash away a nice buck."

"Not a chance, Jenny."

"You got that little room back there and I notice it has a sofa."

"That's for if a man and woman don't have no place else to go," said Jay. "And they gotta be people I know. Another thing, I don't charge them. If I charged them the cops'd raise their take. You got pipe dreams, Jenny. You wouldn't make any seventy-five, a hundred a week here. Not my customers."

"Let me go to work and I'd show you."

"No," said Jay. "Oh, I ain't saying you couldn't pick up a few dollars. Any place that sells booze, it don't take a very smart hustler to make coffee and cakes. Even the old men I got coming in here, you could hustle them, but they don't have the ten dollars to spare, and you're a ten-dollar girl. Some of my old guys make a sawbuck stretch out for a whole week, and you'd take it away from them in ten minutes. No."

"I could make twenty dollars a day, six days a week."

"No dice, Jenny. The whole place'd change."

"It's nothing much now," she said.

"Not to you, maybe."

"Well what the hell are you so stuck up about it? They

(*48*)

call it the Bucket of Blood, for God's sake."

"Not any more. They used to, but not as much."

"Why don't you give *me* a break?" she said.

"A break, yeah, but I don't want to ruin a business I built up."

"I'll give you half, Jay. I tell you what I'll do. I'll bet you five dollars I can hustle the next guy comes in, I don't care who he is or how old or anything."

"Sure you can. You can hustle me, but that ain't saying you're gonna work here."

"You're a mean little bastard. Next Sunday go some place else."

"You don't have to take it personal."

"Well, I do, see? And next Sunday, stay away. We don't have to work Sunday if we don't want to. Sunday we can have anybody we want to, and I—don't—want—you, see?"

"That's your privilege. Have a steam?"

"The hell I will, now or any other time," she said.

He was sorry to break off with Jenny, and amidst his regret was deep appreciation of the compliment to himself and to his business in her willingness to marry him. It was easy to find a woman who would marry a man with a successful business, but Jenny had been willing to be a partner, to bring to the partnership her earning ability. It was a high compliment indeed, and it made little difference whether it flattered his business or himself, since one was the same as the other. He wondered how many other Detweilers in the town had had this satisfaction.

There was no one else in the saloon, and he was pleased that that was so. He poured himself a steam and raised his glass and faced the door. "Good luck, Jenny," he said.

THE BUTTERFLY

Mrs. Benner opened the newspaper wide and raised it in front of her. "I don't want to discuss the matter—*no—more*," she said. "I have no wish to discuss the matter and that's final."

"Mom, that's no way to be," said Hilda Benner Vogel. "Discuss it? We didn't discuss anything. You just said your say and then hide behind your paper."

"Hide? I don't have anything to hide. If it's hiding, you ought to be the one to hide." She lowered the paper. "As long as you're living in this house, just as long as I pay the electricity and the taxes and I'm the one forks over at the supermarket, you'll listen to me."

"All right, I'll listen. I'm willing to listen, Mom. But don't just say something and my God, I'm willing to listen but you don't *say* anything."

Mrs. Benner moved from side to side, shifting her weight in the chair as she lit a cigarette. It was a filter-tip cigarette but from long habit she spit an imaginary fragment of tobacco from her lower lip. "Willing to listen? When are you willing to listen? Hilda, you gotta get work and that's all there is to it. It isn't I mind the drain on my finances. You don't eat that much, and the heating for one room isn't that much extra. But as long as you got nothing to do you're going to get into some kind of trouble. Idle hands are the plaything of the devil. I never seen that to fail. There's not a family I know that whether it's a man or a woman, boy or girl, if they don't have work, they're the ones that get into trouble."

"I *agree* with you—"

"I didn't ask you to agree with me, Hilda. I'm stating a fact, only you don't seem to know it. Thirty-three years of age but some ways you never learned any more responsibility than a kid sixteen. Last night you come home at ten of three. Ten of three this morning. Ten of three on a Monday night? A Tuesday morning? In this neighborhood that's late for a Saturday night, let alone a Monday or Tuesday."

"If they're all asleep they wouldn't know *what* time I came home," said Hilda.

"See? You don't want to listen. You just want to give me an argument."

"I don't want to give you any argument. You asked me who it was and I told you."

"You told me some man named Tom Reese, but who's that? I don't know any Tom Reese. I never heard of him. What does he do for a living? I suppose he's married."

"Yes, I told you that."

"And how old is he? Did you tell me that, too? If you did, I don't remember, I was that upset you coming home at three o'clock in the morning with a married man."

"He's around thirty-eight or -nine."

"You still didn't answer my question, what he does for a living. Does he have a job?"

"He's getting a job."

"Oh, another one. Birds of a feather flock together. Maybe while he's looking for a job he can look for one for you, too."

"I couldn't do his kind of work. If I could I would. He makes plenty when he's working. He's a steeplejack."

"A what? A steeplejack? That paints church steeples?"

"And other jobs like that on tall buildings. But he has to lay off on account of the weather."

"Why don't he get work in Florida, then?"

"He just came back from there. As soon as the weather gets good he has a job down at the shore, Atlantic City."

"What company does he work for?"

"No company. He works independent."

"Oh, inde*pen*dent."

"Pop was independent till he sold the store. There's nothing wrong with working independent if you can. I'd rather be my own boss any day."

"Yes, but Pop built up a business from nothing or the chain wouldn't have bought him out. Don't compare your father with some fly-by-night steeplejack. How many children does this Reese have?"

"Two."

"Well, just you be careful he don't make it three. I'm not that hard up for a grandchild, believe me."

"That won't happen."

"Where did you meet this Reese?"

"He was at that party I went to at Stella Cosgrove's."

"His wife was there?"

"Yeah, she was there."

"But he liked you in preference to her?"

"Well, he asked me for a date."

"What kind of a looking person is she, the wife?"

"Well, I don't hold a candle to her for looks, but she has a lousy disposition."

"Oh, he liked you because you were more the retiring kind."

"Maybe. I don't know. Yes, I guess so."

"But he doesn't sound like any retiring kind himself, asking you for a date the first time he ever laid eyes on you."

"He isn't. He's not the retiring kind."

"A boozer?"

"No. He can't, on account of his job."

"Oh, but he likes women. Was he married before?"

"Yes."

"Did you tell him about Roy?"

"I told him I was married but separated. He said he could tell that by looking at me."

"Yes, I guess he could, a man like that. Some of them can take one look at a woman and tell you all about them, whether they're married or separated, or a widow. *I* can usually tell. Do you have another date with Reese?"

"Tonight."

"Oh," said Mrs. Benner. "Tonight, huh?" She scraped the end off her cigarette and picked up her newspaper. "Then you won't be home for dinner?"

"No," said Hilda.

"Some men can get away with it," said her mother.

Shortly after seven-thirty the doorbell rang and Mrs. Benner went to answer it. "Good evening," she said. "Will you come-in-sit-down?"

"Yes ma'am, thanks," said Tom Reese.

"I'm Hilda's mother. She's near ready but take off your coat."

"Thanks," said Reese. He was wearing an overcoat, very short, hardly came to his knees, the type that was advertised as suburban or sports-car. The upper part of the garment was dark blue, the rest of it grey. The material was something like a tweed, and it was very new. As he walked he seemed to be bow-legged and he was a shorter man than he had given the impression of being. He was very thin, still somewhat sunburned, and had blue eyes and cheekbones that stood out. He offered Mrs. Benner a cigarette, which she accepted, and when he held up a lighter she noticed the back of his hand was tattooed in a design that was interrupted by the cuff of his white shirt.

"I notice you have a tattoo," she said.

"Which one?" he said. He raised the sleeves over his right arm and displayed a dragon that went up to his elbow, and he showed her the tattoo on his left arm, a fouled anchor with a line that wrapped around his arm to the wrist. He kept his cigarette in his mouth while showing her the decorations, and breathed out smoke as he described them. "I got some others, too," he said. "But I guess I won't show you *them*."

"Did it hurt when they did it?"

"Sure, but not bad. I had these since I was seventeen years old. The first couple days they fester and itch, that's worse than the needle. They do it with an electric needle. But the worst part is the itching. Oh, and it don't look very appetizing the first few days."

"I'll bet it doesn't," she said. "Can I offer you a drink of something?"

"Don't touch it. I get high enough in my work, you know what I mean? Did Hilda tell you, I'm a steeplejack."

"High enough in your work, so you don't get high on the ground?"

"That's it. You got a beautiful house here, Mrs. Vogel."

"Benner. Mrs. Benner. Hilda's married name was Vogel."

"Sure. You don't look old enough to have a daughter her age."

(54)

"I am, though. Not saying how old she is."

"She told me. That's why I can't believe it."

"Well, appearances are sometimes deceitful."

"Yeah, and it's how old a person feels. My grandfather got married for the third time when he was seventy-four years of age. He married a woman forty-five and he outlasted her. People don't get enough fresh air, that's what it is. I'm the first one in my family didn't go to sea, and stay at it, that is. I went to sea when I was sixteen but I got better money as a rigger so I give it up. But my father, my grandfather, and a whole bunch of uncles all went to sea, some in the Navy, some not. Tattooing runs in the family. That's how I happened to have these. I understand my grandmother had a tattoo on her leg where it wouldn't show. Except to him, if you know what I mean."

"I wouldn't have it done for any man."

"You don't know. Maybe you would. A lot of women are tattooed."

"The ones in the circus you mean."

"Not only them. Regular women. Women like you."

"Not like *me*, I can tell you," said Mrs. Benner. "I wouldn't be tattooed no matter how much you paid me."

"The best work is a fellow in London. London, England. He's famous. One of these days I'm thinking of flying over there and letting him do a job on me, if he's still alive. I don't know whether he's still alive."

"Well, don't ask me to accompany you, because I wouldn't have it done no matter how much you paid me."

"You be surprised how many women got tattoos on them. I had a friend, a girl friend in Frisco, and she made me take her to a tattoo artist."

"She must have been high."

"Well, she was. She had a few in her, but it was on her

mind when she was sober, too. She kept asking me when was I, so I finally took her to a tattoo artist in San Francisco. A Chinaman."

"Where did she have it done?"

"In San Francisco . . . Oh, you mean where on her?"

"Yes."

He grinned. "Well, you'd have to be pretty well acquainted before you could get a look at it."

"Even if she had one of them Bikinis?"

"With a Bikini you could see it."

"Imagine taking off your clothes and letting some Chinaman. Were you there?"

"Was I there? She wouldn't of done it if I wasn't there."

"What was it? What kind of a design?"

He chuckled. "You know what it was? It was a butterfly."

"Well, go ahead and tell me. *Where* was it?"

"Where was it? Well, I tell you. If she was a steer, it was like she was branded."

"Branded, she sure was. Branded for life. Every time a man asked her—I guess we better change the subject. High up?"

"About halfway. It'd show in a Bikini but not a regular bathing suit."

"Did you pay for it?"

"Forty-fi dollars."

"Forty-five dollars for a thing like that. You don't care how you get rid of your money."

"I'm a spender."

"I don't mind a spender if you get value received. You're a nice dresser, and I thought maybe you'd be coming here in blue jeans. But forty-five dollars just because some foolish woman wants a butterfly on her rear end."

"Many a time I spent forty-fi dollars more foolish than that."

"Oh. You mean value received," said Mrs. Benner. "And she wanted it done? You didn't put her up to it?"

"That's not my motto, Mrs. Benner. My motto is always make the woman ask for it. Always make the woman ask for it, then she don't blame you later."

"Sensible if it works. Don't you ever ask for anything yourself?"

"Never."

"That's a funny way to go through life," said Mrs. Benner.

"Well, the way I look at it, we pretty near all want the same things, only I figured out if you make the other person ask first, they can't blame you if it don't work out."

"Is that business, too, or just personal relations?"

"Oh, business is altogether different. I mean personal."

Hilda appeared, and they left immediately, so quickly that Tom Reese carried his overcoat on his arm. Mrs. Benner followed them to the porch and saw them drive away in a large station wagon with a Florida license plate. She had somehow expected a Cadillac, but maybe he used the station wagon in his business. It had different kinds of racks on the roof, and steel angle-irons along the sides where he could probably hang ladders and things. But it was a well taken care of car.

It was not like Hilda to come rushing in like that. You could almost say she was bossy, rushing in like that and interrupting a conversation. Mrs. Benner enjoyed talking to Tom Reese, even if she didn't agree with him on some things; and it occurred to her that Hilda could have been eavesdropping. If so, the thought must have run through her mind, as it had through her mother's, that Tom Reese had as much as said that Hilda had asked him for a date, not Tom her. Hilda was not a liar; she was an unusually truthful girl, for a woman, but Mrs. Benner would almost bet that if she had a tape recording of the original conversation it would show that Hilda had asked Tom to take her out, maybe without even realizing it. Some little thing, like saying, "I don't have anything to do Monday night," and then Tom saying, "All right, do it with me." Tom Reese *was* a liar, Mrs. Benner believed. A liar in that he would not feel bound to tell the truth. A man so clever about women would have no trouble outsmarting a girl like Hilda.

Hilda came home shortly after eleven. As the front door opened Mrs. Benner could hear the station wagon zooming away. He probably had not even got out of the car.

"You're home early," said Mrs. Benner.

"That's what you wanted," said Hilda.

"Where'd you go?"

"We went to a motel," said Hilda.

"You look here, young lady—"

"You asked me where we went and I told you. If you asked me last night I would of told you the same thing."

"I could of guessed that much. Tomorrow night the same."

"*That's* where you're *wrong*. Tomorrow night he's going to ask *you*."

"It's a good thing you're out of my reach or I'd give you a good slap in the face."

Hilda, still wearing her coat and with her handbag looped over her wrist, stalked out of the room and ran up the stairs. Mrs. Benner lit a cigarette and stared at the TV. The man was drawing curvy lines across a map of the North American continent and accompanying his drawing with references to Bismarck, Denver, and Galveston, but

Mrs. Benner did not take in what he was saying. The lines he was drawing were all so female, so buxom and female, and now as he drew another line his hand moved as though in a quick caress, as though he were creating sections of a woman's torso that she could only anticipate until the line was drawn.

She got to her feet and snapped off the TV. She went around turning out lights because she knew that once she got to the second story she would not want to come down again. In a few minutes the first floor was dark and Mrs. Benner climbed the stairs and she could see that the light was on in Hilda's room.

Hilda had not taken off her coat. Her aluminum suitcase lay open on the bed and was partly filled with clothes.

"What are you, going somewhere?" said Mrs. Benner.

"Looks that way."

"You going for the night, or what?"

"For the night and all the rest of the nights," said Hilda. "My things in the wash, you can send them to me."

"Where to?"

"I'll send you a postcard."

"You don't have any money. How are you going to live?" said Mrs. Benner.

"I'll get something."

"But what?"

"Oh, stop asking me questions. Something."

"You got a better chance of getting something here, where you know people, than if you went away some place."

Hilda said nothing.

"That's the whole problem, Hilda. What I been trying to drum into you, only you won't listen. If you don't have work, something to do, you get miserable."

Hilda stopped packing and stood erect. "What were

you talking about before I came down tonight, you and Tom Reese?"

"What were we talking about? He was telling me about his tattoo."

"I thought as much. And the woman with the butterfly on her behind?"

"Yes, he told me that."

"Huh."

"What do you mean, huh?"

"What do I mean? I mean you're gonna be like that woman in Boston."

"What woman in Boston?"

"That got herself tattooed."

"You mean San Francisco."

"Boston. Boston, Massachusetts."

"He told me San Francisco. Maybe there was two of them."

"Maybe there was two hundred of them. Maybe there wasn't any. But I know this much, I'm not gonna stay around here and watch my own mother make a fool of herself. You ought to hear what he said about you."

"What did he say about me?"

"I'll tell you what he said. He said he bet me inside of two weeks you'd have a butterfly tattooed on you."

"Huh."

"So go on have a date with him tomorrow night. You won't have to go to any motel. I won't be here. And don't forget to tell me when you get the butterfly tattooed on you."

"Up and down these stairs all day, I think I'll sell this place," said Mrs. Benner.

"Didn't you hear what I said?"

"I heard what you said, Hilda, and it's in one ear and out the other."

"Are you sick or something?"

"I don't have to be sick to be disgusted, the kind of men you go out with. You go to a motel the first night you go out with him, no wonder he can talk dirty about your own mother. Do you want some money?"

"I have thirty dollars."

"You'll need more than thirty dollars, that won't last you three days if you want to live decent. You want to live decent, or don't you?"

Hilda was silent.

"You can't go any place this hour of the night, alone. You can go to the bank with me in the morning and I'll draw out some money for you. A woman can't stay decent in this world if she don't have some money to fall back on." Mrs. Benner went to the bed and picked up the aluminum suitcase and turned it upside down. "Your stuff'll be back from the laundry tomorrow. Put these things away for the night, anyway. And for God's sake take off your coat."

Hilda opened the closet door and hung up her coat.

"Straighten it out," said Mrs. Benner. "You gotta learn to take care of your things, or you won't have any-thing."

CLAUDE EMERSON, REPORTER

For thirty years Claude Emerson got up every morning at six o'clock, put the coffee on, shaved himself with one of his two straight razors, took a cup of coffee in to his wife, and then went back to the kitchen and sat at the table and drank two cups by himself. He would sit there, staring straight ahead, slowly stirring the coffee between sips, and when he had finished the second cup he would put on his glasses. There was a small mirror on the kitchen wall, and he would stand in front of it while putting on his collar, in which his necktie was already inserted. He would knot the tie and pull it a little to one side, a little to the other, until he was satisfied that it was in the right place, then he would smooth it down with the palm of his hand, throw back his shoulders until the tie bulged the right amount, and *then* he would insert his stickpin at the right place, slide the safety catch over the pin, and draw away to inspect his work. His next move would be to put on his toupee, which took less time but no less care than the tying of his tie. In thirty years and more Claude Emerson's toupee had deceived no one. It had never quite matched the color of his own hair, which went gradually from an orangey red to a reddish grey. Claude Emerson was always a little behind the natural color changes. He bought a new toupee every five or six years, but he could not afford to keep up with nature. Indeed, he had never been able to afford even one first-class matching job. His friends, his wife, and Peter Durant, his barber, urged him to abandon his toupees, but Claude Emerson refused because, he said, he always caught cold when he went without one.

And so, every morning, there was that part of his personal ritual; putting the toupee in place, smoothing it down gently with the palms of both hands, the final adjusting pull over one ear. After that, his coat and waistcoat, which he put on together, and the business of his watch and chain, which he could do while on his way to the clothes-tree in the front hall. He would put on his seasonal hat and the outer wear appropriate to the weather—rubber coat, gumshoes, umbrella—and he was ready for the street.

On very few mornings he failed to find someone to walk with, and he tried not to walk with the same man on successive mornings. His companions were the bookkeepers and store clerks and men who worked in the offices of the railroads and the coal companies, white-collar men like himself, but whose jobs were nowhere near as exciting as Claude Emerson's. "I'd like to have gone in the writing game," they would often say. "But I was never much of a speller."

Claude Emerson would reply consolingly: "Well, with me it was always arithmetic. When I was in High they tried to teach me bookkeeping, but I could never strike a trial balance."

Most of his morning companions were men who *had* learned bookkeeping, but their work did not furnish much of a topic for conversation. Claude's work, on the other hand, was of the stuff that conversations are made on: last night's meeting of the Borough Council; yesterday's burglary; the untimely passing of a Civil War veteran; a two-alarm fire in the Sixth Ward; tax millages; church picnics; a new movie theater; the Burton Holmes lecture; the gilding of a church steeple; the birth of twins; the price of strawberries; the new uniforms for the band. To the man who spent his days perched on a bookkeeper's high stool, the life of Claude Emerson seemed full of variety and stimulation; and Claude Emerson thought so too, for he loved his work.

He was a big man: six foot two, never less than two hundred twenty pounds. In High he had not liked football, but because of his size he had had no choice but to play. He lacked aggressiveness, but he stood head and shoulders over most high school players, and in helmet and nose-guard, shoulder harness and kidney pads, he was valuable to the team even before the game began. For four years he heard opposing players say, "Get a look at that big son of a bee. I'll bet he's a ringer." Claude's own coach would say to him: "Just watch the center, Emerson, and as soon as the ball's snapped back, fall forward, *fall forward!*" In Claude Emerson's football days there was no forward passing and not much running around the ends; the principal play was the center rush, and Claude's bulk made him worth two line players, leaving, as it did, one extra guard free to engage the opposing line players on every scrimmage. In spite of the hard-rubber noseguard-mouthpiece, Claude lost four front teeth during his playing career, but he gained a reputation as a stalwart son of Old High which lasted all his life, and, better yet, football introduced him to his lifework; he was paid $1.50 for his reporting of the out-of-town games in which he played.

The paper had no sports section or regular sports writer in those days. Claude Emerson's account of the previous Saturday's game seldom appeared before Tuesday, and often did not appear until Wednesday. Nevertheless his stories usually ran a full column in length, and when he was ready to graduate from High he was taken on as a general news reporter at $1.50 a week. At the end of two years, when his salary had reached $3.50 a week, he asked to be raised to $10; he was keeping company with Clara Stahlnecker, a high school classmate, and her father would not give his consent to Clara's engagement until Claude was earning $60 a month and had at least $200 in the bank. The editor of the paper, though heartily approving of marriage, could not see his way clear to a salary jump from $3.50 to $10, and took the opportunity to caution Claude against such an impulsive step as matrimony at the age of twenty or twenty-one. "Think these things over, Emerson," said Bob Hooker, the editor.

"I did think it over, Mr. Hooker," said Claude Emerson. "And I guess I have to tell you, I can get ten dollars at the *Telegraph*."

"I don't believe you," said Hooker. "When did they tell you that?"

"Four or five months ago."

"Bosh! If that was true you would have said something then."

"I almost did, but I was hoping I'd get a bigger raise this time."

"Even if you're telling the truth, which I doubt, you realize that the *Telegraph* is on its last legs? So go on over to them, but don't come back looking for work here when the *Telegraph* shuts down," said Hooker. "I'll give you six dollars a week and a dollar-a-week raise every six months."

"Two years before I get ten? No sir, I can't wait that long."

"You haven't got the Stahlnecker girl in some kind of trouble?"

"I don't have to stand for that kind of talk," said Claude. "Now I quit!"

From time to time during the next dozen years Bob Hooker would try to re-hire Claude Emerson. To more and more citizens of the town Claude Emerson was becoming a symbol, the only symbol, of newspaper reporting. They saved their news items for him and would give them to no one else. They would stop him in the midst of his morning rounds and shyly hand him articles they had written. "You fix it up so it reads right, Claude," they would say, and he would do so. They were fascinated and not antagonized by the changes he would make, and when they saw their items in print, written in Claude Emerson's ornate style—"the festive board groaned under the weight of delicious viands" —they became members of Claude's small army of volunteer reporters. Nor was it only the humble who relied on Claude Emerson for the proper presentation of news items; doctors and bankers trusted him; lawyers and clergymen had confidence in him; rich old ladies, who had heard of him through their medical and spiritual and financial advisers, would make their rare announcements only to Emerson, that nice young man at the *Telegraph*. He was summoned to the homes of certain citizens who had never spoken to Bob Hooker, homes to which Mrs. Hooker had never been invited. In such surroundings Claude Emerson was awkward and perhaps over-polite, but he also had the big man's dignity, and he confined his questions to the matter in hand. He seemed to know instinctively that these ladies felt it their duty to make public the information they gave, while wishing to keep out of the papers themselves. "I don't want this to look as if it came from me," they would say, and so Claude Emerson would begin his story: "Word has been received here of the untimely passing of John W. Blank, former town resident, who for the past forty years has made his home in St. Paul, Minnesota," or, "Through the generosity of a donor who wishes to remain anonymous, a handsome, new, mahogany Chickering piano has been installed in the Parish House of Trinity Church." Claude Emerson's stories appeared without a byline, but Bob Hooker recognized the Claude Emerson touches. In an Emerson story an oyster was always a succulent bivalve and every funeral had a cortege, but all the names and the middle initials were always there and invariably correct.

"Claude, I'd like you to come in and see me one of these days," said Bob Hooker, in his first attempt to re-hire him.

"I don't know if that would look right, Mr. Hooker," said Claude.

"Then I'll say it now, here. I'll pay you twenty a week," said Hooker.

"I'm getting better than that at the *Telegraph.*"

"I don't believe you, but if you are, you won't be getting it for long. That rag is on its last legs."

Several times in the next seven years Claude Emerson had reason to know that the *Telegraph* was having financial difficulties. His pay envelope contained $12.50 and not the full $25. "That's as much as I could scrape together, Claude," said George Lauder, the editor and publisher. "I'll give you my note, but right now things are slow. They should pick up after Labor Day. I'll give you my note, or I'll give you some stock, but I advise you to take my note. Gives you a better claim in case things don't get better around here." Things never got much better at the *Telegraph,* and they would have been much worse without Claude Emerson, who, as in his football days, did the work of two men. The difference now was that he liked what he was doing, and George Lauder was not a coach who failed to appreciate him. It was a sad day for Claude Emerson when George Lauder, unable to face another slow summer, drank a pint of cheap whiskey and put a bullet through his heart. He owed Claude Emerson $412.50 in back wages. The money was uncollectible, since Claude Emerson had never taken one of George's notes and for more than a year George had failed to keep any books. The bank realized as much as it could on the sale of the equipment, and Claude Emerson, literally with hat in hand, went to call on Bob Hooker.

"Well, you see, Claude," said Hooker. "I've got this young lady, a college graduate, that does all the social-and-personals. I don't pay her anything. She's doing it for the experience, and she works like a mule. When she leaves I'll get another like her."

"I didn't want to apply for social-and-personals," said Claude Emerson.

"All you have to do is look at the paper to realize I have no other place for you. The other jobs are filled by fellows you know."

"Well, if you hear of anything elsewhere in the county—"

"Why don't you put an ad in Fernald's Exchange, Springfield, Mass.?"

"No, that'd be a waste of money for me. I'll have to look for something else, maybe up at the court house."

"You mean give up reporting?"

"I guess I'm going to have to," said Claude Emerson.

The threat of this waste of a good reporter was too much even for Bob Hooker. "I wouldn't want to see you do that, Claude," he said. "I'll tell you. I can pay you twenty dollars a week and a commission on any new advertising you bring in."

"Couldn't you make it twenty-five? I have the two children starting school. I tried to sell ads for George Lauder, but I was never any good at it."

"Well, you're a family man, and you're not a drinker," said Bob Hooker.

"No, Mr. Hooker! That's not it. I'm good at my job! I get more news than any two reporters in town. You know that. I could go uptown this minute and get five or six items that won't be in your paper tonight."

"Say, you're pretty sure of yourself."

"About that I am. I didn't use to be, but think how many times I had items in the *Telegraph* that you never had. Or maybe had them a day late."

"I never expected you to get conceited," said Hooker.

"Let me say this, will you, please? The *Telegraph* stopped printing three weeks ago tomorrow, but I made my rounds every day, just the same as usual, just as if the paper was coming out that afternoon. And every day I got at least one story that you would have run on Page One. Let me show you some, here in my pocket. I'm not conceited, but when it comes to getting the news, I don't have to take a back seat for anybody. No, Mr. Hooker, I have to start at twenty-five, and no selling ads." He rose, and the sweat ran down from beneath his toupee. He wiped his forehead with a bandana handkerchief and blew his nose loudly. His speech to Hooker had left him momentarily without a sense of direction, and he made for the wrong door.

"That's the toilet," said Hooker.

"Oh, excuse me," said Claude Emerson. "Well, good day."

"All right, Emerson. I'll start you Monday. Twenty-five a week."

"Is it all right if I start today? I have a story."

(69)

"What is it?"

"The Second National bought the Eisenhauer property at Main and Scandinavian. They're going to move there and put up a five-story office building over the bank."

"That's just a rumor."

"The papers were signed last night. I got that from J. Edward Stokes himself."

"I saw him this morning. He didn't say anything to me about it."

"I saw him this morning, too, and he gave me the whole story. I asked him if he'd keep it quiet for a few days, and he kept his promise . . . Do you want a few lines on Dr. and Mrs. English getting back from their trip to Egypt?"

"When they get back."

"They're back. I was with him earlier this afternoon. He has some very clear pictures of him and the missus in front of the Pyramids. Both riding camels. I talked to Father McCloskey. He has his silver jubilee on the twenty-fourth day of next June, and plans are under way—"

"All right, Emerson. Go on upstairs and go to work," said Hooker. "The other door."

That was in 1908, a year that could be said to mark the beginning of the golden era in the career of Claude Emerson. He was thirty-three years old, an age at which he had grown up to his size. His face had lost the last of the baby-fat look that remained with him through the mid-twenties. He had become, in more than one sense of the word, a prominent figure, instantly recognizable at council meetings, fires, parades, and his volunteers could easily find him. For the same reason it was easier for those who wished to avoid him to keep out of his sight; but few citizens had anything to fear from Claude Emerson. What he knew, he knew, and his inside information was considerable, but the paper he worked for was not a scandal sheet. Even in the heat of the primary election campaigns, when the rules of fair play and reticence were suspended, the paper refrained from publishing the dirtier truths about the opposition candidates. A candidate for the Republican nomination could expect to be called a grafter and an incompetent, and the paper would ask, in large type, what this faithless public servant had done with his share of the looting of the public treasury; but it was never hinted that the man had spent any of the money on women or booze. That sort of accusation was harder to take back when and if the man under attack happened to win the nomination. If there had ever been a threatening Democrat the paper would have used—invented, if necessary—anything it had on the man. Democrats, however, were so few in number that they could not present a formidable candidate. Some Democrats registered as Republicans in order to vote Republican in the primaries, in the fantastic hope that the weaker Republican would be nominated and thus give the Democratic candidate a tiny chance in the November elections. There were some spiritual Democrats who had never voted for a Democrat in the primaries. There were, to be sure, a few Democrats who had never voted for a Republican at any time.

Within two weeks of Claude Emerson's return to the *Standard,* Bob Hooker's paper, there was a noticeable increase in the paper's circulation. It was the custom to place a pile of papers just inside the front door, where workmen could pay their pennies and pick up a copy on the way home.

"We're getting new readers," said Bob Hooker to Claude Emerson, late one afternoon. "We're selling fifty to sixty more papers off the pile, every evening."

Claude Emerson smiled. "Oh, yes. Yes indeed."

"A lot of them I don't recognize," said Hooker. "Who are they? Friends of yours that followed you from the *Telegraph?*"

"I'll tell you who most of them are. They're Democrats. They used to read the *Telegraph*. Now they read the *Standard*."

"Then they *did* follow you? I knew George Lauder was a Democrat, but don't tell me you're one."

"No sir, but I know most of them. Most of those men, you can tell by looking at them, they work in the car shops. I cultivated them. They didn't read the *Standard* when I worked here before, but these past years when I worked for the *Telegraph* I made a practice of chatting with them during lunch hour. It wouldn't surprise me if you got another fifty or seventy-five taking the paper on home delivery."

"Maybe we could get them to vote the right way, in time."

"I don't know about that. Not these fellows," said Claude Emerson.

It was a poorly kept, impossible to keep, secret that the *Standard* was subsidized by the Coal & Iron Company. It was known as a scab rag, a company sheet, anti-labor, anti-union. It had no circulation in the mining patches, and even in the town its circulation was smaller than the opposition paper's. But the Coal & Iron Company subsidy was one of the two factors that made the *Standard* a superior paper. In losing years the deficits were covered, and in profitable years improvements were made. The other factor in the *Standard*'s favor was Bob Hooker himself, who was actuated by greed and inspired by his love for the newspaper business. The greedy man had begun life as a poor boy, whose formal education ended with grammar school. He was of Yankee and Pennsylvania Dutch stock, a common enough combination in the anthracite region. Among his ancestors was an early president of Yale, and on his mother's side there were numerous Lutheran clergymen. His father, however, was a drunkard who died young, and Hooker's mother supported herself and her son with work as a seamstress until her eyesight gave out and she had to take in washing and ironing. She died of consumption in the year that her son finished grammar school. He was a frail boy with an outsize head, and the only job he could find seemed cruelly unsuitable inasmuch as he suffered from defective vision. The job was printer's devil, paid him a dollar a week and a cot to sleep on in the back of the shop. In spite of his bad eyesight he learned his trade quickly and well, and he read his mother's Bible from habit every day, learned three new words out of the dictionary every day, and on Sundays he read every line of all the out-of-town newspapers that he was able to store up during the week. At sixteen he got a job as printer on the *Standard,* and at nineteen he owned it.

As the new owner of the paper he wrote his own editorials in a day when small-town newspapers ran no editorials or meekly reprinted the political opinions of the metropolitan dailies. The small-town public was usually startled to find a local reference in an editorial, and the *Standard,* and its youthful publisher, attracted the attention of the educated citizens. Under the influence of Henry Wadsworth Longfellow and William Cullen Bryant the young editor wrote a weekly poem in which he introduced the local place-names of Indian origin—Lantenengo, Nesquehela, Taqua, Swatara, Mauch Chunk—and on other days he wrote short paragraphs with the standing head, This & That, which failed as humor but were of local, topical interest.

Bob Hooker was only five years older than Claude Emerson, and had had four years' less schooling, and yet there never was any question as to who was in command. The power rested in something other than the authority to hire and fire, although both men were continually conscious of that authority. The two men had remarkably similar backgrounds. Claude Emerson was a Mayflower descendant, a genealogical fact that was passed down to him by his father and mother and almost never mentioned outside the family. (Once in a great while someone would ask Claude: "Is that a baby ring?" and he would touch the smooth-worn gold ring on his little finger: "No, it belonged to my father," he would say.) Alexander Emerson, though not a drunkard, had died at a fairly early age, leaving a wife and fourteen-year-old son Claude. Alexander's widow had a mortgage-free house on Scandinavia Street and her husband's life savings from his job as cashier-bookkeeper with a dry-goods concern. She did not touch her inheritance. She returned to her old job of teaching seventh and eighth grades in the public school, and continued to teach until Claude married the Stahlnecker girl. The then newlyweds lived with her in the Scandinavia Street house for the first eighteen months of their marriage, at which time the senior Mrs. Emerson suffered her third stroke and passed on. She was very tall for a woman—slightly taller than her husband—and everyone said she tried to do too much; coming home tired after the long hours in the classroom, and pitching in to do a lot more than her share of the housework. She had never got used to letting Clara Stahlnecker sweep and scrub and cook, and possibly Clara should have taken a firmer stand, but Clara was so tiny compared to Mrs. Emerson, and Mrs. Emerson all her life was accustomed to giving orders, not taking them. No one could possibly blame Clara, and, after a time, no one did. Some of the neighbors thought Claude could have been firmer with his mother.

The obvious differences in the respective backgrounds of Bob Hooker and Claude Emerson were inherent in the similarities, the principal difference, of course, being the considerable fact that Bob Hooker was practically a homeless waif while Claude Emerson, at the same period in his life, enjoyed the love and protection of his mother. And yet Claude, compelled by the accident of his size to play a brutal game in which he took no pleasure, may have been no better off than Bob Hooker, who at least was no more uncomfortable than the child Mozart. One thing was certain: that Claude Emerson, protected and loved throughout his boyhood, inspired affection in later life, even or perhaps especially among men who treated him with something less than complete respect. No one, on the other hand, was ever known to speak with affection of Bob Hooker, even those men who treated him with respect. Claude was not particularly conscious of inspiring affection, but Bob Hooker was aware of it and mystified by it. Why was that overgrown clod so popular? He was almost a clown, with his ridiculous unmatching toupee, his squarish derby from September to May and his planter's Panama from May to September; his big, pigeon-toed feet and his dainty short steps: his black undertaker's suit with its pockets bulging with wads of copypaper. Claude Emerson's popularity was particularly galling after such incidents as the visit of old Mrs. W. S. Hofman. Her barouche and sorrel pair stopped one morning in front of the *Standard* office, and Bob Hooker rushed out to greet her.

"Good morning, Mr. Hooker," she said. "I have something for Mr. Emerson. A little item that I think might be of some interest."

(75)

"Emerson's uptown on his morning rounds, but I'll be pleased to take it," said Hooker.

"Oh, he is? Do you expect him back soon?"

"No, not for another hour or so," said Hooker. "But I'll be glad to see that it's taken care of. Would you care to come in my office?"

"Thank you very much, but it'll keep. Mr. Emerson knows how I—he usually comes to my house, but since I was in the neighborhood. If it's convenient I'd like him to stop in this afternoon. Half past five, we usually meet. But thank you, Mr. Hooker. All right, Clancy. We'll go to the bank, now, please."

It was no consolation to Bob Hooker that Claude Emerson not only would be treated almost as a servant but that he would conduct himself almost as a servant. It was no comfort, either, that Mrs. W. S. Hofman saved her news for the *Standard*. The irritating fact was that Claude Emerson had a place in Mrs. W. S. Hofman's scheme of things while Bob Hooker had not. The old lady had not even been rude; she had treated him with automatic, impersonal, infuriating politeness, and closed the door of her barouche in his face.

The power, the strength, that Bob Hooker exerted over Claude Emerson was the strength of envy, and it endured because Bob Hooker refused to acknowledge its existence. Instead he kept Claude Emerson on his payroll year after year, raising his salary when necessary, working him hard, diluting his compliments on Emerson's industry with humorously tolerant remarks about his cliché-ridden literary style. Claude Emerson had never pretended to be a writer. He learned early that there was a set journalese phrase for nearly every detail of every event that made a news item, and when he had acquired them all he saw no reason to originate another batch. The people read what he wrote, they understood what he was saying, and they were subtly complimented by his frequent use of elegant expressions. It was nicer to have your daughter united in the bonds of holy matrimony than merely married; the last sad rites were so much more appropriate than a funeral; and Jupiter Pluvius, with his torrential downpours, was more exciting than a two-inch rainfall. It was supposed to be a private, mild, office joke when Bob Hooker would say, in the presence of the other reporters, "Well, I noticed in yesterday's paper that that robber brandished a wicked-looking blue steel automatic." He would not mention Claude Emerson; he did not have to. "Anybody here ever see a holy-looking black automatic?" The city editor and the other reporters would laugh, and so would Claude Emerson. No one, not even Claude, thought Bob Hooker was being cruel. "Emerson's an excellent reporter," Hooker would say privately to the city editor, "but I have to jack him up once in a while. Inclined to get a swelled head."

In spite of Bob Hooker's criticisms in the office Claude Emerson retained his self-confidence "on the street." Again and again he was paid the ultimate compliment by a civic organization to a reporter: they would hold up the start of a meeting until he made his appearance. It was almost as high a compliment as its corollary: "Don't let Claude Emerson find out we're having this meeting." It was finally through a compliment, the second-grade kind, that Claude Emerson became vulnerable to an act of revenge by Bob Hooker.

It was now 1926. Claude Emerson's silver anniversary as a member of the Fourth Estate had passed unnoticed. His son and daughter were married, his wife was content with a daily box of Lowney's, Samoset, Page & Shaw's or Whitman's to assuage her craving for candy, and at $40 a week Claude Emerson was the best-paid reporter in town. He was fifty-one years old and without realizing it he had written the history of the town for all there was of the Twentieth Century and a few years beyond. He had recorded marriages of a hundred young persons whose births he had written up for one paper or another. He had covered all the details of the rebirth of the town from a borough to a third-class city, and he had written the story of the passing of the last horse-drawn fire-fighting equipment. He had seen the vanishing of news value in items concerning local reception of radio programs from Kansas City, Missouri. An Old High teammate had a Princeton son who was on Walter Camp's Second All-America team, and the *Standard* not only had a regular sports department but carried accounts of golf tournaments at the country club. The new hotel was no longer a novelty, and three Philadelphia brokerages had branch offices, complete with stock quotation boards, competing for local investors' business. Two county judges posed for photographs in white linen knickerbockers, and four state troopers went to prison for accepting bribes from bootleggers. The largest and oldest brewery was now an ice cream plant. Bob Hooker was one of the newest members of the Union League in Philadelphia. War was so much a thing of the past that there were only two officers left in the National Guard companies who had seen service on the Mexican Border and in France. A sound Yankee was President of the United States and a sound Pennsylvanian was Secretary of the Treasury . . . The town had no archivist, but it did have Claude Emerson, and his word was accepted as final in the settling of bets. ("I say it was 1911, you say it was 1910. We'll ask Claude Emerson.") In a peculiar, intangible sense he owned the town, the town was his, because he possessed so many of the facts of its life.

Then one morning in 1926, having given Clara her

eye-opener cup of coffee, and adjusted his toupee, and taken his bumbershoot out of the hall stand, he fell in step with Marvin F-for-Frederick Nerdlinger, a friend who lived two squares west on Scandinavia Street. Marvin worked in the laboratory of the Coal & Iron Company. He and Claude Emerson had been classmates at Old High, and the Coal & Iron gave Marvin a job as soon as he graduated. There was even some talk of sending Marvin to Lehigh for college chemistry and physics, but Marvin did not want to waste a lot of time on English and history and the other stuff they made you take in college. Now, at fifty-one, he had college graduates working under him at the lab, although they did not as a rule stay with the company after two years.

"Morning, Marvin," said Claude.

"Claude," said Marvin Nerdlinger, without breaking stride.

"A light precipitation," said Claude, holding his umbrella over his shorter friend.

"Thanks, I don't mind a little rain," said Marvin. "You weren't around yesterday."

"Should I have been?"

"Might have been worth your while, I expected you," said Marvin.

"You had a story for me?"

"No, I didn't, but I thought you'd be around trying to get one."

"Come on, now, Marvin. Don't tantalize me. Something happened. What was it?"

"Fourth of July came early this year."

"Fourth of July? You had an explosion? Anybody hurt?"

"Not hurting any more. Never have another moment of pain."

"Who? You mean someone was killed?"

"All I said was the Fourth came early this year. The rest you'll have to find out for yourself."

"That's what I'm trying to do."

"Oh, no. Not me. I said as much as I'm going to."

They parted company at the corner of Main and Scandinavia, and Claude Emerson hurried to his office and the telephone. After calls to the hospitals, the Coal & Iron doctor, the coroner's office, and the fire chief, Claude Emerson said to Frank Carter, the new city editor: "I'm up against a stone wall."

"I wasn't listening," said Carter. "What stone wall?"

"I understand there was an explosion yesterday over at the C. & I. lab. That's over on Coal Street. They keep it separate from the main building."

"What do they do there?"

"Well, a lot of things. Chemical things. I don't understand much of it, but one thing I know they do do, they analyze dynamite and caps. The lab is a little stone building near the car shops. Built of stone and brick. Walls two feet thick. Looks like a guardhouse. They're not allowed to have it in a residential or business area."

"Then why don't you go there and have a look?"

"I will, but the way I always work, on a story like this I don't go and ask them if the thing happened. We know it happened."

"You're sure of that?" said Carter.

"I'm sure. And I'm sure a man was killed. I'd like to have the man's name and some of the details before I go there. The more I have, the less they can deny."

"They can't deny it if a man was killed."

"Oh, can't they?" Claude chuckled. "Wait till you're here a few months. You'll find out they can deny anything. Do me a favor, don't tell the boss I'm working on this."

(80)

"If he asks me, I'll have to tell him."

"I understand that, sure. But wait till he asks you. He won't be in for another hour or so, but when he comes in just don't say anything. By that time I may have some facts."

"Are you going to get me into trouble?" said Carter.

"Just stay out of it and you won't get in any trouble."

"Why do they want to be so secretive? Accidents happen all the time. Miners get killed every day, it seems to me."

"This is a different matter. They never had a man killed at the lab, to my recollection, and when this gets out it's going to make people nervous. You're not supposed to keep any dynamite in the city limits. That's an old ordinance from the borough days. Gibbsville Supply Company had an explosion back around 1892, two men killed and a conflagration that gutted three buildings. There was hell to pay, and they passed an ordinance. No more dynamite in borough limits. It's right down there in black and white."

"Well, get after it."

"I'll do that little thing," said Claude Emerson.

Police Sergeant Biddle said there was nothing on the blotter, but he avoided looking at his old friend. "Anyway, it's not a police matter, Claude."

"I know. The fire chief. But Billy McGrew is making himself scarce. I've been after him all morning."

"Go have a look in his book. If there was an alarm turned in, he has to keep a record of it. What time was this supposed to happen?"

"You know darn well when it happened."

"Not a police matter, I told you. You start calling me a liar and I'll kick your big ass out of here."

"I don't have a big ass, and you didn't use to, before you were promoted to sergeant."

At the word sergeant, Biddle looked up. As much as to any politician he owed his chevrons to the daily favorable mentions he had got from Claude Emerson. "Is there anybody out there?"

"No," said Claude Emerson, peeking out in the hallway.

"This didn't come from me, mind you?"

"Hell, you know me better than that," said Claude.

"Somewhere between four P.M. and a quarter after, we got a still alarm. Fire reported at 220 South Coal. Billy McGrew answered it in the chief's car, and the combination truck from Perseverance and some other apparatus in the First and Second Ward. The usual still alarm equipment. When they got there the fire was out, or under control. But there was some scraps of a human body, what was left of it, scattered all over the lab. Name of the man, Kenneth W. Cameron. Age twenty-seven. Married. No children. Employed as chemist by the C. & I. Home address, 22 North Frederick. Moved here from Wilkes-Barre about six months ago. Cause of death, accidental explosion of unknown chemicals. The rest you're gonna have to find out for yourself. Now don't say I never gave you anything."

"I won't say anything, not about you, anyway. What did you say your name was? John J. Jones?"

"Huh? . . . Oh, I catch on. Well, you better not," said Sergeant Biddle.

The deputy coroner was an undertaker, Miles T. Wassell, and Claude Emerson found him in his office in back of the funeral parlor. "Morning, Miles. I hear you won't have much to work with, that young fellow yesterday."

"What young fellow was that, Claude?"

"Oh, I thought the deputy coroner was supposed to know all these things. Well, that'll have to go in my story.

'Deputy Coroner Miles T. Wassell was not informed of the fatal accident to Mr. Cameron.' "

"You better not print that or I'll sue you."

"Then you better tell me what you know—that I didn't find out already, and without any help from you, Miles. I don't have to tell you, the coroner's records are public property. How much dynamite did they have at the lab?"

"I didn't say they had any."

"Then what caused the explosion? Maybe he was making tea and put too much sugar in it."

"I don't know anything about any dynamite."

"Or anything else, so it appears. But remember, if you want to try to make a fool out of me, it'll be tit for tat."

"The man was killed by some unknown chemicals exploding."

"You don't have enough of him for an autopsy. When is the inquest?"

"I'm waiting to hear from the Coroner."

"Yes, I'm waiting to hear from him, too. You can tell him that when you talk to him. Is he taking personal charge?"

"Yes."

"I see. You're under orders to him, then. Well, you just tell him I tried to reach him this morning, and I'm not going to try again. I can be reached at the *Standard* after twelve noon."

The windows of the laboratory were boarded over and a Company policeman stood in the doorway. He was a stranger. "You can't go in there," he said.

"Why not? I'm going to see Mr. Nerdlinger."

"You work for the Company?" said the policeman.

"No, I didn't say I did."

"Then you're not allowed in. I got orders to keep

everybody out. Does Nerdlinger know you're coming?"

"He was expecting me yesterday."

"Well, that was yesterday. I wasn't here yesterday, all I got is my orders for today. What are you, a salesman?"

"Tell Mr. Nerdlinger that Mr. Emerson is here. And tell him I don't enjoy standing out here in the rain."

"Well, I guess you can stand here in the doorway. Wait here a minute, but don't go inside. You're not allowed inside till Nerdlinger says it's okay. Emerson?"

"Claude Emerson."

"Claude. Huh. Claude. All right, Claude, stand here, but don't go any farther, or as big as you are I'll throw you out in the gutter."

"Don't talk that way. Captain Wingfield wouldn't like it."

"You know Captain Wingfield? Are you a friend of Captain Wingfield?"

"I'm a friend of everybody's, unless they try to throw me in the gutter. Yes, I know Cap Wingfield, very well indeed. I knew him before he worked for the Company."

"Are you a lawyer?"

"Listen, go on in and tell Mr. Nerdlinger I'm here, and stop asking me questions, will you?"

Still in doubt, the policeman went inside, and as he opened the door Claude got a strong whiff of the odor of chemicals and stale smoke, but the policeman closed the door too quickly for a good look at the laboratory. Claude tried the door; it was locked.

The policeman returned. "He can't see you. He's busy," he said.

"Well, I'm willing to wait, but not long," said Claude. He made a sniffing noise. "Sure is some smell."

"It's a hell of a lot worse in there," said the policeman.

(84)

"Would you mind going back in and ask Marvin—that's Nerdlinger—ask him when he can see me?"

"He didn't sound like he was going to see you. He just said to tell you he was busy."

"Nonsense. What is there to do in there today? Clean up, but he can do that any time."

"No, they have to do it today. They found a piece of the fellow's jaw this morning."

"I didn't think there was that much of him left."

"Oh, that was just talk," said the policeman.

"I thought he was blown into a thousand pieces."

"Nah. From his waist down you wouldn't know he was hurt. The trunk and the head were all blown apart."

"Did you have to look at him?"

"Hell, I seen worse in the army. I dug a grave for worse. Yeah, I saw him. The undertaker put him in a canvas bag last night, the bottom half of him and the big hunks. The piece from his jaw, they found that up on the top shelf where they keep them glass jars, look like Mason jars."

"Oh, I understood all the glass was broken."

"Nah. Dynamite acts funny. You take now for instance a Mills grenade. That goes off and all those little squares, they go in all directions, every which way. But there's a lot of stuff in that labbatory, it wasn't even touched. Smoky, from the fire, but all in one piece."

"There was one report that it was nitro-glycerin."

"Dynamite. This poor son of a bitch was making some kind of a test, and—hyuh, Captain. Friend of yours here."

Captain Thomas L. Wingfield, chief of the Coal & Iron Police Division, stood in the rain and stared at Claude Emerson. "What are you doing here, Emerson?"

"Trying to get in to see Marvin Nerdlinger," said Claude.

"Have you been gabbing to this man?" said Wingfield to the policeman.

"No, I just got here," said Claude.

"You shut up, Emerson. You, Chapman. What was that about some son of a bitch making a test? What have you been telling this fellow?"

"Now wait a minute, Cap," said Claude.

"You didn't let this fellow get inside, did you?" said Wingfield, ignoring Claude.

"Who is he, this fellow?" said Chapman.

"He's a God damn reporter."

"You God damn son of a bitch!" said Chapman. He went at Claude Emerson with both fists driving into Claude's belly. One punch was enough; Claude Emerson had not been physically attacked since high school days, and he was fifty-one years old.

"Cut that out," said Wingfield, and the beating stopped. "Emerson, you're sticking your nose in where you ought to know better. Go on, get out of here."

"I have to sit down a minute," said Claude. "Can't get my breath." He lowered himself to the stone stoop.

"Let him sit there," said Wingfield.

"Solar plexus," said Claude Emerson.

"You ought to know better," said Wingfield. "Get up and walk around. It'll do you good."

"I don't know if I can."

"Go on in and bring him a drink of water," said Wingfield.

"Yes sir," said Chapman, and went inside.

"What the hell is the matter with you, Claude? Bob Hooker isn't going to print anything about the accident. He's on the Company payroll the same as me."

"I know."

(86)

"This Chapman is a bully-boy, as tough as they come. The next thing would have been the boot for you. One of the toughest men I have."

"Could you send around and get me a taxi?"

"Where do you want to go? Home? I'll drive you there."

"The office."

"I advise you to go home and go to bed, and stay there. You took a couple of mean punches. He goes in there like a pile-driver, with both hands. Come on, I'll drive you home."

"No, I have to go to the office, Cap. I'm getting my breath back."

"I wish this wouldn't have happened," said Wingfield. "Fellows our age, that's real punishment." He helped Claude to his feet and they got in Wingfield's car. It was only about seven blocks to the *Standard* office, and the cold rainy air helped to revive Claude, but he and Wingfield maintained silence until the car stopped at the office. "I wouldn't have had this happen for the world, Claude. You know that. But you should have known better."

"Both doing our jobs, Cap. Thanks for the ride."

"I wish I could fire Chapman, but the trouble is I need him."

"Doing his job, too. So long, Cap," said Claude.

He had to stop and rest a couple of times on his way up the stairs, and when he reached the newsroom it was immediately apparent to Frank Carter and the others that he was not well. "Are you all right?" said Carter.

"Had a kind of an accident, you might call it. I'll be all right after I had a little rest." He hung his hat and raincoat and umbrella on the clothes-tree, and made his way to his desk. "I got a lot on the explosion, but I need more. Did you get anything on it?"

Carter reached in the wire basket and took out two

pieces of paper, one typewritten, one in pencil. "I got this," he said, handing it to Claude. "The Boss wrote the story *and* the head."

"A Number 30 head? For this story?" said Claude.

"Read the story. A 30-head is all it's worth," said Carter.

Claude read aloud:

"Kenneth W. Cameron, age 27, of 22 North Frederick Street, was fatally injured yesterday while conducting an experiment in the laboratory at 220 South Coal Street. The accident occurred, according to eyewitnesses, when Cameron apparently misjudged the proportions of chemicals in a test he was conducting as part of a safety program.

"Cameron, who recently came here from Wilkes-Barre, was the son of Mr. and Mrs. James D. Cameron, of that city. He was a graduate of the Rensselaer Polytechnic Institute, at Troy, N. Y. He was a member of Sigma Chi and Sigma Xi, the latter an honorary fraternity. In addition to his parents, his wife, formerly Miss Nancy Benz, of Nanticoke, survives. Funeral arrangements have not yet been completed. Burial is expected to be in Wilkes-Barre."

"And that's all? That's it?" said Claude Emerson.

"And the head. 'Chemist Dies in Safety Test,' " said Carter.

"And the Boss wrote it all himself," said Claude. "Where are you going to run it?"

"Page three."

Claude Emerson handed the story and headline back to Carter. "I had a little more than that," he said.

"I'll bet you did," said Carter.

"I even had the name of the company Cameron was working for. I see the Boss doesn't mention that."

"I noticed that, too, Claude," said Carter.

"I hope the Boss didn't have as much trouble getting his story as I did mine," said Claude.

"What happened?"

"Ran up against a stone wall. Not the same one I mentioned earlier. Although it was, in a way," said Claude. "Frank, I don't want to leave you short-handed, but I'm going to have to take the rest of the day off. Would you do me a favor and call the cab company? I don't feel much like walking. Or anything else."

"Listen, I'll get one of the boys to drive you home. The circulation department has a car."

"Any other time, but today I'd rather take a taxi. This is the first time in thirty-two years I wished I'd been a bookkeeper."

"Not you, Claude," said the city editor.

THE ENGINEER

Work on the big dam had been suspended in 1917 and '18, but after the War the engineers began to arrive in considerable numbers. They were all sorts, running in age between the middle twenties and the early fifties; college men and practical men; married and single; brilliant and barely competent; construction men, electrical men, supervisory men, financial men; men who had worked together in far corners of the world, men who were meeting for the first time; the ambitious, the washed-up, the healthy, the drunkards, the womanizers, the cheats, the gipsies, the dedicated, the dullards, the mysterious, the dependable. Some came and did their jobs and were off and gone in a month or two; others, on jobs that took longer, brought their families; and a few stayed on and became residents of the town, usually because they had had some mining experience and found work in one of the independent coal operations. But whether they left in a month or stayed forever, as a class they were a positive addition to the life of the town. They were educated, well-traveled men; scoundrels or worthy citizens, they were The New Engineers in Town, and no other group of men ever enjoyed quite the same welcome. If some of them abused the welcome, they were usually punished by their confreres' ostracism or efficiently banished by the Company.

They all came to a town already respectful of engineers as a class—the successful and the mediocrities among the native-born mining engineers prepared the way for the new men. And except for the gipsies, the chronically footloose, they could look around and see that for an engineer it was not a bad place to be. Indeed, several of them partnered up to form small engineering firms of their own, with the town as home base, and a couple of those firms are now in the hands of the second generation, not getting rich but getting by.

But in the early Twenties the New Engineers were all strangers in the town, fresh or not so fresh from Cornell and Case and M.I.T., from Wyoming and Montana and Alabama universities, and from Sweden and Scotland and Turkey and France. They took rooms in the Gibbsville Club and the Y.M.C.A., in the hotels and boarding houses, whatever they could get that was appropriate to their position and pay. A man who had had five servants in China was lucky when his bed got made in his boardinghouse on North Frederick Street; and another man who as a colonel had rated his own batman now had to polish his own shoes. But as a group they were adaptable.

Chester L. Weeks arrived in town in 1921, after most of the first wave had gone on to other jobs, and the big generators were in. He checked in at the American House, the oldest and largest hotel, but not the best and by no means the worst. "You understand," he told the desk clerk, "as soon as there's a room with a private bath, I want it. I'm going to be here for some time."

"We understand that, Mr. Weeks," said the clerk. "As soon as Judge Boxmiller checks out."

"How soon do you think that'll be?"

"Well, that's hard to say. Another two-three weeks. He's an out-of-town judge, from over Nesquehela County.

There's some special case he's hearing, I don't exactly know what."

"But when he leaves, I can have the room with bath— and hold on to it? I don't want to give up my private bath every time a judge hears some special case."

"No, this don't happen but once every two-three years."

"Good. Now I have a lot of pressing, and laundry."

"You can give all that to Jimmy, he'll take care of it for you. You can have your laundry back the day after to-morrow."

"Not before then?"

"Well, if Jimmy wants to take it home, his wife can do it special if you're in a hurry."

Chester L. Weeks turned to the colored man beside him. "Are you Jimmy?"

"Yes sir, that's me. Jimmy."

"Is your wife a good laundress?"

"Don't like to brag, but she does the best work I know. All hand work, fifteen cents a shirt."

"And how late is the barber shop open?"

"Oh, ha' past eight, nine o'clock, depending," said Jimmy.

"What time do they open in the morning?"

"In the morning?" said Jimmy.

"They're open around eight o'clock in the morning," said the clerk.

"Fifteen cents for a shirt, eh?" said Weeks.

"Maybe she do it for—twelve?"

"Or maybe she'll never do it again, if she doesn't do good work this time," said Chester Weeks.

"She do good work, that I guarantee you," said Jimmy.

"Do you know what I've been accustomed to paying for a shirt?"

"No sir."

"One cent."

"One cent! A penny! You couldn't even get that low a price from the Chinaman."

"This *was* a Chinaman. In China."

"Oh, in China. That's different. Everything cheaper over there, so I'm told. Them Chinamen, they eat rats and rice. I wouldn't like that. Who'd ever want to eat rats and rice?"

"I have. It can be quite a delicacy."

"Not me. Rice I don't mind. I eat lots of rice, but don't give me no rats with it."

"You probably wouldn't like sheep's eyes."

"Sheep's eyes. You mean eyes out of a regular sheep? Ha ha ha ha. Listen to you talk. Sheep's eyes. Mister, now I *know* you joking me. Mister?"

"What?"

"What else you eat?"

"Oh—fried grasshoppers."

"Fried grasshoppers. Ha ha ha ha ha. What else?"

"Bamboo shoots."

"Bamboo shoots. Ha ha ha. You ever eat any—any—I don't know."

"Thigh meat. I got sick from it."

"What that, thigh meat?"

"Thigh meat, from a man's thigh. They said it was pork, but it wasn't pork."

"Huh? You ate a man?"

"I ate part of a man."

Jimmy was disturbed, and very near to anger.

"Some of the places I've been, and the things I've eaten, it was better not to ask what they were. What are we waiting for? Oh, the rest of my luggage."

"It's coming by Penn Transfer, Mr. Weeks. You don't have to wait. I'll send it up as soon as it gets here. One trunk and one large suitcase?"

"All right, send it up."

In the silent ride up the elevator and the walk to Chester Weeks's room Jimmy decided that no disparagement of his color had been intended by the newcomer, and his anger subsided.

"I'll unpack these bags," said Weeks. "You can take the dirty linen with you, then come back and get the rest when my trunk arrives. Do you send my suits out or are they done here in the hotel?"

"We got a tailor in the basement, he does them."

"No creases in the sleeves, will you tell him?"

"Yes sir. No creases in the sleeves."

"Does your wife know how to wash a linen suit?"

"Yes sir. Sir?"

"Yes?"

"What that sign there, say Raffles?"

"That's the name of a hotel. Singapore. Asia."

"You was in Asia?"

"China's in Asia."

"Oh, yeah. Yeah. Raffles. Some name for a *ho*tel, hey?"

"Some hotel, too."

"Man!"

"What?"

"Look at them guns. Mister, how many guns you got?"

"Three. Just these. This one's a Webley. English. This one is French, and this one's American."

"All countries."

"Well, three. That's so it would be easier for me to get ammunition. Couldn't always get American cartridges everywhere I went. And some places I couldn't get British, and so on. But I could usually get one of the three."

"Was you in the War?"

"Yes. At least I was in the army. Were you in the army?"

"Yes sir, I was a lance corporal. Orderly in the Quartermaster Corps. Served ten months at Frankford Arsenal. Honorable *dis*charge."

"Frankford Arsenal? Where's that?"

"Philadelphia, P A, sir."

"Oh, yes. Here, will you hang these up, please?"

"Hmm. Silk. I never saw a suit made out of silk."

"They won't do me much good when winter comes. How cold does it get here?"

"Oho. Cold. Hot in summer, cold in winter. In the mountains, here. Trolleys don't run. Snow plows get stuck. River gets froze. Poor people don't get enough heat. Children take sick and die. Men got no work. Get drunk and fight, every night, not only Saturday. Folks stay home, ain't got shoes, can't even *look* for work. Men like me, got a steady job in a *hotel*, they let us take home stale bread for our neighbors. But winter's no good for us, no good at all."

"Why do you come North?"

"Sir, I didn't come North, I was born North. My pappy was born North, *his* pappy born North. We's always here in town, since *I* can remember."

"Then why don't you go South?"

"Huh. South. You can freeze there, too. Wintertime ain't no good anywhere if you don't have wood in the stove and bread in the box. It don't get cold in China?"

"You bet it does. And hot."

"Huh. Guess I'll stay here."

"You might as well. Who polishes the shoes?"

"Me. They got another boy in the barber shop, but the people in the rooms, I shine them."

"Do you take the laces out?"

"When they ask. I run them under the tap and rinse 'em out to look nice and fresh. I do it right. But some don't ask."

"Well, I ask."

"Yes sir, I seen that."

"I like to have my things just so. If I gave you a fixed sum every week would you see to it that my shoes are always polished, and my clothes in order? My hats brushed and so on?"

"Like a valley?"

"Yes."

"A fixed sum? How much is that, a fixed sum?"

"Two dollars a week?"

"Two dollars—I don't know. I got a lot of work to do."

"Five dollars."

"Five? Yes sir, I can do it for five. I come in early or stay late for five. I tend to your shoes, take your suits down when you need a press. Brush your hat. Brush it with a brush, no whisk broom."

"All right, five dollars a week. Here."

"Six dollars?"

"Five dollars for your first week, the other dollar is for today. And don't think I always tip a dollar, because I don't."

"No sir. Thank *you* sir."

The hotel staff and, very soon, the friends of the hotel staff were fascinated by the latest member of the corps of engineers. There had been other strange ones, nutty ones, but this Weeks man was the first they ever heard of who had eaten human flesh; a white cannibal. Chester L. Weeks in a week's time attained a celebrity among the hotel and domestic servants and their friends in advance of his first invitations from the resident engineers and non-engineers of the town. But that is not to say he went unnoticed. It was summer, and the business and professional men of the town wore their Palm Beaches and mohairs, and a few of the rich wore linen suits; but Chester L. Weeks had a tropical wardrobe that was just different enough to attract attention every day, everywhere he went. He changed his suit every day, from spruce, crisp linen to luxurious silk; from Panama to Leghorn to Bangkok to sailor, with puggree bands and the colors of remote clubs to add brightness to his headgear. The stuff was not new, but the style and the variety were new to the town, and in those first days the men with whom Chester L. Weeks had to do business were so bedazzled by his wardrobe that they were slow in realizing that he was no mere dude. He was quick, sharp, and knew his business. The other engineers had dressed very conservatively, casually, or even shabbily; but then Chester L. Weeks was not, strictly speaking, an engineer. He had an engineering degree, and he worked for an engineering firm, but he was essentially a financial man. He was not exactly an accountant, although he discussed accounts; he was not a purchasing agent, although he was keenly interested in prices; he was certainly not a lawyer, but he knew the language of contracts. Nor did he come under the head of the fairly new and somewhat suspect designation of efficiency engineer. One thing was certain: he was not the kind of engineer who put on hobnailed boots and carried a transit on his shoulder.

Whatever the precise nature of his job, he seemed to rate on equal terms with the supervising engineer of the entire hydroelectric project, J. B. Wilcey, who had been in charge of the dam building and the plant construction since the earliest blueprint stage, and who was now something of a fixture in the town, with a good-sized house, a wife who played bridge and tennis, and two children in private schools. Jess Wilcey took Chester L. Weeks around and introduced him to the top men of the business and financial community, who did not fail to notice that Wilcey's manner indicated a willingness to please Weeks. "Thank you, Jess," Weeks would say, politely but unmistakably telling him to go and leave him with the new contact. It did not take long for the business men to get it through their heads that this new fellow, with his blue shirts and linen neckties and highly polished oxfords, was very well thought of in the home office back in New York. The concurrent stories that had somehow got around, to the effect that Weeks had once escaped from Chinese bandits and had seen a companion slaughtered to provide food, probably had enough basis in fact, the business men believed, to prove that dude or not, his manhood could not be questioned. It was hard not to question the manhood of an American who carried his handkerchief in his sleeve.

He was a rather small man, with no extra fat on him anywhere, the skin drawn tight over his cheekbones and a mouthful of large, even teeth. He was nearly bald, and on his face and pate and hands, in a fading suntan, were numerous large freckles or liver spots. He had a sharp nose and thin lips that he had a habit of moistening while he studied a business paper. His concentration was intense and he was liable to be impatient when it was interrupted, but his memory, especially for figures, was remarkable. "Thirty-two cents a foot, I think you said," he would say to a business man, referring to a minor detail of a large sheet of figures.

"I can easily look it up," the business man would say.

"Never mind. It was thirty-two," Weeks would say. "But couldn't you have saved us money on those shipping costs? Why the Lehigh Valley instead of the Pennsylvania?

We had our own trucks, and the Pennsylvania railhead is only four miles farther than the Lehigh Valley. But you took this roundabout way because the Lehigh Valley was four miles closer to the dam. Just at a guess I'd say that made a difference of between eight and ten thousand dollars, without having a table of freight rates at hand."

"You're right except for one thing."

"Where am I wrong?"

"You weren't here, so you don't happen to know that the Pennsy was having a strike. A rump strike."

"Then I apologize. It must be very annoying to have me come here, a total stranger, and start right in by questioning your judgment. I'll be more careful in the future. Next time I won't go off half-cocked. But that doesn't say there won't *be* a next time."

He was as unconcerned over the obvious fact that he antagonized some reputable business men as he was by the admiration of others. ("Show the son of a bitch whatever he's entitled to see, but keep him away from me.") The respect that was shown him automatically by virtue of his position in Wadsworth & Valentine was followed by respect he quickly earned on his own, in his relentless preoccupation with facts and figures and his apparent passion for work. "Don't you ever take time off to relax?" said Jess Wilcey, after two weeks of Chester L. Weeks and his zeal.

"Am I going too fast for you, Wilcey?" said Weeks.

"No, but there's no use killing yourself. You don't have to do it all in a month. In fact, you can't. And my wife's waiting for you to say the word, when we can entertain for you."

"That's very nice of her. Tell her any time from now on. The usual Company dinner?"

"Yes, I guess that's what it'll have to be, the first one.

You haven't met any of the wives, have you?"

"No. How many are there?"

"Six," said Wilcey. "Seven couples and you."

"All right, tell Mrs. Wilcey she can get that over with any time next week or the week after."

"Do you want to join the clubs? You almost have to join the Gibbsville Club, but what about the country club?"

"I'll join it. Company pays for it."

"I don't imagine you want to rent a house, but any time you want to move out of the American House you can probably live at the Gibbsville Club, or my secretary will find you an apartment."

"I like the American House. It's a bit broken down, but I like the atmosphere. How many Company dinners do I have to go to?"

"Just ours. The other wives will ask you to Sunday afternoon tea, but you know which ones you have to go to. Then whenever you're ready, Maria—"

"I know. The dinner to meet the natives. You seem to like it here."

"Yes, I do. We both do."

"Have you had any good offers to stay?"

"Yes, although you have a hell of a nerve to ask that question."

"Well, I *have* a hell of a nerve. That's no news to you, Wilcey. Don't tell me you haven't had a half a dozen letters telling all about me. I've had to play Company politics, too, don't forget. I found out all I could about *you* before I came here. That's part of the fun of working for a big company."

"I don't consider it fun. I stay out of Company politics as much as I can."

"Then you'd better seriously consider that local offer, because when you get to where you are and I am, that's when the Company politics is playing for high stakes."

"I'm a construction man."

"Then I don't have to worry about *you*, since you're planning to settle down here."

"I didn't say that."

"You didn't have to, and I could almost tell you what your next job'll be. But that's fine with me, Wilcey. You and I make about the same money, and the next step up is for you, or me, or McDonald, in Manila. You've eliminated yourself, so it's between McDonald and I. That ought to make for harmonious relations between you and I. Fine. Excellent."

Wilcey smiled. "Where did you learn your politics? In China? I was only out there for one year. Maybe I should have stayed longer."

"You're a construction man, Wilcey. And a good one. You stick to that. Ten years from now we may be able to do business."

"When you're president of Wadsworth & Valentine?"

"Chairman of the board. You're the type of man they make president. I don't want it. I want to settle down in New York. Well, now we understand each other perfectly. I thought we'd be six months getting around to this conversation. I hope you're as relieved as I am."

"I wouldn't say we understand each other perfectly, Weeks. But we made progress."

"I stand corrected. Let's say we understand each other as well as we ever have to. And you're a little keener than I gave you credit for."

"Thanks."

Maria Wilcey's Company dinner for Chester L. Weeks went according to protocol except that the guest of honor was the last to leave.

"Where do you get Scotch around here?" said Weeks.

"I got this through the Gibbsville Club."

"Pretty good. It actually tastes like Scotch. Mrs. Wilcey, may I congratulate you on a very nice dinner party? I hope it wasn't too dull for you."

"No, it went off pretty well, I thought. I'm sorry we couldn't have a young lady for you, but next time there'll be all local people and the town is full of attractive girls. Withering on the vine, I may say."

"I look forward to that."

"So are they," said Maria Wilcey. "They've all been wondering who you were, and by the way they've heard the most awful stories about you."

"I have a spotless reputation."

"No you haven't. Morally, yes, but did you know that you're supposed to be a cannibal?"

"A cannibal, did you say?"

"It isn't a subject I cared to bring up at a dinner party, especially a Company dinner party. But I've been asked whether it was true."

Weeks smiled. "Well—I once partook of human flesh. It was fed to me as pork, but I knew damn well it wasn't. That was in Borneo, when a party of us were sent looking for oil. But how did that get all the way back here? Oh, of course. I know. The bellboy at my hotel. What other damage to my reputation?"

"Do you carry a revolver?"

"No, but I know where that started, too. Same source."

"And you never were a spy," said Maria Wilcey.

"I was a military intelligence officer."

"But not a spy, running from one country to another."

"I've run from one country to another, but always for the greater honor and glory of Wadsworth & Valentine, Incorporated."

"Isn't that a military ribbon you wear?"

"It's the Croix de Guerre, but I got that in France three years ago. I think I'll stop wearing it, now that I'm back in the States."

"You didn't get it for spying?"

"No. My company happened to be next-door neighbors to a French outfit, and they gave all the American officers the Croix de Guerre. Our colonel got the Legion of Honor, and their colonel got the D. S. M. The French outdid us in courtesy, but of course they always do."

"He's lying to you, Maria. He got the Distinguished Service Cross," said Jess Wilcey.

"But not for spying, and that's what Mrs. Wilcey wanted to know about. I wouldn't have made a good spy. Too obvious. Too secretive."

"You had a very good war record. One of the best," said Wilcey.

"Well, all right, I did, but I'm not trading on it," said Chester L. Weeks. "Although of course I always wore my medals whenever the British wore theirs, in China. I have the Military Cross, and that did me no harm—or the Company."

"You're all for the Company, aren't you?" said Wilcey.

"I'm all for Chester L. Weeks, just as you're all for J. B. Wilcey."

"If the truth be told," said Wilcey.

"How long have you been with the Company?" said Maria Wilcey.

"Twelve years, with time out for the army. Do you want to know my age, Mrs. Wilcey? Thirty-seven. Your husband could have told you that."

"He didn't tell me anything about you, except that you were coming, and that you were here." Maria Wilcey was annoyed. "I heard much more about you from outside sources."

"A full description of me—or pretty full—was sent to your husband at least a month before I got here. It always is. You know how the Company works."

"Yes, but you obviously don't know how Jess works."

"Mrs. Wilcey, my job here is going to take about two years, then I'll be sent somewhere else. Maybe back to China. Mexico. We're going to have to see a lot of each other these next two years, and suddenly I seem to have gotten off on the wrong foot with you. Was it that remark about my age?"

"Yes."

"Well, I apologize. You see, I'm accustomed to wherever I go, the Company wives take it upon themselves to play Company politics with me, as happened several times this evening. Then they want to marry me off to their sisters. Well, I don't want to play Company politics with the wives. And I'll be damned if I want to marry their sisters. So I'm on my guard at all times, and if I was rude to you, I'm sorry."

"Well, let's have another Scotch-and-soda and forget about it," said Wilcey.

"First I want to know where I stand with Mrs. Wilcey. Do you accept my apology?"

"Of course," said Maria Wilcey.

"Thank you. Now I'll tell you something. I think you are the most charming, and probably the most intelligent Company wife I've met in many years. I would have thought so anyway, but I might not have told you so if we weren't going to be friends. Wilcey, think twice about taking that other job. I hate to see this charming lady wasted on this town."

"She likes it here," said Wilcey.

"You will too, when you've been here a while, Mr. Weeks."

"Not if I can help it. Your husband knows which way I'm headed."

He refused a lift home, and when the Wilceys had turned off the porch light they could hear the precise tapping of his heels on the sidewalk as he marched homeward. "Listen," said Maria Wilcey. "He even walks like a pouter pigeon."

"A pouter pigeon—"

"I know. Hasn't got leather heels. But isn't he a strutting little man?"

"Oh, I guess he's all right."

"I'll turn Mary Beth Huber on him. She's the last thing he'd expect to encounter here."

"Why do you want to do that?"

"Because he's so darn patronizing about this town."

"So were you, at first."

"So I was."

Mary Beth Huber, the most widely traveled young woman in the town, and soon to be off on another trip, sat next to Chester L. Weeks at Maria Wilcey's second dinner party. At the meat course she announced: "I refuse to apologize for monopolizing this man, but he has news of friends of mine I haven't seen in aeons. Now, Mr. Weeks, tell me about Jack and Lydia Banning-Douglass. Did they ever patch it up?"

"No. She went home, and he stayed in Hong Kong."

"And married the Russian? I can't believe *that*."

"No, she was around Shanghai for a while, then she disappeared."

"I didn't think that would come to anything," said

Mary Beth. "Did you ever know Hans van Blankers?"

"Van Blankers? Was he with Shell?"

"I don't think so."

"Where would I have known him?"

"In Bangkok."

"Oh, well you see I haven't been there since before the War."

"No, he was there after the War."

"My particular friends in Bangkok were the Van Egmonds."

"Still there. I had a Christmas card from them last year."

"So did I. Picture of a Dutch boy and Dutch girl skating on the canal."

"And the windmills in the background. Homesick, and afraid to go home after so many years. Just like so many of our friends out there. Did you find that to be the case?"

"Almost invariably, if they stayed in one place. The people that shifted around, or got home every two or three years, they didn't want to stay put. But some of the others you couldn't budge."

"And no wonder. I don't imagine they could live on the same scale back in England, or Holland."

"Although it was the women that usually wanted to go home."

"Well, that's understandable, too. Nobody ages very well in the tropics, but it tells more on the women. Physically, I mean. Are you going back?"

"I just got here, don't send me back so soon. I've just unpacked. Truthfully, I don't know. I'll be here about two years, then I don't know what comes next. We never do, especially we bachelors."

"If you had your way what would you do?"

"Oh, I have my way, Miss Huber. I'm not doing anything I don't want to do. But I suppose you mean if I had the money to do everything I want to do?"

"Yes."

"I'd go on working. I'd be doing more important things than I'm doing now, but working just as hard, using the same brains."

"The tropics haven't affected your ambition."

"I haven't spent all my time in the tropics, and in any case I wouldn't use that as an excuse for laziness. My offices in Hong Kong and Shanghai were no more uncomfortable than my office here. The electric fan was a great invention. The electric fan, used in conjunction with the paperweight."

"I'm going abroad next week. I'll be very much interested to see how you like Gibbsville when I get back."

"Where are you off to?"

"I'm taking my mother to the French Riviera. We'll take trips to North Africa, but I don't expect to see any of our mutual friends. I might go out that way again next year. It would be fun to. Did you play polo in China?"

"Yes, some."

"Then you must have known a man called Pat Dinsmore."

"I was wondering how you happened to miss Pat."

"Oh, I know, Mr. Weeks. But you must admit he has charm."

"Carloads of it."

"I fell for it, just like all the others, before and since. Was he a friend of yours? Do you hear from him?"

"Hear from him? He can barely read and write. No. I don't expect to hear from him. As for his being a friend of mine, he doesn't need friends. He has charm. But I suppose if I wrote to him I'd get an answer, some time in the next year."

"Don't on my account. But how is he?"

"Well, I saw him in June. He came to a stag farewell party for me, and that was one night he left his charm at home."

"And I guess that wasn't the first time. But you forgave him. Why *do* we, people like that? We're so intolerant of little faults in nice people, and yet we're prone to overlook big faults in people like Pat Dinsmore."

"Since you honor me with your confidence, I'll tell you that I never did forgive Pat Dinsmore. And if you ever do see him again, please don't mention my name, when I'm not there to defend myself. Will you promise me that?"

"Of course. Not that I ever expect to see him."

In her remaining days at home Mary Beth Huber did more than dispel some early suspicions that Chester L. Weeks was somehow phony. Especially among the younger men of the town, and particularly among those who had gone to good prep schools and colleges, the social judgment on him was severe. They conceded that his engineering degree from a Western Conference university was probably authentic; Wadsworth & Valentine would have checked on that. They accepted the Wadsworth & Valentine opinion of his professional ability. But his manners and his taste in clothes were a little wrong—and therefore all wrong. The word of Mary Beth Huber, world traveler, was indisputable in fixing Chester L. Weeks's previous social position in the Far Eastern polo and gin sling world. And yet he was not right. He made no claims that were probably false; he made few claims at all, and in two spheres of admirable activity—his work, and his war record—he did not take the credit he was entitled to. The same kind, and a lesser degree, of offense had been given when the leading bootlegger's younger brother had blossomed forth in a five-hundred-dollar raccoon coat. The fact that Chess-turr (they dragged out his name derisively) did not lie and that his credentials were valid was frustratingly infuriating, and it was not particularly pacifying to call him a wet smack and let it go at that.

He was at his most offensive at the bridge table. He was exceptionally good in a community where the standard of bridge was high. He would sometimes, after the fourth or fifth trick, lay down his hand and say, "I'll give you the king of clubs and a diamond trick. The rest are mine," and pick up a pencil to mark the score.

"Let's play it out," someone would say.

"Why? If you insist, all right, but I assume you're going to follow suit. All right, *let's* play it out." He was, of course, always right in such cases, and he was annoyingly over-patient with slow players.

"Is that your lead, Mrs. Walker?" he would say.

"Yes. The ten of hearts."

"I see the ten of hearts, but I want to make sure it's your final decision. Mrs. Walker has led the ten of hearts. From dummy, Mr. Weeks plays the queen. The queen of hearts, Mr. Forbes. Your king, Mr. Forbes? My ace. And now I lead my jack in the same suit. The jack of hearts, led. Mrs. Walker. The knave."

"Oh, dear."

"Why don't you play your four of hearts, Mrs. Walker? *Or* your five. I'm almost sure you have one or the other, because I see that little deuce and that little trey sitting over there in dummy. Ah, the four! Thank you, Mrs. Walker. From dummy I shall play the little deuce. And Mr. Forbes, I count on you to have the six-spot. Yes, the six. Nice distribution, isn't it? But I don't think we'll try that again. What's that they say about the children of London?"

"The children of London are starving because their fathers wouldn't lead trumps."

"I *thought* you'd know that, Mrs. Walker."

At least once a week he would play at a dinner-and-bridge or a bridge-and-supper, and if in the course of the evening there was always someone to feel the sting of his sarcasm for a wrong bid or an unreturned lead, no one could deny that Chester L. Weeks had the game to back it up. He played regularly in another foursome of two other men and a woman who were generally conceded to be the bridge sharks of the town, and he was equally tyrannical with them, although in this foursome the others fought back. The game was never played for high stakes; a quarter of a cent a point, in stag games at the Gibbsville Club, was the limit. But social prestige and the entree to certain formidable houses were reward enough for a man in his first winter in the town. And as he improved his position it seemed foolish and futile to maintain a hostility toward him that was based on little more than a hunch that he was somehow a faker. At the end of his first year in the town he had demonstrated his superiority in bridge, which could not have been faked; he was respected by the men of business and, obviously, by the Company that employed him; he really had played some polo in China; he had some first-class military decorations for bravery under fire. It was ridiculous to say that no one knew anything about him; no one knew very much about any of the new engineers' pre-Gibbsville history, and because of the special animosity toward him, more questions had been asked about his background than about any other man's in the Company. In a year's time the active animosity toward him practically vanished because it had become a bore, and it disappeared without having done anything to mollify or appease the young men who contemned him. They could have beaten him at golf and tennis, but he not only declined their invitations to play; he wondered aloud why presumably grown men wasted their energies on such silly pastimes. Then, to prove that he was not merely anti-sports, he won a mile race against a recent captain of the Penn swimming team.

All this was observed and duly noted by the mothers of nubile young women, most keenly by those mothers whose husbands had accurate information on Chester L. Weeks's personal finances. He was a long way from wealthy, but he was making fifteen thousand a year and his capital was somewhere around a hundred thousand. He was, moreover, thirty-eight years old, and according to Maria Wilcey, next in line for an important position in the home office in New York. He had distributed his attentions evenly among the young women of good family, and he had been classified as elusive; but no conscientious mother believed that an elusive bachelor was a confirmed one, and Blanchette Moseley was the conscientious mother of Ida Moseley, age twenty-five, graduate of Miss Harper's School for Girls, near Ardmore, and of Wellesley College. Blanchette Moseley was convinced that her Ida was just the kind of girl who ought to appeal to a man like Chester L. Weeks. *"You've* got to do something about it, Adam," she admonished her husband.

"All right, but what?" said Adam Moseley. "We've had him here for dinner a couple of times."

"Oh, *that.* So has everybody else. Get him interested in the bank."

"Oh, positively. I can just see the expression on certain faces when I say we ought to put this new fellow on the board. Apart from the fact that Weeks doesn't own a single share of bank stock."

"Wedding present."

"Well, if you want to give him your stock, that's all right with me."

"You don't have to give it to *him,* do you? We can give it to Ida."

"Bee, we don't want to get in any money competition to buy a husband for Ida. She'd hate that, and anyhow, we wouldn't necessarily win that kind of a competition."

"Have a talk with Ida and see how much she'd hate it. She thinks Chester's the most interesting man that ever came to town."

"In some ways he is, but how does he feel about Ida?"

"He has to be prodded, that's all. They have a lot in common. Don't forget Mary Ku."

"Mary Ku? Oh, that Chinese girl."

"Ida's best friend at Wellesley. Through her Ida knows a lot about China. And Ida loves to travel."

"I know that, all right. But so does Mary Beth. I'll do anything and everything I can, but first Weeks has to show some interest."

"He does not! That's exactly where you're wrong. He's so set in his ways that he'll never marry anybody if somebody doesn't prod him."

"You keep saying prod him. I don't quite know what you mean."

"Let's invite him on a trip, away from here."

"Just the four of us? You can't just up and invite him to go along on a trip with us and Ida."

"You don't have to do it that way. Take him up to the camp and Ida and I'll come along later."

"Well, that might work out. If he'll go."

"Ask him. He's not going to hear it by Ouija board."

"It won't look right if it's just he and I. I don't know him that well. I ought to ask a couple other men."

"Ask as many as you please, but not their wives and daughters."

An invitation to spend three or four days at Adam Moseley's camp with two or three men of equal substance would not be taken as a black mark on Chester L. Weeks's record at the home office. Jess Wilcey, for example, had not been given such an invitation until he had lived in Gibbsville three years. "I can guarantee you a buck if you know which way to point a rifle, and there's some trout fishing. In the evening we usually get up a game of bridge or poker. What size shoe do you wear?"

"Eight-B," said Chester L. Weeks.

"Then I guess I can fix you up with all the clothes you'll need. Not very dressy up there, you know. But plenty of hot water. You'll want a hot bath, especially after that first day in the woods. I notice you're a Scotch drinker, and we also have plenty of Canadian ale. We can leave here the afternoon of the fourteenth, about three hours' drive. Have a good dinner and turn in early so we can be up first thing in the morning. You familiar with the Thirty-O-Six? That's the rifle most of us use."

"Know the rifle very well."

"Good. I have four of them, and you can take your pick. Or you can use a different one every day till you get the limit. Our limit, that is. Our limit's one buck to a man. That's over the legal limit, but it's fair. The game wardens use common sense."

"I haven't brought down a deer since I left Michigan."

Here, at this precise point, by naïvely accepting an invitation he considered a simple compliment, Chester L. Weeks had made a decision he would regret throughout the rest of his life. On Wednesday afternoon Adam Moseley picked him up in his Dodge coupe. They arrived at the camp approximately three hours later, to be greeted by the other hunters, Samuel D. Lafflin, a Wilkes-Barre coal operator, and Malcolm Macleod, division superintendent of the Pennsylvania Railroad, both good shots and good bridge players. They had a steak dinner, cooked by Moseley's guide and caretaker; three rubbers of bridge after dinner, and a good night's sleep. They left the cabin at five-thirty in the morning, and were back at eleven, Lafflin having got his buck in the first hour. Toward dusk MacLeod, Moseley, Weeks, and the guide went out again, and Weeks shot his buck while there was still enough light for a good photograph of the animal and the overjoyed hunter. "Another fifteen minutes and you wouldn't have gotten him," said Moseley. "I'm going to make you a present of his head, mounted. I know a good taxidermist in Allentown."

"Why wouldn't I have gotten him fifteen minutes later? Too dark?"

"Yes. You could have still seen him, all right, but I wouldn't have let you shoot. If you'd missed, you know. Buck fever. A spent bullet from a Thirty-O-Six could kill a man a mile away and you'd never know it."

"But I didn't miss, and anyway I don't get buck fever."

"No, you certainly don't," said Moseley.

"We have two more days," said Weeks. "If you and MacLeod don't get your deer by Saturday afternoon, is it permissible for me to take another shot?"

"Well, yes. But you have to let MacLeod have first shot. That's the usual understanding."

"And what about you?"

"You can have my shot."

"Thank you."

In spite of Moseley's guarantee, no more deer were shot, but Weeks remained keyed up until late Saturday afternoon. His disappointment at not getting a second kill was offset by his being, with Lafflin, one of the two lucky hunters, and the arrival of Mrs. Moseley and her daughter in the middle of the afternoon furnished him with a new audience. "Do you shoot, Mrs. Moseley?" he said, at dinner.

"Only with my camera. Ida has. Ida got her first deer when she was fourteen."

"Fifteen, Mother," said Ida Moseley.

"Your first? And how many have you shot since then?"

"Six, here. Two years ago, in Maine, I shot a moose." She pointed to a head over the fireplace. "That one. Everybody thinks that was Daddy's, but it wasn't. It was mine. Daddy *wishes* it was his, but it isn't."

"I don't wish it was mine," said Moseley. "I just wish it had been T.R., instead of a poor inoffensive moose."

Blanchette Moseley's apprehension that Weeks might resent the feminine invasion of the stag party was unfounded. Rather, he seemed to be stimulated by the presence of women, and he was gracious and entertaining until after lunch on Sunday, when they were all ready to leave for home. "I wish I could spend a month up here," he said.

"It's all yours, if you can persuade Wadsworth & Valentine to give you a vacation," said Moseley. "But it'd probably get pretty lonely up here with only Joe Mossbacher to talk to. He doesn't have much to say."

"The less he said the better. Maybe I might even send him away."

"I don't know," said Moseley. "It'd be quite a change for you, you keep pretty busy."

"Isn't that what I want? A change?"

Blanchette Moseley easily maneuvered Weeks into Ida's car for the homeward journey, and herself into Adam Moseley's Dodge. "It went off very well," she said.

"Nothing forced, nobody got self-conscious."

"No, but don't count on me for any more coopera-
tion. I don't like this fellow."

"Oh, now what? I knew you had something plaguing
you."

"I don't want him for a son-in-law. No, it's not
that. I don't want Ida to be his wife, that's what I don't
want."

"I hope you'll respect Ida's wishes in the matter.
You'll get a very different story from her. What terrible
thing did you find out about him?"

"It's nothing you'd understand."

"Irritating. What is there that you'd understand that
I wouldn't, pray tell?"

"The effect it had on him when he killed his buck.
Right away he wanted to go on a killing rampage. He
wanted to kill Mac's buck and mine."

"You didn't get one, neither did Mac."

"No, you wouldn't understand it at all. He's the kind
of a fellow that comes up here and kills three or four deer,
as many as he can kill, and leaves them to rot. Doesn't
even bother to skin them out."

"You were willing to let him stay here a month."

"That was a safe invitation. There's something about
this man's character, I don't pretend to know what it is, but
I don't want to see him married to Ida."

"Well, I hope for Ida's sake that she can overlook
these mysterious flaws in his character. And don't you
help her go looking for them."

"We're going to have snow," said Moseley. "They're
having a blizzard in Montana, I read."

"Oh, pish and tush, Adam Moseley."

Ida Moseley had her friends, and throughout that

fall and winter Chester L. Weeks was so frequently asked to call for Ida—he would walk to her house, and they would proceed to parties in her car—that it began to be taken for granted that he would be her escort at the social functions of the younger set. She was not so beautiful that habitual propinquity to her was likely to turn a man's head; there was no compelling urgency in a friendship with Ida Moseley, and no unbearable suspense was created for her friends. With Ida it was said you could have a good time without getting serious, and plainly Chester Weeks had a good time with Ida, a jolly good time. But Ida was unable to confide in even her closest friends that Chester had misbehaved, made passes, got fresh, or stayed late at her house. He was of course an older man, a man of the world who had himself under control at all times and one who was more likely to protect a girl's reputation than some of the young bachelors and young husbands in Ida's set. It was somehow understood that he *probably* had secret affairs with some of the women in the town who were understood to have secret affairs with men like Chester L. Weeks; those well-dressed dressmakers and nurses and manicurists who went out with traveling salesmen but rarely were seen in public with town men. It would have been so easy for him to have just that kind of extremely private life while living at the American House. He had refused to take advantage of the vacancies at the Gibbsville Club when they occurred, and the American House was known to be lax about women visitors in men's rooms. And Chester himself, so secretive and so independent and self-sufficient, was just the kind of man who would be too discreet to patronize one of the whorehouses but would make elaborate, secret arrangements for his pleasure. Without a doubt he had had concubines in China, and on the word of Mary Beth Huber he had moved in a fast set on the other side of the world.

Among the older men and women, contemporaries of Adam and Blanchette Moseley, the belief in Chester Weeks's clandestine affairs was so fixed that they expressed some cautious concern for Ida's future: if, as seemed reasonable to suppose, he were eventually to marry Ida, would he give up his other women? Ida pretended to be a sophisticated girl, but did she know what she might be getting into? A man like that could ruin a nice girl's life, and for all her sophistication—reading books by Schnitzler, shooting crap with the young men, driving her Hudson Speedster at eighty miles an hour, and the black silk one-piece bathing suit that had got her a strongly worded note from the club—Ida was a nice girl. Friends of Adam and Blanchette Moseley hoped Ida would not make a fool of herself over this man, and they would be glad when his two years were up and he went away.

Not much was left of his two years at the end of that second winter, and Ida Moseley faced the spring in a mood that sickened her because she would not treat it as desperation. Every day was lost time, and the first of August less than four months away. Chester thought he knew where he was going next: the Company had already asked him how he would feel about being "loaned" to the Irish government.

"Would you like that?" said Ida.

"Hard to say," said Chester. "It could be a big step forward, or it could turn out to be a waste of time. One thing that would interest me."

"What?"

"Well, the language. In China we used to hear that Gaelic and one of the Chinese dialects—I forget which—

had words in common. I'd know as soon as I heard them. And of course living in Ireland is much cheaper than living here. I'd save a lot of money there."

"You never worry about money."

"I don't worry about it, but I think about it."

"When would you go, if you went?"

"I get a month off in August, then I report to the home office. Probably the middle of September, late September."

"Won't you be at all sorry to leave Gibbsville?"

"No. I'm not like Jess Wilcey. He's staying here, you know."

"Yes, I know. Maria told me."

"And that's why he's staying. Because Maria likes it. And I guess he does too, although it's Maria that makes the decisions."

"You don't like Maria."

"No. A man as good as Jess shouldn't stop here. He should have made at least one more step upward."

"You've made a lot of friends here."

"Name two. You, but who else?"

"Oh—dozens. You've been one of the most popular men we've ever had. You could be going somewhere every evening if you wanted to."

"Only to escape another kind of boredom. If I had to, I could finish up my job here in four or five weeks. I'm 'way ahead of my schedule. As a matter of fact, I've thought about doing just that, finishing up and taking a leave of absence before the Irish job."

"What other kind of boredom did you mean?"

"Sitting in my room with no work to do."

"Before you go I want to see your room."

"Why? There's nothing to see. Half a dozen prints, and

a mantelpiece full of photographs. But my own furniture's in storage in New York."

"I'd still like to see it, where you've lived for nearly two years."

"No. Can you imagine the buzzing if you were seen leaving the American House?"

"Well, naturally."

"If I had my own things it might be worth it. I have some really lovely pieces I picked up in China. Some jade, naturally. And some tapestries that date back to the twelfth century."

"Haven't you any of the jade here?"

"Four pieces, minor items in my collection because I know what hotel chambermaids can do. But the good stuff is stored in New York till I have a house there. Has to be a house. No apartment for me."

"I still want to see your room at the American House."

"It can't be done. Your mother would not approve."

"What if I went there with her?"

He smiled. "Sure, if your mother's interested in brass beds and Grand Rapids rockers."

"Tomorrow, after dinner?"

"Day after tomorrow. I'd offer you dinner, but they don't set a very good table at the American House. You and your mother come in any time after half past eight."

At nine o'clock on the second evening Ida Moseley appeared in the hotel lobby, went to the house telephone, and was connected with Chester's room. "We're downstairs," she said.

"Come right up," he said.

He stood in the hall outside his room, and said nothing when she walked past him through the doorway. He closed the door.

"This could get you in all sorts of trouble, Ida," he said.

"Well, I'm here, so it's too late to do anything about it now," she said. "Don't be cross, Chester. Give me a drink."

"I'll have to send downstairs for some ice. That means the bellboy, getting a good look."

"Jimmy Scott? I've seen him already. Jimmy used to work for us, in our garden. Just give me whiskey or gin and some water from the tap. And a match, please."

He lit her cigarette and made two Scotch-and-waters. She took off her hat and tossed it in a chair.

"What exactly did you have in mind, Ida?"

"I wanted to put you in a compromising position."

"Compromising positions are passé, but endangering your own reputation is just damn foolishness. And that's all you're doing."

"Well, let's have a drink on it."

"It won't be your first, either."

"No, I sneaked a few at home. Is it noticeable? I only had two. No, three. I had a brandy with Daddy, and two by myself."

"Where's your car?"

"Parked down the street in front of the bank. Why?"

"Finish your drink, and we'll go for a ride."

"No hurry."

"That's just the point, there is. If we go now, right this minute, you might be able to get away with it. Not even that evil-minded night clerk could accuse you of much in five minutes."

"Oh, you have a portable. Have you got any new records?"

"Ida, let's cut out the nonsense."

THE CAPE COD LIGHTER

"Now, you've made your honorable gesture, honorable Chester. Honorable Chester with the honorable gesture. But having done so, your conscience is clear and I, for one, would like another Scotch. How about you?"

"No more, for me or you,"

"Don't be an Airedale. I'm not some sixteen-year-old virgin, unacquainted with the facts of life. Surely you don't think I'm so hopeless that I could reach the age of twenty-five without being seduced. I wouldn't call that a compliment, not a bit. Chester?"

"What?"

"Don't make me talk this way. I don't want to get tight. But I have to have something to get up my nerve. If you knew the times I wanted you to kiss me. And if you had, you could have gone the limit. Did you know that? Is that why you didn't kiss me? You could tell that, couldn't you?"

"I suppose so."

"You know so. I don't know whether I love you or not. I think I do. But whether I do or not, I'm sort of hypnotized by you. And that's just as good or just as bad as being in love. I don't care a *thing* about that other boy. He was just a—well, he was a *darling* boy. I won't say anything against him. And I admit it, I was crazy about him. But with you it was sex without being sex, if you know what I mean, and you probably don't. Or maybe you do. Do you?"

"Yes."

"Oh, you do? Then you knew about me, and you didn't want to start something. See, that's where Neddie was inexperienced. Neddie was the boy. He never would have understood that, but you do. That's where you're experienced. All those women, probably Chinese girls and heaven knows what all. You know we're a lot alike, you and I. You were probably seducing me all that time without even holding my hand, and I felt it. I knew what you were doing. You learned that in China, didn't you? I read it somewhere, something to that effect. Or India. It takes immense concentration. But I have a lot to learn, haven't I?"

"Yes, you have."

"I'll be with you in a minute," she said. She went to his bathroom, and came out in a few minutes, wearing her slip and shoes. "I'm still a bit shy," she said.

"So I see."

"You hurry, though, please? And while you're in there I hope you don't mind if I turn out the light."

"I'm not going in there, Ida."

"All right. Come here and kiss me, darling."

He sat on the edge of the bed, took her in his arms, and kissed her. "There," he said.

"No, I think the light's too strong," she said. "It's the light, it's much too strong. And take off your coat. Your coat and vest, take them off."

"No, Ida, I'm sorry."

"I'll take off this slip."

"No, don't."

"I have a nice shape, I really have."

"I know you have. It's quite lovely."

"One of the best in my class."

"I'm sure."

She smiled. "But you don't have to take my word for it."

"I'd rather," he said. "I'd really rather, Ida."

"Don't you want to *see* me?"

"I don't really want to see you."

"You want to wait a while?"

"It isn't that. Seeing you won't make the slightest difference. Nothing will."

She was silent. She gazed thoughtfully at the brass posts at the foot of the bed, and she frowned. Then she remembered that her hand was on his shoulder, and she took it away.

"You mean you can't?" she said.

"I can't because I don't want to."

"Oh."

"It isn't you, Ida. You're very sweet. Very sweet. And I'm sorry."

"Wouldn't you just like to lie here with me, gently?"

"It wouldn't be any use, and I wouldn't like it. No, I don't want to."

"Is it men?"

"When it's anything, yes."

"But that's terrible, Chester. I feel so sorry for you."

He smiled. "That's because you're nice. You are nice, you know."

"I never guessed. You know—I'm supposed to be pretty blasé."

"Well, now I guess you will be. When you've had time to think it over."

"I don't need time. And I don't like being blasé."

"No, it isn't much."

"It's nothing. Really nothing."

"And now I'm nothing, am I?"

"I don't know. Kiss me again."

He kissed her cheek. She shook her head. "It's much too much for me to understand. I'll have a drink, please."

He went to the table, and while his back was turned she slipped past him to the bathroom. She came out fully dressed, and accepted the glass he held out for her. She sat down and gave him a quick smile, but looked away from him.

"Is this one of the jades you brought from China?"

"Yes, not a very good one."

She put it down without examining it very carefully. "I don't know anything about jade. I have one in my room at home that's supposed to be pretty good. Given to me by a Chinese friend of mine."

"Mary Ku," he said.

"Yes, you've heard me speak of her. She's been here. Everybody adored her."

"Go on home, Ida. Don't make talk-talk."

She finished her drink quickly. "I think I will. Are you coming for dinner Friday?"

"No, I don't think so."

"You can if you want to."

"No."

"I guess you're right, really."

"If I sent you one of my good jades would you keep it?"

"Oh, you know I'd like to, but—"

"Say no more."

"I need a little time to straighten things out in my mind. Oh, heavens, Chester. *You* know."

"Of course."

"Goodnight," she said.

Her car went off the road at a turn about five miles north of Reading, some time around half past ten. It was quite possible that she was blinded by the headlights of a bootlegger's truck, but no one knew why she was so far from home, and alone, at that hour of the night. But they found a considerable amount of alcohol in her stomach, and that was when the questions led back to the American House. Dr. Mary Ku came all the way from Massachusetts General to attend the funeral.

THE FATHER

Miles J. Berry, forty-two, assistant foreman and head mechanic at the Clinton Motor Company, Trenton, New Jersey, entered the kitchen of his home on the outskirts of Trenton, took a can of beer out of the refrigerator, put the can and a glass on the kitchen table, pushed his cap to the back of his head, and let go with a long sigh. From the second story came his wife's voice. "Is that you, Miles?"

"Yes, that's me, Miles. Who the hell'd she expect?"

"Wha'?"

"I said yes it was me."

"There's a letter for you, I put it on top of the TV. It looks like it was from one of your sisters."

"Which one?"

"Wha'?"

"Which one?"

"I do' know. I didn't open it."

"But you're sure it's from one of my sisters."

"Wha'?"

"How'd you know it was from one of my sisters?"

"I seen the postmark on the envelope. Nyack, New York, and it isn't your mother's handwriting."

Miles Berry sipped his beer and lit a cigarette. Slowly he reached down and untied his right shoelace, then untied his left shoelace. He had another sip of the beer, then pulled the laces out of the top eight eyelets of both shoes, took the shoes off and pulled his socks away where they were stuck to his feet. He sighed again. "Ah, Christ," he said.

"What are you beefing about now?"

He had not heard his wife, in her canvas wedgies, coming downstairs, and now she stood at the dining-alcove door, with a bundle of dirty laundry in her arms. "I wasn't beefing," he said. "Where's Ava?"

"She's out, I guess."

"She's out you guess? We don't have all that big a house. She's out or she's in."

"She's out," said Vilma Berry.

"Where, out?"

"Where? At a friend's, maybe. Or down at Al's. The kid's young, she has to have some relaxation."

"You ought to keep her out of that Al's. I know that Al. I knew him ever since I was a kid and any joint he runs I don't want my kid hanging around."

"Then you tell her. What's the harm in having a Coke and maybe smoking a couple cigarettes?"

"You look inside of one of those cigarettes and maybe you won't find any tobacco."

"What are you, inferring they get reefers at Al's?"

"Not inferring anything."

"Well, if you want to give her an order to stay out of Al's you do it. But Ben Lightner the cop's daughter goes there, and if there was reefers for sale Ben ought to know about it."

"Ben is a traffic cop. What does he know where they sell reefers?"

"All right, all right, all right. If you got information you ought to report it."

"I didn't say I have any information. I just said I know Al. I went through school with him and I was in the army with him."

"Whenever your feet hurt you start getting strict with Ava. Why don't you buy a new pair of shoes instead of torturing your feet with those clodhoppers? Then we'd have a little more peace around here."

"Wuddia want me to do? Wear loafers to work? I gotta wear shoes that keep my feet dry. It might inarrest you to know we *wash cars* at the garage, not to mention oil and grease on the floor. I can't wear any other kind of shoes and keep my feet dry."

"Well, I just wish you'd find some solution. You got your bad feet from the army. Make them give you the right shoes."

"It's too much red tape."

"You got anything you want to put in the laundry?"

"No."

"You want to wear what you got on to work tomorrow?"

"Yes."

"It wouldn't hurt you to wear a clean shirt and pants."

"What's wrong with what I got on?"

"Because this is the day I put them in the laundry, otherwise you'll be short next week. You'll want clean next Monday, and I won't have them for you. You got two clean pants in your drawer and two clean shirts, but you'll need clean next Monday to start the week in. Wednesday you'll want clean, Friday you'll want clean, Monday you'll want clean, but you'll only have dirty. How'd you get those so dirty today?"

"I thought you were suppose to wash on Monday? My mother always did her washing on Monday."

"Listen, I got a system worked out, so don't start screwing it up after all these years. The least you can do is go to work with a clean shirt and pants, and nobody can say I'm not a good housewife. This washer isn't big enough for all the laundry I have to do."

"Three people and this house? Wuddia want, the Stacy-Trent washing machine? We only got three people and the sheets and towels. What's so big about that?"

"Because I send my daughter to school clean and my husband to work clean and I do the marketing clean, and anybody comes into this house don't see a lot of dirty towels—you know how many towels you use up in a week? And since you took to wearing that long underwear."

"You rather I got pneumonia?"

"Oh, you're just beefing about anything and everything. Why don't you go read your letter from your sister?"

"Curiosity killed the cat."

"Well, what's *she* writing you a letter for? If she has anything to say why doesn't she say it over the phone, those Friday night calls from Nyack. Collect. God Almighty, you'd think you were living in South Dakota somewhere, and they never saw their brother Miles."

"Well, they don't hardly."

"There's nothing stopping you from taking the car and driving up to Nyack any Sunday you want to."

"Nothing but fifty thousand cars on the Turnpike. I don't get any pleasure out of driving that way."

"Go read your letter."

"When I finish my beer," he said, finishing it.

The letter was leaning against a light blue, temporarily empty flower pot on top of the television apparatus. The handwriting was that of Dot Berry, Miles Berry's older sister. The envelope almost matched the color of the flower pot, and Berry held it up to the light because he could tell it contained two items, one besides the notepaper. Good old Dot.

He tore open the end of the envelope and took out the contents, the notepaper and an old newspaper clipping. Whenever Dot wrote him she always enclosed a newspaper clipping or something like that. The clipping seemed to be from the *Daily News,* although he was not sure. It was a photograph taken in 1943, and it showed four-and-a-half teen-age girls, some grinning, some in the midst of rolling their eyes, huddled together behind a sign that said: "Frankie Boy Is the Most— The Sinatra Swooners Trenton N. J." The caption gave the names of four of the girls, and the second girl from the left was Vilma Schrock, 17, Trenton.

"For God's sake," said Miles Berry. He read the caption again. The girls, it read, had been waiting outside the Paramount Theatre in New York City since seven o'clock in the morning, and at the time the picture was taken they had been waiting four hours and probably would have to wait four more, because the kids who were already in the theater were refusing to leave when the show was over. Vilma Schrock, 17. And he knew the others, too. Mary D'Isernia, 16; Carmen Quisenberry, 17; Rosemary McEntegart, 17, and Betty Dougherty, 16. They were all married, all living in or near Trenton, with their husbands and a total of about fifteen or sixteen children. He read Dot's note:

Dear Milo:
I came across this old paper underneath a pile of stuff in the attic. I guess it was when Mom used to save up Dick Tracy to send you before

you went over seas. She does not remember why she saved it altho we looked all thru the paper to see if there was some article in it. You were over seas when this picture was taken & did not know Vilma then. Therefore we did not save the paper on acc't of Vilma being in it. Just a coincidents. I bet she gets a big laugh out of it today.

Mom is better. Will phone Fri.

Sincerely,

Dot

There she was, the way she was at seventeen, looking as though she were about to charge the photographer and bite him. She had better teeth than the other girls in the picture, but did she have to look like a charging tigress? The photographer probably had said something disparaging about Frankie Boy, to get her reaction.

The kitchen door swung open and Ava came through. "Hi," she said.

"Hi," he said.

"What are you reading?"

"I got a letter from your Aunt Dot."

"Aunt Dot? What does *she* want?"

"She doesn't want anything. She isn't like some people, the only time you—"

"I know, I know, I know. The only time you hear from them is if they want something. I know. What's the matter with the TV?"

"Who said anything's the matter with it?"

"Well, turn it on, then. Gee, Pop. Wuddia, just sitting here?"

"What channel do you want?"

"Six."

"What's on Six?"

"Clutch Cargo."

"Clutch Cargo? What's that?"

"Oh, here we go again. You say it in that tone of voice and I know what's next. Why don't I watch Hunkley Hinkley Brinkley. Pop, I got all the homework I need, without watching Hinkley Hunkley Brinkley."

"This is the time when you ought to be learning something, instead of hanging around Al's all afternoon. I don't like you hanging around Al's."

"Where else do you *want* me to go? I suppose Jimmy's."

"What's Jimmy's?"

"See, you don't even know which places are all right."

"What's Jimmy's?"

"It's another candy store two squares up past Al's. It's where the Emperors hang out. Johnny D'Isernia and Chip Quisenberry. Them."

"I know all about them all right. You stay away from them."

"Then how do you know so much about them if you never heard of Jimmy's?"

"I know enough."

She appeared about to say something, but she kept silent and proceeded to the front hall and up to her room. He could tell when she reached her room: her record-player began to broadcast the melancholy, despairing music that her generation loved, and soon her thin little voice, thin but true, joined in the tune. She could not be thinking of the words she was singing along with the boy vocalist; something about his little sweetheart, his little dove, lying dead on the highway. But her voice went along with the music, and Berry found that there were tears in his eyes, for Ava and for Vilma Schrock, 17, but mostly for Ava. And for every father, too, but mostly for Ava and the years ahead.

THE FIRST DAY

On Monday morning at ten minutes of eight Ray Whitehill entered the Ledger-Star Building, walked quickly through the business office and on to the news room, and came to a halt at Lester Bull's desk. "Hello, Les, here I am," said Ray Whitehill.

"Good for you, Ray. Welcome back. Let's see, I'll take you over and introduce you to the only other member of the staff that's in so far. Or do you know her? Mary McGannon."

"No, I've never met her."

At the last desk in a row of five a young woman was at a typewriter, copying from a notebook, which she peered at through heavy glasses.

"Mary, this is Ray Whitehill. Ray, Mary McGannon."

The young woman quickly removed her glasses and stood up. "Oh. Well, goodness. How do you do? Welcome back, Mr Whitehill."

"Thank you."

"Needless to say, I've heard a lot about you, and we're all so glad you're going to be on the paper again."

"That's very nice of you. What have you got there? A P.T.A. meeting?"

"Well, just about. The League of Women Voters, but the names are almost the same."

"Get them right," said Whitehill. "And always remember that Mrs. J. Stanton Keene spells her name with three e's and the other Keens get along on two."

"Oh, Mrs. J. Stanton isn't with us any more," said the young woman. "She's been out of circulation over two years."

"You mean *more than* two years," said Whitehill. "I didn't know the old girl had cooled."

"Mary writes it *more than,* but in conversation she always says *over,*" said Bull.

"Yes, she brought down her last gavel two years ago."

"Well, don't let me interrupt you," said Whitehill.

"Will you excuse me?" said the young woman. "I've got forty names to copy before I go on my rounds. Very glad you're back, Mr. Whitehill."

"Very glad to be back, thanks."

The girl put on her glasses and sat down.

"I thought it would be nice to get you your old desk, but it's nowhere around," said Bull. "We got all these new ones in a couple of years ago. All new desks and typewriters."

"My old one would have looked out of place here."

"Yeah, I guess it would, but I asked anyway. So I've put you here, temporarily. If you want to change later I'll get one of the other boys to trade places with you, but you don't want to be over on the sports side, do you?"

"Makes no difference where I sit, Les. Although that's where I started. The sports side. When I first came on the paper I *was* the sports side. I did the whole thing myself."

"Well, we have four men doing it now. You know,

every township has a high school now, with a stadium and a swimming pool, and a band. Scholastic sports really sells papers, we found. More so than the junior college."

"What junior college? You mean to say the town has a junior college?"

"Oh, since 1947. Twelve hundred students, but sportswise they don't cut as much cheese as the high school leagues."

"I've been away a long time."

"Yes, when you left I wasn't even in kindergarten."

"That was 1927."

"I'm thirty-seven. I've been here fifteen years this June. I've never worked anywhere else."

"God knows I have."

"I should say you have. I wish I had your experiences to look back on, but when you're married and three kids you think twice about making a drastic move. And I can't complain. They've treated me very well. When the two papers merged I got this promotion, and I'm in on participation. It would have been fun to get around more, but it looks like I'm here the rest of my life unless there's something drastic."

"Well, this is where I began, and this is where I end up, if that's any consolation."

"Yeah, but I never interviewed Winston Churchill, and I never palled around with Heywood Broun and Damon Runyon. Was it true that Runyon couldn't speak, that he had to write on a pad of paper?"

"Yes, the last years."

"I saw a picture of Heywood Broun, he was wearing a raccoon coat and a high silk hat. Did he really dress like that? The unmade bed, somebody called him."

"He didn't care how he looked."

"But he could write. We used to have to read old columns of his. By the way, I've arranged to have the New York papers on your desk every day. The boss said you wanted the *Trib* and the *Times*. They come in around ten o'clock, by mail. Okay?"

"Fine, fine. Thanks, Les."

"You make yourself comfortable, then. I've got to start getting out a paper. Oh, Ray, this is Bud Freedman, our assistant sports editor."

"Hello, Ray," said a young man.

"Hello, Bud." They shook hands.

"Les, I have a story you might like to run on Page One and jump to the sports page."

"What's the story?"

"Marty Moreno's been offered the job coaching the St. Joseph's varsity."

"Why don't you stop? You come in with that story every year."

"This time he's going to take it."

"When he does we'll run it, but never on Page One. Go to work and stop trying to win the Pulitzer prize."

"Where is Marty Moreno coaching now?" said White-hill.

"Queen of Angels. You know Marty?" said Freedman.

"Look in the files, around 1925, and under my by-line you'll find a story that says Marty Moreno has been offered the job of coaching at Villanova. I went for that in 1925, the first year Marty was coaching."

"You're kidding," said Freedman.

"Find out for yourself."

"Thirty-six years ago? Yeah, I guess he could of been coaching then."

"He was coaching, all right. Queen of Angels.

Marty will be coaching with the Queen of Angels when he meets the real one."

"What was that? Let me have that again."

"It isn't all that good," said Whitehill.

"He'll be coaching the Queen of Angels when he finally meets the real one. Wait'll I see him. Will I give him that for a needle? Thanks, Ray." The young man went to his desk.

"Eager," said Les Bull.

"Young," said Whitehill. He went to the assigned desk and inspected the contents: a drawerful of *Ledger-Star* stationery in assorted sizes; typing paper and flimsies and carbons; a neatly folded clean hand towel; an area telephone directory; a box of pencils; a stapler and a package of paper clips. The neat efficiency brought back memories of a room he had once occupied in an *Essex* class carrier, even to the matching pencil and ballpoint pen set. He pulled the typewriter out of its hiding place in the desk, and the typewriter was almost new. He rolled a couple of pieces of paper into the typewriter and tapped out his byline. He saw Les Bull looking up from his work and smiling.

"Attaboy, Ray," said Bull. "That's good to hear."

"My byline," said Ray Whitehill. "That may be as far as I'll get, today."

"Hang in there," said Bull.

One by one the other members of the staff reported for work, all strangers to Ray Whitehill except John J. Wigmore, the county editor. The others wasted little time in the amenities, and Whitehill made no attempt to hold them in conversation, but John Wigmore was a contemporary, had started on the paper a year ahead of Whitehill. He kept his hat on and he was smoking a cigar. "Ray, it's like old times to see you back," said Wigmore. He sat on Whitehill's desk. "Do you recall the big fire of '26?"

"I sure do," said Whitehill. "That was the first time you ever let me cover a news story."

"Yes, and I guess you might say that gave you your start. Hadn't been for that you'd still be covering basketball. Not really, though. You'd have been discovered sooner or later. They couldn't keep you down, Ray. You had the old zing, the old razzmatazz, and you could write. If I'd been able to write worth a damn they wouldn't have put me on the desk."

"The boy editor," said Whitehill.

"I was the youngest city editor in this part of the State. Now I'm damn near the oldest. Where you living?"

"I took a room at the 'Y' temporarily."

Wigmore looked from right to left, lowered his voice and said, "If you're looking for a nice apartment, I can fix you up."

"What's the angle, John?" With Wigmore there was always an angle; that much had not changed.

"Oh, no angle, exactly. Strictly legitimate. You pay rent. But this new apartment building just went up at Fourth and Market."

"I noticed it."

"A little trouble with the building inspector that I happened to be instrumental in fixing up for the Roach brothers. They're the ones put up the building. So naturally I know Jerry Darby, the building inspector, and I got him together with the Roach boys. Now it's all straightened out."

"I imagine the builders are very grateful."

"Well, their apartment house could have sat there empty for six months or a year if somebody didn't take some action. Where they made their mistake was antagonizing Jerry right at the beginning."

"Were you the bag man, John?"

Wigmore smiled. "You know, the funny thing is, no money changed hands. Not a nickel." He studied the end of his cigar. "Now just between you and I, Ray. Jerry has a daughter just got married and it wouldn't surprise me if her new house was built with surplus materials from the apartment building. It's a brick house, and so's the apartment, and I understand she got the same make of refrigerator and dishwasher you'll find in the apartments. Surplus, of course. Hard to trace. But that way everybody's happy."

"And what's your end?"

"Don't worry about me, Ray. My old motto, ask me no questions and I'll tell you no lies. But anyway, there's only two vacancies left and I can get you one for a hundred and a quarter that somebody else'd have to pay two-fifty. Do you have your own furniture?"

"In storage," said Whitehill. "New York."

"We'll send a truck for it," said Wigmore. "Like to have you meet the Roach boys. They're going to be doing a lot for this town, Ray."

"Why not? I'll be glad to meet them."

"Then I'll tell them to hold one of those apartments for you? They're both the same identical size and layout, so whichever one they hold won't make any difference. And you're more or less a prestige tenant, so don't have any hesitation."

"Just a mild payola?"

"Just a mild. Well, I gotta get to work. Where you having lunch?"

"Having lunch with the boss, at the University Club."

"Lousy food, but it's the University Club. I usually eat at the hotel. Are you going to join the University Club, Ray?"

"I don't have to. I was made an honorary member in 1943."

"Oh, that time you came back and lectured. They made you an honorary member. Does that still hold good?"

"As far as I know."

"Don't have to pay any dues, then, hey?"

"Nope."

"That makes you and the boss the only members in this shop. And you're in for free. Pretty nice, pretty nice."

"At those prices," said Whitehill.

The New York papers were delivered punctually, but in the time before their arrival he had written nothing more than his signature. The other staff members were busy at their typewriters and telephones, and when they spoke it was only to each other. They were a little in awe of him, he knew, and they could not know that that was not what he wanted now. He wanted to be made to feel at home in what had been his professional birthplace, but most of them had not been born when he was already too big for the paper and the town. He had felt more at home in bureaus in Hong Kong and Helsingfors, in tents and Quonset huts in the western hemisphere; he had been more at ease with Nehru and Ben-Gurion than with the assistant sports editor of the *Ledger-Star*. He could not concentrate on the available newspapers, the exchanges from the nearby cities in the State, and when the New York papers arrived he read them eagerly, like letters from friends, which indeed they were in at least a manner of speaking. He knew Lippmann as Walter, Alsop as Joe, Reston as Scotty, and to them he was Ray or Whitey. He read the papers and some of his confidence came back to him, and he thought of a piece he might write for the morrow's *Ledger-Star*. But now it was time to keep his date at the University Club, with the boss.

It was a three-story, red brick and white trim building, just off one of the main streets, and he could remember when it was being built, then later when he would go there to cover banquets, then—in 1943—when he went there as guest of honor. The biggest men in town had been there that night, listening respectfully to his report of the fighting against the Germans in Italy. He spared them nothing, that night. They needed to be told some hard, ugly truths after the let-down that followed Mussolini's surrender. When he sat down they were momentarily silent, but then spontaneously they rose and burst into applause and he knew he had done some good. They made him an honorary member and gave him a Revere silver bowl, and the president of the club said how appropriate the bowl was, although accidentally so. "None of us knew beforehand that Ray was going to be a modern Paul Revere," said the president. "But he sure is riding and spreading the alarm, and we'll always be grateful to him."

Ray Whitehill entered the club and started to give his name to the sixtyish attendant. "Don't you remember me, Ray? Al Redmond."

"Aloysius Patrick Xavier Redmond, for God's sake," said Whitehill. They shook hands and Redmond took his hat and coat. "Do they let you play pool here?"

"Tell you the truth I could beat most of them, even with my eyesight the way it is. You're here to stay now, Ray?"

"I think so. I hope so. Maybe we can get in a game sometime."

"Bring your money, I could always give you fifty to forty," said Redmond. "Mr. D. B. Otis would like for Mr. Whitehill to meet him in the bar. I guess that's one place you could always find your way to, Ray. Anyhow, it's to the end of the hall and down them stairs."

"Thanks, Al. See you soon," said Whitehill.

Dexter Otis was standing with his back to the bar, and as soon as he saw Whitehill he waved and pointed to a table for two against the wall. "Got wedged with a bore, and I don't even know his name," said Otis. "Will you have a drink, Ray?"

"No thanks."

"You don't drink anything at all any more?"

"Two years."

"That long, eh? Well, I seldom do during the daytime. Let's order, shall we? I'm going to have the sausage cakes and mashed potatoes. If you stick to the plain things the food here's all right, but otherwise, no. I noticed you're an honorary member, so you'll probably come here a lot, but don't expect fancy dishes."

"I'll have the sausage cakes. Yes, they made me a member in '43."

"I was in the Navy then. I guess that was when I first began to read your stuff. You were doing a lot of magazine stuff."

"Quite a lot. That, and the radio."

"And you sold one book to the movies."

"Two."

"Do you mind if I ask you a personal question?"

"No, go right ahead," said Whitehill, sensing what the question would be.

"Where did it all go, the money I mean, the dough you made?"

"Well, I sometimes wonder myself. I was married twice and divorced both times, and I had a daughter by my first wife. Her education took quite a bit, although I don't regret a nickel of that. I guess I don't regret any of it."

"But weren't you living on an expense account a lot of the time, when you were overseas?"

"Very few guys got rich that way. All that seemed to do was help us acquire expensive tastes."

"Have you any idea how much money you made?"

"All told? You mean since I left the old *Star?*"

"Yes."

"Well, I never stopped to figure it out, but thirty-four years. Over all I probably averaged twenty-five thousand a year in salary. How much would that be?"

"Uh, that would be eight hundred and fifty thousand."

"Books. Lectures. Radio. And two movie sales. And I had that television show a few years ago. I don't know, Dexter. I'd have to put it down on paper. Maybe a million. Taxes always gave me a lot of trouble."

"But you made around two million dollars."

"Yes, I guess I did."

"You make us look like chiselers at the *Ledger-Star*. I wish we could pay you more."

"I'm satisfied. I may not be worth what you are paying me. I may not work out at all."

"Well, we both agreed to try it for a year."

"A year should be plenty long enough," said White-hill. "I just don't want you to keep me longer than a year if you're not satisfied."

"Well, frankly, we couldn't afford to, but we're hoping that by the end of a year's time you'll be syndicated. With your name, your reputation, once you get back into the swing of things—we discussed all that."

"And I'm glad to say you're more optimistic than I am."

"The way we see the picture, Ray, the paper's making money, no doubt about that. We have a monopoly, and some people will tell you that's not a good thing. But one paper that makes money is better than two that are losing money, and that's just about the way it was when my Dad bought the *Star*. The *Star* was on its last legs, and the *Ledger* hadn't shown a profit since the end of the war. So Dad merged the two papers and four years ago we began to see daylight. But what we've got we want to hold on to. It isn't only circulation-wise. It's readership-wise. We could throw the paper into every mailbox in the county and still go out of business, that's what circulation counts for. It's readership, the competition from TV. Do we pull, or don't we? It comes down to this fact, namely, do Sam Jones and his wife Minnie want to read the *Ledger-Star* six days a week? As long as they do, we stay in business. Now we have a lot of good features, syndicated stuff, but it lacks the local identification. That's why when you wrote me for a job we decided to gamble on you, to give us local identification and a well-known name. Confidentially, Ray, you're getting more than anyone else on the paper, and it's a gamble, even if it doesn't seem like much compared to what you've been accustomed to. Les Bull, our managing editor, doesn't know what you're getting. You're not on the regular editorial budget. You come out of the executive budget." At this point the sausage cakes were served.

"Well, as you say, Dexter, it's a gamble. Maybe Minnie Jones isn't going to like me."

"That we'll have to wait and see, but just go at it relaxed, as if you had all the time in the world, and I think you'll get a good response. We'll be able to tell in a month or six weeks, but you mustn't be discouraged if some of them don't know you, your reputation. Some of the younger ones don't, you know."

"A lot of them don't."

"I probably shouldn't say this, considering that you used to hobnob with F.D.R. and Hitler and Stalin, but you realize, Ray, those names are ancient history to a young housewife that wasn't born when the Japs hit Pearl."

"Yes, I realize that. My daughter isn't much older than they are. She's a young housewife."

"Then you know that. They don't even remember Korea very well."

"I didn't go to Korea. I was having booze trouble then. Booze trouble, wife trouble, income tax trouble. And I panicked whenever I looked at a typewriter."

"But you straightened yourself out. You made a lot of money after that."

"Yes, I went back to work. That was when I covered the Berlin airlift."

"When was that, Ray?"

"What I just said. When the Korean trouble started I was having trouble with my wife and I took to the bottle, but I got straightened out, and then I went over and covered the Berlin airlift."

"No. I think the Berlin airlift was before the Korean trouble. I'm pretty sure of that, Ray."

"Was it? Wait a minute. Yes, I guess it was. You're right."

"I wouldn't correct you on a thing like that, only I happen to remember wondering whether I'd have to go back in the Navy."

"It was before the Korean business, you're right."

Throughout the rest of the meal the conversation was awkward and forced. Young Dexter Otis had embarrassed himself, but it was his own fault. How could he expect a man to remember everything that had happened in those crowded years? Dexter Otis, probably a j.g., if that, at the very moments when Mitscher and Nimitz and Halsey were welcoming their friend Ray Whitehill to the Pacific Ocean Area. Would Eisenhower give a grin of recognition upon seeing Dexter Otis? Bradley? Patton? Clark? De Gaulle? Montgomery? Was he ever even sneered at by Goering, barked at by Mussolini? Of course not.

"I beg your pardon, Dexter."

"I was just asking you, in your lapel. Is that the Legion of Honor?"

"Legion of Honor, that's right. I don't often wear it, or any of them."

"How many have you got?"

"I guess about six. Purple Heart. Air Medal. Oh, I guess I have maybe six or seven." He chuckled. "Sometimes I put one on when I want to spruce up a bit, like today, my first day in the new job. Then maybe I go for two or three months without taking them out of the box. The only time I never go without this is in France. The French like you to wear it. They figure it's a courtesy to them when an American wears their decoration."

"Well, it is."

"But not many people around here know what it is, so I think I'll put them all back in the box. All that's in the past anyway, and I'm more interested in the future. As you say, Minnie Jones doesn't care what I did ten, twenty years ago."

"That's a good, healthy way to look at it, Ray."

Plainly the man was pleased to be relieved of his embarrassment. "It just occurred to me, Dexter. I have all the medals, in storage in New York. What would you think if I donated them all to Franklin High? That's where I went. Might be good promotion later on. I have the medals and in addition I have, oh, plaques and scrolls and diplomas, not to mention autographed pictures. It might have some promotional value, and I had four walls from floor to ceiling filled with the stuff. That way the stuff would have some historical value, instead of just gathering dust. And underneath, of course, a discreet little plate to remind everybody that yours truly is a staff member of the *Ledger-Star*. Oh, we'd get that in."

"Yes. Yes, I think it might be good."

"I have a very wonderful picture of me with the old man. Churchill. Completely informal, relaxed. We wouldn't want any Hollywood stuff, would we? I have any number of pictures of me with movie people. And a lot of other celebrities. Writers. Ballplayers. But I was thinking I could give the other stuff to Franklin High, and we might make use of the Hollywood and sports people somewhere in the Ledger-Star Building. You know, it does no harm to remind the old home town that a character named Ray Whitehill was on a first-name basis with the most famous people in the world, and has the pictures to prove it."

"Right. Well, we have plenty of time to talk about that, Ray. I have to go to a meeting, if you'll excuse me."

"Of course. I think I'll stay and have another cup of coffee," said Whitehill.

The younger man departed, and Ray Whitehill sat alone, he knew not how long. The waitress came to him and said, "That coffee must be cold, Mr. Whitehill. Let me give you some fresh."

"All right, thanks," he said. But it would take more than coffee, more than anything he could name, to put warmth where he felt a chill.

JURGE DULRUMPLE

On long trips—to see the cherry blossoms in Washington, to hear the music in the Berkshires, to visit relatives at distant points—Miss Ivy Heinz and her friend Miss Muriel Hamilton sang two-part harmony, not only because they loved to sing but as a safety measure. Muriel Hamilton had never learned to drive, and their singing kept Ivy Heinz from getting too drowsy. They sang well together, especially considering that both were natural altos. Muriel Hamilton carried the melody, since it was a little easier for her to get out of the lower register and also because she was more likely to know the words. Ivy Heinz could go awfully low, and sometimes for a joke she would drop down in imitation of a man's bass, and whenever she did that, just about *every* time she had done it, Muriel Hamilton would say, quickly, without a pause in the singing, "George Dalrymple."

"No, *no!*" Ivy would say, and they would laugh.

Any mention of George Dalrymple was good for a laugh when Ivy Heinz and Muriel Hamilton got together. It was an extremely private source of amusement, sure-fire or not. Shared with a third party it would have been an act of cruelty to George because an explanation of the laughter would have involved revealing a secret that concerned only

George and the two women. It went back to a time when all three were in their middle twenties, the summer in which George Dalrymple proposed first to Muriel Hamilton and then, a month later, proposed to Ivy Heinz. Neither girl had been enormously complimented by a proposal from George Dalrymple, but they knew that from George's point of view it was a compliment, a terribly serious one that was no less serious or sincere because he had gone so soon from Muriel to Ivy. George Dalrymple was a serious man, a fact that made it fun to have a private joke about him, but in public you had to treat such seriousness seriously.

Other people, in discussing George Dalrymple or even in merely mentioning his name, would often lower the pitch as far down as they could get. They would pull their chins back against their necks, and the name would come out, "Jurge Dulrumple." His speaking voice was so deep, his enunciation so economical, that his vocal delivery was his outstanding characteristic, more distinctively his than those details of appearance and carriage and manners that he might share with other men. There were, for example, other men just as tall and thin; others who swayed their heads from side to side independently of their bodies when they walked; and others who were as quickly, instantly polite in such things as standing up when a lady entered the room, lighting a girl's cigarette, opening doors. George did all these things, but what set him apart was his way of talking, his words coming from down deep in his mouth and expelled with a minimal motion of his lips. His friends, such as Ivy Heinz and Muriel Hamilton, knew that he was not self-conscious about his teeth, which were nothing special but all right; and it was not in George Dalrymple's character to go around talking like a jailbird or a ventriloquist. George Dalrymple talked that way because he was serious and wanted people to realize that everything he said was serious.

When George came back from his army duties in the winter of 1919 he was twenty-three years old. His military service had largely consisted of guarding railroad bridges along the Atlantic Seaboard, a task he performed conscientiously with the result that he was discharged a corporal. If the woor—the war—had lasted six months longer he would have been a second lieutenant and probably sent to Brest, France, or some such point of debarkation; his congressman had been practically promised the commission by the War Department. But once the Armistice was signed George was anxious to get out of the Urmy and resume work at the bank. He had already lost practically two years, and in the banking business it was wise to start early and stick to it. The time he had put in at the bank before he was drafted was now just about matched by the fifteen months he had spent protecting the railway systems from German spies. The bank took him back at a slight raise in pay and with full credit in seniority for the time he had been in the service of his country. It was a pleasant surprise to find that one of the newer bookkeepers at the bank was none other than his high school classmate, Muriel Hamilton.

Two of the women who had been hired during the hostilities were let go, as they had been warned they would be, but Muriel Hamilton was kept on. The recently inaugurated school savings plan, for children in the public and parochial schools, owed at least some of its success to Muriel Hamilton and her ability to get along with children. She was painstaking and patient, and the bank officials put her in complete charge. Once a year she went around and gave a talk to all the classes from seventh grade to senior high, and the bank could see the results immediately. No one was more surprised than Muriel herself.

In her four years at High she had been so near to failing in Public Speaking—which almost no one ever failed—
that it had pulled down her general average and kept her
out of the first third of her class. George Dalrymple's marks
in Public Speaking were as bad as Muriel's, but his other
subjects kept him in the first ten in a class of eighty-five
boys and girls, the largest class in the history of G.H.S. It
surprised no one that George Dalrymple, on graduation,
had a job waiting for him at the Citizens Bank & Trust. His
high school record merited the distinction, a fact that delighted his father, the assistant cashier. John K. Dalrymple was not a man who would have forced his son on the
bank.

In his pre-army days as a runner at the bank George
Dalrymple and his father always walked home together for
noonday dinner. Each day John K. Dalrymple would take
the opportunity to review George's morning activities in
detail. The father had George repeat all the conversations
he had had with the tellers at the other banks, and he would
suggest ways of improving the impression he created in the
banking community. "It's all very well to have the light
touch," John Dalrymple would say. "But it can be carried
too far. It's better to be all business at your age. Time
enough for ordinary conversation later on." There was no
actual danger that George might get a reputation for frivol-
ity, but he was young and did not know all the ropes, and
his father did not want George's natural gravity to be affected by nervous unfamiliarity with the work.

John Dalrymple, as assistant cashier, did not have to
stay as late as his son, and they did not walk home together
at the close of business. But as soon as George got home he
would get into his overalls and join his father in the
flower garden, or, during the cold months, in the odd jobs
about the house that John Dalrymple claimed kept him

from getting stale. Father and son had very little time together in the evenings; John Dalrymple liked to stay home and read, while George had choir practice one night, calisthenics and basketball at the "Y" two nights, stamp club another, Sunday evening services at the Second Presbyterian Church, and the remaining evenings he spent with his friend Carl Yoder. Sometimes the boys would be at the Yoders' house, sometimes at the Dalrymples', and once in a while they would take in a picture show if it was Douglas Fairbanks or a good comedy.

It was a terrible thing when Carl passed on during the influenza epidemic. George could not even get leave to come home for the funeral. In fact, there was no real funeral; the churches and theaters and all such public gatherings were prohibited during the epidemic; the schools were closed, and you could not even buy a soda at a soda fountain. The death rate was shockingly high in the mining villages, but death by the wholesale did not affect George Dalrymple nearly so much as the passing of funny little Carl, the Jeff of the Mutt-and-Jeff team of Dalrymple and Yoder in the Annual Entertainment at G.H.S., senior year. George Dalrymple knew that things would not be the same at home without Carl trotting along after him everywhere they went.

One of the first conversations he had with Muriel Hamilton at the bank was about Carl Yoder, their classmate, and George was quite surprised to discover how fond she had been of Carl. "I always thought it was mean to call him The Shrimp," she said. "He didn't like it, did he?"

"No, he certainly did not," said George. "But he wouldn't let on to anybody but me."

"I didn't like it either, because remember in the Annual Entertainment when he wore girl's clothes? I loaned him that dress. And if Carlie was a shrimp, then that made me one too."

"Oh, yes. I remember that dress. That's right, it was yours. But that wouldn't make you a shrimp, Mure. Girls aren't as tall. I never think of you as a short girl."

"Five feet two inches."

"That makes me ten inches taller than you and ten inches taller than Carl."

"Oh, I thought you were taller."

"No, it's because I'm skinny, and so much taller than Carl. Just six feet and maybe an eighth of an inch."

"I never saw you in your uniform."

"Well, you have that treat in store for you. I'm going to be marching in the parade, Decoration Day."

She was a girl, not a short girl, and soon after that first conversation he formed the habit of walking part way home with her after the bank closed for the day. He would say goodnight to her at Eighth and Market, slowing down but not stopping when she entered her house. His new duties at the bank included opening up in the morning, a full half hour before Muriel reported for work, and he did not see her in the evening after supper except by accident. His schedule also had been rearranged so that his and his father's lunch hours did not coincide, and George was not entirely displeased. His father's questions about army life indicated a belief that it had been far more exciting and sinful than was actually the case. Some aspects of army life had disgusted George and he hoped never again to see some of the men in his company; the bullies, the drunkards, the dirty talkers, the physically unclean. George Dalrymple had come out of the army a somewhat coarsened but still innocent young man; he had lived closely with men who really did so many of the things that George and Carl Yoder had only heard about. He had heard men tell stories that they could not possibly have made up, and some of the stories were told by men about their own wives. Nevertheless George Dalrymple had no inclination to discuss that sort of thing with his father. It would have been almost as bad as discussing them with his mother. The war was over, he was through with the army, he had not liked being a soldier, but the whole experience was his own, a part of him, and to speak of it to his father would be an act of disloyalty to himself and the army that he could not explain to himself but that he felt deeply. It was private.

The time would come, he knew, when it would be no more than the right thing to invite Muriel Hamilton to a picture show and a soda afterward. If, in those circumstances, she showed another side of her, he would start keeping company with her and, eventually, ask her to marry him. She was exactly his own age, but he did not know any younger girls. She was what some people called mousy, but she was very well thought of at the bank, and he liked her femininity and her neatness. As soon as there was a tiny daub of ink on her finger she would scrub it off; she never had a hair out of place; and he was sure she used perfume, although that may have been perfumed soap. He had watched carefully the tightening of her shirtwaists over her bosom, and concluded unmistakably that marriage to her would be a pleasure. She had not been one of the prettier girls at G.H.S., and yet she was not by any means homely, and it was remarkable that she was still single while other girls, less attractive, were already married. She belonged to a group that called themselves the H.T.P.'s, who went to the pictures and had sodas together and had been doing so since senior year. One of the group dropped out to get married, and shortly thereafter it became common knowledge that H.T.P. stood for Hard To Please. Now the only ones left of the original H.T.P.'s were Muriel Hamilton and Ivy Heinz.

Muriel so readily accepted George Dalrymple's first invitation to take in a show that he felt sorry for her. She was not really an H.T.P.; she was merely waiting to be asked. They went to the movies, they had a soda. "There'll be a trolley in about seven minutes," said George.

"A trolley, to go eight squares?"

"I forgot to ask you before," he said.

"The only time I ever take the trolley is if it's pouring rain and I'm going to be late to work," she said. "I like walking. It's good exercise."

"So do I, now. I got pretty tired of it in the army, but that was different."

Watching the movie, they had not had any conversation, and now, walking her home, he began a story, about his army duties, that he had not finished when they reached her house. She stood on the bottom of their front steps while he hurried the story to an ending. "Well, thank you for taking me to the movies, George. I enjoyed it very much," she said.

"The pleasure was all mine," he said.

"See you tomorrow," she said.

"Bright and early," he said. "Goodnight."

He said no more than good morning to her the next day. He was determined not to let their outside relationship alter their conduct at the bank. Nevertheless he waited for her when the bank closed, and he soon discovered that their relationship had been altered. "George, I, uh, maybe I ought to wait until you ask me again, but if you have any *intention* of asking me—to go to the movies, that is—then maybe we oughtn't to walk home together every day. Walking home from work, that's one thing. But having a date, that's another. And I don't think we ought to do both. Maybe that's rather forward of me, but if you had any intention of asking me for a date?"

"Yes. Yes, I see."

"Half the people at the bank knew we had a date last night."

"Oh, they did?"

"You can't do anything here without everybody finding out about it."

"Well, personally I don't mind if they find out about that."

"But I do, George. Walking home from work, that's just politeness, but when a fellow and a girl have dates at night in addition, then that's giving them something to talk about."

"I'd be willing to give them something to talk about, but that's up to you, Mure."

"It is and it isn't, if you know what I mean. It all depends on whether you were going to ask me to go out with you in the evening. But if you were, I'd have to say no. And I don't want to say no."

"On the other hand, I don't want to give up walking home with you."

"Then we haven't solved anything, have we?"

"Not exactly," he said. "But maybe I can solve it. How would it be if we kept on walking home every day, but didn't have *regular* dates? Most fellows and girls have date-night on Wednesday, and when they start going real steady, he goes to her house on Sunday."

"We're a long way from that," she said. "All right. We'll walk home after work, as usual, and if you want to take me to a picture, you say so and sometimes I'll say yes and sometimes I'll say no. Is that all right with you?"

"Anything's all right that you agree to."

They violated the agreement immediately. He saw her every Wednesday night, and on Sunday evenings he walked home with her and Ivy Heinz. He and Ivy would say good-night to Muriel, and he would then walk home with Ivy. But though Muriel had never invited him inside her house, Ivy simply opened the door and expected him to follow her, which he did, on the very first night he walked home with her. She called upstairs: "It's me, Momma. I have company."

"All right, but if you're going to play the Vic don't play it too loud. It's Sunday. And don't forget, tomorrow's Monday morning."

Ivy wound up the Victrola and put on Zez Confrey's "Kitten on the Keys."

"Do you still dance, George?"

"Oh, I'm terrible."

"Well, we can try," said Ivy.

He knew as soon as he put his arm around her waist that the dancing was only an excuse. She stood absolutely still and waited for him to kiss her. They kissed through three records, one of them a non-dance record of Vernon Dalhart's, and at the end of the third she stopped the machine and led George to the sofa, stretched out and let him lie beside her. She seemed to be able to tell exactly when he would be about to get fresh, and her hand would anticipate his, but she kissed him freely until the court house clock struck eleven.

"I-vee-ee? Eleven o'clock," her mother called.

"You have to go now," said Ivy.

Sunday after Sunday he got from Ivy the kisses he wanted from Muriel, and after several months it was more

(*159*)

than kisses. "Next Sunday you come prepared, huh?" said Ivy, when their necking reached that stage.

"I am prepared, now," he said.

"No. But next Sunday Momma's going to be away and I'll be all alone. We won't have to stay down here."

He had grown fond of Ivy. From the very beginning she had understood that he was in love with Muriel and had never brought her into their conversations in any way that would touch upon her disloyalty to her friend or his weakness of character. Nor was she jealous of his feeling for Muriel. Nor was Muriel so much as curious about what might go on after they said goodnight to her on Sunday evenings. But fond as he was of Ivy, it was her taking him to bed with her—his first time with any woman—that compelled him to propose marriage to Muriel. He had no doubts about himself now, and among the doubts that vanished was the one that concerned his marital relations with Muriel. As husband he would be expected to know what to do, but before the night in Ivy's bed he had not been sure himself.

He took Muriel to the picture show on the Wednesday following the Sunday in Ivy's room, and when they got to Muriel's house he said, "Can we go inside a minute?"

"It's after eleven, George."

"I know, but I didn't have much chance to talk to you. I wish you would, Mure."

"Well, I guess they won't object, a few minutes. But you can't stay after half past eleven."

His manner did not show it, but he had never been so sure of himself or wanted Muriel so fiercely. He stood behind her as she was hanging up her things on the clothes-stand, and when she turned and faced him he did not get out of the way. "I want to kiss you, Muriel."

"Oh, George, no. I noticed all evening—is that what you were thinking about?"

"Much more, Muriel. I want you to marry me."

"Oh—goodness. You're standing in my way. Let's go in the parlor."

She switched on the parlor chandelier and took a seat on the sofa, where he could sit beside her. She let him take her hand. "Did you just think of this?"

"Of course not. I've been thinking about it for over a year," he said. "Maybe longer than that, to tell you the truth. You're an intelligent girl, and you know I've never dated anyone else."

"As far as I know, you didn't. But I never asked you and you never told me. You could have been having dates with other girls."

"Maybe I could have, but I never did. Ever since I got out of the army the only girl I wanted to be with was you. And that's the way I want it to be the rest of my life. I love you, Muriel."

"Oh, George. Love. I'm afraid of that word."

"You? Afraid of the word love? Why, you, you're so feminine and all, love ought to be—I don't know."

"Well, marriage, I guess. I guess it's marriage I'm afraid of."

"I guess a lot of girls are, but they get over it. Your mother did, my mother did, and look at them."

"You have so many wonderful qualities, George, but I don't think I could ever love you the way Mama loves Father. And your parents. It's nothing against you, personally, it's just me. And any fellow."

"My goodness, you love children."

"You mean when they come in the bank? But that's what they are. Children. You're a man, George."

"Don't tell me you're a man-hater."

"No, not a man-hater. Heavens. But I could never—I never want to get married! Why don't you help me? You know what I'm trying to say. I wouldn't like a man to—I was afraid you were going to kiss me, in the hallway. *That*. That's what I'm trying to tell you. I could never have children. When we were in High didn't you use to feel the same way about girls? I used to think you did. You never went out with girls, George. You and Carlie had more fun than anybody."

"But I always liked girls."

"Well, I liked boys, too, but I never wanted to be alone with a boy. You know how old I am, and I've never kissed a boy in my whole life. And I never will."

"You're wrong, Muriel. You'll fall in love with one some day. I wish it was going to be me."

"How wrong *you* are. I wouldn't let you sit here if I thought you were like the others." In the conversation she had taken away her hand, and now she put it back on his. "I want a man for a friend, George, but that's all. When I was little I read a story about a princess. She was forced to marry this king or else he'd declare war on her father. I couldn't do that. I'd sooner kill myself."

"Why?"

"Don't ask me why. I think all girls feel that way, underneath. I don't think they ever get used to some things, but they pretend to because they love their husbands for other reasons. I could love you that way, George, but you wouldn't love me. You wouldn't be satisfied with just being nice. You'd have to be a man and do those things that are so ugly to my way of thinking."

"But girls have desires, Mure."

She shook her head. "No. They only pretend. Most

girls have to have a man to support them, but if they had a job they'd never get married. I have a job and Ivy has a job, so we didn't have to have a man to support us."

"The rich girls on Lantenengo Street, they don't need a man to support them."

"Not to support them, but that's the way they stay rich. The rich girls marry the rich boys and the money all stays together."

"I hear some pretty funny stories about some of those girls."

"Yes, but most of them drink, and the men take advantage of them. The girls are nice, but when they take too much to drink they're not responsible. That's why the men up there encourage them to drink."

"Well, I know very little about what goes on up there, but at the rate they're spending it, some of them won't have it very long."

"I feel sorry for the women. I don't really care what happens to the men, especially one of them."

"Did something to you?"

"Not to me, but to a girl I know. One of the H.T.P.'s. One night at the picture show, he did something. Don't ask me any more about it because I won't tell you. But they're all alike, up there."

"You'd better not say that at the bank."

"Oh, I should say not. But whenever that man comes in I think of what his wife has to put up with. And they're supposed to be the people everybody looks up to. Rich, and educated, the privileged class."

"I wouldn't be like that, Muriel."

"I know you wouldn't, George. But maybe men can't help themselves."

"It's a good thing we talked about this."

"Oh, I wouldn't have married you, George. Or anybody else."

"I was thinking of something else. You make me wonder about women, how they really feel. You're a woman, and I guess you ought to know."

"We just don't have the same feelings men do."

"Then if women all had jobs the whole race would die out."

"Yes, except that don't forget women love children and they'd still go through it all to have them."

"Would you?"

"No, I don't love children that much."

"What do you love, Mure?"

"What do I love? Oh, lots of things. And people. My parents. Some of my friends. The music in church. Singing with our old bunch. Nature. I love nature. I love scenery, a good view. Flowers. Nearly all flowers I love, and trees on the mountains. The touch of velvet, like this cushion. And I love to swim, not at the shore, but in a dam if the water's not too cold. And my one bad habit. Smoking cigarettes."

"Now I never knew you smoked."

"I don't get much chance to, except when I go to Ivy's. Mrs. Heinz has something the matter with her nose, some condition, and we can smoke one right after the other and she never catches on. If my parents knew I smoked they'd disown me."

He looked at her hand. "Muriel, some day the right fellow will come along, and all these things you said tonight, you won't even remember thinking them."

"Don't say things like that, George. You don't know me at all, what I really feel. Nobody does, not even Ivy."

"Your trouble is, you're just too good, too innocent."

"Oh, I don't like that, either. You meant it as a compliment, but it shows a great lack of understanding. Of me, that is. You think that some fellow with wavy hair—"

"Maurice Costello."

"Or Thomas Meighan. I'll meet somebody like that and forget the things I believe. But you're wrong. I'd love to have Thomas Meighan for a friend, but honestly, George, I'd just as soon have you. At least I know you better, and I don't know what I'd ever find to talk about with Thomas Meighan." She looked at him intently. "George, I don't want to put you off proposing to someone else. You'll make some girl a good husband. But when you do find the right girl, if you want to make her happy, don't be disappointed if she doesn't like the kissing part of married life. You know what I mean, and it isn't just kissing."

"I know."

"A friend of mine, a girl you know too, she got married, and now she comes to me and cries her heart out. 'You were right, Muriel,' she says. 'I hate the kissing.' I used to try to tell her that she wasn't going to like it, but she wouldn't believe me. She said if you love a person, you don't mind. Well, she loved the fellow she married but now he hates her. Isn't that awful? And I feel just as sorry for the fellow, George. He can't help it that he has those animal instincts. All men have them, I suppose. I guess even you, because I admit it, I had that feeling earlier that you were going to want to kiss me, and that's the first step. I've always known that about boys, and that's why I've never let one kiss me."

"Well, I guess we'd better not have any more dates."

"Oh, we couldn't now. And maybe you'd better not wait for me after work tomorrow. I've told you so much about myself, I don't know how I'm going to look at you in the morning."

(165)

"Do you feel naked?"

"George! Oh, why did you say that? Go home, go home. Please go, this minute." She was in angry tears, and he left her sitting on the sofa.

At the bank in the morning she seemed cool and serene, but he was not deceived. At moments when once she would have given him a bright, quick smile, she would not look at him. In the afternoon he stayed behind longer than usual, to give her a chance to leave well ahead of him. On Sunday night she was not at church, and he walked home with Ivy.

"You can't come in," said Ivy. "My mother's still downstairs."

"Then she must be sitting in the dark," he said.

"All right, you can come in, but it won't be any use," she said.

He put a record on the Victrola, but she braked the turntable. He put his arms around her, but she turned her face away and sat in a chair where there was not room for him. She lit a cigarette before he could get out his matches. "Muriel told you, huh?" he said.

"Sure. She tells me everything. I don't tell her everything, but she tells me. Now you'd better leave her alone."

"Oh, I will. She's a man-hater."

"Just finding that out? And what if she is?"

"At least you're not."

"Maybe I should be."

"Oh, she handed you some of her propaganda," said George.

"Think back to one week ago tonight, George Dalrymple. Then Monday, Tuesday, and Wednesday you proposed to Muriel."

"Ivy, you knew all along that some day I was going to ask Muriel to marry me."

"No I didn't. I thought you'd find out that she was never going to marry anybody. You had a lot of talks with her."

"Not about that subject. What's the matter with her?"

"Does there have to be something the matter with her?"

"Well, there's nothing the matter with you. You want to get married some day."

"Maybe I do and maybe I don't."

"Yes you do. What if I asked you to marry me?"

"You didn't ask me."

"Then I do ask you. Will you marry me?"

"No."

"Well, maybe that's because you're sore at *me*. But you're going to marry somebody."

"There you're wrong."

"You'll have to have somebody."

"I have somebody—now."

"Who?"

"Wouldn't you like to know?"

"That's why I'm asking you. Harry Brenner?"

"No, not Harry Brenner."

"Chick Charles?"

"Not him, either."

"Oh, that new fellow in the jewelry store."

"Wrong again."

"I can't think of anybody else you had a date with. Is it a married man?"

"Give up, stop trying."

"All right, I give up. Who is it?"

"That's for me to know and you to find out."

"Don't be sore at me, Ivy."

"I'm not really sore at you, George."

"Yes you are, but when you get over it, let's take in a movie next week?"

"No. Thanks for asking me, but I'm not going to see you any more."

"You're sore about Muriel. Well, I couldn't help it."

"Honestly, George, I'm not sore about Muriel. Not one bit."

"Well, I'm going to keep my eye on you. I want to find out about this mystery man."

"It's a free country, George."

On the next Wednesday night he happened to be at the movies with Harry Brenner's brother Paul, and sitting two rows in front of them were Ivy Heinz and Muriel Hamilton. Later, at the soda fountain, George walked over and reached down and picked up the girls' check. "Allow me, ladies?" he said.

"Oh, no, George, you mustn't," said Muriel.

"My treat," he said. "I guess thirty-two cents won't break me." He paid the cashier on the way out, and stood on the sidewalk. The girls stopped to thank him again, and Muriel, somewhat ill at ease, made some polite conversation with Paul Brenner. George, in his muttering way, spoke to Ivy. "Using Muriel as a disguise, eh?"

"Curiosity killed the cat," said Ivy.

It was a long time, many Wednesdays, before George Dalrymple allowed himself to believe that Ivy was not using Muriel as a disguise. But they were just as nice about his secrets, too.

JUSTICE

There was nothing in or about the house that had been in being more than four years, nothing that gave promise of lasting more than five. The land itself, I knew, had been bulldozed and shoveled into its present contours to provide the setting for the house, which was split level on several levels. For the most part the house was made of glass, stained woods, and aluminum. I had heard that the house alone cost ninety-five thousand dollars, but driving up to it for the first time, seeing it from a distance, I could not help thinking that it looked like an advertisement for a trailer. Trailer advertisements have a way of looking like ads for children's playhouses, and I suppose that what made me think of trailers was that general air of impermanence. Or maybe it was the other way around. The roof supports on the front terrace of the house were thin poles of aluminum, as though they were meant to be folded and tucked away when the trailer, or the house, moved on in the morning. The whole house, or so it seemed on my first look, could be folded according to a trailer designer's plan, and driven off to Maryland or Arizona or Florida or Oak Ridge, Tennessee.

I knew that at one time a man could have stood on the site of the house and seen General George Washington and his Continentals. The view from the house was superb: rolling country, still largely held by dairy farmers whose family names were repeated in the names of the townships and "corners" and villages of the countryside. I was sure that Harry Rupp and his wife and children had never looked out from their terrace and tried to imagine Washington and his men in the snow. But it didn't matter. Barbara Rupp, with her contact lenses, could not see that far, and from what I came to know of their children, they hated history, which they called "social studies." As for Harry, his imagination was active enough but he had trouble recalling any date prior to Pearl Harbor . . .

I parked my car, that first day, and climbed the steps to the terrace level, where Mrs. Rupp was sunning herself and Harry was standing, in Hawaiian print shirt, plaid shorts, blue ankle-length socks, and huaraches. He had a cigar in his left hand, which he held rather daintily high. "Hi, Mr. Daniels," he said. "You didn't have to come all the way out here."

I was a little out of breath.

"Steps are pretty steep," said Harry Rupp. "But they keep my legs in condition. Sit down a minute. Like you to meet my wife. Barbara, this is Mr. Daniels. He's the chairman of the hospital drive."

"No, only the special-gifts committee," I said.

"Make yourself comfortable, Mr. Daniels," said Barbara Rupp. She was wearing wrap-around sun glasses and I don't think she saw me very well. She barely raised her head from the deck chair.

"You have quite a place here, Mrs. Rupp," I said.

"Well, it's what *we* wanted," she said, closing her eyes.

"She did most of the work. I gotta be away a good deal of the time. What would you say to a little libation? Smoke a cigar?"

"Well, a Coke or something like that," I said. "I don't often drink in the daytime. And I'll have a cigarette in a minute or so."

Rupp poured a Coke and handed it to me.

"You live in the town, Mr. Daniels?" said Barbara Rupp, without opening her eyes.

"On the edge of town," I said. "Lakeside Road. It used to be called Kouwenhoven Road."

"I know where it is. How many acres do you have?"

"We have four and a half acres."

"Four and a half acres? Oh, you must live in that big old fieldstone. That's a nice property."

"Thank you."

"Is that your family home?"

"Yes, I was born there. It's been in my family a long while, though not in its present form. My grandfather added on to it. He had a large family."

"They're coming back, according to some people, but I wouldn't have more than two," she said. "If you get one of each, what else do you have to prove?"

"Yeah," said her husband. "Well, Mr. Daniels, what did you have me down for?"

I smiled. "Well, I don't know that we had you down for any set sum. My job is to tell you what we're trying to do at the hospital, and then rely on your generosity."

"I know about that pitch, Mr. Daniels. But what did you have beside my name, in pencil? What was Harry Rupp supposed to be good for?"

"You must have had some experience in this sort of thing," I said. "Very well. We had two figures for you. One was a thousand, the other was fifteen hundred."

"You gave yourself plenty of leeway," said Rupp.

"Not really," I said. "We had you down for a thousand, but the fifteen-hundred figure was for you and Mrs. Rupp."

"Count me out," said Barbara Rupp.

"Well, I'll go for a thousand."

"That'll be fine," I said. "But what about you, Mrs. Rupp? I'd like to put you down for something. Say two-fifty?"

"I'll bet you would. No, when I said count me out, I meant count me out altogether."

"I see," I said. I stood up. "Well, Mr. Rupp. Thank you very much. You've been more than generous, and I won't take up any more of your time. I'll leave this folder with you, in case you'd care to learn about what we're doing at the hospital. And on the back page, the address and so forth. Where to send your cheque."

"Don't leave any folders, will you please?" said Barbara Rupp. "Harry can make out the cheque to the hospital and send it to you direct, can't he?"

"Of course," I said. "Well, thanks again. And nice to have seen you both."

"Well, one of us, anyway," said Barbara Rupp.

I had, of course, acted under instructions: never have an argument with a potential donor. Barbara Rupp was not exactly a potential donor, but her husband had given freely and generously, and would go down on our list as a favorable prospect in years to come. "Oh, and thanks for the Coke," I said, on my way down the steps.

Our community is not a large one, but I literally did not see Barbara Rupp again until the hospital had its drive a year later. Occasionally I would encounter Harry Rupp at our little golf club, but my friends and I had a table of our own in the smoking-room and our golf matches were made up of men from that group, all considerably older than Harry Rupp and his friends. I was sometimes in the club when Harry Rupp was there, but we did not always speak.

When I was again given Harry's name for my special-gifts list I said to him, at the club: "Harry, may I come out and see you, possibly this weekend?"

"Going to cost me a thousand dollars, Norman?" he said.

"At least that, I hope."

"Tell you what I'll do. I'll send you a cheque and spare you the trip," he said.

"Well, of course if you'd prefer. But I was also hoping I could get Mrs. Rupp to change her mind."

"What the hell, you can try. I'll tell her you're coming out Sunday afternoon. Make it late, around five. I won't be there, because our kids got some other kids for Sunday lunch, and then they slop around the pool. But by five she'll be by herself."

"Oh, why don't I do it some other time?"

"Listen, either way it's gonna be a waste of time, whether you go this Sunday or a week from Thursday."

She was wearing a playsuit, and her face and body were dark brown from the sun. "Harry said you were coming," she said. "But the answer's gonna be just the same."

"Yes, he warned me. But I can't think of a better way to spend at least part of Sunday afternoon than trying to collect money for the hospital."

"Don't you go to church?"

"Yes, I do as a rule."

"Church is another one of those things like hospitals."

"How so?" I said.

"Neither one of them will ever get a nickel out of me. Harry does it because it's deductible tax-wise, but also because it looks better if you're in business."

"Is that the way you feel about all charities?"

"In other words, don't I give to charity? No."

"I should think Harry would encourage you to, if only for tax purposes."

"That's a phony. I don't want them to get my money, even if I do get a little deduction for it. If you're not related to me, or you're not some close friend of mine, I wouldn't give you five cents if you were starving. That's not personal. I mean anybody. I don't know you, so I got nothing against you. But I wouldn't give you any money whether it was for you or the hospital or your Aunt Tillie."

"Well, it's an interesting point of view."

"And you're dying to know why. Shall I tell you why you'd like to know, Mr. Daniels? Because everybody wishes they had some excuse to stop giving away money. Take away that tax deduction and the charities would starve to death inside of six months."

"There again, an interesting point of view. I don't happen to agree with you, though."

"How do you know you don't? You didn't take time to think about it. You got it ingrained in you from your parents and *their* parents, give to charity. So you give. That's all."

"Haven't you ever given to any charity?" I said.

"Are you asking for the hospital or for your own information?"

"My own information, I guess. The hospital is a losing cause, it seems to me."

"Then I'll give you the information. You want to fix me a scoop? I'll have a bourbon on the rocks and you help yourself." She lit a cigarette and seated herself in one of those things that pass for chairs and that look like a salad bowl on a tripod. "Yes, I used to give to charity. Just like everybody. The Salvation Army. The Red Cross.

Somebody got married in the store—I was working in a department store—I chipped in. Or if I saw some blind man on the street, even if I was sure he was a phony. A dime. A quarter. Then I got in an automobile accident and they kept me waiting in the hall. They didn't pay a God damn bit of attention to me till I almost died on the stretcher. Then they had the nerve to charge me for blood transfusions, irregardless of my two brothers and friends of mine from the store were donating blood. I was in that hospital six weeks and when I came out I was minus the sight of one eye. I had a concussion. What they call a concussion of the brain. Nothing wrong with my brain, but my eyesight. It finally cleared up so I could see out of that eye, but the hospital ate up all my insurance and what I had saved up. So that's when I stopped giving money to charity."

"Hospital facilities—" I began.

"Sure, sure, sure. And it was right after the war. Sure, sure. Don't *you* give me that. I can recite it backwards and forwards."

"I thought you might have some philosophical reason, some principle based on objective reasons. But it isn't that, is it? It's just a very unfortunate experience. If you'd been bitten by a dog, you probably would have a prejudice against dogs. You don't deny that the hospitals do some good, Mrs. Rupp?"

"I don't deny anything, friend. Harry's got it made now, and if I have to go to a hospital, my bills get paid. But that's all they get out of me. Or any other charity. They can all go to hell."

"Well, fortunately most people don't feel that way," I said.

"You mind if I say something? You're a stuffed shirt," she said. "You're a real stuffed shirt, Daniels."

"Quite possibly," I said. "And not very good company, so I think I'll take my leave, if I may tear myself away."

"Sit down, for Christ's sake," she said. "I don't insult a person unless I like them. You know what I do? I ignore them. I'm not saying I like you as much as some people. I only saw you these two times. But there's two kinds of a stuffed shirt. Those that are stuffed shirts because that's all they are, and those that act like stuffed shirts but aren't. You're the latter."

"I see. But you'll concede, won't you, that when you tell a man's he's a stuffed shirt, he's not likely to wait around long enough to discover that there are *two* categories of stuffed shirt. Tell me why you like me. I may not like your reason for liking me, and then I *will* be a stuffed shirt."

"I think you're regular. You're all manners and politeness and all that, but get you with a load on and you'd be just like anyone else."

"Well, I can't help but feel you have a point. However, I don't often get a load on."

"Let's get stiff," she said.

"No thanks," I said. "As a matter of fact, Mrs. Rupp, I have to take my wife to a cocktail party and should leave this minute."

"What's she like, your wife? How old is she? How old are you?"

"I'm fifty-five. My wife is younger than that."

"A lot younger? Ten years younger?"

"Not ten years, but let's not get too precise."

"Do you have any children?"

"Two daughters. Both married. One in Philadelphia, one in New York." I stood up.

"You know something?" she said, getting out of her salad bowl.

(*176*)

"What?"

"Fifty-five's not so old."

"It's not so young, either," I said.

She moved toward me until her body was actually resting against mine. "I could get you to stay here," she said.

"Yes, if I didn't leave right this minute, you could."

"And you'd be glad you stayed," she said.

"No, there I think you're wrong. I'd be sorry, and so would you."

"You mean on account of Harry."

"Harry, in your case. My wife, in mine."

"You never cheated?"

"If I say no, you won't believe me."

"You're damn right I wouldn't," she said. "Well, go ahead go. I won't detain you, Mr. Daniels. I'll let you chicken out this time."

"You're right. That's exactly what I am doing," I said. "One question. Why me?"

"Ah, you want a little flattery, don't you?"

I laughed. "I guess so."

"Well, I tell you, honey. It's your grey hair. Will that satisfy you?"

"You know, you're quite a naughty woman," I said, smiling.

"Ho-ho. You can say that again. Why do you think Harry has me stashed away up here?"

I left her, and for a few days I seemed to have come to life again. They were disturbing days, full of disturbing thoughts, and when I attempted to treat the thing lightly, to laugh off the episode and its immediate effect on me and on the even tenor of my ways, I was only partially successful. The only thing to do *was* to laugh it off, I told myself, but in honesty I knew that I was not so invulnerable that my sense of humor could banish the thoughts that disturbed me. I felt her in her playsuit resting against my body, and that was all too real. So real that, as I have said, I came to life again. But in a week or so the routine of my life took hold once more. The disturbing thoughts became less disturbing and intruded less frequently. My business affairs, my home life, my social life, the afternoons of golf and the comradeship of my old friends, what I had done for so many years, what I had *been,* came to my rescue. Now I could look upon the episode with amused tolerance. When I was safe again I encountered Harry Rupp at the club. He apparently had been away on business. "Hi, Norman," he said. "I understand you got nowhere."

"I got absolutely nowhere at all," I said.

"She's tough," he said. He was standing naked with a towel wrapped around his middle, and his hairy chest and shoulders and arms and back and belly made me think of him as not a man alone but as a partner to her. I had never before been so close to a naked man whose wife had offered herself to me. I cannot explain what I felt; it was almost but not quite as if I were he but he was not I. His hairy body had done what I had refused to do but had been tempted to do, and my body had felt the very beginnings of what his body had felt completely and often. I was glad the towel covered his middle. I think I would have stared at him and he would think I was something I am not.

I was safely away from her, and I could calmly ask myself why I had even for a moment been so affected by her that for nearly a week she had been disturbingly in my thoughts. I had no reason to like her. Beyond a slight curiosity as to her reasons for being opposed to charities, she had not interested me. She was a woman I could have seen at the supermarket; one of many women I could have seen on the half-fare special Wednesday trains; overdressed, over-talkative, undistinguished; spending their husbands' new money in a competition among themselves. In her playsuit, with its white ruffled edges and gingham material, she was making a foolish effort to be girlish in spite of having produced two children who were in their early teens. Her figure was of the kind that I describe negatively as not bad rather than positively as good. During the war, when I was stationed in London with the Air Force, I had had two brief, meaningless affairs with women who had the same sort of figure: they looked much better in clothes than out of them, and would not take off their brassieres while the light was on.

Those women in London had faded in my memory (and in my conscience) as completely as the details of the paperwork I was then doing for the Air Force. With a strong effort I suppose I could recall an evaluation of some of our daylight bombings over Germany, and with the same effort I could recall the name of one, but not both, of the women. I knew, as a private statistic, that I had been unfaithful to my wife, but if my wife guessed it she never let on, and after the war she had no grounds for suspicion. I came home and got busy and did rather well in my real estate business, and we settled once again into the kind of life we had lived before the war. When the materials were available we repaired and improved our house, we saw our friends, I took part in the less demanding community activities, we watched our daughters through adolescence and young womanhood, and we acquired three grandchildren. We even interceded when two friends of ours talked wildly of getting a divorce, and they have been kind enough to say that Millicent and I kept them together.

With Harry Rupp at the golf club Saturday after Saturday, I cannot say that I forgot about her. Whenever I saw him, I would instantly think of her, but my mind would be occupied with the brief conversations he and I had, and that happened often enough so that I can truthfully say that the encounters with Harry had the curious effect of reminding me of her existence but reducing her to unreality. Harry seldom spoke of her, unless it was to mention her in connection with a trip he had taken with her, or some such joint activity. He rarely mentioned her by name, and I had become so sure of myself that I was able to do so. He said, one afternoon: "I see your wife's in the ladies' semifinals."

"Yes," I said. "Never got that far before. Barbara never plays, does she?"

"Golf? The most exercise she gets is bending over to paint her toenails. Oh, maybe swim the length of the pool. But no sports. Nothing competitive, you know what I mean. She just likes to sit."

"Well, the way I played today I'd have been better off just sitting," I said.

"Yeah, but that don't happen very often. I can belt them off the tee, but Jesus I wish I had your short game."

"I didn't have it with me today," I said. "See you, Harry."

"Right, Norm. Right."

For a while after that conversation whenever I heard their names or had other reason to think of them I would get an instant mental picture of Barbara Rupp in her playsuit, sitting in the sun and bent over to paint her toenails. The picture somehow offended me: the land that had been intact for a million years, now capriciously bulldozed and gouged out to make a site for a silly house for a silly woman, who had nothing better to do than decorate herself with paint and let the sun darken her skin to falsify her age. I had not set foot inside her house, but town talk was that she had all sorts of trick lighting, and built-in loudspeakers for a high-fidelity phonograph, and the very latest electrical appliances and deep-freeze units. They of course had television antennae as complicated as the radar installations on an aircraft carrier, and I gathered that her interior furniture was of a piece with the salad-bowl chairs on the terrace. It had cost ninety-five thousand dollars to build the house; that figure was a matter of public record. How much more was spent on furniture and gadgetry was anyone's guess. Knowing Harry, and after my two interviews with her, I was sure they filled the house with items from catalogs; funny toilet paper and tricky highball glasses and that sort of thing. They had been living in our neighborhood about four years, and the wives of my close friends had yet to meet Barbara Rupp. Some of them had not even seen her, and their initial curiosity about the Rupps' house had subsided.

The men, of course, were acquainted with Harry Rupp. He was already a rich man when he came to inspect building sites; from absolutely nothing he had built up a business that fascinated me, as any simple, fabulously successful enterprise fascinated me. During the war, while working in a defense plant, he sold black market cigarettes and candy to his fellow workers, then wangled a concession to serve coffee and doughnuts in the plant, legitimately. Thereafter he never again had to lie about his source of income; he became a sort of concessionaire in small, then larger, industrial plants, supplying and managing and taking a good profit from cafeterias and executive dining-rooms. He came to our town with a top credit rating and an impressive amount of loose cash. He was a big man, direct and even blunt, according to those of my friends who had dealings with him in his early days in town. But as one of them said to me, "He's a fellow that's definitely on his way to much bigger things. You sense that after talking to him for five minutes." He was away a good deal of the time, usually arriving home on Friday afternoon. In his blunt fashion he told the right men that he and his wife had no social ambitions, but that he wanted to get his kids in the private schools and he himself wanted to play golf. "After that," he said, "you can forget about us." He almost immediately fitted into a group of men at our golf club that consisted of several retail merchants, two young doctors and a dentist, the Catholic priest, the district manager of the telephone company, and one of my younger competitors in real estate. Among them were the best golfers in the club and the hardest drinkers, and they shook dice not only for drinks but for sums of money that caused some alarm among the older members of the house committee. "Somebody's going to get hurt," the committee chairman said.

"True," I said. "But we already have rules against gambling on club property. We either enforce the rules and stop gambling entirely, or we just look the other way. Then when someone does get hurt, they may come to their senses."

As it happened, Harry Rupp, who everyone knew had plenty of money, rescued the house committee from the embarrassing predicament. "This game's getting too damn big for fun," he announced one afternoon. "I don't mind thirty or forty bucks, but when we get up around two hundred dollars on the table, I begin to take it seriously. Furthermore, we got Father Mulcahy sitting here like a bump on a log. One of these days he's gonna get in the game, and that's the day the bishop better count the Sunday collections. So wuddia say, fellows? Wuddia say we don't play for any paper money?" Rupp was the only man who could have done it, and I found out later that my friend the committee chairman had spoken to the priest, who then spoke to Rupp, and that Rupp's immediate reaction had been favorable. "Woodburn," he said, referring to the telephone company manager, "is too nice a guy to get in trouble over a lousy dice game. But I seen him turn pale last week when he dropped seventy-fi' dollars. He don't have that kind of money. I'll break it up."

That was the kind of man Harry Rupp was among men, and then as chairman of the hospital's special-gifts committee I learned a little more about him, but what I learned was really only more of the same: his quick generosity to the hospital drive was to be expected of the kind of man I had seen in the golf club smoking room. Moreover, his sort of heartily virile man's man would not necessarily be guilty of basic disrespect in calling his wife "tough" or even in speaking scornfully of her laziness. His attitude toward his wife, and toward women, had only been hinted at in Barbara's remark: "Why do you think Harry has me stashed away up here?" The remark could have more than one meaning. It might be flirtatiousness on her part; it might have been the plain truth; it might have been indicative of resentment or loneliness or boredom. But it told me almost nothing about *Harry's* attitude, and toward the end of that summer it became important for me to know just what his attitude was.

As always, there was that one day in late July or early August that Nature sends us creatures as a reminder that autumn will come. August and September can be warm, but we have been given that brief warning, although we highly intelligent human animals seldom act upon it. I took no deliberate action on it, to be sure, but I found that inexplicably I was having a recurrence of my disturbing thoughts of Barbara Rupp. I think it was because autumn could be sensed, and in the autumn I would not see her. When I had seen her it was spring or early summer, and for me she did not exist in cold weather. How can I explain to myself what happened to me? I came to life again, as I had before, but this time it was the thin chill of a distant autumn and not the recollected pressure of a real woman against me that brought me to life so desperately. I hardly even thought of *her;* I thought of myself. And then I began thinking that this new life would remain incomplete if I did not go back again to that hideous house. This new life I was feeling was hideous, too, but I had lost any sense of beauty that I had ever had. Yes, I thought, killed by an early frost, and to hell with it. One thing killed, another thing come to life; and what was gone was truly gone and better gone and useless. Only this hideous new life was not dead.

I have never been a devious man. In our business, waiting is half the game, and since Millicent and I both have small private incomes, I could always wait till I got my price before selling a piece of property. In my personal life I was equally secure: Millicent and I were completely compatible, understood each other perfectly, lived in an atmosphere of mutual respect, and were, of course, very much in love. My London episodes can be properly attributed to physical necessity and wartime strain; and since they occurred at a distance of three thousand miles and during a universal moral blackout, I did not get involved in deviousness. But now I seemed to have developed a talent for intrigue. Through the most casual questions I determined that Harry

Rupp would be absent from home from Monday through Friday of the second week in August and that his two children would not yet be home from summer camp. I drove out to the Rupps' house.

To my momentary dismay Barbara Rupp was not alone. She introduced me to a young woman who was the wife of a young farmer nearby. With my new talent encouraging me I recovered quickly from my first disappointment. "I don't want to make a nuisance of myself, Mrs. Rupp," I said. "But I have a client's interested in building a house like yours. Would you mind if I just paced off a few measurements to give me some idea?"

"Help yourself," said Barbara Rupp. "You want a tape measure?"

"No thanks," I said. "I'm used to making rough estimates. You ladies forget all about me."

"I was just leaving," said the farmer's wife.

"You're not gonna leave me all alone with Mr. Daniels," said Barbara Rupp.

The farmer's wife tittered out of embarrassment for me and my decrepitude.

"I hope I'm not *quite* that harmless," I said, as stuffed-shirtedly as I could sound.

The farmer's wife went down the steps, accompanied by Barbara Rupp, while I, with pencil and paper in hand, paced off the dimensions of the terrace. Barbara Rupp returned to the terrace. "You could have got that information by phoning Harry," she said.

"I happen to know he's away."

"What is it? Just an excuse to see me?"

"Yes," I said.

"Yeah, I thought so. I saw the look on your face when you spotted Dora. You know I have two kids."

"I know they're not home from camp," I said.

"Oh, this is for real, huh?" she said. "Wuddia you, been brooding over the pass I made at you?"

"I'm here," I said.

"Well, yeah," she said. She looked at me. "Yeah."

"Can't we go inside?"

"Sure. Why not?" she said. "You want a Coke? I think you better have a *real* drink."

"So do I," I said. I fixed a bourbon on the rocks. She already had a long drink in her hand. She sat in a bright green chair and stretched her legs on the matching hassock.

"What brought this on? A little domestic quarrel with your wife?"

"Not a bit. I just wanted to see you. Had to see you."

"Yeah, that's better, because if it was only a fight with your wife it isn't worth it. A wife getting suspicious, and that's what she'd be. I don't care what you fight about, right away the wife starts getting suspicious. I got myself to think about, too."

"Does Harry trust you?"

"No, and I don't trust him either, but you picked the only time of the year when I don't have two bodyguards age fifteen and thirteen. Hell, I know Harry never passes up anything, but I have to behave myself. I used to wrap hamburgers when Harry and I were just getting started, and I'm not taking any chances of losing out on a deal where he has over eight hundred people working for him."

"You don't seem to be getting much out of the deal now."

"Who says I'm not?"

"I didn't mean financially," I said.

"Neither did I," she said.

(*186*)

"Oh."

"You don't think I was waiting seventeen years till you came along. I said I had to behave myself, but that's for Harry's benefit. I wouldn't give a hoot in hell for a woman that just waited around while Daddy-O was out cutting up . . . Now I got you thinking about your wife."

"It's quite true, you have."

"You want to think about her some more?"

"No."

She put down her drink. "Then why don't you try one on for size? A nice kiss."

She stood up and I took her in my arms and kissed her.

"Say, you're hungry," she said.

"Yes," I said, and we went to her room.

The strangest thing was that I was new to myself, as new as she was new to me. The self-reproach and the disgusted weariness I had expected did not occur. I did not want to leave her, and because I did not want to leave her I knew that I never would leave her entirely. She put on a pale blue kimono and walked with me to the terrace door. "Maybe in a week or so," she said. "I have ways of getting rid of my little bodyguards. And listen, don't worry about Dora. She owes *me* a few favors."

"Are you planning to tell Dora?"

"I don't have to tell her. All we ever talk about is men anyway."

"I know her father-in-law."

"So do I. A damned sight better than you ever will. So there's nothing to worry about there, either, Daniels."

"Don't call me Daniels," I said.

"I'll call you whatever comes into my head," she said.

But she was not destructive. She was me, and if she

had continued only to be me the affair might have had a self-destructive effect on me. But it soon became a shared experience, and one day she said, "Harry says I'm getting quieter."

"Well, are you?"

"With him I am."

"Does that mean he's getting suspicious?"

"Just about. He has an old trick he tries. Like out of the blue he'll suddenly mention some fellow's name, and watch for my reaction."

"Has he mentioned my name?"

"Not so far. But all the names of his golf friends. He had it kind of narrowed down to Woodburn there for a while. But don't you start getting careless."

"Never fear."

"Don't say never fear. Always fear. Because I'm apt to get careless. I'm smarter than Harry Rupp, but him noticing that I'm getting quieter. That was careless. But you know what the trouble is, Norman. You know why I'm getting careless."

"Why?"

"I'm the next thing to falling in love with you."

"You are, Barbara?"

"Just about. It's all I can do to fake it with that ox any more. I didn't use to mind. Enjoyed it, in fact. What's two men when the one don't mean any more than the other? Dora's father-in-law Wednesday night, Harry Saturday night. I don't hate Harry Rupp. I think the world of him, in some ways. But I never told him I loved him since we got the Schwarzberg contract, that was our first big contract. Some nights he didn't get three hours' sleep. Architect plans. Bank loans. Unions. Wholesalers. And me big as a house with Harriet. We had a semi-detached in Kew Gardens. You would of thought he had the entire responsibility for the atom bomb. Huh. Two years later he wouldn't renew with Schwarzberg. They weren't *big* enough any more. He said he was doing it for me and the kids, but not Harry. Harry's a born big shot. The only trouble is, I don't like it when he big-shots me. Him or anyone else."

I smiled. "I'll try to remember that."

"You better more than try, Norman. I could turn on you," she said.

She was now contentedly in my thoughts, where before she had been a source of disturbance. We saw each other on an average of once a week, usually at her house, but when Harry did not go away we would meet at Dora's. My real estate business is a modest operation, not requiring the services of a full-time secretary, and my office is in the second-floor rear of a two-story building on a side street. In the morning there is no one but me to answer the telephone, and it is normal for me to be seen in all parts of town and the nearby countryside, afoot or in my little car. My recently discovered talent for intrigue was being given few tests.

I say she was contentedly in my thoughts and that is true, and I am mindful of a certain ambiguity in the statement. Her confession of love for me did not come as a surprise. A man knows those things. I was able to recognize, for instance, the difference between her somewhat crude tenderness and Millicent's habitual gentleness. Millicent's behavior, her gentleness, was universal, not limited to her relations with me. Barbara, on the other hand, was learning tenderness for the first time. She loved her children, in her special way, but she sometimes would compare their childhood with her own. She had had to drop out of high school to go to work at sixteen, and the contrast between her children's private schools and summer camps and luxuries, and her struggles to earn a living, was a source of resentment. "I don't begrudge it to them," she said. "Harry has the money. But if I don't slap them down once in a while, they start correcting my grammar and all." And slap them down she did, with the result that their father's weekly home-comings were fun for him and the children, but not for their mother. For that and other reasons it was not so remarkable that she should turn to other men and finally to me.

I could not tell her that I loved her. I had never said that to anyone but Millicent, and it was the one thing of the old me that the new me withheld from Barbara. No, there was one other: she was fascinated by my affairs in London and coaxed me for all the details, and I saw no reason not to tell her as much as I remembered. She was correspondingly revealing concerning the men she had known before and since her marriage to Harry Rupp. But I refused to discuss Millicent on such terms, and my refusal infuriated Barbara. As a matter of fact my apparent loyalty to Millicent was not solely based on a question of taste; Millicent and I, as I have said, "understood" each other, but when I said that, I was speaking of the mutuality of a successful marriage. Actually there had been times in my marriage when I did *not* understand Millicent, when it seemed to me that she was taking advantage of her femininity to behave capriciously. Millicent was the last woman in the world I would call neurotic, but on several occasions she pretended that I had been neglecting her and then, with beautiful inconsistency, locked me out of our room! As for the kind of detail Barbara Rupp sought, there was nothing much to tell.

And I could not bring myself to pay Barbara the compliment that I could have done in all sincerity: that she, and not Millicent, was the woman in my life. I had every intention of staying married to Millicent as long as I lived. I would maintain the same courtesy toward her and protect her from gossip and scandal. But she would have to find her own reasons for the change that had taken place in our relationship, and I was sure she would do that. My hair was grey, my golf handicap had been raised, I needed new glasses every year, a fourth grandchild was on the way, and it was not unusual for me to go to two funerals in the same week. It was my own secret, not even shared by Barbara, that in a few days I would build up such a fierce desire for her as nothing in my old life—the early days with Millicent, the wartime days in London—had prepared me for. I had laughed, with my friends, over jokes about "the last call to the diner," and *l'age dangereux*. The jokes, though I laughed, had always seemed to be in questionable taste, possibly because I have always felt that a man's dignity is more important than his demonstrated virility, and the jokes demonstrated just the opposite at the cost of his dignity. Such jokes, however, usually concerned an aging man and a young girl, and Barbara Rupp was not a young girl. She was a woman who did not have too far to look for a dangerous age of her own. And, as she had said, fifty-five was not so old. There was this, too: that since she had fallen in love with me, we were in this thing together.

I now come to the part of this story that is the most difficult to tell. It is told by the old me, about the man whom I have called the new me; and while they are essentially separate and distinct persons, who will believe that they are not one and the same? The old me and the new me had the same name; I signed my cheques the same way, and the bank never questioned them. The new and the old occupied the same pew in church, and no one noticed when the old became the new. And the old me, now writing, can reveal the innermost thoughts of the new me without taking any so-called literary license. My insistent plea that the old me and the new be considered separately is not the whimpering of a coward: what happens to me happens to the outer me, the only me that the world can see. Nevertheless, I have the same right as anyone else to be judged fairly. I intend to write this all down and destroy it immediately, but I have come to believe that there are many things we do not fully comprehend. I believe that a man can be two men, can even have two souls, for I was two men and have had two souls. And I believe that if I put this all down, somehow the truth will get into the air, even though I destroy these pages immediately and without showing them to anyone. If I tell the truth, sparing neither myself nor anyone else, it will show in my face and in my actions, and people will at least be less positive that my punishment is completely and unquestionably just. If I can create some doubt, this painful confession will have served its purpose.

Barbara abandoned her attempts to extract information of an intimate nature on the subject of my relations with Millicent, and I was glad that we had buried that bone of contention. But without at first seeing any connection, I next had to resist her wish to *meet* Millicent. She had no desire to advance herself socially; but she was increasingly curious, to the point of obsession, about Millicent, about the woman who had been my wife for nearly thirty years. Once again I took a firm stand. "You warned *me* against getting careless," I said. "But this is simply asking for trouble. Your paths haven't crossed, so why should they now, after five years?"

"I want to meet her, and I'm going to."

"I forbid you to do any such thing," I said.

"Forbid me? Who the hell do you think you are? You sound like a God damn schoolteacher."

She wasted no time. The very next afternoon, when I got home from work, Millicent said: "You should have been here earlier. I had a caller. Mrs. Harry Rupp."

"What the devil did she want?"

"I don't know. I thought maybe you'd know. She said she wanted to talk to me about the hospital, serve on one of the committees. But she didn't impress me as the kind of woman that wanted to do any work. She had some other reason."

"Wanted to have a look inside our house," I said.

"Not from what I've heard of hers," said Millicent.

"No, and not from what I've seen of it."

"She mentioned that you'd been there twice."

"I went there to collect money, remember?"

"Oh, I remember."

"Well, are you going to try her out?"

"No," said Millicent. "She wouldn't fit in."

"I don't think she would, either." I said. "What did you tell her?"

"Well, I hope you don't mind, but I said I'd got the impression from you that she wasn't really interested in charities."

"You shouldn't have said *that*, Millicent."

"I wouldn't have, ordinarily. But I wanted to get rid of her, so I wasn't exactly polite. If she wanted a look at this house, she got it, but I don't imagine she'll pay me a second visit."

I was incensed at Barbara for her defiant disobedience, and she was furious at me for the snub Millicent had given her. She appeared in my office on the morning after her visit to Millicent, and said things that could be heard down the hall, things that, overheard, could leave no doubt about the character of our relationship. I fought back with complete silence, until she had run out of vituperation for Millicent and for me. Then I got up and opened the door and looked down the hall. No one was in the hall, and I said, "Now go, and never come here again." What I wanted most was for her to leave the building unrecognized. It was about a quarter to eleven in the morning, a busy time in the building, but there was no one in the hall or on the stairway, and she left.

My reputation, of course, was endangered. I held out no foolish hope that she had not been overheard. All I could hope was that people in the neighboring offices would not identify the woman who had been in my office. That hope was not an entirely foolish one, since it was possible for her to go downstairs and out the rear door to the parking lot, and that is what she did.

But the damage to my reputation had been done. Next door to my office was a tailor's establishment, conducted by a man who had often been behind in his rent. I had had to warn him so many times that there was no cordiality left in our daily greetings. But at noon that day he grinned and smirked. The other two rooms on my floor were rented to a milliner who was not renewing her lease but was moving to a larger store on the main street. The tailor's daughter worked for her as a saleslady, and there was no chance that the three of them would miss this opportunity to wag their tongues.

As a rule I lunched with friends of mine in the coffee shop of the hotel, and I could now tell, from day to day, the progress of the gossip about me. It was two weeks before anyone actually said anything, but if I happened to miss a day at our table, the next day I could detect uneasiness and small silences that revealed they had been discussing me in my absence. The first man to come out with it was Millicent's brother, Harvey Crimmons, who was a lifelong friend. He walked back to my office with me after lunch. "Norm, are you in any trouble?"

"You wouldn't ask me that if you didn't know I was," I said.

"It's going to get to Millicent," he said. "It's spreading like wildfire. Norm, I'm no saint, and if I can help you, say so. Is there anything *to* this talk?"

"I don't know what the talk is, by this time, but you're referring to a visitor I had in my office a couple of weeks ago?"

"Raised hell because you cut off her money or something," said Harvey. "Nobody can figure out who it is you're keeping."

"That's the story, is it?"

"I'd go to Millicent if I were you. I think I know my sister pretty well."

"Harvey, I couldn't bring myself to tell her. And yet the minute she hears anything at all, she's going to guess who the woman is."

"Then you're only postponing it. It's like the dentist. You're going to have to go sometime."

"It isn't really like the dentist, Harvey."

"No, not really, but——"

"It isn't just one tooth. It's several sets of teeth, if you want to think of it that way," I said. "And nobody's going to look very pretty when this dentist gets through."

"I still say tell Millicent before someone else does."

"I'll think about it some more, but thanks anyway," I said.

I stopped in at the tailor shop. "Why, hello there, Mr. Daniels. What can I do for you?"

"Schneider, you're going to have to find another room," I said. "I want you out of here by the first of the month."

"Where can I find a place in that short time? I gotta look, and find some place is in my price range. Why are you kicking me out, Mr. Daniels?"

"You're not a good tenant, and you haven't lived up to the agreement. Three times in the last eleven months you've been behind, and I could have kicked you out the first time."

"You talk about good tenants, Mr. Daniels. I could talk about bad landlords. Noisy ladies cursing and swearing in the landlord's office, that's no good for business."

"That's what I wanted to make sure of, Schneider," I said. "Be out of here by the first of the month. You'll get a registered letter tomorrow."

"It wasn't only me that heard her," said Schneider.

"The first of the month, Schneider," I said. I was satisfied that he had not identified my visitor and that the milliner and her saleslady were likewise in the dark. Why was that important?

Because I wanted to be with Barbara again. For whatever time we had left, I wanted to be with her. Before Millicent learned the truth, before Harry Rupp learned the truth. I was convinced that no one knew it was Barbara who had made the stormy scene in my office. If I could see her only one more time, then it had to be that, but that it had to be. And I was not sure that it would be only one more time. Harry Rupp, for instance, might hear gossip about me, but he would not place me under suspicion. As for Millicent, if she guessed the identity of my mistress, I would lie to her, not lies of denial but lies that promised never to see Barbara again. I had no intention of giving up Barbara Rupp. Once again she was me, in my blood, and once again I was thinking of myself rather than of her. It was just like before, when I had come to life again, except that now I knew it was for the last time, whether that meant one afternoon or meetings over a period of months.

The shady character I had become dropped in at the golf club, not to play golf but to learn a few things about Harry Rupp. I must say he behaved astonishingly well. He made no mention, direct or indirect, of my new status. No one, as yet, had treated the gossip as a subject for humor in my presence, but Harry Rupp was always unpredictable, to say the least. I did not for a second doubt that he had heard the gossip; his group were as fond of gossip as a woman's sewing circle. But however much he may have joined in the gossip and jokes when he was with his cronies, he gave absolutely no indication that he had heard anything that reflected on my character. As for his suspecting that Barbara was involved, the notion was preposterous: Harry Rupp was not a man who could so convincingly hide his feelings. At all events, I ascertained that he would be absent on one of his usual Monday-to-Friday trips, and on the following Tuesday I telephoned Barbara from my office. I came right to the point. "I'll be at your house at half past one," I said.

"Are you crazy?" she said. "You know what I heard about you? You're supposed to be mixed up with a married woman!" She chose the wrong time to be funny.

"One-thirty," I said.

The autumn, that by a hint of its coming had started this thing, was now here, with colors so gorgeous that it was hard to believe there had ever been a summer or ever would be a winter. As I drove out along the country roads to that trailer-camp house I actually forgot that an unpleasant scene would occur at the end of my drive. But I was shaken back to reality by the sight of Dora's car in the driveway.

Barbara and Dora were drinking coffee in the "family room," a room so designated for no other reason that I could make out than to distinguish it from the livingroom. Both women simultaneously raised their eyelids as I entered, both expressing the same disapproval and hostility. They waited for me to speak.

"I see we're going to be chaperoned," I said. "Or were you just ready to go, Dora?"

"I'm staying," said Dora.

"Would you care to join in the fun?" I said, hoping to shock her.

"I'm here to protect Barbara," said Dora.

"What from? She hasn't needed your protection thus far."

"She sure does now," said Dora.

"Harry didn't go away," said Barbara. "He only went to Newark. He'll be back this afternoon."

"And I'm staying right here till he gets back," said Dora.

"What made him change his mind at the last minute?" I asked Barbara.

"How should I know? But that's the way it is," said Barbara.

"Was it your idea to have Dora here?"

"Partly mine, partly Dora's."

"Well, I certainly haven't got much to talk about with Dora here," I said. "I'll be in my office every morning except Thursday. Will you phone me?"

"No, she won't," said Dora.

"Dora, you're rapidly becoming a bit of a nuisance," I

said. "Barbara and I have a lot of things to talk about—"

"You son of a bitch, don't you see she's scared stiff?"

"Are you scared stiff, Barbara?"

"Harry was never this way before," said Barbara. "Maybe he didn't even go to Newark. And he was suppose to go to Newport News. He was suppose to be there just about now. But he called up and cancelled his appointment, in front of me. He won't hardly talk to me."

"Well, let's see what he does tomorrow," I said.

They took that as my parting remark. They looked at me in silence, and said nothing when I left.

I never saw Barbara again, and I have no better information as to the later events of that day than has any other reader of the newspapers. No one else ever knew what happened that afternoon after Harry Rupp came home and Dora left. The driver of the school bus saw Harry Rupp, alone at the foot of the driveway. Rupp told the busman to take the Rupp daughter to Dora's house (the boy was at boarding school). That was at approximately four-ten. At five o'clock Harry telephoned the state police and told them to come and get him. Barbara, beaten and choked, was stretched out on the sofa in the family room

I, of course, was never charged with any crime, and even when I was made to testify as a material witness the State objected so often to the defense questions that a transcript of the trial contains only a few pages of my testimony. But if ever a man was on trial, it was I. The jury found Harry Rupp not guilty, but I was convicted of an unnamed crime by my friends and fellow townsmen. I was convicted and sentenced before I ever took the stand, and the district attorney was a fool to go against the weight of public opinion. I do not know what kind of reasoning it is that blames me for the murder of Barbara Rupp, the breaking up of

Harry Rupp's home and business, the disgrace to my children and grandchildren. The only person who could legitimately claim to have suffered by my infidelity was Millicent, but she and my children no longer bear my embarrassing name. For Millicent the scandal was a release, the divorce proceedings were humorously perfunctory, and she married a man who, I am told, is another Harry Rupp with fifteen years added. They live in a place called Petoskey, Michigan.

Perhaps it is too late for any real good to come of this confession. I did not expect to be judged fairly during the near-hysteria of a murder trial, with one of the New York papers referring to me as "Barbara's aging aristocratic lover." I, an aristocrat? My ancestors fought and died two centuries ago to free this land from the aristocrats, and down through the years my family have stood for justice and fair play. For that very reason I hoped, throughout my ordeal, that when the trial was ended and my fellow townsmen came to their senses, they would see this thing in its true light. I naturally released my clients from our business commitments, with the expectation that they would return to me voluntarily. Indeed, I counted on their return as the first indication of a general return of sanity after the orgy of gossip and persecution. But I have been disillusioned on that score. Younger firms, and newer firms, seized the opportunity of my temporary retirement, and timidity has overcome my former clients. My last dealings in real estate have been the sale of my house, that had been in my family for five generations, and the business property in which I had my office. I am barely able to afford my small room in the hotel, which is situated two stories above the bus terminal. I gave my golf clubs to the pro in part payment of my account with him when I resigned from the club. And Millicent extracted her pound of flesh, down to the last ounce.

I walk the streets of this old town as a convicted criminal, waiting for a word or a sign that justice is being tempered with mercy. Friends of a lifetime speak to me when they cannot avoid doing so, but they never stop to chat, although I have given them openings. It is not so much that I need their companionship; it is rather that I want to be helpful. I know that one of my lifelong friends is going to need the kind of help that I could give him; every morning and afternoon he drops in for a chat with the comely young woman who sells tickets at the bus station. If I could tell him that people have no time for compassion—but perhaps he too feels that he is coming to life again. The young woman is certainly prettier than Barbara and has a much better disposition. I go to the bus station about once a week to weigh myself. Every man over forty-five should watch his weight.

THE LESSON

To the young half of the people in the little church the name
Godfrey Gaines meant almost nothing. He was Mr. Gaines,
father of two of their number, and a sufficiently close friend
of the deceased to be selected as an usher at the service. But
it had been a long time—the lifetime of the young people
in the church—since Godfrey Gaines had done or been anything to attract the attention or stimulate the curiosity of
anyone born after 1930. The young people were there to
pay their last respects to Mr. Barton, father of the Barton
twins and a man whom it was easy to call Rex. People of
all ages called him Rex, and in the church that day were
twenty or thirty young people who throughout their lives
had called him Uncle Rex. As for Mr. Gaines, Godfrey
Gaines, it so happened that none of his nieces or nephews
had made the trip East to attend Rex Barton's funeral, and
therefore no one present had ever called him Uncle Godfrey.

It was a little strange, or so it seemed to the young
people, to see how many of the older half of the congregation greeted Mr. Gaines with warmth. The fathers, the actual uncles, all shook his hand and whispered something;
the women, the mothers, the actual aunts quite obviously
expected to be kissed, and were kissed. All this was strange

because he was a stranger to the young people, but it was also strange because there was nothing about him now that called for any demonstration of affection or pleasurable greeting. Mr. Gaines, Godfrey Gaines, was not what you would call a distinguished-looking man, and in his blue serge suit and black four-in-hand he could easily have been mistaken for a paid pallbearer or one of Walter J. McIlhenny's assistants. The young people knew Johnny Gaines and Miriam Gaines Loomis because Johnny and Mimi had been brought up by their mother and stepfather, who lived in the neighborhood. It was known that Johnny's and Miriam's father was to be an usher at Rex Barton's funeral, and he thus escaped being identified as a paid pallbearer or an undertaker's assistant. But it was all pretty strange, to see Johnny's and Mimi's father, whom most of them had never seen before; to see him so warmly greeted by the older people; and for him to be an usher and thereby presumably to have been an intimate friend of Rex Barton. And perhaps the strangest thing of all was that Godfrey Gaines was such an ordinary-looking man.

The young people watched him with his contemporaries, recognizing them, failing to recognize them, being recognized by them. When recognition occurred it was with a quick smile, a smile as close to elation as the circumstances would permit, and the young people, seeing the smile, had a clue to the warmth of their parents' greeting. When Godfrey Gaines smiled the fathers and mothers and uncles and aunts seemed to be remembering good times, memories that needed the appearance of Godfrey Gaines for the reawakening. A father would whisper something to Mr. Gaines and Mr. Gaines would grin and nod; the mother would kiss Godfrey Gaines, sometimes putting both hands on his shoulders as she did so. Then they would all remember where they were, the solemnity of the occasion, and the mother, the woman, would take Godfrey Gaines's arm and be led to her pew. Mr. Gaines would leave them then and come down the aisle, an ordinary-looking man who could have been mistaken for one of McIlhenny's lugubrious helpers.

The little church was known to them all. Three generations were represented on this day: Rex Barton's generation, and the preceding and succeeding generations. No one had ever seen a speck of dust on the woodwork or a smudge on the brass, and only the most faithful of the faithful noticed the difference when the floor matting was changed. Everything else was the same, year in, year out, and by some mystery of time and human association, even Godfrey Gaines began to fit into the hour. In the midst of the prayers and hymns, the friends and relations, the banks of flowers and the sacred furniture, Godfrey Gaines was one minute a stranger and the next minute a member. Everyone was extraordinarily conscious of time and the passage of it outside the church and down to the moment of entering a pew and becoming part of the congregation; but then time was suspended, minutes and fractions of hours ceased to be the measure of time. Outside, and in the past, there were years and more years or fewer, and when the service ended there would be other years, many or few, but during the ceremony a man in the pew ahead had never been anywhere else, a woman across the aisle had been there throughout eternity. And the young people had known Godfrey Gaines all their lives.

McIlhenny's six men marched beside the casket as Brendan McIlhenny, at one end, pushed it down the aisle. Mrs. Barton and the twins and their husbands darted across the transept and out a side door, and after a moment of hesitation the first pews' occupants commenced to leave. They gathered on the steps of the church and on the sidewalk. ("Are you going back to the house?" "No, nobody is. Mrs. Barton and the others are leaving right away for Manchester, Vermont. That's where he's being buried.")

Godfrey Gaines got his coat and hat out of a limousine and put them on, then went back to the gathering on the church steps. He looked for and found a group of five: his former wife, her husband; his son, his daughter and her husband.

"You're staying with Tom and Edie?" said his former wife. She was standing very close to her husband and holding the collar of her coat close to her throat.

"Staying with Tom and Edie," said Godfrey Gaines. "How are you, Bill?"

"Pretty well, thanks," said Bill Whitehill, calmly.

"Our friend here looks very well," said Godfrey Gaines.

"I wish you wouldn't refer to me as our friend," said Miriam Whitehill.

"All right," said Godfrey Gaines. "I was being polite, that's all. I thought you were going to invite me for lunch or something."

"Far from it," said Miriam Whitehill. "I only wanted to be sure where you were staying."

"So you wouldn't go there?" said Godfrey Gaines.

"Something like that," said Miriam Whitehill.

"But would it be all right if Johnny and Mimi went to Edie's for lunch?"

"I'm sorry, but I can't, Father. I have to be in New York this afternoon," said Johnny Gaines.

"Where do *you* have to be, Mimi?" said Godfrey Gaines.

"I'll go with you," said his daughter. "George is driving back to town with Johnny, but I can go to the Taylors', if that's what you want."

"That's what I do want. Very much. In fact, it's all I

want. Let's go." Without another word to the others he turned and led his daughter to the limousine. "Mr. Taylor's house, please," he said to the chauffeur. "Cigarette, Mimi?"

"No thanks. I've given them up."

"Permanently?"

"I guess so. Haven't had one in four months . . . I'm having a child."

"Well, that's good news. Congratulations. What do you want?"

"I don't care. A boy, I suppose. I'm sure George would like to have a boy, and call it George the Third."

"Not if he knows his American history. When is it due?"

"Probably the second week in June."

"How does your mother feel about being a grandma?"

"She's looking forward to it. All her friends already are."

"Yes. That would be her reason."

"Oh, Father. Must you? You two, still so bitter after twenty-five years. Why don't you grow up?"

"Would you speak that way to her?"

"I have."

"In her hearing?"

"I'm not afraid of Mother, or I wouldn't be here now. I didn't ask her permission to come with you."

"No, you didn't. And she didn't like it a damn bit."

"Well, I'm not going to like it either if all you're going to do is make cracks about her."

"All right. I'll stop. But I want to point out that she's had all these years to make cracks about me. And don't tell me she didn't take advantage of that opportunity."

"I wouldn't think of trying. She's made you sound like such an awful son of a bitch that you couldn't possibly live up to it. She made you seem like Errol Flynn."

"Errol Flynn? That's reaching for one."

"No. What made me think of him was when he died, Ma said he couldn't have been any worse than you."

"A charming thing to say to a man's daughter, you have to admit that."

"She didn't exactly say it to me. To George."

"Well then it was nice of George to pass the information along to you."

"He thought it was funny. Don't criticize George."

"Did you think it was funny?"

"In a way. I only remembered Errol Flynn dressed in a pirate's costume, I think it was. And I can't picture you as a pirate."

"I have to weigh that remark. How do you picture me?"

"As you are. And every once in a while I come across a picture of you in a football suit. Did you see yourself in *Sports Illustrated* last fall?"

"Every time that picture's reprinted people send it to me. Sure, I saw it. But you never knew me when I looked like that. My Errol Flynn days, you might say."

"I can't imagine Ma falling for a football type."

"She didn't. By the time she knew me I was a golf type. Although my football reputation had preceded me."

"Lefty Gaines."

"Only because I learned to pass with my left hand. I was never lefthanded in anything else, but I spent a whole summer practicing forward passes with my left hand, and that was really how we beat Yale my sophomore year. When we played Harvard they were ready for me, in spite of the no-scouting agreement. I always used to rib Rex Barton about that. At first he maintained that Harvard hadn't broken the agreement, but I finally got him to admit that some kind alumnus had managed to convey the essential information. Well, what the hell, it was a ridiculous idea anyway. All you had to do was read the Sunday papers, the play-by-play. The New York *World* had charts of the big games."

"Were you an All-American?"

"Second. I lost out to a fellow at the University of Michigan. I'm sure Walter Camp had never seen him play, but I guess it was a fair choice."

"Only you don't really think so."

"Of course I don't, but I'm so used to saying it, I can say it in my sleep. You don't really care anything about football, do you?"

"Not very much. Sometimes people used to ask me if you were my father."

"Not very often, I'll bet. At least not people your age."

"Nobody my age, but a few years older, and of course the father of boys I went out with."

"Then why do you encourage me to talk about it? Not that I needed much encouragement. You were being nice to the old man."

"Why not?"

"Well—yes. Why not? Do you think I've had a rough time, Mimi?"

"Yes, I do."

He took his daughter's hand and looked at it, and then he put it back on her lap. "I have," he said. "But God damn few people know how rough. How did you?"

"I don't know, exactly. Stories. Not exactly stories, either. All the people around here liked you, but they talked about you as if you were dead. Uncle Rex didn't, but a lot of the others did. I knew you didn't have any money, and I heard about your divorce."

"That was in the papers."

"Yes. You married that woman to annoy Ma, didn't you?"

"Well—that may have been part of the reason. I didn't have to marry her, God knows. Nobody did. And she wasn't a bad dame. The only trouble was, she saw me with men, men that knew me as Lefty Gaines. She thought if she married me, my men friends would give her a background. Do you know what I mean? These Yale guys and Harvard guys and Princeton friends of mine, they were the big money and the social leaders of the town. But when I married Jenny my friends' wives never had us to their houses, and she began to think I was some kind of a phony. She wanted like hell to be respectable, and that's where I failed her. She took me for plenty, too, but I had no right to expect anything else. She was, let's face it, a whore."

"That was easy to guess."

"And that's what she is now. A madam. She runs a whorehouse in Kentucky. She's married again, so I don't have to pay her any more alimony. But she took me for everything I had when I walked out on her. It wasn't much by Bill Whitehill's standards, but it was all I had, and I had a hard time getting on my feet again. Your Uncle Rex helped me there. Not with money. With a job."

"I never knew Uncle Rex to be tight-fisted."

"Don't get the wrong impression. He never was tight-fisted. He'd have let me have any amount of money, within reason. But I didn't ask him for money. Him or anyone else. You know, when you get in a jam your friends will often let you have five hundred or a thousand in the hope of getting rid of you. I know. I've done it myself. But a job is a different story. So I called Uncle Rex on the phone and I put it to him straight. All he had to do was pick up the phone and I'd have a job. Rex was a director of a lot of big corpora-

tions. 'What kind of job, Lefty? What do you want to do?'
And I told him, not just some stopgap kind of job. I wanted
something where I could get a whole new start, and I
thought the place where I'd fit in best was in some kind of
personnel work. Well, to make a long story short, that's how
I happened to get with Midlands Incorporated. I knew less
than nothing about food processing, but all my life I had a
knack of dealing with people. It's mighty interesting work,
too. I make twenty thousand dollars a year. Maybe your
husband makes that much, a little over half my age. But
that twenty thousand represents four big raises in ten years.
I started at ten. So they like me. I get results."

"That's wonderful, Father."

"I come back here and see the old crowd I used to
know before you were born. Some of them probably expected to see me with my tail between my legs. Beaten. Ab-
ject. But I don't think I gave that impression, do you?"

"Not a bit."

"Were you—you weren't embarrassed or anything,
were you? I can't tell about Johnny. A son takes his
mother's side instinctively, and I don't know whether he had
to go back to New York or not."

"He really did. I happen to know he did. He said so
before the service."

"Well, I'm glad he wasn't just ducking me. I'd hate to
think he didn't have any more character than that. I'm sure
Bill Whitehill's been a good father to him and all that, but
I know Bill, and if Johnny was only making up some excuse,
Bill Whitehill wouldn't have much respect for him. You get
along with Bill all right, don't you?"

"Very well."

"Bill's all right. I won't say anything against Bill. Not
everybody that inherited as much money as Bill came

through as well as he has. He always did everything by the book. He was in love with your mother long before I entered the picture, and when she married me instead, he took it with good grace. You *could* say he was biding his time till the roof fell in, but I never held that against him. Your mother was very lucky she had Bill to turn to. So were you, for that matter. And Johnny."

"Father?"

"What?"

"I probably shouldn't ask you this."

"If it's what I think it is, don't ask it," said Godfrey Gaines.

"How will I know we're thinking of the same thing?"

"Because there's only one question you could ask me that you'd have to soften me up first. When you say, 'I probably shouldn't ask you,' there aren't that many things that you're curious about."

"You *are* good about people," said Mimi. "Up to a point."

"Up to a point? What do you mean by that?"

"Well, you guessed the nature of what I was going to ask you, and you refused to hear the question. But where you're not good is that you don't know me."

"Not as well as I'd like to," said Godfrey Gaines.

"Thanks, but I'm not going to be diverted by compliments. Up to a point you know people, Father, but you don't know that you can't stop me from asking the question. Was it Mrs. Barton?"

"Was what Mrs. Barton?"

"Was Mrs. Barton the one that made Mother so bitter? Was Mrs. Barton your girl?"

Godfrey Gaines smiled faintly. "You have it all figured out, haven't you?"

"Yes, I think I have."

"All the wisdom of your years, all the sophistication of Long Island. You just have to know, don't you? Is that why you came along with me?"

"Not entirely, Father. But for years I've suspected that Mrs. Barton was the one that came between Mother and you. She always seemed the logical one."

"You looked over the field, and Mrs. Barton seemed the logical one."

"Yes. She must have been beautiful when she was young."

"She was indeed, and in my view she still is."

"Then I'm right. It was she?"

"No," said Godfrey Gaines.

"Is this a gentlemanly denial? Are you going by the book, too?"

"No. But I kissed Mrs. Barton once."

"Is that all?"

"That's all," said Godfrey Gaines. "I kissed her once, and then I went away."

"It doesn't sound like you at all, Father."

"No. It doesn't sound like Errol Flynn, either, I imagine." He leaned forward. "Driver, don't go to Mr. Taylor's right away. We want to drive around a while. Just take us anywhere till I tell you." Godfrey Gaines pressed the button that raised the glass division in the front seat, and looked at his daughter. "I haven't been a very good father, Mimi. I've been a lousy father. In fact, practically not a father at all. Bill Whitehill's been your father, not I, and he's a man that goes by the book. Always goes by the book. Which is all right, most of the time. But there comes a time when you have to throw the book away. I have a lesson for you, and it isn't in the book. Okay?"

"Of course."

"The first rule in the book, of course, is that a gentleman doesn't talk. Right?"

"And the rule that's broken most often."

"Right. And now your father is about to break that rule, because it's much more important for a father to teach his daughter something about life than it is for him to observe the rules."

"I'm waiting with bated breath, Father."

"All right," said Godfrey Gaines. "After you were born, and it seemed like the time had come for your mother and I to resume normal relations, she decided to go away for a while. The doctor had told me it was all right for us to sleep together, but your mother begged off. I had another talk with the doctor, and he said that while your mother was physically able to have relations with me, still it wasn't unusual for a woman after her first child to—to be reluctant. Unwilling. Indifferent. And in some cases he said the whole idea was repulsive to a wife, especially if she'd had a bad time in her pregnancy. That wasn't the case with you, at least physically. Your mother didn't have a particularly bad time having you, but then as Jerry Murphy, Doctor Murphy, said, we couldn't overlook the psychological factor. So your mother went South for four months. She was to be gone two weeks, originally, but that became a month, then two months. Then four. She'd never say she was staying another month, and several times when I said I wanted to join her, she said she'd be home the next week and there was no point in my going South. Then she'd stay another month.

"Well, I didn't suspect anything wrong, but I was young and vigorous and a couple of times I more or less picked up where I'd left off with a girl I'd known before I was married. In plain language, I slept with this girl several times while your mother was in the South, and in some way or other your mother found out about it. I don't know to this day how she found out, and it really doesn't matter. The point is, when your mother came home she accused me of being unfaithful, told me the girl's name and where she lived, and had me dead to rights. No use denying it. Her facts were too good. I asked her if she wanted a divorce, and she said she'd have to think it over. She thought it over for quite a while. She took so long, in fact, that I began seeing the girl again, and one day I realized that it had been a whole year since I'd last slept with your mother. I was never the most sensitive man in the world, but it dawned on me that this was getting to be a hell of a marriage. I was crazy about you, but you weren't the most brilliant conversationalist at that age. Goo and gah were about the extent of your conversation when you weren't yelling your head off. And it was just about that time that I realized that I wasn't in love with your mother any more. We were living in the same house and we went everywhere together and entertained a lot. But don't forget I was still kind of on trial. She was still thinking it over, whether to get a divorce or not, and finally one day I asked her what she'd decided, and she said it didn't really make all that difference unless I wanted one. That was the first inkling I had that she knew I'd been seeing the other girl again. Then, just a shot in the dark, I asked her if she was seeing anyone, and she said yes, she was. I couldn't believe it. I wasn't in love with her any more, but no man wants to feel like a chump, and believe me I did. I regret to say that I threatened to kill her and the guy. I hit her, and she ran to her room and locked the door and telephoned the Bartons. It was about eleven o'clock at night, but the Bartons came over and Rex more or less took me in hand and Mrs. Barton went in and pacified your mother. It was decided that the best thing would be if Rex and I went in town and spent the night at the club, which we did.

"Oddly enough, the quarrel seemed to be just what we both needed. I returned home next afternoon, full of remorse and apologies, and your mother said it wasn't all my fault, that I'd had provocation, and I don't remember who first suggested it, but we decided to take a trip together and see if we couldn't make a fresh start. That lasted about three weeks, or just long enough for me to bring up the subject of the other guy. She said it was part of the bargain that we weren't to talk about what had happened before, but if that was part of the bargain, I certainly didn't remember it. In fact, I didn't remember any bargain. We returned to Long Island, and shortly after that your mother announced that she was having a baby. Johnny. It should have occurred to me that she'd gone into the second-honeymoon very enthusiastically, considering that we'd been on the verge of very serious trouble. But I didn't say anything. The reason I kept quiet was because I was secretly ashamed of myself. I'd got her pregnant, but I really didn't love her. The only love in my life was you, saying goo and gah."

"Hadn't I progressed beyond goo and gah by that time?"

"Conversationally, you were in a rut."

"I was practicing up to be a good listener," she said.

"Maybe."

"All right. So you'd got Mother pregnant," she said. "Or someone had."

"Really, Mimi."

"Well, isn't that why she went away on this second honeymoon?"

"Listen, kid, I don't mind not going by the book, but you *want* me to throw the book away."

"Father, all this talk about the book, going by the book, that came from you."

"Then I guess I don't know how to talk to you," said Godfrey Gaines.

"Yes you do. I'm enjoying the conversation, but when you talk about Bill Whitehill and yourself and this non-existent book, I wonder where you've been the last twenty-five years. You were married to a woman that runs a whore-house. I should have thought—well, go on with your story, Father."

"I don't know how to. In my job I have to give a lot of talks, but there I know my audience. This time I don't."

"Well, try. Assume that I take it for granted that you weren't responsible for Mother's pregnancy. Who was?"

"Rex Barton," said Godfrey Gaines. He looked at her again.

"That doesn't surprise me."

"God, in your way you're as smug as I thought I was."

"But Father, I've known for *years* that Uncle Rex and Mother were a thing. Who around here doesn't know it?"

"Bill Whitehill?"

"Maybe he does and maybe he doesn't."

"Has he got somebody?"

"Well, if he hasn't it's only because he doesn't want anybody."

"What about *you*, Mimi?"

"What about me?"

"You and George?"

"Have I got somebody? No. But I happen to like George."

"Gee, that's a positive declaration," said Godfrey Gaines. "That's the old-time religion."

"Don't be sarcastic, Father. You had the old-time religion, you and Mother, and where has it got you? Twenty-five years of hating each other, not to mention a home broken up, and you marrying a whorehouse madam. That's the book you keep talking about. Well, you can have it."

"What would George do if he found out this child wasn't his?"

"What do you mean, found out? He wouldn't have to *find out*. I'd tell him."

"If you knew," said Godfrey Gaines.

"Father, ask the driver to take us to the Taylors'."

Godfrey Gaines did so, and the car wound along the roads that long ago and now once again had names that seemed so odd—Muttontown, Matinecock, Skunks Misery. Godfrey Gaines could not have found his way now, where the chopped-up estates had lost all identity.

"Father. When did you kiss Mrs. Barton?"

"Oh, you want to go back to that? Well, when I went to say goodbye to her. Your mother and Rex Barton were off somewhere together, and I decided I wouldn't be there when they got back."

"Did you know they were together, or just guess?"

He smiled. "I was like you. He seemed the logical one."

"Why?"

"Well, she'd turned down Bill Whitehill, the other logical one, and that left Rex Barton. And who did she rush to the phone to when I threatened to kill her? Oh, hell, it had to be Rex. He was all over the place anyway."

"Where was I?"

"In the nursery, where you belonged. I had no intention of taking you away, then or later. Personally I considered your mother a slut, but what did I know about raising a one-year-old daughter?"

"So you went to see Mrs. Barton."

"I told her I was leaving Miriam, and she said I was making a great mistake. I'll never forget it. 'Rex will get over it, and so will she.' That was the first I ever knew that Mrs. Barton was hep to the jive."

"Oh, Father. Not slang. Not *that* kind of slang."

"All right," said Godfrey Gaines. "She knew where they were, and she offered to make Rex come home, but I said no. Then she suddenly became very attractive to me, Mrs. Barton, and I suggested that she and I go away together. She laughed. She said she'd do a lot of traveling if she went away every time she got that kind of an offer. But she said no. 'I like you, Lefty,' she said. 'And maybe this is a good idea, your going away. But if you do go, don't ever come back. Don't *ever* come back,' she said. 'Cut them all out of your life, all of us,' she said. So that's what I did."

"And you kissed her."

"Actually it was more like she kissed me. It wasn't a pass on either side. It was affection. So I stayed away—till she sent for me, the day before yesterday. I guess most people around here wouldn't have thought of me to help give Rex Barton a send-off, but she did. And I guess she must have had her reasons. I didn't even ask. There's nothing I wouldn't do for Cyn Barton," said Godfrey Gaines.

"If you ask me, you've done quite a lot," said his daughter.

MONEY

The money was divided three ways: Ellen Brosnan got her widow's share, and as soon as possible she left town and went back to Buffalo, New York, where she had originally come from; the remaining two-thirds was split between Nan Brosnan and her sister Marietta Brosnan Kelly. The whole thing amounted to about two hundred thousand dollars, quite a sum in those days, but the distribution did not cause much talk in the town. A few said Ellen Brosnan was lucky to get anything, but they were quickly reminded by the knowledgeable that under the law it was almost impossible to cut Ellen off. It could be done, they said, but she would have had to agree and it would have had to be so stated in Clete Brosnan's will. He would have had to say that Ellen had been provided for during his lifetime (and God knows that would have been the truth) and consequently consented to accept the nominal sum of one dollar in exchange for waiving her dower rights. All were unanimous that the way Clete disposed of his estate was the best way: give Ellen her third and let her go back to her Buffalo, New York, without any excuse for making a fuss, and let the Brosnan girls enjoy life in peace and quiet, gratefully remembering their brother with Month's Mind and Anniversary Masses said for him and a simple urn of Indiana limestone to mark his grave. He had not had much peace and quiet during the latter portion of his life, but at least he could rest in peace now—that was what *"requiescat in pace"* meant, wasn't it, after all?—with Ellen back in Buffalo and Nan and Marietta home and keeping the name up. All were unanimous that Clete had managed to bring about in death the kind of order and dignity that he had so longed for in life.

They got a good price for the house in Oak Road. The house was only five years old, well built of the best materials and with all the latest modern conveniences. Electricity everywhere, and two full-sized bathrooms. A high antenna for the Stromberg-Carlson so that Ellen could get Kansas City and Chicago as clearly as other people could get Pittsburgh and Schenectady. The garage door lifted easily with one hand instead of being a swinging door that had to be swung outward into the driveway. The Vic was an Orthophonic, and Ellen was the only housewife on Oak Road who had a telephone extension in her kitchen—although for the time she spent in her kitchen it seemed like a waste of money. Ellen even had an electric contraption for polishing the hardwood floors, although no one thought for a minute that Ellen was the one who pushed the contraption around. That was a job for her maid. A maid—for a house containing eight rooms and no children, where there were seldom any visitors to take care of but always fresh candy in the cut-glass jars, where there was a baby grand piano with no one who could play a note. Completely furnished, rugs and all, the house brought twenty-eight thousand dollars, which had to be divided up three ways under the terms of Clete's will. "I'd as soon let her have the whole thing," said Nan Brosnan.

"Well, not me. I wouldn't. I'd as soon she got none

of it," said Marietta Kelly. "She already got more than she's ever entitled to."

"Yes, but she's going to get all's coming to her or we'll have some shyster lawyer hauling us into court."

"I didn't mean we should try any funny business. What Clete wanted we have to conform with. But if she got what she was entitled to, a roll of toilet paper'd be sufficient."

"It doesn't come by the roll in that house," said Nan Brosnan.

"Just a figure of speech," said Marietta.

"I know. And don't think I was having generous thoughts, lamb. If I let her have the whole thing, it'd only be to get rid of her, to have nothing more to do with her whatsover . . . I'll say this for her. You'll hardly find a mark on any of the furniture, not a scratch, and in some ways the stuff is better than new."

"Why shouldn't it? At our place it's just the opposite, but I brought up my three children in our place. Why shouldn't her stuff look new? A hired girl with nothing to do but clean and dust—and run that electric floor polisher. You'd think she was getting ready to give a ball."

"And it's what killed Clete, too. Those slippery floors," said Nan Brosnan. "That spill he took the summer before last, Clete was an old man after that. Never the same."

"Oh, we can't blame her for that, Nan. Clete was delicate from as far back as I can remember. True, he got a bad shaking up, but when was Cletus Brosnan ever a Gene Tunney? You or I could always put him down, as children."

"He wasn't a muscular man, but he made up for it in brains," said Nan.

"With only the one blind spot, but men are easily

swayed. I ought to know, with a husband and three sons."

"You don't have to be married to know that," said Nan. "I didn't enter the convent at some tender age."

"I wasn't inferring anything, Nan. Don't always have a kind of a chip on your shoulder when the subject comes up about men."

"I didn't think you were inferring, lamb. But it's you with your husband and three sons that sometimes you act a *little* superior. I see all kinds of men at the office, away from their women, and many's the time I'm glad I never married. A woman in an office sees an entirely different side of things. I know I wouldn't want to be talked about the way some men talk about their wives, or have my husband say the things I've had married men say to me."

"Well, the more credit to you, Nan."

"Thanks. Just don't feel sorry for me."

"I don't. There've been times I envied you, and you know that."

"Well, we're not dependent on anyone now, you or I," said Nan Brosnan. "We can do as we please now, if we want to."

"Yes, and I hope you stick to it, your decision."

"To quit my job? Nothing'll shake me now, lamb."

"Oh, that I'm sure you'll do. I was thinking of your other decision."

"To give up my room? Well, if you still want me."

"Still *want* you?"

"You didn't say anything these last couple of weeks. I thought maybe you talked it over with Luke and he was against it."

"Good heavens, no. We got all that extra room, what's the use of paying room rent when we have all that extra room?"

"Well, I was thinking it over."

"Oh, Nan, there you go again with that chip on your shoulder. In other words, why didn't we ask you to stay with us before? Well, the only answer I could give to that question is the truthful one. We never thought of it before. You seemed content boarding at Bess Stauffer's, a few minutes' walk to your office. Me asking you to come live with us has nothing to do with your legacy, Nan, if that's what worried you."

"I'm not saying it did."

"No, but it stands to reason that's what you were thinking, your remark about thinking it over. After all, Nan, I have as much as you have from Clete, so don't start conjuring up some ulterior motive. It never would have occurred to me to ask you to live with us, only you said you were giving up your job, and then I thought why does Nan go on living at Bess Stauffer's, downtown? It was too far a walk from our place as long as you had your job, but if you're not going to an office every day, why not keep me company? I get lonesome for someone to talk to. I sound like another Ellen but it's true. You devote your whole life to making a home for a husband and three boys and then the boys all go off and get married and all those years you didn't make any friends of your own."

"You? You have a lot of friends, friends by the dozen."

"No. I have neighbors and acquaintances but not a single close friend. Don't confuse me with Luke, Nan. Luke has the Knights and the Legion he goes to and always some kind of a political thing, but I never could join the Daughters or the Auxiliary when they wanted me to, and now I don't want to."

"They want you now, surely."

"Since the news of Clete's will, indeed they do. But

I was always careful who I made friends with, and this is the time to be more careful than ever. That's a good thing for you to keep in mind, too, Nan."

"Oh-ho! Don't think I won't."

"Especially look out for men, Nan."

"The fortune-hunter type of man I can see through a mile away."

"I'm glad to hear that, Nan. Very glad to hear it. There's no more pitiful a figure than a woman suddenly come into money and no one to ward off the leeches and sponges."

"I can spot one of them a mile off. Don't forget, I've been a bookkeeper since I was seventeen years of age."

"I know, but with we Brosnans the heart often rules the head. Look at Clete and Ellen. Suddenly at almost forty-five years of age one of the cleverest businessmen in the county, Cletus Brosnan, J. Cletus Brosnan, what does he do but become infatuated with a pretty face in a nurse's uniform. If he could have seen her the first time dressed in something else there might be a different story to tell. But I had to sit there one day and listen while he told me about this angel of purity."

"Angel of purity is what he said to me, too. Did you ever think she was that?"

"Her? You're not seriously asking me that question, Nan. That kind of a bust development, I was sure she had one or two children."

"Oh, you can't tell anything by that. Remember Sister Mary Alexander?"

"I do. But in a black habit she still looked more like an angel of purity than Ellen in her white nurse's uniform. Could you ever picture Ellen in a nun's habit?"

Nan laughed. "No, that I couldn't."

"We have fun together, Nan. You come and stay with

us. You'll get used to Luke, if that's worrying you. Once in a month of Sundays he comes home stewed to the gills, but he always has enough sense to sleep in the cellar those nights. 'If you come home in that condition,' I tell him, 'you don't deserve better than the dog. Sleep it off in the cellar,' I tell him. But that's only maybe once or twice a year."

"I've never seen Luke with one too many."

"That's the Legion. The brewery sends them good beer, a couple halves at a time, and they don't stop drinking till the barrels are empty. At that I'd rather have him get drunk on good beer than take a chance on going blind from bootleg hootch."

"Oh, any day. And if not blind, I heard of some that died of convulsions."

"Luke won't often take a drink of whiskey. He likes his beer, but the hard liquor he leaves for the younger fellows. He has that much sense, and that's something to be thankful for."

"You got the best of the Kelly boys. Clete always had only the nicest things to say about Luke. And I remember during the war people saying Luke didn't have to go, but he went."

"Well, there'd always been a Kelly in the Civil War and the Spanish-American, and our boys weren't old enough, so he went. He couldn't have gone if we didn't have Clete to help out, but Clete was glad to. You remember."

"I do. Clete was mortified when they wouldn't take him, but at least he could make some contribution."

"Mind you, it wasn't much. Two thousand, and Luke paid it all back. It took him five years, but he paid back every cent. Oh, yes. Every red cent. Luke was bounden determined he wouldn't go through life owing money to his brother-in-law."

"I never knew that. I never knew that at all."

"See? Here we are, sisters, living in the same town all our lives, and there's so many things we don't know about one another." Marietta Kelly was abruptly silent.

"What, lamb?" said Nan Brosnan.

"*Please* come and live with us, Nan."

"What's the matter? Is there something wrong? Tell me."

Marietta nodded. "I'd tell you, but I took my oath. You'll find out soon enough, God help us."

Nan Brosnan, in the weeks of accustoming herself to her new surroundings and leisure and to the constant close company of her sister, respected the mysterious oath Marietta had given. There were times when she had the guilty suspicion that Marietta had invented a crisis in order to persuade her to become a member of the Kelly household. But against that was the genuineness of Marietta's entreaty; it was not like Marietta to show any sign of weakness. In years gone by Marietta had taken things from her older sister, taken them without permission, stolen them on occasion; and when she asked favors she had always managed not to say please. Nan Brosnan could not remember ever hearing Marietta say please, and if she had actually uttered the word, the implication that the word carried was never in her tone. The word "please," and its significance as a sign of weakness, convinced Nan that Marietta had taken an oath and that the oath was necessary to hide a real, a desperate secret. Marietta was cheerful and chatty, sarcastic and revealing, but in those early weeks she did not again refer to the oath. It took weeks, but Nan Brosnan discovered that among all the persons and things that Marietta was so eager to talk about, one topic was omitted: not once, not ever, did Marietta tell a story that had Luke Kelly for the principal character. She told wonderfully funny stories about school days and the eccentricities of some of the nuns; stories about departed curates that she would never have told in front of a third person; anecdotes about her three sons growing up, and hearsay gossip about the inside maneuverings and machinations in the Legion Post and the Knights of Columbus Council. But Luke Kelly was never made the principal character of these reminiscences, and once Nan Brosnan discovered this omission she realized that the thing that troubled Marietta surely concerned Luke. Her mind leaped to a suspicion that it concerned Luke and Ellen, but as she listened further to Marietta's criticisms of Ellen, Nan Brosnan dismissed the suspicion: Marietta despised Ellen, but she was not jealous of her for any reason that had to do with Luke.

Nan grew fonder of Luke. Living in the same house with him she surprised herself with her quick acceptance of Luke as a sort of living substitute for Clete. He would never be Clete; he was too jolly and careless about everything; his manners, his appearance, his outlook on life made him totally unlike Clete. Clete was hardly out of bed in the morning before he was shaved and wearing collar and tie, and if you ever saw Clete in his shirtsleeves it was only because he was doing some handyman chore about the house. His coat went back on the minute he finished the chore. But Luke would come down in the morning needing a shave, carrying his coat and vest and collar and tie, rubbing his whiskers, scratching himself wherever he felt the need and without regard for Nan's presence. "Hello, girls. You got the old man's breakfast ready?" he would say. "Nan, what are you doing up at this hour? You're supposed to be a lady of leisure. Go on back to bed." He would put an elbow on the table and rest his head on his hand as he spooned up big globs of Cream of Wheat, and while waiting for his eggs and bacon he would sit and smile sadly at Nan. "No rest for the weary, Nan," he would say. Sometimes in the interval between cereal and eggs he would stand up and put on his collar and tie. He would finish his breakfast and say, "Goodbye, girls. Anybody phones, I'll be at the barbershop." He was a collector for a furniture company, which allowed him to bring a Dodge coupé home at night, and he would be out of the house by half past eight, although he seemed to be dawdling and delaying. It was just that his way of doing things, unlike Clete's way, made him seem to be wasting time when he really wasn't. One morning the sisters were in the kitchen, and at eight-fifteen he had not made his appearance. "Will you go up and see if he went back to bed? He wasn't up when I came down."

"I thought I heard him moving around," said Nan. "I'll call him. I don't feel right about going up."

"If he went back to bed, calling won't waken him."

"Then you go up. I'll fry the eggs," said Nan.

Marietta was gone about five minutes. She returned to the kitchen and looked at her sister. "I can't move him. He's lying on the floor in the bathroom."

"Who do you doctor with?" said Nan.

"Young Michaels. The number's one-three-five-oh. But I think it's too late."

"They'll know where he is."

"Too late for Luke, I mean. I think he's gone."

"*No,* lamb. I'll phone Michaels and maybe he'll bring a pulmotor. You go on up with Luke."

Nan admired Marietta's calm without understanding it, but she understood it better when Marietta said, "It's what I've been expecting. What we both been dreading."

"The oath you took?"

"He had the one stroke, but he made me swear to keep it secret. He wanted to be Post commander and he was afraid they wouldn't vote for a man'd had a stroke."

"Go on up with him, lamb."

Marietta shook her head. "I can't, Nan. It isn't him," she said. "You can put the eggs back in the icebox, unless *you* want them."

"Oughtn't somebody to be up there with him? You phone Michaels and I'll go upstairs."

"Will you, then? You can wait out in the hall. But I just can't go up there, Nan."

Everyone said what a brave woman Marietta was throughout her ordeal of the next few days. When they compared notes they found that no one had seen her break, although some noticed that at the requiem Mass, while Joe Denny was singing "Beautiful Isle of Somewhere," she put her handkerchief to her eyes under her heavy veil. But that was the closest to a display of emotion that anyone saw during those days. "A brother and a husband in less than a year's time," they said. "It's lucky she's got her three boys."

"And Nan. It isn't as if she was all alone in the house."

"And at least they won't have any money worries."

Luke's insurance and the house and his savings came to nowhere near the size of Clete's legacy, but Marietta for the first time in her life could be considered comfortably well off. The boys were all self-supporting in more or less distant cities, and before they returned to their homes Marietta spoke to them about money. "Thanks to your Uncle Clete and your father, you won't have me to worry about. Aunt Nan and I'll be living here and sharing expenses. So you don't have to support me. Use your money to raise your own families."

The two older boys nodded silently, but the youngest,

Bob, spoke up. "I was counting on a thousand dollars from Dad," he said. "I was *counting* on it, Mom. He as much as promised it to me."

"He didn't say anything in his will," said Marietta.

"I know, but when I married Polly, Dad said he was sorry he could only give me a hundred bucks for a wedding present. He told me he was paying off Uncle Clete and a hundred was all he could spare. He said he'd make up for it some day."

"I don't hear the others claiming a thousand dollars," said Marietta. "And as far as that goes, I don't hear *anybody* offering to chip in for the funeral expenses."

"Oh, wait a minute, Mom," said Gerald, the oldest brother. "The funeral expenses come out of his benefits from the Knights."

"Partially only," said Marietta. "If you want to see the bills, I'll show them to you when they come in. Are you going to say Dad promised you a thousand, too?"

"Well, he told me the same as he told Bob," said Gerald.

"And me," said Ray, the middle son.

"It's funny I never heard about any of these big promises, although Dad and I never had any secrets from one another. Especially about financial matters. And you, Robert, you're a strange one to bring it up, considering how we scraped and pinched to send you to pharmacy school."

"If I had a thousand dollars I could use it for downer money to open my own drugstore," said Bob.

"A thousand dollars to open a drugstore?" said Marietta.

"And Polly's father willing to go on my note, and the little I managed to save."

"If it wasn't for your Uncle Clete I'd have to sell this

house and you'd all have to chip in to support me. Or I hope you would. It certainly would look nice if I had a son owner of a drugstore and another son a telegraph operator for the United Press and another son making carpenter's wages, and not enough from the three of them to keep me out of the poorhouse."

"Poorhouse? Bushwah!" said Bob. He stood up. "Dad made me a promise, and Jerry and Ray, too, and Dad always kept his promises. But I promise *you* something, Mom. This is the last time you'll see me in *this* house."

"Sit down, Bob," said Gerald.

"Don't have a fight over money with Dad hardly—" said Ray.

"Oh, go to hell," said Bob. "Stick around, maybe she'll give you my share."

"That calls for a—" Gerald began, but Bob went out.

"Sit down, Gerald," said Marietta. "I won't have any rough stuff in the house of the dead. Let him go, and I hope he keeps his promise, because I don't want any son of mine in my house that talks that way to his mother."

"He was telling the truth, though, Mom," said Ray. "Dad said the same thing to me he said to Bob."

"I don't doubt it for a minute, that Dad would say those things. But where the money was going to come from, that was another matter entirely. All the years we were married he used to say he was going to take me on a trip to Ireland. Five years from now, ten years from now, he used to say we'll go back and pay a visit to Roscommon and Waterford and look up the Kellys and the Brosnans and the Dooleys. But the only trips anybody ever made was when Dad was delegate to the Legion conventions. I never held him to any of those promises, although dear knows I'd of welcomed a trip anywhere. You'd a wonderful father, you boys, but he had a forgetful habit of saying we were going to do this and going to do that and then the whole thing would completely pass from his mind. He'd mean it at the time, but I soon found out it was like playing some kind of a game. 'Sure,' I'd say, 'we'll visit Ireland five years from now,' but when the five years were up I had more sense than to remind him. I'm surprised he didn't promise you *five* thousand, but it shows how little you understood your father if you took those things seriously. Paying back your uncle, getting rid of the mortgage on this property—it cut him to the quick that the only money I ever had of my own had to come from my brother, not from him."

"Oh, let's drop the subject of money," said Gerald.

"Well, if you two honestly believe I'm holding on to money that rightfully belongs to you—if you honestly believe that? I'll give each of you five hundred as soon as Lawyer Phillips finishes with the legal end, and five hundred apiece next year or the year after. But not Robert. Robert's behavior in this house today puts him beyond the pale. Let him and his Polly and her father start their drugstore, and luck to them. Is that agreeable to you?"

"Whatever suits you, Mom," said Gerald.

"You, Ray?" said Marietta.

"The same for me," said Ray.

"I'll do the best I can for the two of you," said Marietta. "And don't forget, I'm not going to live forever, either. Just remember, no man knows the day or the hour."

Nan Brosnan joined her sister in double mourning. "As long as you wear black I'll wear it too," said Nan.

"Not you," said Marietta. "I'll always wear black, but a year's plenty long enough for you. You won't be criticized."

"I wasn't afraid of that. It's the way I felt about Luke. The next thing to a brother."

"Well, when the year's up for Luke I'll wear a little white in my hats, and you can start wearing colors."

"Well, we'll see," said Nan.

"I'm sure if you took a trip to Buffalo, New York, you wouldn't find a certain Mrs. J. Cletus Brosnan in widow's weeds. Oh, did I tell you? She sent Monsignor fifteen dollars for Masses for Luke. Imagine the gall! Never a word to me, never as much as a bunch of forget-me-nots for the funeral. But fifteen dollars for Masses."

"Well, it's one way of showing spite, if you want to look at it that way. Or maybe something's come over her since Clete passed on. Maybe she's finally learning to appreciate him, now that it's too late."

"Yes, and maybe she's having a high old time with poor Clete's money and what's fifteen dollars?"

"For me it's a lot of money when I think of how much you have to have in capital to get fifteen dollars' income."

"How much?" said Marietta.

"Well, fifteen dollars is three hundred dollars at five per cent."

"Yes, I guess it is," said Marietta. "It doesn't seem like much, does it, to only get fifteen dollars from three hundred."

"You don't get anywhere near that much from the bank."

"You hear about so many that are making money hand over fist in the stock market. Oughtn't we to go in the stock market, Nan?"

"I've been thinking about it. I was always afraid to when I only had my salary and my building-and-loan."

"Well, find out more about it. You're better at business than I am. Who do you go to for advice on such matters? Who did Clete go to?"

"A fellow named Ralph Fexler."

"Who's he? I never heard of him."

"He manages the local office for Westmore & Company. That's a New York stockbroker firm. Fexler goes around with the country-club outfit. He's a young fellow in his early thirties, I'd say."

"Oh, you know him?"

"I know him to say hello to, from coming in the office. He knew me as Clete's sister. Don't worry, you'll be hearing from him."

"Clete trusted him?"

"Oh, he's honest. Westmore & Company's a big firm, and a lot of the country-club outfit buy their stocks through Fexler. He'll be around to see us one of these days."

"Maybe we're losing money by not going to see him," said Marietta.

"Well, I had the same thought, but I didn't want to say anything till things got more settled. But now don't get the idea that everything you put money in guarantees a hundred-per-cent profit. You don't hear as much about the ones that lose money in the stock market."

"Oh, I know that much."

"Well, as long as you do. It's taking a chance when you buy a stock, lamb. If I lost all my money I'm pretty sure I could get a job, but I was a head bookkeeper. I wouldn't go in too deep if I were you. A little at a time. Risk five hundred or a thousand, and if you make a profit reinvest it. If you lose it, well, you learn by experience."

"That sounds like a very sensible idea, Nan. But don't you think maybe we ought to get started? Couldn't you go to see this Fexler man?"

"Not go to see him. He has a big office all full of men smoking cigars and watching the stock market."

"Watching the stock market?"

"A blackboard with the names of the stocks, and young Jimmy Shevlin—"

"Jule Shevlin's boy?"

"Uh-huh. Young Jimmy up there marking down the latest prices with a piece of chalk. I was never inside the place, but I often had to pass it and I could see in."

"Jule Shevlin'd never let her Jimmy work in a place if it wasn't reliable."

"Oh, I said it was reliable, and Clete did business with them for years, years. But I wouldn't just walk in and ask for Fexler. I'll write him a little note and tell him we were interested. If I put up five hundred and you put up five hundred it'd only be a thousand, small potatoes to Fexler, but he knows there's more. And remember this, lamb. He's a broker, and makes a little every time whether we buy or sell. He knows that between us there's over a hundred thousand dollars, and he'd love to have us for customers. You watch. When I tell him we're interested he'll come running, even if it's only a thousand to start with."

Marietta Kelly was quite taken with Ralph Fexler. "Did you notice his complexion?" she said to Nan. "Skin like a baby's. And isn't it nice to see a young fellow wear a stiff collar these days? I noticed his hands, too. He'd hands like Monsignor's. Clete had hands like that."

"And Ray, and Bob. Maybe Jerry would have, too, but a carpenter gets his hands banged up with a hammer, I guess," said Nan. "Anyway, we're in the stock market, lamb. Is it a thrill for you? It is for me."

"I feel as if it was the first day of school and Mom bought me a new dress," said Marietta.

(235)

They made money: their thousand-dollar investment grew to fifteen hundred in a year's time—"Makes bank interest look sick," said Nan—and along the way they learned about margin trading. They also overcame their shyness about sitting in the big room surrounded by men smoking cigars watching Jimmy Shevlin. One day Marietta was offered a cigarette by a man sitting in the next chair. "I believe I will," she said and grinned at Nan.

"So will I," said Nan Brosnan.

They added another fifteen hundred to their fund. Although their accounts were kept separate, they bought and sold the same shares in the same amounts, and calculated their winnings and losses in terms of a joint account. They were at the office of Westmore & Company nearly every day, all day, and when the market was being particularly active they had sandwiches and coffee sent in, just like the big traders among the men. They were at the Westmore office one day and heard the town fire whistle blow five times. "Five times," said Marietta. "That's the Fourth Ward, our Ward."

"Oh, good Lord," said Nan.

"What?"

"I'll be back in a minute," said Nan. She went to a telephone booth, and when she came back she was holding her hand over her breast and shaking her head. "It's our house, lamb. It's my fault. I'll pay you back, every cent."

"The fire? My house?"

"Maybe Mr. Fexler'd drive us there in his car," said Nan.

On the way to the house in Fexler's car she explained. As soon as she heard the alarm she remembered that on the way down to the office she was almost sure she'd left a cigarette burning in the kitchen. "I couldn't be altogether sure," she said. Marietta was very angry, but she did not want to say anything in front of Mr. Fexler.

"Fire must be out," said Fexler. "Here come two of the engines. The hook and ladder and the chemical."

The chief's car and another engine were standing at the curb. The house showed no damage, looked the same as usual except that the front door was open and a hose line ran from the fire plug, through the doorway, to somewhere inside the house. "Thank God," said Nan.

"Wait'll we have a look inside before thanking God," said Marietta.

"I'd be glad to wait for you ladies," said Mr. Fexler.

"No, no, that's all right. Thank you very much for being so accommodating," said Marietta.

"Well, let me know if I can be of any assistance," said Mr. Fexler.

Ed Sharp, the fire chief, was in the hall when the sisters entered. He shook his head. "Don't you know better than to leave a curling iron attached? For God's sake, if you're going to curl your hair, at least disconnect the thing when you're done with it. You got off easy this time, but—"

"How do you know it was the curling iron started it?" said Marietta.

"It's my job to know, that's how," said Ed Sharp. "Your God damn fire started in the bathroom and your God damn curling iron was the only thing hooked up. That was a dumb thing to do. Who do you insure with?"

"Joe Denny," said Marietta.

"Well, lucky he's a friend of yours."

"Do we get the insurance?"

"If it was up to me you wouldn't, anybody that would do a dumb thing like that. You got all that money, why don't you spend some of it on a permanent wave? Yeah, you'll get your insurance, this time. But I hope they make you pay double after this."

"Who discovered the fire, Ed?" said Nan Brosnan.

"The woman next door. Schrope. She noticed the smoke coming out the bathroom window, and she knew there was nobody home. Nobody home, I'll say. Nobody home." He made a revolving-wheel gesture with his finger over his ear. "Ten more minutes and this house would have been a vacant lot."

In her total humiliation Marietta could extract some consolation from the fact that even if the insurance company refused to pay, she had made enough money in the stock market to cover the damage. It was not as easy as that to take the blame away from Nan and assume it herself. "Well, why don't you say it? Say it was my fault," said Marietta.

"It could have been mine," said Nan. "I feel just as guilty."

"Like hell you do. You're standing there telling yourself I blamed you and all along it was my fault. Well, what if it was my fault? What's to stop me from putting a match to my own house if that's what I wanted to do?" Aloud, but to herself she added: "We ought to had the whole house rewired years ago. Luke was right." Then, to Nan she said: "Would you be willing to chip in to have the whole house rewired?"

"Well, being's you don't charge me any rent, sure. But why do we put money in this house? Why don't you sell it instead of putting good money in it?"

"And live where?"

Nan shrugged her shoulders. "Depends. An apartment is big enough for just the two of us. Or, if you want to splurge, we could buy a house on Oak Road."

"Oak Road," said Marietta. "Oh, if we could get back Clete's house, wouldn't that be delicious, Nan? Nan, we're rich. The two of us worked hard all our lives. Aren't we entitled to enjoy ourselves with the time we got left?"

"Clete's house has gone up since we sold it. But we might be able to get it back, if we offered that young couple a quick two or three thousand profit. How high would you want to go? They paid twenty-eight thousand. We could offer them thirty."

"I'll go to thirty-five! It's an investment, isn't it?"

"Well—nobody's going to refuse a seven-thousand-dollar profit on a twenty-eight-thousand investment. That comes to a twenty-five-per-cent profit in less than two years. If you want it that much, it's all right with me. But there we get into a legal problem. Who takes title to it? You, or me?"

"I will. I have more money than you have."

"Oh. You want to buy the whole thing yourself?"

"As I think it over, yes. I'm not crowding you out, Nan, but I think I ought to be the one to own the house, and maybe you wouldn't object to paying me a little rent."

"Like for instance, how much?"

"What did you pay at Bess Stauffer's?"

"I paid Bess fifteen a week for my room and breakfast and supper. That's sixty a month, seven-twenty a year. You wouldn't have any trouble getting a mortgage."

"Well, what do you think of the idea?"

"Well, it isn't what I started out thinking about, but maybe it's better for all concerned," said Nan.

"You'll always have a home with me, Nan. You know that," said Marietta.

Lawyer Phillips strongly advised against it, but within two months the purchase had been made and the sisters took up residence in the house their brother had built.

"They must be crazy," their friends said. But even Lawyer Phillips was forced to admit that luck was on their side. A woman paid ten thousand dollars for Luke Kelly's old house and immediately converted it into six apartments. "Maybe that's what you should of done," said Nan. "She's going to have between two and three hundred a month from Luke's house."

"I'm satisfied," said Marietta. "I'm not out of pocket, and I own Clete's house. That's the real satisfaction, us living in Clete's house. Wait till Ellen hears that. Us sitting in her chairs. Can you still play the piano, Nan?"

"I guess I could pick it up again if I practiced."

"Have a few lessons. I'll make you a present of them," said Marietta.

"No, I wouldn't take lessons at my age, but I'll practice and see if it comes back to me. I'll buy some music at the five-and-ten."

"You practice your piano, and do you know what I'm going to do? I'm going to practice how to drive a car."

"Are you going to buy a car?"

"I am. An Essex coop. I told Jim Denny if I could learn to drive inside of a month, I'd buy one. I start tomorrow. Living out here one of us has to learn to drive a car, and I know you wouldn't care to."

"I might. I'm not as afraid of them as I used to be."

"Then so much the better. When Jim takes me for my lesson, you come along."

"No, you learn and I'll watch you."

"Yes, I can practically drive now, from watching Luke. He wouldn't let me drive, because the Dodge belonged to the store, but he showed me how everything worked. I understand the gearshift is different in an Essex, but the general idea is the same."

(240)

"You'll learn in no time," said Nan.

She began to feel deserted already. She would never learn to drive a car, and her eyesight was so bad that if anything happened to her glasses she would not be able to see the radiator cap. No matter what Marietta said to re-assure her, Nan Brosnan felt far less at home in Clete's house than she had in Luke's. It was not only the mere act of paying rent in Clete's house—which she had not done while living at Luke's. Nan enjoyed spending money when she had it to spend. But her first mention of a house on Oak Road was a chance remark, not intended to interest Marietta specifically in Clete's house. She had not gone to the house very often while Clete was alive, not nearly as often as Marietta and Luke had been. The married couples had made a pretense of conviviality in the early years of Clete's marriage, partly because it was the right thing to do, and partly because Ellen had bought some, but not all, of her furniture through Luke, which meant a small commission for Luke even at reduced prices. In a sense every article of furniture in the house meant some-thing to Marietta, either as a chair that had been bought through Luke, or a rug that Ellen had bought at Wana-maker's, and thus an item that contributed to Marietta's hatred of Clete's wife. There was little in the house that Marietta did not, as it were, know personally. In the final two years of Clete's life, when Ellen was supposed to be carrying on with the manager of the hotel, nothing new was added to the house furnishings. But Nan was accus-tomed to living in surroundings that had been chosen by other women: her mother, Bess Stauffer, Marietta, and now Ellen Brosnan. In what would soon be fifty years she had never bought so much as a footstool for herself, and now that she could afford to furnish a whole house she had neither the inclination nor an established taste to express in purchases of sofas and tables and draperies. For more than thirty years she had been making her neat little figures in ledgers, under lighting conditions that were not of the best, and now if she took off her glasses a picture on the wall was only a blurred square outline.

"Jim Denny says I'll be driving in a week," said Marietta, returning from her first lesson.

"Then we can start going to Westmore's again," said Nan.

"Well, I don't know about that, Nan," said Marietta. "Do you want to?"

"Don't you?"

"Well, we don't have to, you know. And I don't think it looks right, two women going there every day."

"We've been doing it, and we weren't the only women there."

"No, we weren't, but I don't have to tell you who one of the women was."

"But we never had to sit near her, and she never tried to get friendly or anything."

"No, and a good thing she didn't. But she was there every day and for a long time we didn't even know who she was. But believe you me, all the men knew. The worst madam in the county."

"Well, there was old Mrs. Lucas, she went every day."

"As queer as Dick's hatband," said Marietta.

"And Sylvia Levy."

"Yes, but always with her husband. Levy was there most of the time, but she only came up a little while in the morning and just before the market closed. I don't want to start going every day."

"Why? Since we're living on Oak Road?"

"All right, yes. Since we're living on Oak Road. We're not on a party line here, Nan. If Ralph has anything to tell us, like for instance a margin call, he can get us here almost as quick as if we were there in the board room."

"We can't be watching the board from here."

"Well, if you miss it that much, I'll take you down every day, but I won't promise to stay."

"What are you going to do?"

"I don't know, but one sure thing I'm not going to spend the whole day sitting in Westmore's office."

"Why don't you join the country club and learn to play golf?"

"Well, I'll tell you this much, sitting around a board room all day isn't going to get us in any country club."

"You and I could sit on the *steps* of the country club and they wouldn't ask us in if it rained kangaroos. If that's what you're thinking."

"Nan, we don't have to have a fight over this. If you want to go, I'll take you down in my car. And I'll bring you back in the afternoon."

"I can walk down to Market Street and take the trolley, and I can take the trolley home, thanks just the same."

So it came about that for a few weeks Nan Brosnan every morning boarded the trolley, spent four or five hours at Westmore & Company's office, and took the trolley home. She went stubbornly, hoping that with the renewal of the habit the zest would return. But without Marietta it was not fun. It was only business. Work. And often there were stretches of hours at a time when nothing happened that was of interest to her financially. The men who once had made casual conversation now no longer chatted with her in that way they had of talking about the market while never taking their eyes off the board. Now they would bid her the time of day, but without Marietta she was left alone. Marietta was not very pretty; the most that could be said for her was that she was vivacious and had good legs. But whatever she had to offer, in the board room it was what had impelled the men to stop for a chat.

On a Friday afternoon Nan Brosnan made up her mind to discontinue her visits to Westmore & Company. She got off the trolley and walked up the hill to Oak Road. The garage was empty, and she let herself in the front door. She was tired, and some of her weariness was caused by apprehension. Marietta had not stopped being cross with her. Her decision to abandon the trips to Westmore's was a victory for Marietta, but nothing pleased Marietta.

In the livingroom Nan took off her shoes and started to go to the kitchen, but she made only one step and the rug slipped away. For the briefest moment she had a sense of exhilaration while both feet were in the air, and even at the very moment that her leg was breaking the pain was slower in coming than her understanding of what was happening to her. The pain came fully and strong and she forced herself to look at her leg, just above the ankle, where blood was coming. "Mother Mary, Mother of Jesus, let me die," she said. "Get me out of here." Her prayer was not answered.

THE NOTHING
MACHINE

Her dress and the modified beehive coiffure deceived no one
about her age, and were not meant to. It was a compara-
tively simple matter to fix the important dates of her career
and of her life: her class in college, so many years as a copy-
writer and copy chief, so many years with one agency as
account executive, so many years as vice-president of one
firm and then another. She did not claim to be forty or
forty-five, but her record spoke for itself and her chic proclaimed her determination to quit only when she was ready
and not one minute before. The only thing was—more and
more she liked to have Monday and Tuesday and Wednesday evenings to herself, to whip up her own dinner, to read
a while, to work if she felt like it, to watch what the competitive accounts were doing on television, to take a warm
bath in a tub of scented water and go to bed at a time of
her own choosing. All she had she had worked for, fought
for, fought dirty for when she'd had to. She had gone
through those years when they said terrible things about
her, and she had known they were saying them; but now
that was past, and she was up there where they had to respect her—or be respectful to her—and they gave her
plaques now, and wanted her name on committees. "Oh,

Judy's tough all right," they said. "But she had to be, to get where she did in this rat-race. There aren't many men around that started the same time she did."

Judith Huffacker waved a pink-gloved hand at the chairman of the board. He raised his hat and shook it in farewell, and then was hurried along by the passengers behind him. That was that, and she turned to the man at her side. "Where can I take you?"

"Well, I was going to suggest *I* take you to dinner. It's a little late, but some place like the Oak Room. How would that suit you?"

"No. No thanks. I've had a long day, but I'll drop you anywhere you say."

"Oh, come on. Have dinner with me. I don't want to go back to Detroit and admit I couldn't talk the famous Judith Huffacker into a dinner."

"Admit it to whom?"

"Any of the guys you know and I know."

"Like who, for instance?"

"Well—Jim Noble. Ed Furthman. Stanley Kitzmiller. You want me to name some more?"

"Production men. Don't you know any advertising men?"

"Sure, but I thought you'd be more interested in your impression on production men. You're aces with them."

"I'm glad to hear that."

"The ad men, of course, but that goes without saying."

"Not always, you may be sure. All right, let's go to the Oak Room."

When they were under way he said, "This your car?"

"Yes, are you impressed?"

"Naturally. I'm always impressed when people spend

their own money when they don't have to. You could have had the use of one of our cars, couldn't you? Don't you rate that executive-car deal? I'm sure you do."

"Yes."

"And it takes a certain amount of guts to drive around in a foreign car when you're working with an American manufacturer."

"You put it correctly. I'm working with them, not for them. I've worked with a lot of them, don't forget, and if your company doesn't like my taste in cars, if that's going to make the difference, they can either get me fired or take their business elsewhere."

"Nobody'd fire you at this stage."

"They wouldn't call it that, but that's what it would be."

"Do you mind if I call you Judith?"

"No, I don't mind. What do I call you?"

"Van," he said. "At the plant they call me B.B., but my outside friends call me Van."

"What is B.B. for?"

"Benjamin Brewster Vandermeer is the full handle. Now I can ask you, who was Huffacker?"

"He was my second husband."

"Oh, you were married twice? I didn't realize that. Are you divorced?"

"Twice. But Huffacker's dead. He died some time after we were divorced. I kept on using his name because I'd had three names in ten years and it was getting to be confusing."

"Have you any children?"

"I have a daughter, married and living in Omaha, Nebraska. I have two grandchildren. And I own a Mercedes-Benz."

"I don't want to sound oversensitive, but do you resent my asking you these questions?"

"Well, resent isn't the word exactly. Or maybe it is. I've spent so many years working with men, and with some success, working on equal terms. I don't like it when a man asks me the kind of questions he wouldn't ask another man. If you came to my house for a social visit it'd be different, but we've been together since nine o'clock this morning, talking some pretty technical stuff and all the give and take of a business conference. But as soon as we get alone together, you want to know about my sex life."

"You're absolutely right."

"Well, give up, because you're not going to find out."

"Oh, that isn't what I meant. When I said you were absolutely right I meant you were right to be annoyed. But you're kind of a legend, you know. You must be aware of that."

"Fully. I've read enough about myself to know that. And I've heard enough, too. The kind of stuff that *Fortune* can hint at but wouldn't dare come out and say it."

"Well, I can take the hint. Let's just be a couple of guys that haven't had anything to eat all day, and are hungry and irritable. All right?"

"Fine."

"*I've* been married twice and *I* have two grandchildren. Now we're even, okay? I don't own a Mercedes-Benz, but I think they make a hell of an automobile. Now we've traded information just about fact for fact."

She wished she had not consented to have dinner with this man. All day he had been easy to work with because he had been brisk and efficient and bloodless. He had the right answers in his mind or readily available in his batch of papers, and it was not his job to relate his facts to the

(248)

field of theory in which she functioned. At the airport he could have left her for a few minutes and in that brief time been lost in the crowd. She regretted that just that had not happened, so that she would now be on her way to her comfortable apartment and a warm, fragrant bath. She had had to change her mind about him too often: from a nothing-machine, with his quick mind and attaché case, to a lonesome out-of-towner, to one of the Detroit boys who gossiped about her, to a man who could express himself in sarcastic terms that compelled her respect. She very nearly told him she had decided to drop him at the Plaza, but the words she uttered were in a conciliatory tone: "You don't get to New York very often?"

"About once a month," he said. "Our department has a dinner at the University Club, usually on the second Monday. But I go back to Detroit the same night if I can."

"Oh, yes. I knew about those dinners. We have them, too, but I don't always have to go," she said.

"I suppose they do some good. For my part, they have a dubious value. I don't get home till around two o'clock in the morning and I like my sleep. But departmental dinners must be worth it or the company'd do away with them."

"They can be a bore, all right," she said.

"I don't need the inspirational presence of my fellow man," he said. "I can perform just as well over the telephone and the teletype, and those big martinis they serve at the University Club, they certainly do promote frank discussions. Here we are."

At the table he said, "They all seem to know you here, customers *and* waiters."

"I've been coming here a long time," she said.

"I'll tell you one thing. Whether you like it or not, you didn't get that reception because you were vice-president of an ad agency. That was for a good-looking woman. Shall we order?"

It was unexpectedly smart of him to have noticed the quality of the reception, but he was not making it easier for her to like him. He put his elbows on the table and clasped his hands and looked about the room. "All these people that I've never seen before and probably never will again. I don't suppose I'll see you again, either. At least not for a year."

"I guess not. You're originally from the Middle West, aren't you?"

"Hell, that's written all over me. Yes, I've lived in Wisconsin, Illinois, Indiana, Ohio, and Michigan. I was born Wisconsin. My father was a preacher, that's why we moved around so much. I graduated from Purdue and got a job near Indianapolis . . . Oh, here's somebody I don't want to see." He raised his water glass in front of his face, but he had been seen and recognized.

"Hyuh, there, Van. Do you remember me? Charley Canning?" The newcomer was in his middle fifties, dressed with expensive care by no tailor on this side of the Atlantic. He seemed sure of his welcome and had his hand out.

"Oh, hello there."

"*Hello* there? Have I changed that much, or have you got a lousy memory? Charley *Canning,* from Humphreysville. Or maybe I'm wrong. You *are* Benjamin Vandermeer?"

"Yes, and I lived in Humphreysville, but I can't seem to place you."

"Well, for Christ's sake, don't crack your brains trying. You know damn well who I am, but maybe you have your reasons for wishing I didn't remember you. Good day, sir." Canning stared angrily at Vandermeer and at Judith Huffacker, then went on his way.

"Why did you do that? He seemed all right, and he knew you were doing it deliberately."

He nodded. "I did it deliberately."

"But why? He doesn't know why you did it."

"No, and he wouldn't understand if I told him," he said. "I haven't seen that fellow in thirty years. If I told *you* why I snubbed him you probably wouldn't understand either . . . I didn't order any wine. Are you used to having wine with your dinner?"

"Forget about the wine, and stop being evasive. I want to know why you disliked that man so. If it's not too personal."

"It isn't personal, in the sense of his doing something to me. Consciously, deliberately doing something to me." He looked at her quickly. "All right, I'll tell you.

"I went to live in Humphreysville, my first job after I graduated from Purdue. It's a little town about fifteen miles from Indianapolis, population about twelve-fourteen hundred, and I was assistant county engineer. A kind of a maid-of-all-work and utility outfielder. Highways. Water supply. Anything that was on a blueprint or you looked at through a transit. I liked it. I got twelve hundred a year, and that was twelve hundred more than a lot of my classmates were making. And I liked the town, the people. It was like going back home, to any of the other Middle Western towns I'd lived in. And like most Middle Western towns, especially Indiana, they were crazy about basketball, so when the high school coach had to quit, I took over the team. I'd played at Purdue and they knew that.

"Well, we had a pretty good season. Won sixteen and lost eight and came in second in the county league. And at the end of the season they had the usual banquet. My boys, and letter men from other years and a few leading citizens. Small. If we'd won the county league it would have been bigger, but they always had a team banquet regardless of how they came out. The basement of the Presbyterian church, which was used for a lot of community get-togethers because they had a kitchen and plenty of chairs et cetera. We had the high school principal give out the little miniature basketballs, silver. I still have mine at home. And it was a very nice sociable gathering. A lot of kidding among ourselves, replaying some of the games we lost, and recalling funny incidents that happened on our trips. And the whole thing broke up around nine-thirty, quarter of ten, because the boys had dates and the place where they hung out closed at eleven.

"But instead of that, eight of my boys and their dates all got into cars—not *their* cars. They didn't have cars, with one or two exceptions. There were cars waiting outside for them. And they all drove off to a roadhouse down near Indianapolis, where this fellow you just saw gave them another kind of a party. Got them all liquored up, and some of them had never taken a drink before, and when they got home that night some of them were sick, and the girls were crying, and the parents raised holy hell, and the whole town was in an uproar the next day. And that's why I don't like Canning."

"Was anybody hurt?"

"You mean drunken driving? No, nothing like that."

"What did you do?"

"How do you mean?"

"Well, about Canning?"

He shrugged his shoulders. "Nothing. Oh, I could have gone and had it out with him and most likely he would have ended up on the floor. That was what I felt like doing, I'll admit that. But if I didn't know my own boys better than that, that I'd been seeing every day and three-four nights a week for four months. And if they wanted to sneak off and go to a roadhouse with a fellow like Canning, maybe *I* didn't know *them* so well, either. No, I didn't do anything. But as soon as the first job came along, I left Humphreysville and I've never gone back since. A fellow like Canning, he probably got a big laugh out of seeing a bunch of kids get drunk. Canning was a rich guy. His father owned the hardware store and was agent for Deering and Delaval and companies like that. This fellow was a Dartmouth graduate, Phi Psi, I think he was I wouldn't have accomplished anything by mopping up the floor with him, although I admit I was strongly tempted."

"Yes," she said.

He laughed. "Tonight, too. Here in the Plaza Hotel, New York City, I wanted to give him a punch in the nose. That would have been something, explaining that to the New York police. Thirty years later. You would have had to tell your friends you were out with a lunatic, all these people that know you."

"Yes, they'd have thought you were a lunatic. But I don't."

"Well, that's good. I'm glad to hear that."

They talked no more about Canning or Indiana or anything so remote as thirty years ago. He paid the bill and walked with her to her car and they shook hands. "Let me know if you're coming to Detroit," he said. "My wife and I'd be glad to have you stay with us."

"I'll do that, Van," she said. The lie was not as bad as some she had told. It was the most harmless lie imaginable. At home, comfortable at last in her lavender-scented bath, she thought of lies and of truth, and of a life she had not spent with a man who could be so unforgiving of a little thing that had happened thirty years ago. Humphreysville, Indiana. Good God!

PAT COLLINS

Now they are both getting close to seventy, and when they see each other on the street Whit Hofman and Pat Collins bid each other the time of day and pass on without stopping for conversation. It may be that in Whit Hofman's greeting there is a little more hearty cordiality than in Pat Collins's greeting to him; it may be that in Pat Collins's words and smile there is a wistfulness that is all he has left of thirty years of a dwindling hope.

The town is full of young people who never knew that for about three years—1925, 1926, 1927—Whit Hofman's favorite companion was none other than Pat Collins. Not only do they not know of the once close relationship; today they would not believe it. But then it is hard to believe, with only the present evidence to go on. Today Pat Collins still has his own garage, but it is hardly more than a filling station and tire repair business on the edge of town, patronized by the people of the neighborhood and not situated on a traffic artery of any importance. He always has some young man helping out, but he does most of the work himself. Hard work it is, too. He hires young men out of high school—out of prison, sometimes—but the young men don't stay. They never stay. They like Pat Collins, and they say so, but they don't want to work at night, and Pat Collins's twenty-four-hour service is what keeps him going. Twenty-four hours, seven days a week, the only garage in town that says it and means it. A man stuck for gas, a man with a flat and no spare, a man skidded into a ditch— they all know that if they phone Pat Collins he will get there in his truck and if necessary tow them away. Some of the motorists are embarrassed: people who never patronize Pat Collins except in emergencies; people who knew him back in the days when he was Whit Hofman's favorite companion. They embarrass themselves; he does not say or do anything to embarrass them except one thing: he charges them fair prices when he could hold them up, and to some of those people who knew him long ago that is the most embarrassing thing he could do. "Twelve dollars, Pat? You could have charged me more than that."

"Twelve dollars," he says. And there were plenty of times when he could have asked fifty dollars for twelve dollars' worth of service— when the woman in the stalled car was not the wife of the driver.

Now, to the younger ones, he has become a local symbol of misfortune ("All I could do was call Pat Collins") and at the same time a symbol of dependability ("Luckily I thought of Pat Collins"). It is mean work; the interrupted sleep, the frequently bad weather, the drunks and the shocked and the guilty-minded. But it is the one service he offers that makes the difference between a profit and breaking even.

"Hello, Pat," Whit Hofman will say, when they meet on Main Street.

"Hyuh, Whit," Pat Collins will say.

Never more than that, but never less . . .

·　　·　　·

(255)

Aloysius Aquinas Collins came to town in 1923 because he had heard it was a good place to be, a rich town for its size. Big coal interests to start with, but good diversification as well: a steel mill, a couple of iron foundries, the railway car shops, shoe factories, silk mills, half a dozen breweries, four meat packing plants and, to the south, prosperous farmers. Among the rich there were two Rolls-Royces, a dozen or more Pierce-Arrows, a couple of dozen Cadillacs, and maybe a dozen each of Lincolns, Marmons, Packards. It was a spending town; the Pierce-Arrow families bought small roadsters for their children and the women were beginning to drive their own cars. The Rolls-Royces and Pierce-Arrows were in Philadelphia territory, and the franchises for the other big cars were already spoken for, but Pat Collins was willing to start as a dealer for one of the many makes in the large field between Ford-Dodge and Cadillac-Packard, one of the newer, lesser known makes. It was easy to get a franchise for one of those makes, and he decided to take his time.

Of professional experience in the automobile game he had none. He was not yet thirty, and he had behind him two years at Villanova, fifteen months as a shore duty ensign, four years as a salesman of men's hats at which he made pretty good money but from which he got nothing else but stretches of boredom between days of remorse following salesmen's parties in hotels. His wife Madge had lost her early illusions, but she loved him and partly blamed life on the road for what was happening to him. "Get into something else," she would say, "or honest to God, Pat, I'm going to take the children and pull out."

"It's easy enough to talk about getting another job," he would say.

"I don't care what it is, just as long as you're not away

five days a week. Drive a taxi, if you have to."

When she happened to mention driving a taxi she touched upon the only major interest he had outside the routine of his life: from the early days of Dario Resta and the brothers Chevrolet he had been crazy about automobiles, all automobiles and everything about them. He would walk or take the "L" from home in West Philadelphia to the area near City Hall, and wander about, stopping in front of the hotels and clubs and private residences and theaters and the Academy of Music, staring at the limousines and town cars, engaging in conversation with the chauffeurs; and then he would walk up North Broad Street, Automobile Row, and because he was a nice-looking kid, the floor salesmen would sometimes let him sit in the cars on display. He collected all the manufacturers' brochures and read all the advertisements in the newspapers. Closer to home he would stand for hours, studying the sporty roadsters and phaetons outside the Penn fraternity houses; big Simplexes with searchlights on the running-boards, Fiats and Renaults and Hispanos and Blitzen-Benzes. He was nice-looking and he had nice manners, and when he would hold the door open for one of the fraternity men they would sometimes give him a nickel and say, "Will you keep your eye on my car, sonny?"

"Can I sit in it, please?"

"Well, if you promise not to blow the horn."

He passed the horn-blowing stage quickly. Sometimes the fraternity men would come out to put up the top when there was a sudden shower, and find that Aloysius Aquinas Collins had somehow done it alone. For this service he wanted no reward but a ride home, on the front seat. On his side of the room he shared with his older brother he had magazine and rotogravure pictures of fine cars pinned to the walls. The nuns at school complained that instead of paying attention, he was continually drawing pictures of automobiles, automobiles. The nuns did not know how good the drawings were; they only cared that one so bright could waste so much time, and their complaints to his parents made it impossible for Aloysius to convince Mr. and Mrs. Collins that after he got his high school diploma, he wanted to get a job on Automobile Row. The parents sent him to Villanova, and after sophomore year took him out because the priests told them they were wasting their money, but out of spite his father refused to let him take a job in the auto business. Collins got him a job in the ship-yards, and when the country entered the war, Aloysius joined the Navy and eventually was commissioned. He married Madge Ruddy, became a hat salesman, and rented half of a two-family house in Upper Darby.

Gibbsville was on his sales route, and it first came to his special notice because his Gibbsville customer bought more hats in his high-priced line than any other store of comparable size. He thus discovered that it was a spending town, and that the actual population figures were deceptive; it was surrounded by a lot of much smaller towns whose citizens shopped in Gibbsville. He began to add a day to his normal visits to Gibbsville, to make a study of the automobile business there, and when he came into a small legacy from his aunt, he easily persuaded Madge to put in her own five thousand dollars, and he bought Cunningham's Garage, on Railroad Avenue, Gibbsville.

Cunningham's was badly run down and had lost money for its previous two owners, but it was the oldest garage in town. The established automobile men were not afraid of competition from the newcomer, Collins, who knew nobody to speak of and did not even have a dealer's franchise. They thought he was out of his mind when he began spending money in sprucing up the place. They also thought, and said, that he was getting pretty big for his britches in choosing to rent a house on Lantenengo Street. The proprietor of Cunningham's old garage then proceeded to outrage the established dealers by stealing Walt Michaels' best mechanic, Joe Ricci. Regardless of what the dealers might do to each other in the competition to clinch a sale, one thing you did not do was entice away a man's best mechanic. Walt Michaels, who had the Oldsmobile franchise, paid a call on the new fellow.

A. A. Collins, owner and proprietor, as his sign said, of Collins Motor Company, was in his office when he saw Michaels get out of his car. He went out to greet Michaels, his hand outstretched. "Hello, Mr. Michaels, I'm Pat Collins," he said.

"I know who you are. I just came down to tell you what I think of you."

"Not much, I guess, judging by—"

"Not much is right."

"Smoke a cigar?" said Pat Collins.

Michaels slapped at the cigar and knocked it to the ground. Pat Collins picked it up and looked at it. "I guess that's why they wrap them in tinfoil." He rubbed the dirt off the cigar and put it back in his pocket.

"Don't you want to fight?" said Michaels.

"What for? You have a right to be sore at me, in a way. But when you have a good mechanic like Joe, you ought to be willing to pay him what he's worth."

"Well, I never thought I'd see an Irishman back out of a fight. But with you I guess that's typical. A sneaky Irish son of a bitch."

"Now just a minute, Michaels. Go easy."

(259)

"I said it. A sneaky Irish son of a bitch."

"Yeah, I was right the first time," said Collins. He hit Michaels in the stomach with his left hand, and as Michaels crumpled, Collins hit him on the chin with his right hand. Michaels went down, and Collins stood over him, waiting for him to get up. Michaels started to raise himself with both hands on the ground, calling obscene names, but while his hands were still on the ground Collins stuck the foil-wrapped cigar deep in his mouth. Three or four men who stopped to look at the fight burst into laughter, and Michaels, his breath shut off, fell back on the ground.

"Change your mind about the cigar, Michaels?" said Collins.

"I'll send my son down to see you," said Michaels, getting to his feet.

"All right. What does *he* smoke?"

"He's as big as you are."

"Then I'll use a tire iron on him. Now get out of here, and quick."

Michaels, dusting himself off, saw Joe Ricci among the spectators. He pointed at him with his hat. "You, you ginny bastard, you stole tools off of me."

Ricci, who had a screwdriver in his hand, rushed at Michaels and might have stabbed him, but Collins swung him away.

"Calling me a thief, the son of a bitch, I'll kill him," said Ricci. "I'll *kill* him."

"Go on, Michaels. Beat it," said Collins.

Michaels got in his car and put it in gear, and as he was about to drive away Collins called to him: "Hey, Michaels, shall I fill her up?"

The episode, the kind that men liked to embellish in the retelling, made Pat Collins universally unpopular among the dealers, but it made him known to a wider public. It brought him an important visitor.

The Mercer phaeton pulled up at Pat Collins's gas pump and Collins, in his office, jumped up from his desk, and without putting on his coat, went out to the curb. "Can I help you?" he said.

"Fill her up, will you, please?" said the driver. He was a handsome man, about Collins's age, wearing a brown Homburg and a coonskin coat. Pat Collins knew who he was—Whit Hofman, probably the richest young man in the town—because he knew the car. He was conscious of Hofman's curiosity, but he went on pumping the gasoline. He hung up the hose and said, "You didn't need much. That'll cost you thirty-six cents, Mr. Hofman. Wouldn't you rather I sent you a bill?"

"Well, all right. But don't I get a cigar, a new customer? At least that's what I hear."

The two men laughed. "Sure, have a cigar," said Collins, handing him one. Hofman looked at it.

"Tinfoil, all right. You sure this isn't the same one you gave Walt Michaels?"

"It might be. See if it has any teeth marks on it," said Collins.

"Well, I guess Walt had it coming to him. He's a kind of a sorehead."

"You know him?"

"Of course. Known him all my life, he's always lived here. He's not a bad fellow, Mr. Collins, but you took Joe away from him, and Joe's a hell of a good mechanic. I'd be sore, too, I guess."

"Well, when you come looking for a fight, you ought to be more sure of what you're up against. Either that, or be ready to take a beating. I only hit him twice."

"When I was a boy you wouldn't have knocked him down that easily. When I was a kid, Walt Michaels was a good athlete, but he's put away a lot of beer since then." Hofman looked at Collins. "Do you like beer?"

"I like the beer you get around here. It's better than we get in Philly."

"Put on your coat and let's drink some beer," said Hofman. "Or are you busy?"

"Not that busy," said Collins.

They drove to a saloon in one of the neighboring towns, and Collins was surprised to see that no one was surprised to see the young millionaire, with his Mercer and his coonskin coat. The men drinking at the bar—working-men taking a day off, they appeared to be—were neither cordial nor hostile to Hofman. "Hello, Paul," said Hofman. "Brought you a new customer."

"I need all I can get," said the proprietor. "Where will you want to sit? In the back room?"

"I guess so. This is Mr. Collins, just opened a new garage. Mr. Collins, Mr. Paul Unitas, sometimes called Unitas States of America."

"Pleased to meet you," said Paul, shaking hands.

"Same here," said Collins.

"How's the beer?" said Hofman.

Paul shook his head. "They're around. They stopped two truckloads this morning."

"Who stopped them? The state police?" said Hofman.

"No, this time it was enforcement agents. New ones."

Hofman laughed. "You don't have to worry about Mr. Collins. I'll vouch for him."

"Well, if you say so, Whit. What'll you have?"

"The beer's no good?"

"Slop. Have rye. It's pretty good. I cut it myself."

"Well, if you say rye, that's what we'll have. Okay, Collins?"

"Sure."

Hofman was an affable man, an interested listener and a hearty laugher. It was dark when they left the saloon; Collins had told Hofman a great deal about himself, and Hofman drove Collins home in the Mercer. "I can offer you some Canadian Club," said Collins.

"Thanks just the same, but we're going out to dinner and I have to change. Ask me again sometime. Nice to've seen you, Pat."

"Same to you, Whit. Enjoyable afternoon," said Collins.

In the house Collins kissed Madge's cheek. "Whew! Out drinking with college boys?" she said.

"I'll drink with that college boy any time. That's Whit Hofman."

"How on earth—"

She listened with increasing eagerness while he told her the events of the afternoon. "Maybe you could sell him a car, if you had a good franchise," she said.

"I'm not going to try to sell him anything but Aloysius Aquinas Collins, Esquire. And anyway, I like him."

"You can like people and still sell them a car."

"Well, I'm never going to try to make a sale there. He came to see me out of curiosity, but we hit it off right away. He's a swell fellow."

"Pat?"

"What?"

"Remember why we moved here."

"Listen, it's only ha' past six and I'm home. This guy came to see me, Madge."

"A rich fellow with nothing better to do," she said.

"Oh, for God's sake. You say remember why we moved here. To have a home. But *you* remember why I wanted to live on this street. To meet people like Whit Hofman."

"But not to spend the whole afternoon in some hunky saloon. Were there any women there?"

"A dozen of them, all walking around naked. What have you got for supper?"

"For *dinner,* we have veal cutlets. But Pat, remember what we are. We're not society people. What's she like, his wife?"

"How would I know? I wouldn't know her if I saw her. Unless she was driving that car."

They had a two weeks' wait before Whit Hofman again had the urge for Pat Collins's company. This time Hofman took him to the country club, and they sat in the smoking-room with a bottle of Scotch on the table. "Do you play squash?" said Hofman.

"Play it? I thought you ate it. No, I used to play handball."

"Well, it's kind of handball with a racquet. It's damn near the only exercise I get in the winter, at least until we go South. If you were a good handball player, you'd learn squash in no time."

"Where? At the Y.M.?"

"Here. We have a court here," said Hofman. He got up and pointed through the French window. "See that little house down there, to the right of the first fairway? That's the squash court."

"I was a caddy one summer."

"Oh, you play golf?"

"I've never had a club in my hand since then."

"How would you like to join here? I'll be glad to put

you up and we'll find somebody to second you. Does your wife play tennis or golf?"

"No, she's not an athlete. How much would it cost to join?"

"Uh, family membership, you and your wife and children under twenty-one. They just raised it. Initiation, seventy-five dollars. Annual dues, thirty-five for a family membership."

"Do you think I could get in? We don't know many people that belong."

"Well, Walt Michaels doesn't belong. Can you think of anyone else that might blackball you? Because if you can't, I think I could probably get you in at the next meeting. Technically, I'm not supposed to put you up, because I'm on the admissions committee, but that's no problem."

Any hesitancy Pat Collins might have had immediately vanished at mention of the name Walt Michaels. "Well, I'd sure like to belong."

"I'll take care of it. Let's have a drink on it," said Whit Hofman.

"We're Catholics, you know."

"That's all right. We take Catholics. Not all, but some. And those we don't take wouldn't get in if they were Presbyterian or anything else."

"Jews?"

"We have two. One is a doctor, married to a Gentile. He claims he isn't a Jew, but he is. The other is the wife of a Gentile. Otherwise, no. I understand they're starting their own club, I'm not sure where it'll be."

"Well, as long as you know we're Catholics."

"I knew that, Pat," said Hofman. "But I respect you for bringing it up."

Madge Collins was upset about the country club. "It

isn't only what you have to pay to get in. It's meals, and spending money on clothes. I haven't bought anything new since we moved here."

"As the Dodge people say, 'It isn't the initial cost, it's the upkeep.' But Madge, I told you before, those are the kind of people that're gonna be worth our while. I'll make a lot of connections at the country club, and in the meantime, I'll get a franchise. So far I didn't spend a nickel on advertising. Well, this is gonna be the best kind of advertising. The Cadillac dealer is the only other dealer in the country club, and I won't compete with him."

"Everything going out, very little coming in," she said.

"Stop worrying, everything's gonna be hunky-dory."

On the morning after the next meeting of the club admissions committee Whit Hofman telephoned Pat Collins. "Congratulations to the newest member of the Lantenengo Country Club. It was a cinch. You'll get a notice and a bill, and as soon as you send your cheque you and Mrs. Collins can start using the club, although there's no golf or tennis now. However, there's a dance next Friday, and we'd like you and your wife to have dinner with us. Wear your Tuck. My wife is going to phone Mrs. Collins some time today."

In her two years as stock girl and saleslady at Oppenheim, Collins—"my cousins," Pat called them—Madge had learned a thing or two about values, and she had style sense. The evening dress she bought for the Hofman dinner and club dance was severely simple, black, and Pat thought it looked too old for her. "Wait till you see it on," she said. She changed the shoulder straps and substituted thin black cord, making her shoulders, chest, and back completely bare and giving an illusion of a deeper décolletage than was actually the case. She had a good figure and a lovely complexion, and when he saw her ready to leave for the party, he was startled. "It's not too old for you any more. Maybe it's too young."

"I wish I had some jewelry," she said.

"You have. I can see them."

"Oh—oh, stop. It's not immodest. You can't see anything unless you stoop over and look down."

"Unless you happen to be over five foot five, and most men are."

"Do you want me to wear a shawl? I have a nice old shawl of Grandma's. As soon as we start making money the one thing I want is a good fur coat. That's all I want, and I can get one wholesale."

"Get one for me, while you're at it. But for now, let's get a move on. Dinner is eight-thirty and we're the guests of honor."

"Guests of honor! Just think of it, Pat. I haven't been so excited since our wedding. I hope I don't do anything wrong."

"Just watch Mrs. Hofman. I don't even know who else'll be there, but it's time we were finding out."

"Per-*fume!* I didn't put on any per*fume*. I'll be right down."

She was excited and she had youth and health, but she also had a squarish face with a strong jawline that gave her a look of maturity and dignity. Her hair was reddish brown, her eyes grey-green. It was a face full of contrasts, especially from repose to animation, and with the men— beginning with Whit Hofman—she was an instant success.

The Hofmans had invited three other couples besides the Collinses. Custom forbade having liquor bottles or cocktail shakers on the table at club dances, and Whit Hofman kept a shaker and a bottle on the floor beside him.

The men were drinking straight whiskey, the women drank orange blossoms. There was no bar, and the Hofman party sat at the table and had their drinks until nine o'clock, when Hofman's wife signalled the steward to start serving. Chincoteagues were served first, and before the soup, Whit Hofman asked Madge Collins to dance. He was feeling good, and here he was king. His fortune was respected by men twice his age, and among the men and women who were more nearly his contemporaries he was genuinely well liked for a number of reasons: his unfailingly good manners, no matter how far in drink he might get; his affability, which drew upon his good manners when bores and toadies and the envious and the weak made their assaults; his emanations of strength, which were physically and tangibly demonstrated in his expertness at games as well as in the slightly more subtle self-reminders of his friends that he *was* Whit Hofman and *did have* all that money. He had a good war record, beginning with enlistment as a private in the National Guard for Mexican Border service, and including a field commission, a wound chevron, and a Croix de Guerre with palm during his A.E.F. service. He was overweight, but he could afford bespoke tailors and he cared about clothes; tonight he was wearing a dinner jacket with a white waistcoat and a satin butterfly tie. Madge Ruddy Collins had never known anyone quite like him, and her first mistake was to believe that his high spirits had something special to do with her. At this stage she had no way of knowing that later on, when he danced with his fat old second cousin, he would be just as much fun.

"Well, how do you like your club?" he said.

"My club? Oh—*this* club. Oh, it's beautiful. Pat and I certainly do thank you."

"Very glad to do it. I hope you're going to take up golf. More and more women are. Girl I just spoke to, Mrs.

Dick Richards, she won the second flight this year, and she only started playing last spring."

"Does your wife play?"

"She plays pretty well, and could be a lot better. She's going to have a lot of lessons when we go South. That's the thing to do. As soon as you develop a fault, have a lesson right away, before it becomes a habit. I'm going to have Pat playing squash before we leave."

"Oh."

"He said he was a handball player, so squash ought to come easy to him. Of course it's a much more strenuous game than golf."

"It is?"

He said something in reply to a question from a man dancing by. The man laughed, and Whit Hofman laughed. "That's Johnny King," said Hofman. "You haven't met the Kings, have you?"

"No," said Madge. "She's pretty. Beautifully gowned."

"Oh, that's not his wife. She isn't here tonight. That's Mary-Louise Johnson, from Scranton. There's a whole delegation from Scranton here tonight. They all came down for Buz McKee's birthday party. That's the big table over in the corner. Well, I'm getting the high sign, I guess we'd better go back to our table. Thank you, Madge. A pleasure."

"Oh, to me, too," she said.

In due course every man in the Hofman party danced with every woman, the duty rounds. Pat Collins was the last to dance with Madge on the duty rounds. "You having a good time?" he said.

"Oh, *am* I?" she said.

"How do you like Whit?"

"He's a real gentleman, I'm crazy about him. I like him the best. Do you like her, his wife?"

"I guess so. In a way yes, and in a way no."

"Me too. She'd rather be with those people from Scranton."

"What people from Scranton?"

"At the big table. They're here to attend a birthday party for Buzzie McKee."

"Jesus, you're learning fast."

"I found that out from Whit. The blonde in the beaded white, that's Mary-Louise Johnson, dancing with Johnny King. They're dancing every dance together."

"Together is right. Take a can-opener to pry them apart."

"His wife is away," said Madge. "Where did Whit go?"

Pat turned to look at their table. "I don't know. Oh, there he is, dancing with some fat lady."

"I don't admire his taste."

"Say, you took a real shine to Whit," said Pat Collins.

"Well, he's a real gentleman, but he isn't a bit forward. Now where's he going? . . . Oh, I guess he wanted to wish Buzzie McKee a happy birthday. Well, let's sit down."

The chair at her left remained vacant while Hofman continued his visit to the McKee table. On Madge's right was a lawyer named Joe Chapin, who had something to do with the admissions committee; polite enough, but for Madge very hard to talk to. At the moment he was in conversation with the woman on his right, and Madge Collins felt completely alone. A minute passed, two minutes, and her solitude passed to uneasiness to anger. Whit Hofman made his way back to the table, and when he sat down she said, trying to keep the irritation out of her tone, "That wasn't very polite."

"I'm terribly sorry. I thought you and Joe—"

"Oh, *him*. Well, I'll forgive you if you dance this dance with me."

"Why of course," said Hofman.

They got up again, and as they danced she closed her eyes, pretending to an ecstasy she did not altogether feel. They got through eighteen bars of "Bambalina," and the music stopped. "Oh, hell," she said. "I'll let you have the next."

"Fine," he said. She took his arm, holding it so that her hand clenched his right biceps, and giving it a final squeeze as they sat down.

"Would you like some more coffee?" he said. "If not, I'm afraid we're going to have to let them take the table away."

"Why?"

"That's what they do. Ten o'clock, tables have to be cleared out, to make room for the dancing. You know, quite a few people have dinner at home, then come to the dance."

"What are they? Cheap skates?"

"Oh, I don't know about that. No, hardly that."

"But if *you* wanted to keep the table, they'd let you."

"Oh, I wouldn't do that, Madge. They really need the room."

"Then where do we go?"

"Wherever we like. Probably the smoking-room. But from now on we just sort of—circulate."

"You mean your dinner is over?"

"Yes, that's about it. We're on our own."

"I don't want to go home. I want to dance with you some more."

"Who said anything about going home? The fun is just about to begin."

"I had fun before. I'm not very good with strangers."

"You're not a stranger. You're a member of the club, duly launched. Let's go out to the smoking-room and I'll get you a drink. How would you like a Stinger?"

"What is it? Never mind telling me. I'll have one."

"If you've never had one, be careful. It could be your
downfall. Very cool to the taste, but packs a wallop. Sneaks
up on you."

"Good. Let's have one." She rose and quickly took his
unoffered arm, and they went to the smoking-room, which
was already more than half filled.

At eleven o'clock she was drunk. She would dance with
no one but Whit Hofman, and when she danced with him
she tried to excite him, and succeeded. "You're hot stuff,
Madge," he said.

"Why what do you *mean?*"

"The question is, what do *you* mean?"

"I don't know what you're *talking* about," she said,
sing-song.

"The hell you don't," he said. "Shall we go for a
stroll?"

"Where to?"

"My car's around back of the caddyhouse."

"Do you think we ought to?"

"No, but either that or let's sit down."

"All right, let's sit down. I'm getting kind of woozy,
anyhow."

"Don't drink any more Stingers. I told you they
were dangerous. Maybe you ought to have some coffee.
Maybe I ought to, too. Come on, we'll get some coffee."
He led her to a corner of the smoking-room, where she
could prop herself against the wall. He left her, and in the
hallway to the kitchen he encountered Pat Collins on his
way from the locker-room.

"Say, Pat, if I were you—well, Madge had a couple of
Stingers and I don't think they agree with her."

"Is she sick?"

"No, but I'm afraid she's quite tight."

"I better take her home?"

"You know. Your first night here. There'll be others much worse off, but she's the one they'll talk about. The maid'll get her wrap, and you can ease her out so nobody'll notice. I'll say your goodnights for you."

"Well, gee, Whit—I'm sorry. I certainly apologize."

"Perfectly all right, Pat. No harm done, but she's ready for beddy-bye. I'll call you in a day or two."

There was no confusing suggestion with command, and Pat obeyed Hofman. He got his own coat and Madge's, and when Madge saw her coat she likewise recognized authority.

They were less than a mile from the club when she said, "I'm gonna be sick."

He stopped the car. "All right, *be* sick."

When she got back in the car she said, "Leave the windows down, I need the fresh air."

He got her to bed. His anger was so great that he did not trust himself to speak to her, and she mistook his silence for pity. She kept muttering that she was sorry, sorry, and went to sleep. Much later he fell asleep, awoke before six, dressed and left the house before he had to speak to her. He had his breakfast in an all-night restaurant, bought the morning newspapers, and opened the garage. He needed to think, and not so much about punishing Madge as about restoring himself to good standing in the eyes of the Hofmans. He had caught Kitty Hofman's cold appraisal of Madge on the dance floor; he had known, too, that he had failed to make a good impression on Kitty, who was in a sour mood for having to give up the Buz McKee dinner. He rejected his first plan to send Kitty flowers and a humorous note. Tomorrow or the next day Madge could send the flowers and a thank-you note, which he would make sure contained no reference to her getting tight or any other apologetic implication. The important thing was to repair any damage to his relationship with Whit Hofman, and after a while he concluded that aside from Madge's thank-you note to both Hofmans, the wiser course was to wait for Whit to call him.

He had a long wait.

Immediately after Christmas the Hofmans went to Florida. They returned for two weeks in late March, closed their house, and took off on a trip around the world. Consequently the Collinses did not see the Hofmans for nearly a year. It was a year that was bad for the Collins marriage, but good for the Collins Motor Company. Pat Collins got the Chrysler franchise, and the car practically sold itself. Women and the young took to it from the start, and the Collins Motor Company had trouble keeping up with the orders. The bright new car and the bright new Irishman were interchangeably associated in the minds of the citizens, and Pat and Madge Collins were getting somewhere on their own, without the suspended sponsorship of Whit Hofman. But at home Pat and Madge had never quite got back to what they had been before she jeopardized his relationship with Whit Hofman. He had counted so much on Hofman's approval that the threat of losing it had given him a big scare, and it would not be far-fetched to say that the designers of the Chrysler "70" saved the Collins marriage.

Now they were busy, Pat with his golf when he could take the time off from his work—which he did frequently; and Madge with the game of bridge, which she learned adequately well. In the absence of the Whit Hofmans the social life of the country club was left without an outstanding couple to be the leaders, although several couples tried to fill the gap. In the locker-room one afternoon, drinking gin and ginger ale with the members of his foursome, Pat Collins heard one of the men say, "You know who we all miss? Whit. The club isn't the same without him." Pat looked up as at a newly discovered truth, and for the first time he realized that he liked Whit Hofman better than any man he had ever known. It had remained for someone else to put the thought into words, and casual enough words they were to express what Pat Collins had felt from the first day in Paul Unitas's saloon. Like nearly everyone else in the club the Collinses had had a postcard or two from the Hofmans; Honolulu, Shanghai, Bangkok, St. Andrew's, St. Cloud. The Hofmans' closer friends had had letters, but the Collinses were pleased to have had a postcard, signed "Kitty and Whit"—in Whit's handwriting.

"When does he get back, does anyone know?" said Pat.

"Middle of October," said the original speaker. "You know Whit. He wouldn't miss the football season, not the meat of it anyway."

"About a month away," said Pat Collins. "Well, I can thank him for the most enjoyable summer I ever had. He got me in here, you know. I was practically a stranger."

" 'A stranger in a strange land,' but not any more, Pat."

"Thank you. You fellows have been damn nice to me." He meant the sentiment, but the depth of it belonged to his affection for Whit Hofman. He had his shower and dressed, and joined Madge on the terrace. "Do you want to stay here for dinner?"

"We have nothing at home," she said.

"Then we'll eat here," he said. "Did you know the Hofmans are getting back about four weeks from now?"

"I knew it."

"Why didn't you tell me?"

"I didn't know you wanted to know, or I would have. Why, are you thinking of hiring a brass band? One post-card."

"What did you expect? As I remember, you didn't keep it any secret when we got it."

"You were the one that was more pleased than I was."

"Oh, all right. Let's go eat."

They failed to be invited to the smaller parties in honor of the returning voyagers, but they went to a Dutch Treat dinner for the Hofmans before the club dance. Two changes in the Hofmans were instantly noticeable: Whit was as brown as a Hawaiian, and Kitty was pregnant. She received the members of the dinner party sitting down. She had lost one child through miscarriage. Whit stood beside her, and when it came the Collinses' turn he greeted Pat and Madge by nickname and first name. Not so Kitty. "Oh, hel*lo*. Mrs. *Co*llins. *Nice* of you to come. Hello, Mr. Collins." Then, seeing the man next in line she called out: "Bob-bee! Bobby, where were you Tuesday? You were supposed to be at the Ogdens', you false friend. I thought you'd be at the boat."

The Collinses moved on, and Madge said, "We shouldn't have come."

"Why not? She doesn't have to like us."

"She didn't have to be so snooty, either."

"Bobby Hermann is one of their best friends."

"I'm damn sure we're not."

"Oh, for God's sake."

"Oh, for God's sake yourself," she said.

The year had done a lot for Madge in such matters as her poise and the widening of her acquaintance among club members. But it was not until eleven or so that Whit Hofman cut in on her. "How've you been?" he said.

(*276*)

"Lonely without you," she said.

"That's nice to hear. I wish you meant it."

"You're pretending to think I don't," she said. "But I thought of you every day. And every night. Especially every night."

"How many Stingers have you had?"

"That's a nasty thing to say. I haven't had any. I've never had one since that night. So we'll change the subject. Are you going to stay home a while?"

"Looks that way. Kitty's having the baby in January."

"Sooner than that, I thought."

"No, the doctor says January."

"Which do you want? A boy, or a girl?"

"Both, but not at the same time."

"Well, you always get what you want, so I'm told."

"That's a new one on me."

"Well, you can *have* anything you want, put it that way."

"No, not even that."

"What do you want that you haven't got?"

"A son, or a daughter."

"Well, you're getting that, one or the other. What else?"

"Right now, nothing else."

"I don't believe anybody's ever that contented."

"Well, what do *you* want, for instance?"

"You," she said.

"Why? You have a nice guy. Kids. And I hear Pat's the busiest car dealer in town."

"Those are things I have. You asked me what I wanted."

"You don't beat about the bush, do you, Madge? You get right to the point."

"I've been in love with you for almost a year."

"Madge, you haven't been in love with me at all. Maybe you're not in love with Pat, but you're certainly not in love with me. You couldn't be."

"About a month ago I heard you were coming home, and I had it all planned out how I was going to be when I saw you. But I was wrong. I couldn't feel this way for a whole year and then start pretending I didn't. You asked me how I was, and I came right out with it, the truth."

"Well, Madge, I'm not in love with you. You're damn attractive and all that, but I'm not in *love* with you."

"I know that. But answer me one question, as truthful as I am with you. Are you in love with your wife?"

"Of course I am."

"I'll tell you something, Whit. You're not. With her. With me. Or maybe with anybody."

"Now really, that *is* a nasty thing to say."

"People love you, Whit, but you don't love them back."

"I'm afraid I don't like this conversation. Shall we go back and have a drink?"

"Yes."

They moved toward the smoking-room. "Why did you say that, Madge? What makes you think it?"

"You really want me to tell you? Remember, the truth hurts, and I had a whole year to think about this."

"What the hell, tell me."

"It's not you, it's the town. There's nobody here bigger than you. They all love you, but you don't love them."

"I love this town and the people in it and everything about it. Don't you think I could live anywhere I wanted to? Why do you think I came back here? I can live anywhere in the God damn world. Jesus, you certainly have that one figured wrong. For a minute you almost had me worried."

He danced with her no more that night, and if he could avoid speaking to her or getting close to her, he did so. When she got home, past three o'clock, she gave Pat Collins a very good time; loveless but exceedingly pleasurable. Then she lay in her bed until morning, unable to understand herself, puzzled by forces that had never been mysterious to her.

The Hofman baby was born on schedule, a six-pound boy, but the reports from the mother's bedside were not especially happy. Kitty had had a long and difficult time, and one report, corroborated only by constant repetition, was that she had thrown a clock, or a flower vase, or a water tumbler, or all of them, at Whit at the start of her labor. It was said, and perfunctorily denied, that a group of nurses and orderlies stood outside her hospital room, listening fascinatedly to the obscene names she called him, names that the gossips would not utter but knew how to spell. Whatever the basis in fact, the rumors of hurled bric-a-brac and invective seemed to be partially confirmed when Kitty Hofman came home from the hospital. The infant was left in the care of a nurse, and Kitty went to every party, drinking steadily and chain-smoking, saying little and watching everything. She had a look of determination, as though she had just made up her mind about something, but the look and decision were not followed up by action. She would stay at the parties until she had had enough, then she would get her wrap and say goodnight to her hostess, without any word or sign to Whit, and it would be up to him to discover she was leaving and follow her out.

Their friends wondered how long Whit Hofman would take that kind of behavior, but no one—least of all Pat Collins—was so tactless, or bold, as to suggest to Whit that there *was* any behavior. It was Whit, finally, who talked.

He was now seeing Pat Collins nearly every day, and

on some days more than once. He knew as much about automobiles as Pat Collins, and he was comfortable in Pat's office. He had made the garage one of his ports of call in his daytime rounds—his office every morning at ten, the barber's, the bank, the broker's, his lawyer, lunch at the Gibbsville Club, a game of pool after lunch, a visit with Pat Collins that sometimes continued with a couple of games of squash at the country club. On a day some six weeks after the birth of his son Whit dropped in on Pat, hung up his coat and hat, and took a chair.

"Don't let me interrupt you," he said.

"Just signing some time-sheets," said Pat Collins.

Whit lit a cigarette and put his feet up on the window-sill. "It's about time you had those windows washed," he said.

"I know. Miss Muldowney says if I'm trying to save money, that's the wrong way. Burns up more electricity. Well, there we are. Another day, another dollar. How's the stock market?"

"Stay out of it. Everything's too high."

"I'm not ready to go in it yet. Later. Little by little I'm paying back Madge, the money she put in the business."

"You ought to incorporate and give her stock."

"First I want to give her back her money, with interest."

"Speaking of Madge, Pat. Do you remember when your children were born?"

"Sure. That wasn't so long ago."

"What is Dennis, about six?"

"Dennis is six, and Peggy's four. I guess Dennis is the same in years that your boy is in weeks. How is he, Pop?"

"He's fine. At least I guess he's fine. I wouldn't know how to tell, this is all new to me."

"But you're not worried about him? You sound dubious."

"Not about him. The doctor says he's beginning to gain weight and so forth. Kitty is something else again, and that's what I want to ask you about. You knew she didn't have a very easy time of it."

"Yes, you told me that."

"How was Madge, with her children?"

"I'll have to think back," said Pat. "Let me see. With Dennis, the first, we had a couple false alarms and had the doctor come to the house one time at four o'clock in the morning. He was sore as hell. It was only gas pains, and as soon as she got rid of the gas, okay. The real time, she was in labor about three hours, I guess. About three. Dennis weighed seven and a quarter. With Peggy, she took longer. Started having pains around eight o'clock in the morning, but the baby wasn't all the way out till three-four in the afternoon. She had a much harder time with the second, although it was a smaller baby. Six and a half, I think."

"What about her, uh, mental state? Was she depressed or anything like that?"

"No, not a bit. Anything but."

"But you haven't had any more children, and I thought Catholics didn't believe in birth control."

"Well, I'll tell you, Whit, although I wouldn't tell most Protestants. I don't agree with the Church on that, and neither does Madge. If that's the criterion, we're not very good Catholics, but I can't help that. We had two children when we could only afford one, and now I don't think we'll ever have any more. Two's enough."

"But for financial reasons, not because of the effect on Madge."

"Mainly financial reasons. Even if we could afford it,

(281)

though, Madge doesn't want any more. She wants to enjoy life while she's young."

"I see," said Whit Hofman. The conversation had reached a point where utter frankness or a change of the subject was inevitable, and Whit Hofman retreated from candor. It then was up to Pat Collins to break the silence.

"It's none of my business, Whit," he began. "But——"

"No, it isn't, Pat. I don't mean to be rude, but if I said any more about Kitty, I'd sound like a crybaby. Not to mention the fact that it goes against the grain. I've said too much already."

"I know how you feel. But nothing you say gets out of this office, so don't let that worry you. I don't tell Madge everything I know. Or do. She made some pretty good guesses, and we came close to busting up. When I was on the road, peddling hats and caps, I knew a sure lay in damn near every town between Philly and Binghamton, New York. Not that I got laid every night—but I didn't miss many Thursdays. Thursday nights we knew we were going home Friday, salesmen. You don't make any calls on Friday, the clients are all busy. So, somebody'd bring out a quart."

"Did you know a sure lay in this town?"

"Did I! Did you ever know a broad named Helene Holman?"

"I should say I did."

"Well, her," said Pat Collins.

"You don't see her now, though, do you?"

"Is that any of your business, Whit?"

"Touché. I wasn't really asking out of curiosity. More, uh, incredibility. *Incredulity.* In other words, I've always thought you behaved yourself here, since you've been living here."

"I have. And anyway, I understand the Holman dame is private property. At least I always see her riding around with the big bootlegger, Charney."

"Ed Charney. Yes, she's out of circulation for the present, so my friends tell me."

"Yes, and you couldn't get away with a God damn thing. You're too well known."

"So far I haven't tried to get away with anything," said Whit Hofman. "How would you feel about a little strenuous exercise?"

Pat Collins looked up at the clock. "I don't think any ripe prospect is coming in in the next twenty minutes. Two games?"

"Enough to get up a sweat."

They drove to the country club in two cars, obviating the continuance of conversation and giving each man the opportunity to think his own thoughts. They played squash for an hour or so, took long hot showers, and cooled out at the locker-room table with gin and ginger ale. "I could lie right down on that floor and go to sleep," said Whit. "You're getting better, or maybe I'm getting worse. Next year I'm not going to give you a handicap."

"I may get good enough to take you at golf, but not this game. You always know where the ball's going to be, and I have to lose time guessing." They were the only members in the locker-room. They could hear occasional sounds from the kitchen of the steward and his staff having supper, a few dozen feet and a whole generation of prosperity away. The walls of the room were lined with steel lockers, with two islands of lockers back-to-back in the center of the room, hempen matting in the passageways, a rather feeble ceiling lamp above the table where their drinks rested. It was an arcane atmosphere, like some goat-room in an odd lodge, with a lingering dankness traceable to their recent hot showers and to the dozens of golf shoes and plus-fours and last summer's shirts stored and forgotten in the lockers. Whit, in his shorts and shirt, and Pat, in his B.V.D.'s, pleasantly tired from their exercise and additionally numbed by the gin and ginger ales, were in that state of euphorious relaxation that a million men ten million times have called the best part of the game, any game. They were by no means drunk, nor were they exhausted, but once again they were back at the point of utter frankness or retreat from it that they had reached in Pat's office, only now the surrounding circumstances were different.

"Why don't you get it off your chest, Whit?"

Whit Hofman, without looking up, blew the ash off his cigarette. "Funny, I was just thinking the same thing," he said. He reached for the gin bottle and spiked Pat's and his own drinks. "I have too damn many cousins in this town. If I confided in any of them they'd call a family conference, which is the last thing I want." He scraped his cigarette against the ash tray, and with his eyes on the operation said, "Kitty hates me. She hates me, and I'm not sure why."

"Have you got a clear conscience?"

"No," said Whit. "That is, *I* haven't. When we were in Siam, on our trip, Kitty got an attack of dysentery and stayed in the hotel for a couple of days. I, uh, took advantage of that to slip off with an American newspaper fellow for some of the local nookie. So I haven't got a clear conscience, but Kitty doesn't know that. Positively. I don't think it's that. I *know* it isn't that. It's something—I don't know where it began, or when. We didn't have any fights or anything like that. Just one day it was there, and I hadn't noticed it before."

"Pregnant."

"Oh, yes. But past the stage where she was throwing up. Taking it very easy, because she didn't want to lose this baby. But a wall between us. No, not a wall. Just a way of looking at me, as if I'd changed appearance and she was fascinated, but not fascinated because she *liked* my new appearance. 'What's this strange animal?' That kind of look. No fights, though. Not even any serious arguments. Oh, I got sore at her for trying to smuggle in a ring I bought her in Cairo. I was filling out the customs declaration and I had the damn thing all filled out and signed, then I remembered the ring. I asked her what about it, and she said she wasn't going to declare it. She was going to wear it in with the stone turned around so that it'd look like a guard for her engagement ring. So pointless. The ring wasn't *that* valuable. The duty was about a hundred and fifty dollars. An amethyst, with a kind of a scarab design. Do you know that an amethyst is supposed to sober you up?"

"I never heard that."

"Yeah. The magical power, but it doesn't work, I can tell you. Anyway, I gave her hell because if you try to pull a fast one on the customs inspectors and they catch you, they make you wait, they confiscate your luggage, and I'm told that for the rest of your life, whenever you re-enter the country, they go through everything with a fine tooth comb. And incidentally, an uncle of Jimmy Malloy's was expediting our landing, and he would have got into trouble, no doubt. Dr. Malloy's brother-in-law, has something to do with the immigration people. So I had to get new forms and fill out the whole God damn thing all over again. But that was our only quarrel of any consequence. It did make me wonder a little, why she wanted to save a hundred and fifty when it wasn't even her money."

They sipped their drinks.

"The day she went to the hospital," Whit Hofman continued, "it was very cold, and I bundled her up warm. She laughed at me and said we weren't going to the North Pole. Not a nice laugh. Then when we got to the hospital the nurse helped her change into a hospital gown, but didn't put her to bed. She sat up in a chair, and I put a blanket over her feet, asked her if she wanted anything to read. She said she did. Could I get her a history of the Hofman family? Well, there *is* one, but I knew damn well she didn't want it. She was just being disagreeable, but that was understandable under the circumstances. Then I sat down, and she told me I didn't have to wait around. I said I knew I didn't have to, but was doing it because I wanted to. Then she said, 'God damn it, don't you know when I'm trying to get rid of you?' and threw her cigarette lighter at me. Unfortunately the nurse picked that exact moment to come in the room, and the lighter hit her in the teat. I don't know what came over Kitty. 'Get that son of a bitch out of here,' and a lot more on the same order. So the nurse told me I'd better go, and I did." He paused. "Kitty had an awful time, no doubt about it. I was there when they brought the baby in to show her. She looked at it, didn't register any feeling whatsoever, and then turned her face away and shut her eyes. I have never seen her look at the baby the way you'd expect a mother to. I've never seen her pick him up out of his crib just to hold him. Naturally she's never nursed him. She probably hasn't enough milk, so I have no objection to that, but along with hating me she seems to hate the baby. Dr. English says that will pass, but I know better. She has no damn use for me *or* the child." He paused again. "The Christ-awful thing is, I don't know what the hell I *did*."

"I agree with Dr. English. It'll pass," said Pat Collins. "Women today, they aren't as simple as they used to be, fifty or a hundred years ago. They drive cars and play golf. Smoke and drink, do a lot of the same things men do."

"My mother rode horseback and played tennis. She didn't smoke that I know of, but she drank. Not to excess, but wine with dinner. She died when I was eight, so I don't really know an awful lot about her. My father died while I was still in prep school. From then on I guess you'd say I was brought up by my uncle and the housekeeper and my uncle's butler. I have an older brother in the foreign service, but he's too close to me in age to have had much to do with bringing me up. He was a freshman when our father died."

"I didn't know you had a brother."

"I saw him in Rome. He's in the embassy there. Both glad to see each other, but he thinks I'm a country bumpkin, which I am. And since I don't speak French or Italian, and he has a little bit of an English accent, you might say we don't even speak the same language. He married a Boston girl and you should have seen her with Kitty. Every time the Italian men flocked around Kitty, Howard's wife would act as an interpreter, although the Italians all spoke English. But I don't think that has anything to do with why Kitty developed this hatred for me. Howard's wife disapproved of me just as heartily as she did Kitty. We were all pretty glad to see the last of each other. Howard's wife has twice as much money as he has, so he doesn't exactly rule the roost, but in every marriage one of the two has more money than the other. That's not what's eating Kitty." He sipped his drink. "I've been thinking if we moved away from here. Someone told me that this town is wrong for me."

"They're crazy."

"Well, it's bothered me ever since. This, uh, person

said that my friends liked me but I didn't like them back."

"That *is* crap."

"As a matter of fact, the person didn't say like. She said love. Meaning that as long as I lived here, I wouldn't be able to love anybody. But I've always loved Kitty, and I certainly love this town. I don't know what more I can do to prove it."

"As far as Kitty's concerned, you're going to have to wait a while. Some women take longer than others getting their machinery back in place after a baby."

Whit Hofman shook his head. "Dr. English tells me Kitty's machinery is okay. And whatever it is, it started before the machinery got out of place. It's me, but what in the name of Christ is it? It's getting late, Pat. Would you have dinner with me here?"

"If you'll square me with Madge. It *is* late. I'm due home now."

"You want me to speak to her, now?"

"We both can."

There was a telephone in the hall off the locker-room and Pat put in the call.

"I knew that's where you'd be," said Madge. "You could just as easily called two hours ago."

"I'm going to put Whit on," said Pat, and did so.

"Madge, I take all the blame, but it'll be at least an hour before Pat could be home. We're still in our underwear. So could you spare him for dinner?"

"Your wish is our command," said Madge.

Whit turned to Pat. "She hung up. What do you do now?"

"We call Heinie and order up a couple of steaks," said Pat.

It was not only that the two men saw each other so fre-

quently; it was Pat's availability, to share meals, to take
little trips, that annoyed Madge. "You don't have to suck
up to Whit Hofman," she would say. "Not any more."

"I'm glad I don't."

This colloquy in the Collins household resembled
one in the Hofmans'. "Not that it matters to me, but how
can you spend so much time with that Pat Collins person?"
said Kitty.

"What's wrong with Pat? He's good company."

"Because your other friends refuse to yes you."

"That shows how little you know about Pat Collins,"
he said. "You don't seem to realize that he had hard going
for a while, but he never asked me for any help of any
kind."

"Saving you for something big, probably."

"No. I doubt if he'll ever ask me for anything. When
he needed money to expand, he didn't even go to our bank,
let alone ask me for help. And I would have been glad to
put money in his business. Would have been a good investment."

"Oh, I don't care. Do as you please. I'm just amused to
watch this beautiful friendship between you two. And by
the way, maybe he never asked you for anything, but did he
ever refuse anything you offered him? For instance, the
club."

"He would have made it."

"Has he made the Gibbsville Club?"

"As far as I know, he's not interested."

"Try him."

"Hell, if I ask him, he'll say yes."

"Exactly my point. His way is so much cagier. He's
always there when you want him, and naturally you're going to feel obligated to him. You'll want to pay him back

for always being there, so he gets more out of you that way than if he'd asked for favors. He knows that."

"It's funny how *you* know things like that, Kitty."

She fell angrily silent. He had met her at a party just after the war, when he was still in uniform and with two or three other officers was having a lengthy celebration in New York. Whit, a first lieutenant in the 103d Engineers, 28th Division, met a first lieutenant in the 102d Engineers, 27th Division, who had with him a girl from New Rochelle. She was not a beauty, but Whit was immediately attracted to her, and she to him. "This man is only the 102d and I'm the 103d. He's only the 27th and I'm the 28th," said Whit. "Why don't you move up a grade?"

She laughed. "Why not? I *want* to get up in the world."

He made frequent trips to New York to see her. She was going to a commercial art school, living at home with her family but able to spend many nights in New York. Her father was a perfectly respectable layout man in an advertising agency, who commuted from New Rochelle and escaped from his wife by spending all the time he could in sailing small boats. His wife was a fat and disagreeable woman who had tried but failed to dominate her husband and her daughter, and regarded her husband as a nincompoop and her daughter as a wild and wilful girl who was headed for no good. One spring day Kitty and Whit drove to Greenwich, Connecticut, and were married. They then drove to New Rochelle, the first and only time Whit Hofman ever saw his wife's parents. Two days later the newly married couple sailed for Europe, and they did not put in an appearance in Gibbsville, Pennsylvania, until the autumn. It was all very unconventional and it led to considerable speculation as to the kind of person Whit Hofman had married, especially among the mothers of nubile girls. But a *fait accompli* was a *fait accompli,* and Whit Hofman was Whit Hofman, and the girls and their mothers had to make the best of it, whatever that turned out to be.

In certain respects it turned out quite well. The town, and indeed the entire nation, was ready to have some fun. There was a considerable amount of second-generation money around, and manners and customs would never revert to those of 1914. Kitty Hofman and the Lantenengo Country Club appeared almost simultaneously in Gibbsville; both were new and novel and had the backing of the Hofman family. Kitty made herself agreeable to Whit's men friends and made no effort in the direction of the young women. They had to make themselves agreeable to her, and since their alternative was self-inflicted ostracism, Kitty was established without getting entangled in social debts to any of the young women. A less determined, less independent young woman could not have achieved it, but Gibbsville was full of less determined, less independent young women whom Whit Hofman had not married. And at least Whit had not singled out one of their number to the exclusion of all the others, a mildly comforting and unifying thought. He had to marry somebody, so better this nobody with her invisible family in a New York suburb than a Gibbsville girl who would have to suffer as the object of harmonious envy.

Kitty did nothing deliberately to antagonize the young women—unless to outdress them could be so considered, and her taste in clothes was far too individualistic for her new acquaintances. She attended their ladies' luncheons, always leaving before the bridge game began. She played in the Tuesday golf tournaments. She precisely returned all invitations. And she made no close friendships. But she actively disliked Madge Collins.

From the beginning she knew, as women know better than men know, that she was not going to like that woman. Even before Madge got up to dance with Whit and made her extraordinary, possessive, off-in-dreamland impression with her closed eyes, Kitty Hofman abandoned herself to the luxury of loathing another woman. Madge's black dress was sound, so much so that Kitty accurately guessed that Madge had had some experience in women's wear. But from there on every judgment Kitty made was unfavorable. Madge's prettiness was literally natural: her good figure was natural, her amazing skin was natural, her reddish brown hair, her teeth, her bright eyes, her inviting mouth, were gifts of Nature. (Kitty used a great deal of makeup and dyed her blond hair a lighter shade of blond.) Kitty, in the first minutes of her first meeting with Madge, ticketed her as a pretty parlor-maid; when she got up to dance with Whit she ticketed her as a whore, and with no evidence to the contrary, Madge so remained. Kitty's judgments were not based on facts or influenced by considerations of fairness, then or ever, although she could be extremely realistic in her observations. (Her father, she early knew, was an ineffectual man, a coward who worked hard to protect his job and fled to the waters of Long Island Sound to avoid the occasions of quarrels with her mother.) Kitty, with her firmly middle-class background, had no trouble in imagining the background of Madge and Pat Collins, and the Collinses provided her with her first opportunity to assert herself as a Hofman. (She had not been wasting her first years in Gibbsville; her indifferent manner masked a shrewd study of individuals and their standing in the community.) Kitty, who had not been able comfortably to integrate herself into the established order, now rapidly assumed her position as Whit's wife because as Mrs. Whit Hofman she could look down on and crack down on

Madge Collins. (By a closely related coincidence she also became a harsher judge of her husband at the very moment that she began to exercise the privileges of her marital status.) Kitty's obsessive hatred of the hick from West Philadelphia, as she called Madge Collins, was quick in its onset and showed every sign of being chronic. The other young women of the country club set did not fail to notice, and it amused them to get a rise out of Kitty Hofman merely by mentioning Madge Collins's name.

But the former Madge Ruddy was at least as intuitive as Kitty Hofman. Parlor-maid, whore, saleslady at Oppenheim, Collins—the real and imagined things she was or that Kitty Hofman chose to think she was—Madge was only a trifle slower in placing Kitty. Madge knew a lady when she saw one, and Kitty Hofman was not it. In the first days of her acquaintance with Kitty she would willingly enough have suspended her judgments if Kitty had been moderately friendly, but since that was not to be the case, Madge cheerfully collected her private store of evidence that Kitty Hofman was a phony. She was a phony aristocrat, a synthetic woman, from her dyed hair to her boyish hips to her no doubt tinted toenails. Madge, accustomed all her life to the West Philadelphia twang, had never waited on a lady who pronounced third *thade* and idea *ideer*. "Get a look at her little titties," Madge would say, when Kitty appeared in an evening dress that had two unjoined panels down the front. "She looks like she forgot to take her hair out of the curlers," said Madge of one of Kitty's coiffures. And, of Kitty's slow gait, "She walks like she was constipated." The animosity left Madge free to love Kitty's husband without the restraint that loyalty to a friend might have invoked. As for disloyalty to Pat Collins, he was aware of none, and did he not all but love Whit too?

Thus it was that behind the friendly relationship of

Pat Collins and Whit Hofman a more intense, unfriendly relationship flourished between Madge Collins and Kitty Hofman. The extremes of feeling were not unlike an individual's range of capacity for love and hate, or, as Madge put it, "I hate her as much as you like him, and that's going some." Madge Collins, of course, with equal accuracy could have said: "I hate her as much as I love him, and *that's* going some." The two men arrived at a pact of silence where their wives were concerned, a working protocol that was slightly more to Whit's advantage, since in avoiding mention of Madge he was guarding against a slip that would incriminate Madge. He wanted no such slip to occur; he needed Pat's friendship, and he neither needed nor wanted Madge's love. Indeed, as time passed and the pact of silence grew stronger, Whit Hofman's feeling for Madge was sterilized. By the end of 1925 he would not have offered to take her out to his parked car, and when circumstances had them briefly alone together they either did not speak at all or their conversation was so commonplace that a suspicious eavesdropper would have convicted them of adultery on the theory that two such vital persons could not be so indifferent to each other's physical presence. One evening at a picnic-swimming party at someone's farm—this, in the summer of '26—Madge had had enough of the cold water in the dam and was on her way to the tent that was being used as the ladies' dressing-room. In the darkness she collided with a man on his way from the men's tent. "Who is it? I'm sorry," she said.

"Whit Hofman. Who is this?"

"Madge."

"Hello. You giving up?"

"That water's too cold for me."

"Did Pat get back?"

(294)

"From Philly? No. He's spending the night. It's funny talking and I can't really see you. Where are you?"

"I'm right here."

She reached out a hand and touched him. "I'm not going to throw myself at you, but here we are."

"Don't start anything, Madge."

"I said I wasn't going to throw myself at you. You have to make the next move. But you're human."

"I'm human, but you picked a lousy place, and time."

"Is that all that's stopping you? I'll go home now and wait for you, if you say the word. Why don't you like me?"

"I do like you."

"Prove it. I'm all alone, the children are with Pat's mother. I have my car, and I'll leave now if you say."

"No. You know all the reasons."

"Sure I do. Sure I do."

"Can you get back to the tent all right? You can see where it is, can't you? Where the kerosene lamp is, on the pole."

"I can see it all right."

"Then you'd better go, Madge, because my good resolutions are weakening."

"Are they? Let me feel. Why, you are human!"

"Cut it out," he said, and walked away from her toward the lights and people at the dam.

She changed into her dress and rejoined the throng at the dam. It was a good-sized party, somewhat disorganized among smaller groups of swimmers, drinkers, eaters of corn on the cob, and a mixed quartet accompanied by a young man on banjo-uke. Heavy clouds hid the moon, and the only light came from a couple of small bonfires. When Madge returned to the party she moved from one group to another, eventually staying longest with the singers and the

(295)

banjo-uke player. "Larry, do you know 'Ukulele Lady'?"

"Sure," he said. He began playing it, and Madge sang a solo of two choruses. Her thin true voice was just right for the sad, inconclusive little song, and when she finished singing she stood shyly smiling in the momentary total silence. But then there was a spontaneous, delayed burst of applause, and she sat down. The darkness, the fires, the previously disorganized character of the party, and Madge's voice and the words—"maybe she'll find somebody else/ bye and bye"—all contributed to a minor triumph and, quite accidentally, brought the party together in a sentimental climax. "More! More! . . . I didn't know you were a singer . . . Encore! Encore!" But Madge's instinct made her refuse to sing again.

For a minute or two the party was rather quiet, and Kitty had a whispered conversation with the ukulele player. He strummed a few introductory chords until the members of the party gave him their attention, whereupon he began to play "Yaaka hula hickey dula," and Kitty Hofman, in her bare feet and a Paisley print dress, went into the dance. It was a slow hula, done without words and with only the movements of her hips and the ritualistic language of her fingers and arms—only vaguely understood in this group—in synchronous motion with the music. The spectators put on the knowing smiles of the semi-sophisticated as Kitty moved her hips, but before the dance and the tune were halfway finished they stopped their nervous laughter and were caught by the performance. It hardly mattered that they could not understand the language of the physical gestures or that the women as much as the men were being seduced by the dance. The women could understand the movements because the movements were formal and native to themselves, but the element of seductiveness was as real for them as for the men because the men's responsiveness —taking the form of absolute quiet—was like a held breath, and throughout the group men and women felt the need to touch each other by the hand, hands reaching for the nearest hand. And apart from the physical spell produced by the circumstances and the dance, there was the comprehension by the women and by some of the men that the dance was a direct reply to Madge's small bid for popularity. As such the dance was an obliterating victory for Kitty. Madge's plaintive solo was completely forgotten. As the dance ended Kitty put her hands to her lips, kissed them and extended them to the audience as in a benediction, bowed low, and returned to the picnic bench that now became a throne. The applause was a mixture of hand clapping, of women's voices calling out "Lovely! Adorable!" and men shouting "Yowie! Some more, some more!" But Kitty, equally as well as Madge, knew when to quit. "I learned it when Whit and I were in Hawaii. Where else?" she said.

Madge Collins went to Kitty to congratulate her. "That was swell, Kitty."

"Oh, thanks. Did you think so? Of course *I* can't *sing*," said Kitty.

"You—don't—have—to—when—you—can—shake —that—thing," said Bobby Hermann, whose hesitant enunciation became slower when he drank. "You—got—any —more—hidden—talents—like—that—one—up—your— sleeve?"

"Not up her sleeve," said Madge, and walked away.

"Hey—that's—a—good—one. Not—up—her—sleeve. Not—up—your—sleeve—eh—Kitty?"

In the continuing murmur of admiration for the dance no one—no one but Madge Collins—noticed that Whit

Hofman had not added his compliments to those of the multitude. In that respect Kitty's victory was doubled, for Madge now knew that Kitty had intended the exhibition as a private gesture of contempt for Whit as well as a less subtle chastening of Madge herself. Madge sat on a circular grass-mat cushion beside Whit.

"She's a real expert," said Madge. "I didn't know she could do the hula."

"Uh-huh. Learned it in Honolulu."

"On the beach at Waikiki."

"On the beach at Waikiki," said Whit.

"Well, she didn't forget it," said Madge. "Is it hard to learn?"

"Pretty hard, I guess. It's something like the deaf-and-dumb language. One thing means the moon, another thing means home, another means lonesome, and so forth and so on."

"Maybe I could get her to teach me how to say what *I* want to say."

"What's that?" said Whit.

"Madge is going home, lonesome, and wishes Whit would be there."

"When are you leaving?"

"Just about now."

"Say in an hour or so? You're all alone?"

"Yes. What will you tell *her?*"

"Whatever I tell her, she'll guess where I am. She's a bitch, but she's not a fool."

"She's a bitch, all right. But maybe you're a fool," said Madge. "No, Whit. Not tonight. Any other time, but not tonight."

"Whatever you say, but you have nothing to fear from her. You or Pat. Take my word for it, you haven't. She's watching us now, and she knows we're talking about her. All right, I'll tell you what's behind this exhibition tonight."

"You don't have to."

"Well I hope you don't think I'd let you risk it if I weren't positive about her."

"I did wonder, but I'm so crazy about you."

"When we were in Honolulu that time, I caught her with another guy. I'd been out playing golf, and I came back to the hotel in time to see this guy leaving our room. She didn't deny it, and I guessed right away who it was. A naval officer. I hadn't got a good look at him, but I let her think I had and she admitted it. The question was, what was I going to do about it? Did I want to divorce her, and ruin the naval officer's career? Did I want to come back here without her? That was where she knew she had me. I *didn't* want to come back here without her. This is my town, you know. We've been here ever since there was a town, and it's the only place I ever want to live. I've told you that." He paused. "Well, you don't know her, the hold she had on me, and I don't fully understand it myself. There are a lot of damn nice girls in town I might have married, and you'd think that feeling that way about the town, I'd marry a Gibbsville girl. But how was I ever to know that I was marrying the girl and not her mother, and in some cases her father? And that the girl wasn't marrying me but my father's money and my uncle's money. Kitty didn't know any of that when I asked her to marry me. She'd never heard of Gibbsville. In fact she wasn't very sure where Pennsylvania was. And I was a guy just out of the army, liked a good time, and presumably enjoying myself before I seriously began looking for a job. The first time Kitty really knew I didn't have to work for a living was when I gave her her engagement ring. I remember what she

(*299*)

said. She looked at it and then looked at me and said, 'Is there more where this came from?' So give her her due. She didn't marry me for my money, and that was somewhat of a novelty. Are you listening?"

"Sure," said Madge.

"That afternoon in the hotel she said, 'Look, you can kick me out and pay me off, but I tried to have a child for you, which I didn't want, and this is the first time I've gone to bed with another man, since we've been married.' It was a good argument, but of course the real point was that I didn't want to go home without a wife, and have everybody guessing why. I allowed myself the great pleasure of giving her a slap in the face, and she said she guessed she had it coming to her, and then I was so God damned ashamed of myself—I'd never hit a woman before—that *I* ended up apologizing to *her*. Oh, I told her we were taking the next boat out of Honolulu, and if she was ever unfaithful to me again I'd make it very tough for her. But the fact of the matter is, her only punishment was a slap in the face, and that was with my open hand. We went to various places —Australia, Japan, the Philippines, China—and I got her pregnant."

"Yes. But what was behind this hula tonight?"

"I'd forgotten she knew how to do it. The whole subject of Honolulu, and ukuleles, hulas—we've never mentioned any of it, neither of us. But when she stood up there tonight, partly it was to do something better than you—"

"And she did."

"Well, she tried. And partly it was to insult me in a way that only I would understand. Things have been going very badly between us, we hardly ever speak a civil word when we're alone. She's convinced herself that you and I are having an affair—"

(*300*)

' Well, let's."

"Yes, let's. But I wish we could do it without—well, what the hell? Pat's supposed to be able to take care of himself."

"I have a few scores to settle there, too."

"Not since I've known him."

"Maybe not, but there were enough before you knew him. I used to be sick with jealousy, Monday to Friday, Monday to Friday, knowing he was probably screwing some chippy in Allentown or Wilkes-Barre. I was still jealous, even after we moved here. But not after I met you. From then on I didn't care what he did, who he screwed. Whenever I thought of him with another woman I'd think of me with you. But why isn't Kitty going to make any trouble? What have you got on her, besides the navy officer?"

"This is going to sound very cold-blooded."

"All right."

"And it's possible I could be wrong."

"Yes, but go on."

"Well—Kitty's gotten used to being Mrs. W. S. Hofman. She likes everything about it but me—and the baby. It's got her, Madge, and she can never have it anywhere else, or with anybody else."

"I could have told you that the first time I ever laid eyes on her."

"I had to find it out for myself."

There is one law for the rich, and another law for the richer. The frequent appearances of Whit Hofman with Madge Collins were treated not so much as a scandal as the exercise of a privilege of a man who was uniquely entitled to such privileges. To mollify their sense of good order the country club set could tell themselves that Whit was with Pat as often as he was with Madge, and that the three were often together as a congenial trio. The more kindly disposed made the excuse that Whit was putting up with a great deal from Kitty, and since Pat Collins obviously did not object to Whit's hours alone with Madge, what right had anyone else to complain? The excuse made by the less kindly was that if there was anything *wrong* in the Whit-Madge friendship, Kitty Hofman would be the first to kick up a fuss; therefore there was nothing scandalous in the relationship.

The thing most wrong in the relationship was the destructive effect on Madge Collins, who had been brought up in a strict Catholic atmosphere, who in nearly thirty years had had sexual intercourse with one man, and who now was having intercourse with two, often with both in the same day. The early excitement of a sexual feast continued through three or four months and a couple of narrow escapes; but the necessary lies to Pat and the secondary status of the man she preferred became inconvenient, then annoying, then irritating. She withheld nothing from Whit, she gave only what was necessary to Pat, but when she was in the company of both men—playing golf, at a movie, at a football game—she indulged in a nervous masquerade as the contented wife and the sympathetic friend, experiencing relief only when she could be alone with one of the men. Or with neither. The shame she suffered with her Catholic conscience was no greater than the shame of another sort: to be with both men and sit in self-enforced silence while the man she loved was so easily, coolly making a fool of the man to whom she was married. The amiable, totally unsuspecting fool would have had her sympathy in different circumstances, and she would have hated the character of the lover; but Pat's complacency was more hateful to her than Whit's arrogance. The complacency, she knew, was real; and Whit's arrogance vanished in the humility of his passion as soon as she would let him make love to her. There was proficiency of a selfish kind in Pat's lovemaking; he had never been so gentle or grateful as Whit. From what she could learn of Kitty Hofman it would have been neatly suitable if Pat had become Kitty's lover, but two such similar persons were never attracted to each other. They had, emotionally, everything in common; none of the essential friction of personality. Neither was equipped with the fear of losing the other.

It was this fear that helped produce the circumstances leading to the end of Madge's affair with Whit Hofman. "Every time I see you I love you again, even though I've been loving you all along," she told Whit. Only when she was alone with him—riding in his car, playing golf, sitting with him while waiting for Pat to join them, sitting with him after Pat had left them—could she forget the increasingly insistent irritations of her position. Publicly she was, as Whit told her, "carrying it off very well," but the nagging of her Catholic conscience and the rigidity of her middle-class training were with her more than she was with Whit, and when the stimulation of the early excitement had passed, she was left with that conscience, that training, and this new fear.

The affair, in terms of hours in a bed together, was a haphazard one, too dependent on Pat's unpredictable and impulsive absences. Sometimes he would telephone her from the garage late in the afternoon, and tell her he was driving to Philadelphia and would not be home until past midnight. On such occasions, if she could not get word to Whit at his office or at one of the two clubs, the free evening would be wasted. Other times they would make love on country roads, and three times they had gone to hotels in Philadelphia. It seldom happened that Whit, in a moment of urgently wanting to be with her, could be with her within the hour, and it was on just such occasions, when she was taking a foolish chance, that they had their two narrow escapes in her own house. "You can never get away when I want you to," said Whit—which was a truth and a lie.

"Be reasonable," she said, and knew that the first excitement had progressed to complaint. Any time, any-where, anything had been exciting in the beginning; now it was a bed in a hotel and a whole night together, with a good leisurely breakfast, that he wanted. They were in a second phase, or he was; and for her, fear had begun. It told on her disposition, so that she was sometimes snappish when alone with Whit. Now it was her turn to say they could not be together when she wanted him, and again it was a truth and a lie of exaggeration. They began to have quarrels, and to Whit this was not only an annoyance but a sign that they were getting in much deeper than he intended. For he had not deceived her as to the depth or permanence of their relationship. It was true that he had permitted her to deceive herself, but she was no child. She had had to supply her own declarations of the love she wanted him to feel; they had not been forthcoming from him, and when there were opportunities that almost demanded a declaration of his love, he was silent or noncommittal. The nature of their affair—intimacy accompanied by intrigue—was such as to require extra opportunities for candor. They were closer than if they had been free and innocent, but Whit would not use their intimacy even to make casual pretense of love. "I can't even wring it out of you," she said.

"What?"

(304)

"That you love me. You never say it."

"You can't expect to *wring* it out of anyone."

"A woman wants to hear it, once in a while."

"Well, don't try to wring it out of me."

He knew—and she knew almost as soon as he—that his refusal to put their affair on a higher, romantic love plane was quite likely to force her to put an end to the affair. And now that she was becoming demanding and disagreeable, he could deliberately provoke her into final action or let his stubbornness get the same result. It could not be said that she bored him; she was too exciting for that. But the very fact that she could be exciting added to his annoyance and irritation. He began to dislike that hold she had on him, and the day arrived when he recognized in himself the same basic weakness for Madge that he had had for Kitty. And to a lesser degree the same thing had been true of all the women he had ever known. But pursuing that thought, he recalled that Madge was the only one who had ever charged him with the inability to love. Now he had the provocation that would end the affair, and he had it more or less in the words of her accusation.

"You still won't say it," she said to him one night.

"That I love you?"

"That you love me."

"No, I won't say it, and you ought to know why."

"That's plain as day. You won't say it because you don't."

"Not *don't. Can't*," he said. "You told me yourself, a long time ago. That people love me and I can't love them. I'm beginning to think that's true."

"It's true all right. I was hoping I could get you to change, but you didn't."

"I used to know a guy that could take a car apart and

(305)

put it together again, but he couldn't drive. He never could learn to drive."

"What's that got to do with us?"

"Don't you see? Think a minute."

"I get it."

"So when you ask me to love you, you're asking the impossible. I'm just made that way, that's all."

"This sounds like a farewell speech. You got me to go to a hotel with you, have one last thing together, and then announce that we're through. Is that it?"

"No, not as long as you don't expect something you never expected in the first place."

"That's good, that is. You'll let me go on taking all the risks, but don't ask anything in return. I guess I don't love you *that* much, Mr. Hofman." She got out of bed.

"What are you going to do?"

"I'm getting out of this dump, I promise you that. I'm going home."

"I'm sorry, Madge."

"Whit, you're not even sorry for yourself. But I can make up for it. I'm sorry for you. Do you know what I'm going to do?"

"What?"

"I'm going home and tell Pat the whole story. If he wants to kick me out, all he has to do is say so."

"Why the hell do you want to do that?"

"You wouldn't understand it."

"Is it some Catholic thing?"

"Yes! I'm surprised you guessed it. I don't have to tell him. That's not it. But I'll confess it to him instead of a priest, and whatever he wants me to do, I'll do it. Penance."

"No, I don't understand it."

"No, I guess you don't."

"You're going to take a chance of wrecking your home, your marriage?"

"I'm not very brave. I don't think it is much of a chance, but if he kicks me out, I can go back to Oppenheim, Collins. I have a charge account there now." She laughed.

"Don't do it, Madge. Don't go."

"Whit, I've been watching you and waiting for something like this to happen. I didn't know what I was going to do, but when the time came I knew right away."

"Then you really loved Pat all along, not me."

"Nope. God help me, I love you and that's the one thing I won't tell Pat. There I'll have to lie."

It was assumed, when Pat Collins began neglecting his business and spending so much time in Dick Boylan's speakeasy, that Whit Hofman would come to his rescue. But whether or not Whit had offered to help Pat Collins, nobody could long go on helping a man who refused to help himself. He lost his two salesmen and his bookkeeper, and his Chrysler franchise was taken over by Walt Michaels, who rehired Joe Ricci at decent wages. For a while Pat Collins had a fifty-dollar-a-week drawing account as a salesman at the Cadillac dealer's, but that stopped when people stopped buying Cadillacs, and Pat's next job, in charge of the hat department in a haberdashery, lasted only as long as the haberdashery. As a Cadillac salesman and head of the hat department Pat Collins paid less attention to business than to pill pool, playing a game called Harrigan from one o'clock in the afternoon till suppertime, but during those hours he was at least staying out of the speakeasy. At suppertime he would have a Western sandwich at the Greek's, then go to Dick Boylan's, a quiet back room on the second story of a business building, patronized by doctors and lawyers and merchants in the neighborhood and by recent Yale and Princeton graduates and near-graduates. It was all he saw, in those days, of his friends from the country club crowd.

Dick Boylan's speakeasy was unique in that it was the only place of its kind that sold nothing but hard liquor. When a man wanted a sandwich and beer, he had to send out for it; if he wanted beer without a sandwich, Boylan told him to go some place else for it; but such requests were made only by strangers and by them not more than once. Dick Boylan was the proprietor, and in no sense the bartender; there were tables and chairs, but no bar in his place, and Boylan wore a suit of clothes and a fedora hat at all times, and always seemed to be on the go. He would put a bottle on the table, and when the drinkers had taken what they wanted he would hold up the bottle and estimate the number of drinks that had been poured from it and announce how much was owed him. "This here table owes me eight and a half," he would say, leaving the bookkeeping to the customers. "Or I'll have one with you and make it an even nine." Sometimes he would not be around to open up for the morning customers, and they would get the key from under the stairway linoleum, unlock the door, help themselves, and leave the money where Dick would find it. They could also leave chits when they were short of cash. If a man cheated on his chits, or owed too much money, or drank badly, he was not told so in so many words; he would knock on the door, the peephole was opened, and Boylan would say, "We're closed," and the statement was intended and taken to mean that the man was forever barred, with no further discussion of the matter.

Pat Collins was at Dick Boylan's every night after Madge

made her true confession. Until then he had visited the place infrequently, and then, as a rule, in the company of Whit Hofman. The shabby austerity of Dick Boylan's and Boylan's high-handed crudities did not detract from the stern respectability of the place. No woman was allowed to set foot in Boylan's, and among the brotherhood of hard drinkers it was believed—erroneously—that all conversations at Boylan's were privileged, not to be repeated outside. "What's said in here is Masonic," Boylan claimed. "I find a man blabbing what he hears—he's out." Boylan had been known to bar a customer for merely mentioning the names of fellow drinkers. "I run a san'tuary for men that need their booze," said Boylan. "If they was in that Gibbsville Club every time they needed a steam, the whole town'd know it." It was a profitable sanctuary, with almost no overhead and, because of the influence of the clientele, a minimum of police graft. Pat Collins's visits with Whit Hofman had occurred on occasions when one or the other had a hangover, and Boylan's was a quick walk from Pat's garage. At night Whit Hofman preferred to do his drinking in more elegant surroundings, and Pat Collins told himself that he was sure he would not run into Whit at Boylan's. But he lied to himself; he *wanted* to run into Whit.

At first he wanted a fight, even though he knew he would be the loser. He would be giving twenty pounds to a man who appeared soft but was in deceptively good shape, who managed to get in some physical exercise nearly every day of his life and whose eight years of prep school and college football, three years of army service, and a lifetime of good food and medical care had given him resources that would be valuable in a real fight. Pat Collins knew he did not have a quick punch that would keep

Whit down; Whit Hofman was not Walt Michaels. Whit Hofman, in fact, was Whit Hofman, with more on his side than his physical strength. Although he had never seen Whit in a fight, Pat had gone with him to many football games and observed Whit's keen and knowing interest in the niceties of line play. ("Watch that son of a bitch, the right guard for Lehigh. He's spilling two men on every play.") And Whit Hofman's way of telling about a battle during one of his rare reminiscences of the War ("They were awful damn close, but I didn't lob the God damn pineapple. I *threw* it. The hell with what they taught us back in Hancock.") was evidence that he would play for keeps, and enjoy the playing. Pat admitted that if he had really wanted a fight with Whit Hofman, he could have it for the asking. Then what *did* he want? The question had a ready answer: he wanted the impossible, to confide his perplexed anger in the one man on earth who would least like to hear it. He refused to solidify his wish into words, but he tormented himself with the hope that he could be back on the same old terms of companionship with the man who was responsible for his misery. Every night he went to Dick Boylan's, and waited with a bottle on the table.

Dick Boylan was accustomed to the company of hard drinkers, and when a man suddenly became a nightly, hours-long customer, Boylan was not surprised. He had seen the same thing happen too often for his curiosity to be aroused, and sooner or later he would be given a hint of the reason for the customer's problem. At first he dismissed the notion that in Pat Collins's case the problem was money; Collins was selling cars as fast as he could get delivery. The problem, therefore, was probably a woman, and since Collins was a nightly visitor, the woman was at home—his wife. It all came down to one of two things: money, or a woman. It never occurred to Dick Boylan—or, for that matter, to Pat Collins—that Pat's problem was the loss of a friend. Consequently Dick Boylan looked for, and found, all the evidence he needed to support his theory that Collins was having wife troubles. For example, men who were having money troubles would get phone calls from their wives, telling them to get home for supper. But the men who were having wife trouble, although they sometimes got calls from women, seldom got calls from their wives. Pat Collins's wife never called him. Never. And he never called her.

It was confusing to Dick Boylan to hear that Pat Collins's business was on the rocks. Whit Hofman did not let his friends' businesses go on the rocks. And then Boylan understood it all. A long forgotten, overheard remark about Whit Hofman and Madge Collins came back to him, and it was all as plain as day. Thereafter he watched Pat Collins more carefully; the amount he drank, the cordiality of his relations with the country clubbers, the neatness of his appearance, and the state of his mind and legs when at last he would say goodnight. He had nothing against Pat Collins, but he did not like him. Dick Boylan was more comfortable with non-Irishmen; they were neither Irish-to-Irish over-friendly, nor Irish-to-Irish condescending, and when Pat Collins turned out to be so preoccupied with his problems that he failed to be over-friendly or condescending, Dick Boylan put him down for an unsociable fellow, hardly an Irishman at all, but certainly not one of the others. Pat Collins did not fit in anywhere, although he got on well enough with the rest of the customers. Indeed, the brotherhood of hard drinkers were more inclined to welcome his company than Collins was to seek theirs. Two or three men coming in together would go to Pat's table instead of starting a table of their own and inviting him to join them. It was a distinction that Dick Boylan noticed without comprehending it, possibly because as an Irishman he was immune to what the non-Irish called Irish charm.

But it was not Irish charm that made Pat Collins welcome in the brotherhood; it was their sense of kinship with a man who was slipping faster than they were slipping, and who in a manner of speaking was taking someone else's turn in the downward line, thus postponing by months or years the next man's ultimate, inevitable arrival at the bottom. They welcomed this volunteer, and they hoped he would be with them a long while. They were an odd lot, with little in common except an inability to stand success or the lack of it. There were the medical men, Brady and Williams; Brady, who one day in his early forties stopped in the middle of an operation and had to let his assistant take over, and never performed surgery again; Williams, who at thirty-two was already a better doctor than his father, but who was oppressed by his father's reputation. Lawyer Parsons, whose wife had made him run for Congress because her father had been a congressman, and who had then fallen hopelessly in love with the wife of a congressman from Montana. Lawyer Strickland, much in demand as a high school commencement speaker, but somewhat shaky on the Rules of Evidence. Jeweler Linklighter, chess player without a worthy opponent since the death of the local rabbi. Hardware Merchant Stump, Eastern Pennsylvania trapshooting champion until an overload exploded and blinded one eye. Teddy Stokes, Princeton '25, gymnast, Triangle Club heroine and solo dancer, whose father was paying blackmail to the father of an altar boy. Sterling Agnew, Yale ex-'22, Sheff, a remittance man from New York whose father owned coal lands, and who was a part-time lover of Kitty Hofman's. George W. Shuttleworth,

Yale '91, well-to-do widower and gentleman author, currently at work on a biography of Nathaniel Hawthorne which was begun in 1892. Percy Keene, music teacher specializing in band instruments, and husband of a Christian Science practitioner. Lewis M. Rutledge, former captain of the Amherst golf team and assistant manager of the local branch of a New York brokerage house, who had passed on to Agnew the information that Kitty Hofman was accommodating if you caught her at the right moment. Miles Lassiter, ex-cavalry officer, ex-lieutenant of the State Constabulary, partner in the Schneider & Lassiter Detective & Protective Company, industrial patrolmen, payroll guards, private investigators, who was on his word of honor never again to bring a loaded revolver into Boylan's. Any and at some times all these gentlemen were to be found at Boylan's on any given night, and they constituted a clientele that Dick Boylan regarded as his regulars, quite apart from the daytime regulars who came in for a quick steam, drank it, paid, and quickly departed. Half a dozen of the real regulars were also daytime regulars, but Boylan said—over and over again—that in the daytime he ran a first-aid station; the sanctuary did not open till suppertime. (The sanctuary designation originated with George Shuttleworth; the first-aid station, with Dr. Calvin K. Brady, a Presbyterian and therefore excluded from Boylan's generalities regarding the Irish.)

For nearly three years these men sustained Pat Collins in his need for companionship, increasingly so as he came to know their problems. And know them he did, for in the stunned silence that followed Madge's true confession he took on the manner of the reliable listener, and little by little, bottle by bottle, the members of the brotherhood imparted their stories even as Whit Hofman had done on the afternoon of the first meeting of Whit and Pat. In exchange the members of the brotherhood helped Pat Collins with their tacit sympathy, that avoided mention of the latest indication of cumulative disaster. With a hesitant delicacy they would wait until he chose, if he chose, to speak of the loss of his business, the loss of his jobs, the changes of home address away from the western part of town to the northeastern, where the air was always a bit polluted from the steel mill, the gas house, the abattoir, and where there was always some noise, of which the worst was the squealing of hogs in the slaughterhouse.

"I hope you won't mind if I say this, Pat," said George Shuttleworth one night. "But it seems to me you take adversity very calmly, considering the first thing I ever heard about you."

"What was that, George?"

"I believe you administered a sound thrashing to Mr. Herb Michaels, shortly after you moved to town."

"Oh, that. Yes. Well, I'm laughing on the other side of my face now. I shouldn't have done that."

"But you're glad you did. I hope. Think of how you'd feel now if you hadn't. True, he owns the business you built up, but at least you have the memory of seeing him on the ground. And a cigar in his mouth, wasn't it? I always enjoyed that touch. I believe Nathaniel would have enjoyed it."

"Who?"

"Nathaniel Hawthorne. Most generally regarded as a gloomy writer, but where you find irony you'll find a sense of humor. I couldn't interest you in reading Hawthorne, could I?"

"Didn't he write *The Scarlet Letter?*"

"Indeed he did, indeed so."

"I think I read that in college."

"Oh, I hadn't realized you were a college man. Where?"

"Villanova."

"Oh, yes."

"It's a Catholic college near Philly."

"Yes, it must be on the Main Line."

"It is."

"Did you study for the priesthood?"

"No, just the regular college course. I flunked out sophomore year."

"How interesting that a Catholic college should include *The Scarlet Letter*. Did you have a good teacher? I wonder what his name was."

"Brother Callistus, I think. Maybe it was Brother Adrian."

"I must look them up. I thought I knew all the Hawthorne authorities. Callistus, and Adrian. No other names?"

"That's what they went by."

"I'm always on the lookout for new material on Nathaniel. One of these days I've just got to stop revising and pack my book off to a publisher, that's all there is to it. Stand or fall on what I've done —and then I suppose a week after I publish, along will come someone with conclusions that make me seem fearfully out of date. It's a terrifying decision for me to make after nearly thirty years. I don't see how I can face it."

"Why don't you call this Volume One?"

"Extraordinary. I thought of that very thing. In fact, in 1912 I made a new start with just that in mind, but after three years I went back to my earlier plan, a single volume. But perhaps I could publish in the next year or two, and later on bring out new editions, say every five years. Possibly ten. I'd hoped to be ready for the Hawthorne

Centenary in 1904, but I got hopelessly bogged down in the allegories and I didn't dare rush into print with what I had then. It wouldn't have been fair to me or to Nathaniel, although I suppose it'd make precious little difference to him."

"You never know."

"That's just it, Pat. He's very real to me, you know, although he passed away on May eighteenth or nineteenth in 'sixty-four. There's some question as to whether it was the eighteenth or the nineteenth. But he's very real to me. Very."

This gentle fanatic, quietly drinking himself into a stupor three nights a week, driven home in a taxi with a standing order, and reappearing punctually at eight-thirty after a night's absence, became Pat Collins's favorite companion among the brotherhood. George was in his early fifties, childless, with a full head of snowy white hair brushed down tight on one side. As he spoke he moved his hand slowly across his thatch, as though still training it. Whatever he said seemed to be in answer to a question, a studied reply on which he would be marked as in an examination, and he consequently presented the manner, looking straight ahead and far away, of a conscientious student who was sure of his facts but anxious to present them with care. To Pat Collins the mystery was how had George Shuttleworth come to discover whiskey, until well along in their friendship he learned that George had begun drinking at Yale and had never stopped. Alcohol had killed his wife in her middle forties—she was the same age as George—and Boylan's brotherhood had taken the place of the drinking bouts George had previously indulged in with her. "The Gibbsville Club is no place for me in the evening," said George. "Games, games, games. If it isn't bridge in the card room, it's pool in the billiard room. Why do men feel they have to be so strenuous—and I include bridge. The veins stand out in their foreheads, and when they finish a hand there's always one of them to heave a great sigh of relief. That's what I mean by strenuous. And the worst of it is that with two or possibly three exceptions, I used to beat them all consistently, and I never had any veins stand out in *my* forehead."

As the unlikely friendship flourished, the older man, by the strength of his passivity, subtly influenced and then dominated Pat Collins's own behavior. George Shuttleworth never tried to advise or instruct his younger friend or anyone else; but he had made a life for himself that seemed attractive to the confused, disillusioned younger man. Ambition, aggressiveness seemed worthless to Pat Collins. They had got him nowhere; they had in fact tricked him as his wife and his most admired friend had tricked him, as though Madge and Whit had given him a garage to get him out of the way. He was in no condition for violent action, and George Shuttleworth, the least violent of men, became his guide in this latter-day acceptance of defeat. In spite of the friendship, George Shuttleworth remained on an impersonal basis with Pat Collins; they never discussed Madge at all, never mentioned her name, and as a consequence Pat's meetings with his friend did not become an opportunity for self-pity.

The time then came—no day, no night, no month, no dramatic moment but only a time—when George Shuttleworth had taken Whit's place in Pat Collins's need of a man to admire. And soon thereafter another time came when Pat Collins was healed, no longer harassed by the wish or the fear that he would encounter Whit. It was a small town, but the routines of lives in small towns can be restrictive.

A woman can say, "I haven't been downtown since last month," although downtown may be no more than four or five blocks away. And there were dozens of men and women who had been born in the town, Pat's early acquaintances in the town, who never in their lives had seen the street in the northeastern section where Pat and Madge now lived. ("Broad Street? I never knew we had a Broad Street in Gibbsville.") There were men and women from Broad Street liberated by the cheap automobile, who would take a ride out Lantenengo Street on a Sunday afternoon, stare at the houses of the rich, but who could not say with certainty that one house belonged to a brewer and another to a coal operator. Who has to know the town as a whole? A physician. The driver of a meat-market delivery truck. A police officer. The fire chief. A newspaper reporter. A taxi driver. A town large enough to be called a town is a complex of neighborhoods, invariably within well-defined limits of economic character; and the men of the neighborhoods, freer to move outside, create or follow the boundaries of their working activities—and return to their neighborhoods for the nights of delight and anguish with their own. Nothing strange, then, but only abrupt, when Pat Collins ceased to see Whit Hofman; and nothing remarkable, either, that three years could be added to the life of Pat Collins, hiding all afternoon in a poolroom, clinging night after night to a glass.

"What did you want to tell me this for?" he had said.
"Because I thought it was right," she had said.
"Right, you say?"
"To tell you, yes," she said.
He stood up and pulled off his belt and folded it double.

(318)

"Is that what you're gonna do, Pat?"

"Something to show him the next time," he said.

"There'll be no next time. You're the only one'll see what you did to me."

"That's not what I'm doing it for."

"What for, then?"

"It's what you deserve. They used to stone women like you, stone them to death."

"Do that, then. Kill me, but not the strap. Really kill me, but don't do that, Pat. That's ugly. Have the courage to kill me, and I'll die. But don't do that with the strap, please."

"What a faker, what a bluffer you are."

"No," she said. She went to the bureau drawer and took out his revolver and handed it to him. "I made an act of contrition."

"An act of contrition."

"Yes, and there was enough talk, enough gossip. You'll get off," she said.

"Put the gun away," he said.

She dropped the revolver on a chair cushion. "You put it away. Put it in your pocket, Pat. I'll use it on you if you start beating me with the strap."

"Keep your voice down, the children'll hear," he said.

"They'll hear if you beat me."

"You and your act of contrition. Take off your clothes."

"You hit me with that strap and I'll scream."

"Take your clothes off, I said."

She removed her dress and slip, and stood in brassiere and girdle.

"Everything," he said.

She watched his eyes, took off the remaining garments, and folded her arms against her breasts.

He went to her, bent down, and spat on her belly.

(319)

"You're dirty," he said. "You're a dirty woman. Somebody spit on you, you dirty woman. The spit's rolling down your belly. No, I won't hit you."

She slowly reached down, picked up the slip and covered herself with it. "Are you through with me?"

He laughed. "Am I through with you? Am *I* through with you."

He left the house and was gone a week before she again heard from him. He stayed in town, but he ate only breakfast at home. "Is this the way it's going to be?" she said. "I have to make up a story for the children."

"You ought to be good at that."

"Just so I know," she said. "Do you want to see their report cards?"

"No."

"It's no use taking it out on them. What you do to me, I don't care, but they're not in this. They think you're cross with them."

"Don't tell me what to do. The children. You down here, with them sleeping upstairs. Don't you tell me what to do."

"All right, I won't," she said. "I'll tell them you're working nights, you can't come home for dinner. They'll see through it, but I have to give them some story."

"You'll make it a good one, of that I'm sure."

In calmer days he had maintained a balance between strict parenthood and good humor toward the children, but now he could not overcome the guilt of loathing their mother that plagued him whenever he saw the question behind their eyes. They were waiting to be told something, and all he could tell them was that it was time for them to be off to school, to be off to Mass, always time for them to go away and take their unanswerable, unphrased questions with them.

Their mother told them that he was very busy at the garage, that he had things on his mind, but in a year he had lost them. There was more finality to the loss than would have been so if he had always treated them with indifference, and he hated Madge the more because she could not and he could not absolve him of his guilt.

One night in Boylan's speakeasy George Shuttleworth, out of a momentary silence, said: "What are you going to do now, Pat?"

"Nothing. I have no place to go."

"Oh, you misunderstood me. I'm sorry. I meant now that Overton's has closed."

"That was over a month ago. I don't know, George. I haven't found anything, but I guess something will turn up. I was thinking of going on the road again. I used to be a pretty good hat salesman, wholesale, and when I was with Overton I told the traveling men to let me know if they heard of anything."

"But you don't care anything about hats."

"Well, I don't, but I can't pick and choose. I can't support a family shooting pool."

"Isn't there something in the automobile line? A man ought to work at the job he likes best. We have only the one life, Pat. The one time in this vale of tears."

"Right now the automobile business is a vale of tears. I hear Herb Michaels isn't having it any too easy, and I could only move four new Cadillacs in fourteen months."

"Suppose you had your own garage today. Could you make money, knowing as much as you do?"

"Well, they say prosperity is just around the corner."

"I don't believe it for a minute."

"I don't either, not in the coal regions. A man to make

a living in the automobile business today, in this part of the country, he'd be better off without a dealer's franchise. Second-hand cars, and service and repairs. New rubber. Accessories. Batteries. All that. The people that own cars have to get them serviced, but the people that need cars in their jobs, they're not buying new cars. Who is?"

"I don't know. I've never owned a car. Never learned to drive one."

"You ought to. Then when you go looking for material for your book, you'd save a lot of steps."

"Heavens no," said George Shuttleworth. "You're referring to trips to Salem? New England? Why it takes me two or three days of walking before I achieve the proper Nineteenth Century mood. My late lamented owned a car and employed a chauffeur. A huge, lumbering Pierce-Arrow she kept for twelve years. I got rid of it after she died. It had twelve thousand miles on the speedometer, a thousand miles for each year."

"Oh, they were lovely cars. Was it a limousine?"

"Yes, a limousine, although I believe they called it a Berliner. The driver was well protected. Windows on the front doors. I got rid of him, too. I got rid of him *first*. Good pay. Apartment over the garage. Free meals. New livery every second year. And a hundred dollars at Christmas. But my wife's gasoline bills, I happened to compare them with bills for the hospital ambulance when I was on the board. Just curiosity. Well, sir, if those bills were any indication, my wife's car used up more gasoline than the ambulance, although I don't suppose it all found its way into our tank. But she defended him. Said he always kept the car looking so nice. He did, at that. He had precious little else to occupy his time. I believe he's gone back to Belguim. He was the only Belgian in town, and my wife was very sympathetic toward the Belgians."

"Took his savings and—"

"His plunder," said George Shuttleworth. "Let's not waste any more time talking about him, Pat. You know, of course, that I'm quite rich."

"Yes, that wouldn't be hard to guess. That house and all."

"The house, yes, the house. Spotless, not a speck of dust anywhere. It's like a museum. I have a housekeeper, Mrs. Frazier. Scotch. Conscientious to a degree, but she's made a whole career of keeping my house antiseptically clean, like an operating surgery. So much so, that she makes me feel that I'm in the way. So I'm getting out of the way for a while. I'm going away."

"Going down South?"

"No, I'm not going South. I'm going abroad, Pat. I haven't been since before the War, and I'm not really running away from Mrs. Frazier and her feather dusters. I have a serious purpose in taking this trip. It has to do with my book. You knew that Nathaniel spent seven years abroad. Perhaps you didn't. Seven years, from 1853 to 1860."

"You want to see what inspired him," said Pat.

"No, no! Quite the contrary. He'd done all his best work by then. I want to see how it spoiled him, living abroad. There were other distractions. The Civil War. His daughter's illness. But I must find out for myself whether European life spoiled Nathaniel *or* did he flee to Europe when he'd exhausted his talent. That may turn out to be my greatest contribution to the study of Hawthorne. I can see quite clearly how my discoveries might cause me to scrap everything I've done so far and have to start all over again. I've already written to a great many scholars, and they've expressed keen interest."

"Well, I'll be sorry to see you go, George. I'll miss our evenings. When do you leave?"

"In the *Mauretania*, the seventh of next month. Oh, when I decide to act, nothing stops me," said George Shuttleworth. "I want to give you a going-away present, Pat."

"It should be the other way around. You're the one that's leaving."

"If you wish to give me some memento, that's very kind of you. But what I have in mind, I've been thinking about it for some time. Not an impulse of the moment. How much would it cost to set you up in a business such as you describe?"

"Are you serious, George?"

"Dead serious."

"A small garage, repairing all makes. No dealership. Gas, oil, tires, accessories. There's an old stable near where I live. A neighbor of mine uses it to garage his car in. You want to go on my note, is that it?"

"No, I don't want to go on your note. I'll lend you the money myself, without interest."

"Using mostly second-hand equipment, which I know where to buy here and there, that kind of a setup would run anywhere from five to ten thousand dollars. Atlantic, Gulf, one of those companies put in the pump and help with the tank. Oil. Tools I'd have to buy myself. Air pump. Plumbing would be a big item, and I'd need a pit to work in. Anywhere between five and ten thousand. You can always pick up a light truck cheap and turn it into a tow-car."

George Shuttleworth was smiling. "That's the way I like to hear you talk, Pat. Show some enthusiasm for something. What's your bank?"

"The Citizens, it was. I don't have any at the moment."

"Tomorrow, sometime before three o'clock, I'll deposit ten thousand dollars in your name, and you can begin to draw on it immediately."

"There ought to be some papers drawn up."

"My cheque is all the papers we'll need."

"George?"

"Now, now! No speech, none of that. I spend that much every year, just to have a house with sparkling chandeliers."

"Well then, two words. Thank you."

"You're very welcome."

"George?"

"Yes, Pat."

"I'm sorry, but you'll have to excuse me. I- -I can't sit here, George. You see why? Please excuse me."

"You go take a good long walk, Pat. That's what you do."

He walked through the two crowds of men and women leaving the movie houses at the end of the first show. He spoke to no one.

"You're home early," said Madge. "Are you all right?"

"I'm all right."

"You look sort of peak-ed."

"Where are the children?"

"They're out Halloweening. They finished their home work."

"I'm starting a new business."

"You are? What?"

"I'm opening a new garage."

"Where?"

"In the neighborhood."

"Well—that's good, I guess. Takes money, but it'd be a waste of time to ask you where you got it."

"It'd be a waste of time."

"Did you have your supper?"

"I ate something. I'm going to bed. I have to get up early. I have to go around and look for a lot of stuff."

"Can I do anything?"

"No. Just wake me up when the children get up."

"All right. Goodnight."

"Goodnight."

"And good luck, Pat."

"No. No, Madge. Don't, don't—"

"All right. I'm sorry," she said quietly. Then, uncontrolled, "Pat, for God's sake! Please?"

"No, Madge. I ask you."

She covered her face with her hands. "Please, please, please, please, please."

But he went upstairs without her. He could not let her spoil this, he could not let her spoil George Shuttleworth even by knowing about him.

"Hello, Pat."

"Hyuh, Whit."

Never more than that, but never less.

THE PROFESSORS

Free tea and cookies were served every afternoon at five in the Faculty Club. Locally, among the older teachers and those already living on their pensions, the repast was known as the appetite-spoiler: a man who had not been able to put aside much money during his active career could come to the Faculty Club—the F.C.—and stuff himself with tea that was half milk but at least was warm, and with chocolate Hydroxes, and when he went home to supper he was not as hungry as he might have been otherwise. All the men who depended upon the F.C. teas to keep their food budgets in order had an understanding about that, and some of them had become very adept at picking up four cookies with one hand while holding cup and saucer with the other. There were those who stacked the cookies, like poker chips, and there were some who could scoop them off the tray, using their thumbs to slide the cookies back into the palms of their hands. In either case the men would take their tea and biscuits and seat themselves in their accustomed places and devour the first batch in silence, washing it down with the tea in somewhat of a hurry, in order to go back for a second cup and another polite handful before Arthur, the club waiter, would start removing the tea things at half past five.

Arthur had a rude name for these members: tea customers, he called them, although tea was not the word he used. "Two, three lumps of sugar in every cup, and all them sweet crackers," he would say. "It's hardly any wonder they don't have any teeth left. But I rackon most of them don' get to sink their teeth into many sirloins." Arthur had been with the club for forty years and through three university administrations, and was no more in awe of a Nobel Prize winner than of the freshmen's basketball coach. At half past five on the dot he would take away the hot water and the carton of teabags and what was left of the biscuits, and if a professor asked for one more cup of tea Arthur had ways of handling him, depending on the degree of his dislike of the professor. "Sorry, sir, it's after ha' past. Club rule," a refusal; or "Well, I guess I could let you have another cup but I could get myself into trouble." In the latter case the professor would usually give up. There was only one club member who got special privileges from Arthur: Ernest Pangborn, soon-to-retire professor of Romance Languages, who in all his years on the faculty had never had the senior yearbook dedicated to him. But every afternoon, at about five-twenty-seven Arthur would start staring at Ernest Pangborn until he got his attention, and Arthur would point with his forefinger to the carton of teabags and then look up at the Seth Thomas clock, and Pangborn would get to his feet in time to be served the last cup of tea, his third, and only for Professor Pangborn would Arthur open a fresh box of cookies.

"Ernest, you have a drag with Arthur. How do you rate it?" The man who spoke in archaic collegiate slang was Jack Veech, Mathematics Department, a full professor and a few years younger than Ernest Pangborn.

"I'm sure I don't know, and it's probably just as well I don't."

"Why? Why do you say that?"

"Why do I say it? I say it because it's what I mean, Jack. And I mean it because whatever it is that got me in Arthur's good graces, he isn't self-conscious about it and neither am I. But if I knew what it was, I'd think of it whenever I saw Arthur and in all probability I'd have referred to it. Or been at such pains not to refer to it that it would have been just as awkward for both of us. I don't believe in being too analytical about what makes some people like me, those who do, I used to be *very* analytical about what made people *dis*-like me, but I gave that up. They just do. And when there's no overt reason for it, when it's instinctive, or acquired through association, I'm not going to be able to change it. And for quite a long time I haven't wanted to. A few people like me, and those few I place on the side of love. Some others dislike me, and that can be equally mysterious. Not baffling, though. From my earlier investigations I can easily recall standing, as it were, outside myself and disliking me. When I was a young man, for example, I was occasionally complimented by young women on my profile. That, of course, was forty years ago. But when I studied my profile I saw a well-shaped head, a fairly good nose, but a rather in-solent young man. Insolent, and sensual, and surprisingly cruel at least potentially. That was my appearance, which some young ladies admired, and which I sincerely did not."

"I only *asked* you how you got your drag with Arthur."

"I know, and I apologize for the disquisition. My ex-cuse is that the opportunity doesn't come very often. Would you like to have, as they say, equal time? I'll ask you a lead-ing question. Why do you think Arthur is less fond of you than he is of me?"

"I don't know, and I couldn't care less."

"No, Jack, you must care a *little*, and not only because

Arthur Dayton looks out for me. You observed that he does, and the fact irritated you."

"You claim you don't know why he likes you. Therefore I can claim I don't know why he doesn't like the rest of us."

"I don't know the answer to either question. I was only offering you the chance to theorize, which I know you like to do."

"Not on such matters."

"Well, true. It's not the kind of thing a first-class mind ought to be concerned with. Very trivial. Very, very, very, very trivial."

"Is that sarcasm, Ernest?"

"No, not really, Jack. I do concern myself with trivial matters, that in your field would be—well, obstacles. I've often thought, as I gazed at your blackboard after one of your lectures, all that clear thinking, unimpeded by trivial things, and none of it having any meaning for me except that my friend Jack Veech makes a very sloppy *phi*. Your *phi* and your *psi* are written in such haste that if I were one of your students I'd be confused."

"It isn't my Greek letters that confuse them."

"Of course not. But I'm not one of your students, and I'm sure if I were—"

"You wouldn't last very long."

"I was about to say, I wouldn't last very long. In fact I didn't go that high in mathematics. I fulfilled those re-quirements—how did I? After solid I took a year of physics. I guess that was it. I never had to take trigonometry. Now I doubt if I could pass high school algebra."

"You might be able to. They don't use *phi* or *psi* in it to distract you, in case the teacher didn't make them pretty."

"Oh, now, Jack, you're not going to be peevish about that, surely."

"I've seen *your* handwriting, in English, and it's nothing to brag about."

"It's legible, though, Jack. Small, but legible. I formed the habit of writing small to save paper, years ago. But my letters are clear, easy to read."

"Under a magnifying glass."

"Well, no one can say that about your hand. Large, sweeping, flourishing, you might say. Isn't it odd that—"

"That what?"

"Oh, we've had enough of this conversation. I think I'll amble homeward." Ernest Pangborn had come close to remarking how odd it was that he, a tall man, should have such small handwriting, while Veech, who was short, wrote a large, sweeping, flourishing hand.

Pangborn did indeed amble homeward, with a gait that all newcomers to the university were likely to attribute to alcohol and first-year medical students to the onset of locomotor ataxia. Neither opinion was correct; Pangborn could not afford liquor, and his coordination and reflexes were in good condition, but in another day the women students, seeing Pangborn's walk, would say, "Truckin' on down." Veech, on the contrary, walked like a midshipman, one of the lower-class midshipmen who had recently been braced.

But Jack Veech's hatred to Ernest Pangborn was not caused by the difference in height or even by an instinctive dislike of the sort mentioned by Pangborn. The hatred went back to the early days of their acquaintance and Veech's second year on the campus. It was a large university, with a large faculty, and newcomers on the instructor and assistant professor levels often found that they were meeting only the men and women in their field and their neighbors in faculty housing accommodations, houses and apartments for the married teachers, smaller apartments and single rooms for the unmarried. Among such a large faculty there were those who had independent incomes, and they lived where they chose. Men like Jack Veech had more or less to take what was assigned to them, in order of seniority in the teaching profession. It was through this circumstance that Jack Veech made the acquaintance of Ernest Pangborn.

It was in the very early Thirties, and Maizie and Ernest Pangborn were still able to hang on to their house. Maizie had a little money of her own, Ernest Pangborn a little less, which together enabled them to have the house and to travel abroad. They then lived on a scale that was higher than that of full professors and as a sort of punishment for their conspicuous extravagance Ernest was given extra chores. One of the chores was to serve on a committee that assigned living quarters to new teachers, and in the course of determining seniority, Ernest discovered that there was a one-year gap in John Philip Veech's academic history. A whole year was unaccounted for.

A couple of weeks before college was to open, Ernest Pangborn saw John P. Veech on the campus. "Veech, I'm Pangborn. Interested in a Coke?"

"Why, yes. Thanks very much," said Veech.

They took a table in the cafeteria and Veech waited for Pangborn to begin.

"I'm on a committee that decides who is going to live where," said Pangborn. "It's a dull dreary task, and the only thing that keeps it from being duller is to try to be conscientious about it. And I noticed that according to seniority, which is what we go by, two new men get their choice of rooms in West Hostetter before you do. But they're not entitled to that seniority. They're both younger than you, and they took their bachelors' and masters' a year after you did.

You graduated in '26, I believe. Master's in '28. Taught for two years, but in the academic year '30-'31 you apparently vanished from the face of the earth. It couldn't have been a sabbatical, but if it was a leave of absence, you're entitled to first choice of what's left in West Hostetter. There's a corner room left, and as far as I can see, you've got more right to it than the other two. But the record doesn't say what happened to '30-'31. If you were on leave, I suggest you correct the record and then you can have the corner room."

"I wasn't on leave that year," said Veech. "I stopped teaching because I was ill."

"Well, couldn't you have that put on the record? It isn't there now, and if you were ill I think you're entitled to have it so stated, even if it wasn't an actual leave of absence."

"Why should you bother about it if I don't?" said Veech.

Pangborn took the rebuff in silence, drank the rest of his Coke and said, "You may be sure I never will again," and left Veech.

The rudeness was of such a pointless kind that Pangborn did not speak of it to Maizie, therefore to no one, until at a faculty cocktail party he overheard Veech saying, "I've never been sick a day in my life. I have a system of exercises that I do every day, no matter where I am. On shipboard. Even on trains. It's ridiculous for men to let themselves get out of shape. Toxicity affects the brain and nobody can tell me otherwise."

At home that evening Ernest Pangborn said to his wife, "How do you like John Veech?"

"John Veech. Mathematics. The one that looks like an overgrown jockey."

"If you weren't from Kentucky you'd say an overgrown

coxswain. Yes, what do you think of him?"

"Just a quick impression, just right off like that?" She snapped her fingers.

"Yes."

"A man I wouldn't trust. Maybe the soul of honor, as upright as they come, but not a man I would trust. Why?"

"He's a liar." He then told her why he thought so. "His home town is Duluth. I think I'll write to Don Marshall."

"And you give Don my love and tell him he's still my second favorite Beta, even if he didn't think to send us a Christmas card last Christmas."

When Don Marshall's letter arrived a couple of weeks later Pangborn said nothing to Maizie, but something made her think of Veech and she said, "Honey'd you ever hear from Don? Don Marshall? About Mr. Veech?"

"Yes, I heard from him. Veech is a liar, all right. And this is a pretty darn nice university."

"Well, you always said *that*, honey. This little old cow college, you always loved and revered it. Why now specially?"

"Because they gave John Veech a second chance."

"Second chance? Was he here before?"

"No, never here. Michigan. They let him resign. He was arrested in Detroit, contributing to the delinquency of a minor. Found guilty, served several months and got time off for good behavior. Don said it didn't surprise anyone in Duluth."

"He must be awful good scholastically."

"He is, or so I'm told. But I'm darn proud of this old place."

In a year or so Veech got married and at regular intervals became the father of sons, three in number, who were well-disciplined reproductions of Veech. They marched to the model school in the Teachers College, took prizes in junior sports, won merit badges in the Scouts, and stayed out of trouble. Some faculty mothers envied Nadine Veech, who had a husband that was not too damned busy to do his share in raising the three boys; some faculty fathers, in self-defense, referred to the Veech boys as the Junior R.O.T.C. And yet when Vernon, the youngest of the Veech boys, ran away and was missing for two days, the university community suspended all criticism of the manner in which Jack Veech was raising his sons. The concern and sympathy were genuine, and upon Vernon's being restored to his parents the other fathers and mothers, as though by universal agreement, forbade their children to tease the Veech child. He had been discovered, cold and hungry, in an abandoned henhouse on a farm not twenty miles from the campus. He was thirteen years old.

It was one of the many, many times that Ernest Pangborn missed Maizie. If she had been alive he could have talked it out with her, and one silly-seeming comment might have shown him what to do. And if not a frivolous remark, it might be a couple of lines from her favorites, Elinor Wylie, Edna St. Vincent Millay. He knew so well that she would love to be able to say

> I shall stop fighting and escape
> Into a little house I'll build.

or, from Millay, "Standing beside some tumbled shed" or "And I upon the floor will lie/and think how bad I've been." Wylie and Millay she knew as she knew Wodehouse and Bolton and Porter and Berlin, and certain sections of the Book of Common Prayer, including the words that had been said over her in April of that year in the University Chapel.

There would be nothing profound in her comments on the fugitive Vernon Veech, for in her childlessness she was diffident where the problems of parents were concerned, and sensitive to the unuttered disappointment of her husband. He could invent the impossible dialog: "Maybe I ought to go see Veech," he would say.

"If you think you *ought* to, but not just because they got the whole football squad out looking for Vernon. Maybe you'd be better off with the football players. We're such strangers maybe Jack Veech'd order you off his porch."

In the end, though, he went to call on Veech and Nadine.

"Oh—Ernest. Come in," said Veech.

"I won't stay."

"Much rather have you come here than tie up the phone. I wish people would have sense enough not to call us up. They're so damned inconsiderate."

"Their intentions are good, Jack. Some of them just don't think."

"They have nothing to think with, especially the women. Not that the men aren't just as bad. I never realized how many stupid people there are at this place. Oversized Ag school is what it is."

"I'm sorry but I can't agree with you on that, but I know you're upset, understandably. Just say hello to Nadine for me, and if I can help in any way, do call me."

"I just got finished telling you, we want to keep the line clear. But I'll tell Nadine you were here."

"Yes, do, but *don't* call this an oversized Ag school. You don't mean that, Jack. You of all people."

"Did you come here to start an argument? I never meant anything more in all my life."

"Goodnight, Jack," said Pangborn.

After Vernon Veech's adventure quieted down, the boy's father one evening called on Ernest Pangborn in his rooms in East Hostetter. "You've got this place fixed up pretty nicely. You sold your house when Maizie died. You must have got a pretty good price for it, the way the real estate situation is."

"Well, there were mortgages to be taken care of, and the government has that ceiling business. But I wanted to get out of the house. All this, my books and this furniture, I had in my study. The bedroom furniture I left behind, with everything else. I'd like to go away for a year. I have a sabbatical coming and the people in Main Hall will let me go any time I like, but I have difficulty making plans. It's easier just to stay on. How would you like a cup of coffee? I have this little electric thing."

"Never drink it at night, thanks. But you go ahead and have one."

"I will later. I get along with a lot less sleep than I used to." Pangborn was willing to continue the small talk as long as Veech wished to, but Veech was now ready.

"I said something the other night at my house, when you came to see us. You know what I have reference to."

"Yes. I know."

"Since then I've been thinking. You said to me, 'You didn't mean that. You of all people.' Why me of all people?"

"Oh, you *didn't* come here to explain your remark. You want *me* to explain *mine*."

"If you mean did I come here to apologize, I don't make a habit of apologizing."

"Well, it's a habit you could form, to use when necessary."

"And I don't see why I'd apologize to you anyway."

"No, I guess you don't. You could apologize to me for

saying what you did about a place that I happen to love.
But that hasn't occurred to you, so—don't apologize, whatever you do."

"I won't. You can be sure of that. But you still haven't
told me what you meant by 'you of all people.'"

"Are you bluffing, Jack?"

Veech looked at Pangborn. "Bluffing?" He uttered the
word, but only as an echo, not as angry protest.

"You have no feeling of gratitude for this place?"

"Oh," said Veech. "You're referring to something that
happened in Detroit? How did you find out?"

"Not from Main Hall, I assure you. And I assure you,
I've never spoken of it to anyone now living."

"All the years since, that I've been making up for that,
that I've been living a decent life. Those years don't mean
anything?"

"They do indeed mean something. They mean that this
oversized Ag school showed good judgment. But even if
you hadn't vindicated them, I'd love the place because it
gave you a second chance. Were you accepted anywhere
else, Jack?"

"No, I wasn't."

"Then go on home and do something nice for Vernon."

"I've been very nice to Vernon."

"Then by God you've learned *something* here. I didn't
think you had."

"Gratitude doesn't go on forever," said Veech.

"Yes it does. Phony humility doesn't go on forever,
but that only sickens people anyway. Gratitude is something else."

"I ought to be grateful to you for keeping quiet?"

"Oh, Lord, you have no understanding of it, or of me.
Tell me, how were you nice to Vernon?"

(338)

"How was I nice to him? Different ways. I bought him a new bike. I'm letting him go to camp next summer."

"Then you are grateful, aren't you? You're grateful to your son for not dying, for not making more trouble."

"When it comes to raising a family I guess I know more about that than you do."

"That's not the crushing remark you intended it to be, Jack, honestly it isn't," said Pangborn.

"Well, goodbye, Mr. Chips," said Veech. He rose and left, and Ernest Pangborn laughed more heartily than he had in many months. Veech's parting remark could have and should have made him sadder, but Veech had no way of knowing that through outrageous accident he had spoken the name that Maizie used when she wanted to deflate Pangborn. "You're being Chipsy," she would say, and it would cover quaintness, pomposity, prolixity, eccentricities of dress, penny-watching, and even hand-holding during lectures by visiting notables. He went to the door and shouted down the stair-well. "Hey, Jack?"

"What?"

"Touché."

"What'd you say?"

"Never mind," said Pangborn, and returned to his rooms.

Thereafter he often sought the company of Jack Veech, knowing that Veech despised him for doing so, but caring little what Veech felt. He was sure that to Veech he was an ineffectual turner of the other cheek, too ready to forgive, a slob. But when he caught himself in the act of being Chipsy he would know that it was time to bask in the light of the cold, hard intelligence of Jack Veech, and Veech never let him down. Veech could be relied upon to say at least one thing during a conversation that would be so down-to-earth, or pragmatic, or unconsciously cruel that it had the double effect of exposure to a fresh point of view, and, immediately, a reaffirmation by Pangborn of his own point of view. He used Veech because he could not change him, and then he found that he did not want to change him. An association that had really begun with a name, if not a voice, from the grave, now continued because Veech had become a medium. A medium, a confessor, a messenger. Then Pangborn began to notice that as they grew older he was seeing more of Veech than of any other member of the faculty, and that their encounters, their conversations, were not all of his own maneuvering; some of them, then more and more of them, came about through an effort on the part of Veech. Pangborn would be walking across campus and Veech would join him; Pangborn would take his accustomed chair in the Faculty Club, and the chair next to him would be taken by Veech. Only once during that time did Veech depart from the severity of his manner toward Pangborn, but that exception was enough to give Pangborn another look at the man. "Well, we finally got the last of the boys off to college," said Veech one afternoon at the F.C.

"Vernon?" said Pangborn.

"Yes. He started at Kenyon yesterday."

"You sent all three to Kenyon. You didn't go there."

"No, but Nadine's father did, and he's paying the bills. You don't think I could send three sons to a place like that? I don't know how I'd have managed to send them through here, even allowing for free tuition and having them live at home. Well, with Vernon and Victor at Kenyon and Vance in the army, our food bills won't be so high. Nadine said to me yesterday, next Sunday we ought to have a steak and eat it all by ourselves. A nice choice cut just big enough for the two of us. I'm looking forward to it. Then I can start paying some bills. Who knows? I may be able to save some money."

"I always thought you had some."

"My family had some, but I was cut off. Didn't you find that out when you were finding out everything else about me?"

"No."

"I haven't been to Duluth since 1930. My father paid for my lawyers, and he allowed my mother to give me five hundred dollars when I got out of prison. But only on condition I never go back to Duluth. No, I haven't any money. And neither has Nadine. *Her* family weren't giving any money to a jailbird."

"I never knew any of this, Jack."

"Well, you weren't supposed to. I didn't go around broadcasting it, you can be sure of that."

It was another look at the man and at the life he and his wife had led for more than twenty years, close to twenty-five. And Ernest Pangborn did not know what to say. A compliment would be rejected, and a word of pity would be unthinkable. Indeed, the compliment was being paid to Pangborn; Veech honored him with his confidence and accorded him honor more subtly, more truly, by asking no further assurances of his silence. Pangborn did not know what to say, knew there was nothing to say, and while he was thinking he became conscious of Arthur, who was making his end-of-tea-time signals.

"Let me have your cup," said Ernest Pangborn. He picked up Veech's cup and saucer and carried them with his own to the tea table. "For Professor Veech and me, please, Arthur."

Arthur looked up at the clock. "Well—all right," he said.

A SHORT WALK
FROM THE STATION

On a Friday evening in February this year Francis King dozed off just after his train left the 30th Street Station, and he would have slept all the way to Paoli had it not been for Joe Dybert. Joe Dybert shook him gently. "Wake up, Francis," said Joe Dybert. "Show momma the blue."

"Huh? . . . Oh. Oh, hello, Joe. We here?" said Francis King.

"Think you can make it? What'd you have for lunch, boy?" said Joe Dybert.

The two men left the station together, walking in step but without conversation until they reached the street. "Give you a ride up the hill?"

"No thanks," said Francis King. "See you tomorrow."

"Tomorrow's Saturday. You won't see *me* tomorrow."

"What did *you* have for lunch? We're going to your house for dinner tomorrow night. Drive carefully, Mr. Dybert. Drive carefully." Francis King turned up the collar of his topcoat and put on his gloves, but now that he was alone the thought of walking up the short incline to Cardiff Road sickened him. It was only a short walk, three blocks, and the times he had made it automatically surely numbered well up in the thousands; nevertheless his legs weighed a ton. He had no sensation of dizziness, he felt no pain. It was just that he wanted to stand there a couple of minutes.

Friends of his and their wives waved to him and tapped their horns in goodnight salute, all knowing that Francis King never accepted the offer of a lift in the evening. "Forget something, Francis?" said one such friend, on foot and not waiting for an answer.

"Just trying to think," said Francis King, and it was the truth: he was trying to understand the leaden immobility of his legs. He knew he could walk only so far—to Arlington Drive, which was at the bottom of the incline. He knew he could get that far, that his legs would let him get that far, but not beyond. And then, in shame and embarrassment, he saw the truth: it was not the short incline to Cardiff Road that was so formidable; it was the thought of once more, for the many-thousandth time, walking past Lydia Brown's shop with his eyes averted, pretending the shop did not exist, pretending there was no Lydia Brown.

The Tack Room was hideously expensive. Lydia Brown's prices for everything were really out of this world. You could get cashmere things much cheaper almost anywhere on Chestnut Street, and the horse things she still carried—to justify the original name of the shop—cost less on Walnut Street. The presents for men were higher than in the New York stores, the children's things were ridiculously overpriced. But Lydia Brown's friends went on buying from her whenever they could, partly out of admiration for her courage, partly because her old friends approved of the appearance of her shop and the way she kept it up in among the cluster of real estate offices, liquor stores, drug stores, hairdressers' salons in the vicinity of the station. The Tack Room was a convenient and pleasant place to drop in for a cigarette, a cup of coffee in the mid-morning, a cup of tea in the afternoon. Old friends could borrow an umbrella there, leave their bundles there, make a telephone call. The field-stone and white trim house was inviting. And if the mounting block at the curb got in the way of off-side car doors, what were a few scratches nowadays, when every anonymous parking attendant did worse than scratch your door? All her old friends wanted Lyd Brown to stay in business, and she always took it with a smile when they kidded her about overcharging them for chutney and English biscuits and Italian leather and Swedish woodwork. Sometimes in the Philadelphia shops a salesperson would say, "We don't carry that any more. The only place I can think of where you might find it is Lydia Brown's store, the Tack Room, you know?" Everything in the Tack Room was the best.

Francis King made straight for the Tack Room, and climbing the three steps from the sidewalk level did not tax his strength. The shop was brightly lighted by three frosted globes hanging from the ceiling, but as he entered he saw no one. Then, from a room at the rear of the store, Lydia Brown came forth.

"Hello, Francis," she said. "Is there something the matter?"

He nodded. "I don't know what it is. I just want to sit down a minute."

"Would you like a glass of water? Brandy? Can I call a doctor?"

"I just want to sit down a minute. It isn't anything. Not a heart attack."

"I'll get you a brandy," she said.

He sat down and opened his coat, took off his hat and gloves and put them on a display table. She brought him a pony of brandy from the back room, and as he took a sip she lowered the Venetian blinds at all the windows. "I was about ready to close up anyway," she said, and stood in front of him with her arms folded and looked down at him over the rims of her glasses.

"If you could see yourself," he said.

"You didn't look so hot when you came in. What did you have for lunch?"

"You're the second one asked me that. I fell asleep on the train, and Joe Dybert asked me the same question. I had oyster stew, apple pie, and two cups of coffee. What I've had for lunch every Friday for thirty years, with time out for the war. What did *you* have for lunch, Lyd?"

"A chicken sandwich and a glass of milk. Why?"

"I don't know. I just thought I'd ask you. *You* asked *me.*"

She took a chair facing him and lit a cigarette. "Nobody would believe it, that the first conversation we have after all these years consists of what we had for lunch."

"Well, I guess after all these years that's just about all we have to talk about."

"You have a point. How are you feeling?"

"Much better, thanks. I'll leave, don't worry."

"Don't hurry. I have nothing to do till seven."

"And then what do you do?"

"What?"

"I'm not just being inquisitive. I've often wondered what you do when you're not being a business woman."

"Terribly nice of you, Francis. I'm touched."

"You have a nice store," he said.

"I like it."

"You must do pretty well."

"Pretty well. I had the best Christmas since I opened the shop."

"Good."

"Rose helped," said Lydia Brown.

"You don't have to tell me that. I'm the one that pays the bills. Why the smile?"

"The only communication we ever have, your name at the bottom of a check. Francis D. B. King. Francis D. B. King. I remember I used to write Mr. and Mrs. Francis D. B. King, to see how it would look. Lydia B. King. Mrs. Francis D. B. King. Mrs. F. D. B. King. L. B. K. I guess every girl that ever lived did that."

"I did it too. I wrote Mrs. Francis D. B. King with you in mind."

"You did, really?"

"Sure. And Lydia B. King, and Lydia King. I don't remember writing L. B. K., but possibly I did."

"I just can't imagine you being so sentimental. Romantic."

"You forget," said Francis King.

"Do I, indeed? *I*—for*get*. What an unearthly nerve you have, to say a thing like that. The one thing I've never had a chance to do was forget. Do you realize that every morning, when I'm opening up my shop, for close to thirty years I see you walking past here on your way to the train. You've never looked in, not even looked in this direction. But I'm the one that forgets? You don't even see the shop."

"I've always known it was here. During the war I remember I'd be at my battle station, pitch dark in the early morning, and I'd think of how it was at home. I'd think of all the houses in the neighborhood, all the stores. And I always thought of your shop."

"I was hoping you'd be killed in the war."

"What?"

"You find that hard to believe?"

"I find it impossible to believe. By the time the war started it was already a good ten years since we'd had our quarrel. It was one thing to stop speaking to me, but to hate me enough to want me killed, ten years later! I never did anything that bad, Lydia."

"You did to me, Francis. You as good as killed me. Look at me. What am I? Close to sixty years old, no chance of ever having children and I love children. An apartment over my shop instead of a nice home of my own."

"That part isn't hard to understand, being bitter. But hating me enough to want me killed. Do you know, if I'd known that I might have obliged you."

"Oh, come, Francis."

"Oh, yes. When I went out to the Pacific I arranged all my affairs. Made my will, provided for Rose and the children. I put everything in order, so to speak. But I couldn't undo what I'd done to you. I guess it's very seldom a man is so completely in the wrong that there's nothing he can do, absolutely nothing. But I didn't realize you hated me that much."

"Oh, yes."

"And do you now?"

"Right now? This minute? No." She looked away, reflectively. "When you came in here you looked as though you might fall over dead right here."

"That would have been awkward."

"Yes, it would have been. But you asked me a question. Do I hate you now? And the answer is no."

"Why not?"

"You must figure that out for yourself, Francis."

"Because you don't feel anything. Is that why?"

"Yes."

"I looked so nearly dead that you couldn't hate me any more? Is that it?"

"Yes."

"How do I look now?"

"Oh, you're all right now, I suppose."

"Therefore you ought to be hating me again."

She shook her head. "No. Nothing. Absolutely nothing. I'll never hate you again."

Her face was suddenly bright and beautiful, her eyes as blue as her cashmere slip-on and as bright as her necklace of pearls. "Lydia," he said.

"What?"

"Would it be all right if I stopped in again, once in a while?"

"No."

"Never?"

"Never," she said. "I really don't want to see you again, Francis."

"I see," he said. "Well—thanks for the brandy." He rose and picked up his hat and gloves.

"Would you like me to call you a taxi?" she said.

"No thanks," he said.

She held the door open for him, and after he passed through it he heard the spring lock. Even before he reached Arlington Drive she had turned out the lights in her shop, and it was very dark going up to Cardiff Road. Dark and cold, and the wind was strong.

SUNDAY MORNING

Marge Fairbanks had her second cup of coffee and third cigarette, then she put on her zippered arctics and polo coat and went back to the garage. On an impulse that she did not immediately recognize as defiant she started the Fiat, and she was well on her way to the village before she even wondered what had made her take the little car. Her car—that is, the car she was supposed to use—was the station wagon. In the Fairbanks household the station wagon seldom got to the station. It got everywhere else, but hardly ever to the station. Oh, no. The car that was driven to the station every morning, five days a week, and left there in the sun and rain and snow, was the Fiat, the little car that she loved but almost never got a chance to drive. The once bright little Fiat, with its stunning grey paint job and white-wall tires, and its maneuverability and park-ability. She had chosen it and had contributed four hundred dollars toward its purchase, but a month after they bought it Allan expropriated it, and now it was referred to as *his* car. Her car was the Chevy, the station wagon, that was twice as old and twice as big as the Fiat; that needed new floor mats; that got a washing once or twice in the spring and once or twice in the summer; that she tried to keep clean inside but could not seem to, what with dog hair, bobby pins, candy wrappers, matchbooks, Kleenex, comic books, pencil stubs, and the rest of the accumulation of strange articles, souvenirs of family activity and car pool. The inside of the Fiat was not spotlessly clean, but at least it was not disorderly, and the upholstery of the driver's seat was the only place that showed wear.

She passed the Catholic church and waved to Patty O'Brien in her four-year-old mink and her white gloves, but obviously Patty did not recognize her in the Fiat. On a weekday Patty would have waved automatically at the Chevy. Patty, and Kevin, and the O'Brien twins, trying not to be late for the nine o'clock Mass. Marge Fairbanks wondered who felt worse this morning, Patty or Kevin. They must have had to get up at seven-thirty, to be all dressed up and shaved and the children given their breakfast and made to look presentable. The O'Briens' car was nowhere to be seen, although it was probably parked somewhere near; but how had Kevin gotten his car, or had they all come to Mass in a taxi? The Fairbankses had driven the O'Briens home from Ethel Canning's party, somewhere around four o'clock, having persuaded Patty and Kevin that if they were picked up by the police, someone would lose his or her license. With the hangovers they must have, the O'Briens were still risky drivers, but the police never stopped anyone on Sunday morning. Come to think of it, Marge Fairbanks could not remember when she had seen a policeman this early on Sunday morning. A little later, yes, when all the churches would be holding services, but not at this hour.

She pulled up in front of Mr. Goldstein's store and got out. In this weather Goldstein kept the Sunday papers inside. In the summertime the papers were piled on boards in front of the store and you helped yourself, but on a sloppy day like this—rain, snow, gusts of wind—you had to go inside. Goldstein was standing behind the cigar counter.

"Good morning," said Marge Fairbanks.

"No papers," said Goldstein.

"What's the matter? A strike?" she said.

"Don't ask me, all I know is that they didn't deliver. You can have the advance stuff, but the news and sports sections you'll have to come back later."

"Have you any idea how soon they'll be here?"

"Don't ask *me*, Mrs. Fairbanks. Maybe an hour, maybe two hours."

"What do you mean, don't ask *you?* Who else *shall* I ask, if not you? You know I have to drive four miles in and four miles back."

"Lady, don't take it out on me," said Goldstein. "I ain't responsible *how* many miles you drive."

She left the store and got in the car. She was busy lighting a cigarette when there was a startling horn blast behind her. She looked in the mirror and said, "Oh, go to hell," and then recognized the car, Ralph Shipstead's Cadillac. He got out and walked to the Fiat.

"I just told you to go to hell," she said. "Don't you know it's Sunday morning, blowing your horn like that?"

"Jesus, do I know it's Sunday morning. Move over."

"No I won't. Get in the other side, if you want to."

He did so. "You haven't got another cigarette, have you?"

"Yes," she said. "Here."

"I came out without any."

"Well, Goldstein sells them. No papers, by the way."

"I know. I was around earlier and I went back to the house and then I came out without any cigarettes. I must have left them on—I don't know where I could have left them . . . *I* know, I was wearing a different coat. How do you feel?"

"I feel all right. I didn't have much to drink. I never do."

"Well, your boy Allan made up for it. Not to mention ten others. I saw Kevin O'Brien a few minutes ago, trying to park his car. He had a space big enough to park a trailer truck, but he couldn't make it today."

"He had his own car?"

"That's right, you gave them a ride home. Yes, he had his own car. They must have had to take a taxi to Ethel's."

"That was my guess, too. I saw them going into church."

"Then he finally got it parked. Are you going to wait around for the papers?"

"No, I have to go back and get breakfast for Allan."

"No hurry about that, is there?"

"No, but then I have to take the children to Sunday School."

"Thank God ours are away at school. Let's go for a ride."

"I can't. Finish your cigarette and then you have to get out."

"You don't go for me, do you, Marge?"

"Not really, I guess."

"Have you got somebody else—I don't mean Allan."

"No, but you don't think I'd tell you if I had."

"You might. I can't figure you."

"You don't know me. You've only been here a short time."

"Oh, it doesn't usually take me long."

"That's the trouble with you, if you don't mind my saying so. You find yourself irresistible."

"Well, at least you're giving me some plain talk, instead of that housewife routine. I know there's more there than just the housewife, but this is the first time you've ever really talked."

"There's nothing there for you, Ralph, so don't waste your time."

"You're really letting me have it, aren't you? What are you sore about? You're usually very polite and so forth."

"I hate to have people blow their horns at me."

"Mm. That's not it, but I see I'm doing myself no good. You going to be at the club this afternoon?"

"We might. I don't know."

"There's a football game on TV, and the reception's very good at the club. Bunch of us are going to be there. Few drinks. Maybe get up a pool. If you're lucky you might win a buck. I came away with two hundred dollars last week. A hat pool, based on the total score. All luck. You don't have to know anything about football."

"I never win."

"You might this time."

"Heavy *double entendre*."

"Well, what the hell, Marge? The way you said 'I never win.' That sounded like *double entendre*."

"Goodbye, Ralph."

"Thanks for the cigarette," he said.

She headed for home, thinking of her encounter with Ralph Shipstead. He was a loathsome man, who decorated his person with expensive haberdashery and surrounded himself with luxury, but never seemed quite dressed or established. It was not merely a matter of taste in his clothes or in the gadgeted house he had built, with its elaborate high-fi and heated pool and pitch-and-putt golf course. Nor was it that the money for it all had come to him. It was a more positive thing, that he belonged elsewhere, that he should

(353)

not have made money with his cleverness but with his muscles. If a pro football player could have made his kind of money, it would have seemed all right; but his money, she knew, had come from shrewd deals involving depletions and depreciations and dodges. At this moment he wanted her, and it excited her to think that in her present frame of mind he could almost have her. Almost.

She left the village behind her and began the slower drive along the narrow, twisting roads to her house. In a few minutes she was on Monument Road, more than a mile from her house but always when the car was once on Monument Road she would say to herself, "Practically home." She said it now, and she remembered that it was just about here less than an hour ago she had first sensed the involuntary act of defiance that she had made in taking the Fiat. She slowed down until the little car almost stalled, and she was angry with herself for abusing the engine. She stopped the car and switched off the engine, and she immediately understood this unusual act: she was delaying as long as possible her return to her house, and if anyone came along she would wave them on. She would not even offer a lame excuse. "Just go on and don't bother me," she would say—knowing that she would say nothing of the kind. But no one was likely to bother her at this hour. Between here and her house there were only the Martins, who never got their Sunday papers until after church; and the Greens, who always ate Sunday lunch at the club. What else did anyone want to know about the Martins and the Greens? She could tell them. Would anyone be interested to learn that Nannie Martin was thinking of changing to Presbyterian? Would the *Herald Tribune* send a reporter to interview Dixie Green if they knew that Dixie had once had a date with the gentleman who now sat in the White House?

She did not want to go home. The children would be up, messing around the kitchen, impatient because she had taken those few extra minutes to chat with Ralph Shipstead. And Allan would be in bed. Not really asleep, but not ready to get up. She knew how he would look when she went in to ask him if he wanted his breakfast: he would have his arms wrapped around a pillow and his pajamas would be drawn tight across his shoulder blades. Two hours ago he had made love to her and it had been all right. Oftener than not he made love to her on Sunday morning, and it was usually all right. Better than when he made love to her when they got home from a party like Ethel Canning's. After twelve years she had convinced him that she simply did not like to be made love to when he was tight. It had not actually taken twelve years to convince him of that. Twelve years was what they had been married. Five years was what it had taken her to convince him that alcohol did not make him a lover, and she conceded that in that respect he was considerate, even docile. Oh, in a lot of things he was considerate, when he was considerate. He was not mean, he was good about money, he was almost unquestionably faithful to her. By comparison he was a very good husband, and by comparison the children were dreams. But what was *she*, Marge Fairbanks? A secure wife, yes, and a conscientious mother, yes. But what else? But she, she, she? What was she, apart from husband and children, apart from Ralph Shipstead's mechanical lechery for her? And worst of all, what did she want, what could she be, other than what she had and what she was? Was this all? Was it worth it?

The drizzle on the windshield reminded her of tears, and she waited for the thought to bring the tears, but they did not come. She was not even that unhappy. She began to feel foolish and oddly conspicuous on this empty road. She sighed, and then turned the switch and pushed the starter button. The little car tried, but the engine would not start. She looked at the fuel gauge and the needle pointed to the far left. The son of a bitch! He hadn't even bothered to get gas.

She put the keys in her pocket and got out of the car, and as she began the homeward walk she kicked the front tire. It hurt her toe, and now she *could* cry, a little.

THE SUN-DODGERS

Back in the long nighttime of the Twenties and Thirties, when so many of the people I knew had jobs that made them sun-dodgers, Jack Pyne was known derisively as a mystery man. He was even called *the* mystery man, but it was not said in a way that would make you want to meet him or to inquire into the reason for calling him that. We all have our secrets, and Jack Pyne undoubtedly had his, but when he was referred to as a mystery man it was a term of contempt. In our set it was universally known that Jack Pyne made his living by peddling gossip to the Broadway columnists. They paid him no money, but Jack Pyne always had some chorus girls or bit players who paid him twenty-five dollars a week to get their names in the papers. The chatter writers would mention his clients in return for his acting as a spy or a messenger boy or procurer. You would be surprised to learn the names of some of the girls who once were clients of Jack Pyne. You might even be shocked and incredulous.

When business was good Jack Pyne sometimes had three or four clients, some of them paying him more than twenty-five dollars a week, and when business was exceptionally good Jack Pyne might have four individual clients, a second-rate night club, and a Broadway show. The night club seldom paid him any cash, but he was on the cuff there for meals and, within reason, free drinks for newspaper men. There were occasional periods when Jack Pyne probably had an income of close to two hundred dollars a week from the chorus girls and a hundred and fifty dollars a week as press agent for a musical comedy, in addition to the food and liquor he got free from the night clubs. It was in that way that he got the nickname of mystery man. "Who's Jack Pyne hustling for a buck now? The mystery man," someone once said. "Jack Pyne, the man of mystery."

We had favorite joints and favorite tables in the joints, and in the course of a single night, any night, we would move from a favorite table in one joint to a favorite table in one or two other joints, more or less according to a schedule. Jack Pyne always knew where we could be found at any hour between eleven P.M. and six o'clock in the morning. In our group there were, among the regulars, four or five newspaper men, a Broadway doctor, a Broadway attorney, one or two lyric-writers, a playwright, two or three press agents, a bookmaker, a detective from the Broadway Squad, sometimes a Catholic priest, a vaudeville actor turned sketch writer, a salesman for a meat packer, a minor poet, a real estate speculator, a radio announcer. At no time were all these men together at the same table, but they were the regulars of our group. There were other groups: the mobster group, the song-writing and music-publishing group, the gamblers, the minor hoods, and in the course of a night we might be visited briefly by members of the other groups, with the exception of the minor hoods. They kept to themselves because they did not want to go anywhere near a newspaper man; they did not want to be seen talking to a newspaper man. As a group, a class, they were the cruelest, stupidest, most evil men I have ever known, and I was afraid of them. I was not afraid of the big shots; they, with their new importance and power, generally behaved themselves in public, but the smallies, as we called the minor hoods, were unpredictable, reckless, and we knew the stories about them and their savagery. They were not all young men; some of them were in their forties and fifties, and I had a theory that the reason the older ones survived was that they had been out of circulation, in prison, and thus invulnerable to the high mortality rate among smallies.. It was not only a theory I had; some of them had been in prison before Prohibition went into effect and came out to find that highjacking and gang warfare paid better than armed robbery and felonious assault, and not only paid better but were safer in that prosecution had become more difficult and the mobs retained cleverer attorneys. A man who had gone to prison for homicide in 1916 and was released in ten years would discover that in his absence an almost ideal situation had been created. If he could make a connection with an established mob he might easily make a living on a standby basis, with nothing to do but remain on call until the mob had some punishment to dole out. And if the punishment involved murdering a member of an opposition mob, the legal authorities often could not or would not make an arrest. The smallies were killing each other off in private mob warfare, and if you noticed that one of the familiar faces was missing from the smallies' table, you could usually guess why. But you had to guess, most of the time. I didn't know many of them by name, although I knew them by sight, and even when their bodies were found in Bushwick or in Dutchess County, the newspaper photographs did not identify them for me. One man with half his face shot away and curled up in the back of a sedan looks much the same as another man who died in the same circumstances. A man who had been soaked with gasoline as well as stabbed or shot might be the missing face from the smallies' table, but I could only guess.

When the tabloids came out with stories and pictures of a mobster's murder the regulars at our table postponed discussion of it, but we could not help looking at the smallies' table to see how they were taking it. Sometimes their table would be vacant, which usually meant that one or more of the smallies had been picked up by the police and the others were in hiding. The big shots were always at their own table, gabbing away as though nothing had happened, and probably from their point of view nothing had; the murder we were reading about had been ordered weeks before, and the actual killing was old hat to the big shots. This was New York, not Chicago, and it has never ceased to amaze me how few of the real big shots got killed. But of course there is the old saying that generals die in bed, too.

If we often stole glances at the smallies' table, they in turn spent a lot of time staring at us. Plainly they resented us and our presence; obviously they thought we did not belong in the same joints that they frequented—and in a way they were right, but we were sun-dodgers and had no place else to go. If they had had their way they could easily have got rid of us, and without working us over. I know I would not have gone to a joint after being warned off by a couple of those hoods. They had a neat trick of pushing a man to the sidewalk, laying his leg across the curbstone, and jumping on it. No guns, no knives, no acid. They had a hundred other tricks, too, to maim or cripple people, of either sex, who got in their way. But the big shots' visits to our table gave us a sort of *laissez-passer*, which, though it increased the smallies' resentment of our presence, protected us from abuse. I must qualify that statement a little bit: they would not have abused the detective from the Broadway Squad. *He* abused *them*, sometimes beat them up just to keep in practice. But he was a special case, a terrifying man with fist and boot, and not really one of our group. Two things were always, always said of Tommy Callaghan: he was a law unto himself, and he led a charmed life. He has been written about in articles and in fiction, and I think there was even a movie that was more or less based on his career. His attitude and policy were expressed very simply. "I hate hoods," he would say, and he made no distinction between the big shots and the smallies. One of the biggest of the big shots always had to tip his hat to Tommy Callaghan, no matter where they ran into each other; at the fights in the Garden, at the race track, or in a hotel lobby. But this is not a repetition of the legend of Tommy Callaghan. In this chronicle he plays a minor part, and having introduced him I will go on until I need him later in the story.

However, since I have been rambling along with digressions where I felt like making them, I want to put in a warning to those readers who may still retain an impression of those days and those people that may be charming, but has nothing to do with the truth. Broadway really was not populated by benevolent bookmakers who gave all their money to the Salvation Army, and bootleggers who were always looking around for a paraplegic newsboy who needed surgery, and crapshooters who used their tees and miss-outs—crooked dice—in order to finance a chapel. There is something about the words rogue and rascal that brings a smile to the eyes of people who never spent any time with rogues and rascals. And I have never been able to accept the paradox of the prostitute who was faithful to one man. The big shots and the smallies that I saw—and I saw dozens of them—were unprincipled, sadistic, murderous bullies; often sexually perverted, diseased, sometimes drug addicts, and stingy. The women were just as bad, except when they were worse. The picture of a band of jolly Robin Hoods on Times Square is all wrong and not very romantic to those who knew that perhaps the most spectacular gambler of them all was nothing but a shylock—a usurer—and a fixer. And now back to Jack Pyne.

The joint that usually was our last stop before going home was a place called The Leisure Club, Fiftieth Street near Eighth Avenue, on the second story. It had several things to recommend it: it stayed open until nine o'clock in the morning; it was considered neutral territory by the important mob leaders; the booze was basically good liquor that had been cut only once; and it was not expensive. The Leisure offered no entertainment more elaborate than a colored piano player who also sang dirty songs. His name was Teeth, the only thing he would answer to. He played quite good piano, in spite of not having eighty-eight notes to work with. It was a studio piano, and he had to be inventive to do right by Youmans and Gershwin and Kern on an abbreviated keyboard. The dirty songs were the work of anonymous composers, and they were the same dirty songs that could be heard in little joints all over town, or parodies of songs by Cole Porter and Noel Coward. It was rather high-class stuff for a joint like The Leisure, most of it too subtle for the big shots and the smallies, but their girl friends liked it.

The Leisure had not caught on with the Park Avenue-Junior League-Squadron A crowd, probably because they would be flocking to Harlem at just about the same hour that The Leisure was showing signs of action. In any event, The Leisure was strictly a Broadway joint, not for post-

debutantes or squash players. It was for show people, newspaper men, various kinds of hustlers, and mobsters, in addition to the regulars whom I have already mentioned. Since
for most of the customers it was the last place before going
home, it was usually well filled, with no new male faces
from night to night. There were, of course, new girls from
the musical comedies and other night clubs, and women who
had come in from out of town; but some of these girls and
women soon became steady customers too.

At The Leisure our group gathered at a booth in the
middle of a row of booths. When we were more than nine
in number the waiters would put a table against the booth
table as an extension, but that seldom was necessary. We
hardly ever numbered fewer than five or more than nine,
and eight was the most comfortable; four on each side of
the table and two at the open end. I describe the seating
arrangements because I never saw anyone make room for
Jack Pyne. If he joined our table, he had to sit at the open
end. And I never heard anyone actually ask him to sit down.

He would come in, say a few words to the hatcheck
girl, and head for our table. "Hello, there, you muggs," he
would say.

Somebody would say, "Jack," and the others would
nod—or not nod. There was one fellow, a newspaper reporter, who would be a bit more loquacious. "Why, hello
there, Jack. We were just talking about you."

"Oh, yeah? What'd you say?"

"Just saying what a great fellow you were. We just got
finished taking a vote."

"Come off it."

"On the level. We're raising a little purse to send you
on a trip. Where would you rather go, Jack? Devil's Island?
You speak French, don't you, Jack?"

"Lay off, lay off, you muggs."

There was no insult he would not take, whether it concerned his honesty, his morals, his manhood, his appearance, or his methods of earning a living. The newspaper reporter who suggested Devil's Island (and who had first called him a mystery man) would mention an extraordinary sexual perversion and suddenly say, "What's it like, Jack? I hear that's what you go for." Always, when they were making a fool of him, he would pretend to think they were kidding him, as though they would only kid a man they were fond of. But it was all insulting, often straight-factual, and finally not very funny. We all had a crack at insulting Jack Pyne, but he was so totally lacking in self-respect and so completely unable or unwilling to make any kind of retort that we finally did lay off, and he became a bore. I think we began to hate him then. He was a bore, and a terribly cheap individual, and because we had given up the mean sport of insulting him, he convinced himself that he was one of the boys.

We all read the same newspapers and heard the same gossip, and that went for Jack Pyne. He had the same information we had out of the newspapers, but now he had opinions as well. He was one of the boys, and he would hold forth on politics and sports and other topics of the day, and I've never known anyone who could be so consistently wrong about everything. We would sit in glassy-eyed silence while he told us what he thought was going to happen at City Hall or the Polo Grounds or the Garden. And why. If there were only four or five of us at the table we would fiddle with matchbooks, make rings on the table with our highball glasses, and neither look at Jack nor say a word to him. Then when he had said his say we would resume talking, but not about the topic Jack had just discussed. We would not agree with him, we would not contradict him; we would simply ignore all he had said. Almost literally we were giving him the freeze. When our group was larger, when there were so many of us that the waiter added the extra table, Jack Pyne was no problem. The larger group always meant that one of the Broadway columnists was present, and Jack Pyne knew better than to interrupt their monologs. The Broadway columnists were his gods, his heroes—and his bread and butter.

You may wonder why we put up with Jack Pyne. The answer is easy: in the beginning he had been a pathetic clown, and later there was no way to get rid of him. And I guess we were not very selective on the late shift. The meat salesman was no Wilson Mizner, the radio announcer no Oliver Herford, the Broadway doctor no James Abbott MacNeill Whistler. We did not pretend to be the Algonquin Round Table, and there was no test of wit that a man had to pass to be welcome in our group. We were brought together by the circumstances of our jobs and their unconventional hours, and the attraction of convivial drinking. The married men among us never brought their wives, and the rest of us rarely brought a girl. Our conversation would have bored women, and women would have inhibited our conversation. From this distance I could not repeat one of our conversations, not so much because the talk was rough— although it was that—as because it was so immediately topical. It was lively, but evanescent, and the interruptions by Jack Pyne only gave us a chance to get our breath.

Then one night—say around four o'clock in the morning—the character of our meetings began to change. It was not something we noticed at the time, but I know now that the change began when one of the smallies came to our table and said to Jack Pyne, "Hey, Pincus, I want to talk to you." Jack got up and followed the gangster to an empty table. They talked for five minutes or so, and Jack came back to our table and the gangster returned to his group.

"Who's your friend, Jack?" said the newspaper reporter. "I don't remember seeing him before. Don't want to see him again, either."

"I went to school with him. We grew up together," said Jack Pyne.

"He didn't look as if he went to school very long."

"No. I knew him in sixth grade. Seventh grade. Around then," said Jack Pyne.

"He's been away?"

"I'll say he has. He was doing five to ten up the river. He only got out about a month ago."

"What was the rap, Jack?"

"Why, I guess it was felonious assault. I didn't ask him, but I remember hearing about it. I think he was up twice. I don't know. I don't know for sure."

"He knew you. He made you the minute you came in tonight."

"Yeah. Yeah, I guess he did. I guess he was kind of expecting me."

"What has he, got some little broad he wants you to get her picture in the paper?"

"I didn't say that, did I?" said Jack Pyne.

"You didn't say anything, but that's a pretty good guess, isn't it? Your fame has spread far and wide, Jack. You're getting somewhere. Who's the broad? We'll find out, so don't be coy."

"Ella Haggerty. She's in the Carroll show."

"Mixed up with a hood like that? She does better than that, Jack."

"Not now she doesn't, and she better not. He's stuck on her."

"She doesn't need you to get her picture in the paper. I know Ella. You guys know Ella Haggerty."

Some of us did, and some of us didn't.

"I know her myself," said Jack Pyne. "She recommended me. She told Ernie to hire me, and Ernie said he went to school with me."

"Small world. What's Ernie's last name?"

"Black, he goes by. Ernie Black. It used to be Schwartz."

"Well, what the hell? Mine used to be Vanderbilt, but Buckley's easier to remember. I'll tell you something, Jack. Your friend Ernie, whether it's Black or Schwartz, he's got himself a very expensive lady friend."

"I know that."

"You know whose girl she was for a couple of years."

"I know."

"And where he had her living and all that? Those fur coats and diamonds."

"I been to her apartment. I know all that," said Jack Pyne.

"You know all that. Then what's she doing with some smallie like this Ernie Black? You don't go from J. Richard Hammersmith to some cheap hood just out of stir."

"She did."

"She did, but you better find out why, and you better get your money in advance. The way I see it, Jack, you've got nothing but trouble ahead of you. This coffee-and-cakes mobster, he hasn't got enough dough to keep her in bath salts. So he's going to have to get big all of a sudden, and how do you get big in his racket? You know as well as I do. From where he is, you start by killing somebody. That's the only way to make a fast big score. Homicide."

"I know, I know," said Jack Pyne.

"And even then you don't get rich, unless you happen

to kill somebody very big. And if you kill somebody very big, you end up very dead. Jack, you ought to get out of this contract as quickly and as gracefully as you can."

"I can't," said Pyne. "I made a contract."

"Then leave town."

"Sure. Where would I go? My show closed Saturday and I got expenses."

"Well, if you don't want to take my advice, that's up to you," said Buckley.

"Who's the banker tonight?" said Jack Pyne.

"I am," I said.

Jack tossed me a five-dollar bill. "I had two drinks. Give me three bucks change."

I did so, and he left.

"You know," said Buckley. "I wouldn't be surprised if I accomplished something tonight. I think we finally got rid of the mystery man."

"Is that what you were doing?" I said.

"Sure. Everything I said was true, but Pyne hadn't looked at it that way. It just needed me to point out certain disadvantages."

Buckley was entirely correct. Days, then weeks, then years passed, and no more was seen of Jack Pyne. It was as though the sewer had swallowed him up. Our group, I have said, changed in character, and I may be putting too much emphasis on the effect Jack Pyne's disappearance produced. But there is no use denying the coincidence that the only time we were visited by one of the smallies, one of our number disappeared. We didn't talk about the coincidence, but one of the smallies had invaded our territory despite the implied protection we enjoyed from the big shots.

Several months after Jack Pyne vanished a body was fished out of the East River. It was identified as Ernie Black, *né* Schwartz, and the mutilations indicated to police that Black had been tortured in gangster fashion. I advanced the theory that we might soon be welcoming Jack Pyne back to the fold, but I was wrong. Wherever he had gone, he liked it better than The Leisure, and not long after that The Leisure itself was raided and permanently closed. We had to find a new late spot, and in so doing we lost some of our group and recruited some newcomers. Then I changed jobs and got married and moved to Great Neck, and began leading a very different life from the one I had known

That was more than thirty years ago. We have grandchildren now, and my wife and I last year bought a little house near Phoenix, Arizona. I have my retirement pay, a few securities, and an unsteady income from my writing. I occasionally sell a piece to a magazine and I have written two books, one of which did well as a paperback. Our two daughters are married and living in the East, and until about a month ago it looked as though we had it made. We liked Arizona; the climate suited us, we made new friends, we had no money worries, the future looked good. So did the past. Our new friends seemed to be entertained by my reminiscences of the old days, and now and then I could convert my reminiscences into an honest buck. For instance, I wrote a story about Ella Haggerty that I sold as fiction but was almost straight fact. Ella married a clarinet player in 1930 or '31 and shortly after that dropped out of sight. The piano player from The Leisure, the man known as Teeth, went to Paris, France, during the depression and became a great hit. He was married briefly to an English lady of title, and after World War II he was awarded the Medal of Resistance, which must have amused him as much as it did me. I had a letter from him in 1939. He was thinking of writing his memoirs even then, and he

particularly called my attention to his new name—Les
Dents. "It sounds like 'let's dance' if you pronounce it English style but I talk mostly French these days," he wrote.
Only one of the former big shots is still alive. He is living, I
believe, in Hot Springs, Arkansas. My friend Buckley, the
newspaper reporter, was killed in the War. He and another
correspondent, riding in a jeep in Italy, hit a land mine.
His old paper established the Buckley Scholarship at a
school of journalism, a memorial he would object to as he
hated the very word journalism. My friends of the old days
who have survived are in the minority, and Madge and I
have our aches and pains as well as the obituary pages to
remind us of the passage of time, but things were going all
right until last month, when one afternoon Madge came to
my workroom and said a man wanted to see me. "Who is
he?" I said.

"I didn't ask him his name, but he wanted to make
sure you had worked on the old New York *World*."

"Probably a touch," I said.

I went out to our tiny patio, and a man got up to greet
me. He was wearing a white sombrero, the kind that costs
about seventy-five dollars, and a gabardine coat and trousers
that in the West they call a stockman's suit. "You don't remember me?"

"I'm afraid I don't," I said.

"Well, I shouldn't have expected you to. It's a long,
long time," he said. Then, suddenly, he said: "Jack Pyne."

"Jack Pyne," I repeated. *"Jack Pyne?"*

"You think I was dead?"

"As a matter of fact I did," I said.

"Now you recognize me?"

"Yes, of course," I said. "Sit down. What can I get you
to drink?"

"Not a thing," he said. "I just happened to hear in a

roundabout way that you were living out here, so I took it in my head to look you up. I bought your book. You must be coining money. I see it every place I go. Airports. Drug stores. You coulda cut me in." He smiled to show he was joking. "I reccanized Ella Haggerty, and I said to my wife, I said I introduced him to her."

"But you didn't," I said.

"I know I didn't, but it impressed the hell out of my missus. Like we took a trip over to Europe a couple of years ago, and did you ever hear of the famous entertainer, Les Dents? You know who that is?"

"Yes. Teeth, from the old Leisure Club."

"Oh, you knew that. Well, he remembered me right off. I was twenty pounds lighter then. Good old Teeth. He sat and talked with the wife and I for a couple hours, and all those French people and the international set, they couldn't figure out who we were."

"What are you doing now, Jack?"

"Well, I got a couple of things going for me. Different things. I got my money all invested in various enterprises. I only live about ten miles from here. You ought to come and take a look at my place. You have a car, don't you? Or I could send one for you."

"We have a car," I said. "But, Jack, what ever happened to you? You just disappeared into thin air."

"You mean way back? Oh, I just took it into my head one night, what was I wasting my time sitting around those night spots. So I sold my business—"

"What business?"

He shook his head somewhat pityingly. "Jack Pyne. I had one of the first if not *the* first really successful public relations concerns. You know, your memory ain't as good as it ought to be. I noticed a couple things in your book. Sure it was fiction, but you sure did take a lot of liberties.

I mean, didn't you know Ella was my girl? I kept that dame for three years. She cost me a fortune. Maybe you were afraid I'd sue you for libel, but that's not the way I operate. I told my wife, I said this book was about an old girl friend of mine. That was before I read the book, and then she asked me which one was me and I said I guess you were afraid I'd sue you for libel. I wouldn't take an old friend into court. You ought to know me better than that."

"Well, I'll put you in my next book."

"No, don't do that. You don't have to make amends. But you and your wife come out and have dinner at my house and I'd like to straighten you out on those days. You remember Pete Buckley?"

"Sure."

"Always pestering me to meet Ella, but I said to him one night, I was glad to help him out any time he needed a send-in with one of those underworld characters. I knew them all. But it was one thing to tell my mob friends a guy was all right, and a very different story to introduce a thirty-five-dollar-a-week police reporter to my girl. I sent them a cheque when they had that memorial for Pete. Very sarcastic when he made his load, but a great newspaper man when he was sober. Great. No doubt about it." He stood up. "Old pal, I gotta see a couple executives downtown, but you and I are going to have a lot of fun together, cutting up the old touches. Right?"

We have not gone to his house, although we have heard it is one of the showplaces. But we see him a great deal. A great deal. He has found out where we are and he knows when we'll be home. It is a sad thing after so many years to have a house you love seem to turn into a night club table. Suddenly I miss Pete Buckley, too.

THINGS YOU
REALLY WANT

It was Friday, and because it was Friday, promptly at three o'clock the doorman announced that Mr. Miles's station wagon was at the door, and Mrs. Miles's personal maid told the doorman that They would be right down. And in a very few minutes They *were* down: Elsie Miles in her blue windowpane tweed cape and black beret; George Miles in his trench coat with hood and his Tyrolean hat. The motor was running; the heater was functioning. The doorman, Jim, saw to it that the wicker hamper and Mrs. Miles's Noah bag, her small black suitcase, and Mr. Miles's old cowhide and new pigskin attaché cases were nicely arranged on the floor of the station wagon.

"You didn't forget anything?" said George Miles.

"No," said Elsie Miles.

"Well, Jim, we're off," said George Miles.

"Have a nice weekend," said Jim.

George Miles pointed to a double-parked car just ahead. "One of our doctors left his motor running," he said.

"Yes sir, he does that," said Jim. "They all got something on their minds."

"Don't you think you'd better turn it off? Leaving a car unattended, with the motor running."

"He'll only give me a bawling-out," said Jim.

"Next time a police car comes around, just point to the doctor's Pontiac. You don't have to say anything. Just point. They'll take the hint. I think it's outrageous."

"Dangerous, all right," said Jim. "I guess you can pull out now, Mr. Miles. Nothing coming."

"So long, Jim," said George Miles.

"Goodbye, Jim," said Elsie Miles.

"Nice weekend," said Jim.

The next westbound street was two blocks north, and George Miles drove to it in silence. There he was stopped by a traffic light. "Doctors of all people ought to observe the rules," he said.

"No, there's no excuse for it," said Elsie Miles.

"What?"

"I said there was no excuse for it, the way that car was parked."

"Absolutely no excuse," said George Miles. "Aside from all the obvious dangers. Car running away. Some kid stealing it. And filling the air with carbon monoxide. It's the attitude of these doctors."

"*Hey, station wagon. Get the lead out!*" The driver of the car behind blew his horn and yelled, and Elsie Miles giggled.

"The light's changed," she said.

"Christ, *I* know it," said George Miles.

He did not again speak to her. They crossed Manhattan Island and the George Washington Bridge and more than half the width of New Jersey without saying a word.

"I forgot something," he said.

"You did? What?" she said.

"Aren't you going to gloat over it? *I* forgot something, instead of you?"

(374)

"I'm not going to gloat. What did you forget? Is it important enough to go back for?"

"It's important, but I'll be damned if I go back for it," he said. "It's my medicine."

"Your pills? Well then of course we'll go back. I'll drive if you want me to."

"Forget it."

"Not at all forget it. Let's watch for a pay station and the next one we see, we can stop and call the apartment and have Roger bring it out in the other car."

"I let him go home after lunch."

"Then let's just call him at home. He only lives out in Jackson Heights. Dear knows it won't kill him to work a few extra hours. You pay him enough."

"The company pays him."

"Well, then, he *gets* paid enough, whoever pays him."

"Oh, Roger puts in plenty of extra time," he said. "I have a more sensible idea."

"What?"

"When we get to Stroudsburg I'll stop in a doctor's office and get him to give me a prescription. It's just nitroglycerin. If he wants additional information he can phone Jack Cushman."

"Yes, I must say that makes more sense." She looked at him in the late afternoon light. "Do you feel all right?"

"Elsie, I wouldn't be at the wheel if I felt some kind of an attack coming on. I feel fine except that I feel embarrassed. I pride myself on not forgetting things, and I forgot the most important thing I own. Anyway, the most important when I need it."

"There's something I've been meaning to do, and when we get back Monday I'm going to do it," she said.

"What's that?"

"I'm going to ask Jack Cushman to write out a prescription for me. Your pills. And I'm going to carry it with me all the time, wherever we go."

"This is the first time I ever forgot them."

"I didn't intend that as any criticism of you, George. I'm going to ask Jack for two prescriptions. I'm going to have one filled, and carry the pills with me. And I'll save the other prescription."

"All right," he said.

The doctor in Stroudsburg was not in his office, but when he heard that the transient patient was George R. Miles he cut short his supper and arrived at the office in fifteen minutes. He was familiar with the kind of pills George R. Miles had left behind, but to be on the safe side he telephoned Dr. Cushman. "I've had the pleasure of meeting Dr. Cushman, but perhaps you'd better speak to him first," said Dr. Reeber.

"Jack, I'm sorry to trouble you, but I came away without my dynamite pills. I'm in Dr. Reeber's office, in Stroudsburg, P-A. I'm okay, but I didn't want to go up in the woods without the pills. Dr. Reeber is right here. I'll put him on."

Dr. Reeber was a study in dignified restraint, with the great John Cushman at the other end of the line, and George R. Miles in his office. He wrote out the prescription while talking with Cushman. "Thank *you,* Dr. Cushman. Pleasure talking to you again." Reeber tore the prescription off the blank and handed it to George R. Miles.

"How much do I owe you, Doctor?"

"Nothing. I wouldn't charge you anything—"

"Now, now, now, now, now, Doctor. I took you away from your supper, not to mention two long distance calls. I insist."

(376)

"Well—ten dollars."

"Ridiculous," said George Miles. "Make it a hundred dollars and send me a bill." He gave his address.

"Very well, Mr. Miles. I'll send you a bill," said Dr. Reeber. "You and Mrs. Miles on your way up to your camp?"

"Yes, we go there every weekend we possibly can."

"I've hunted over your land. I got a deer there last fall."

"Well, there're plenty of them."

"Yes, Senator Rossbach is a friend of mine."

"Oh, is Karl a friend of yours? You must get him to bring you up there when the trout season opens. You tell him I said to bring you, and be sure and stop in at the cabin. I've had to curtail my fishing and gunning the last couple of years, ever since I sprained my ankle. But we're there nearly every weekend that the roads are clear, October right through June. Then of course we go to the seashore. Well, Dr. Reeber, thank you very much, and don't forget about that bill."

"I'll say goodbye to Mrs. Miles," said the doctor.

Another half hour was wasted in having the prescription filled and in chatter with the pharmacist, who had immediately recognized the name of Reeber's patient. "That'll be fourteen dollars," said the pharmacist. "Be glad to send you a bill, if you like, Mr. Miles."

"Whatever you say," said George Miles. "Send it to the camp, or my New York address."

"Well, I guess you pay your bills from New York," said the pharmacist. "We'll open an account for you, with the address on the prescription."

"Thank you. Goodnight."

"Come in again," said the pharmacist.

Once more they were under way. "It's nice to be known," said Elsie.

"It has its advantages sometimes," he said. "As long as you remember it's the almighty dollar and not your own personal charm."

"Don't be so cynical, George."

"It's not cynical. It's just being realistic. You weren't in there to see Dr. Reeber when he was talking to Jack Cushman. You could see the wheels going around in his head. Apparently he's met Jack Cushman, without making much of an impression. But this time he has me in his office with him, and the next time he meets Jack you can bet he's going to mention tonight's little consultation."

"Other doctors worship Jack Cushman."

"Of course they do. I admire Jack, too. But let's face it, Elsie, I couldn't have got Jack on the phone so quickly if I'd been Joe Blow from Kokomo. Jack knows who I am, don't forget. Just as I know who Jack is and where he stands in his profession. He wouldn't be my doctor if he were just another Reeber."

"George, for all you know, Dr. Reeber may be hiding his light under a bushel."

"For all I know, but *you* don't believe that. Not for a minute, not for a fraction of a second."

"Well—maybe he was over-polite, but this must have been a big day for him. You as a patient, and having a conversation with the great John Cushman. Are you getting hungry?"

"Yes, and I'm looking forward to my four ounces of bourbon. I may even have five ounces. What have we got in the hamper?"

"You'll see when we get there."

"You always say that."

"You always ask the question," she said.

(378)

The caretaker had left everything ready for their arrival; logs and kindling in the fireplaces, ice cubes in the bucket, night lights on in cellar and hallways. "Otto never forgets a thing," said George Miles. "I think when I step down I'll make him chairman of the board."

"Well, if you do, I hope you can sneak me into the first meeting."

"Listen, Otto has such dignity that he could almost carry it off. Put him in a good suit, spend a few dollars in the barber shop. We have men on the board that don't look the part one bit more than Otto does. I suppose I could take him to one meeting and introduce him as the man from Krupp's and get away with it. But that will never happen."

"Why not?"

"Because Otto wouldn't do it. No matter how much I offered to pay him, he wouldn't sacrifice his dignity. In fact, he'd probably tell me to go to hell. When you're as good as Otto, you *can* tell people to go to hell. *I* can't tell people to go to hell, but Otto Lichtenwalner can. Do you realize that all Otto really needs is a hatchet?"

"And a gun."

"No, he doesn't need a gun. With a hatchet or an axe he can make a bow and arrows, with a bow he can start a fire. He can build lean-tos wherever he's going to need them. He can converse in two languages. He can have a well-balanced diet without poisoning himself. Salt-free, too."

"Don't start envying Otto. You go through this about once a year, usually when something's gone wrong at the office. What is it now?"

"Nothing special. Will you have your drink now, or when supper's ready?"

"You have yours and I'll get mine later. You can set the table, if you like," she said.

"That's one thing Otto does forget."

"Deliberately, I think."

"A subtle way of telling us to go to hell. Probably considers it woman's work."

George Miles set the table in the large room, which was furnished in cedar and oaken chairs and sofas, Navajo rugs and animal trophies. He lit the fire, poured a drink, and in five minutes of heat from the blaze he fell asleep with the empty glass in his hand.

She let him sleep for an hour. She had her own drink and a couple of cigarettes. She blew some smoke from the second cigarette under his nostrils, and he opened his eyes. He smiled. "Up to your old tricks," he said. "That'll always wake me. You could have a brass band in here, and I'd sleep through it. But one whiff of cigarette smoke. How long was I out?"

"Just over an hour, I think. About an hour."

"I needed that."

"I know you did, but now come and have supper. Go wash your face and don't go back to sleep, George."

"I could just close my eyes and not move till eight o'clock tomorrow morning."

"And be stiff as a board the whole weekend. Anyway, I'm hungry, so come on, please. Up, up."

"The chairman of the board as stiff as a board. Did I do any talking?" He rose and stretched, went to the kitchen and doused his face in cold water.

"The usual muttering. Why, did you dream?"

"Something about that doctor in Stroudsburg. He was telling me to go to hell and I wanted to hit him, but when I swung at him he drove away in an empty car. An empty car. I knew he was in the car, but I couldn't see him. Nobody was at the wheel."

"It makes more sense than most of your dreams."

(380)

"They make a lot of sense, but I can't put them into words. I forget them as soon as I begin to wake up." He laughed. "Then Jim, the doorman, he began telling me to go to hell. I thought at first it was Otto, but then I realized it was Jim."

"Put some more cold water on your face and come have your supper," she said.

"Oh, squab. Good," he said. "We haven't had that for a long time. Tomorrow let's take a walk down to the lower dam and see what the ice did to the footbridge. Last year, remember, the ice broke it in two."

"Was it last year?" she said.

"No, you're right. It was the year before. *No*, Elsie, I'm right. It was last year."

"I guess it *was* last year."

"Oh, yes. It was definitely last year. Do you want me to prove it to you?"

"I take your word for it," she said.

"It was last year because I wanted to go to work and fix it myself, but I was having to take it easy."

"On account of your sprained ankle," she said. "Why did you have to tell Dr. Reeber you had a sprained ankle?"

"How did you know I told him that?"

"He mentioned it when he was saying goodbye to me. You were putting on your coat."

"Well, why not tell him I had a sprained ankle? That's what I tell everybody."

"That's all right to tell people that don't know any better, but Dr. Reeber is a *doctor*. He *prescribed* for you. He knows you haven't got a sprained ankle."

"I might have a sprained ankle too, as well as a cardiac condition. There's no law of nature that says you can't have both."

(*381*)

"It's so unnecessary, making up stories. Eisenhower had that big operation. Ill-etis. Ill-eyetis. And Johnson, the Vice-President, everybody knows he has a heart condition. Even Kennedy, as young as he is, he was in the hospital for a year."

"That was his back. Elsie, let me handle my own illnesses. Let me decide how much my stockholders should know and shouldn't know. I'm perfectly willing to step down when I reach sixty, and not a word of complaint from me. If they started rooting out all the board chairmen that are in worse shape than I am, you'd see a real industrial revolution in this country."

"I don't know anything about that, George. All I know is you go to extremes to try to prove how healthy you are. Coming here every weekend—does Jack Cushman prescribe that? The long drive, in all kinds of weather?"

"Hap McTaggart drives down to Southampton every weekend, just about the same distance. And he's out there banging away at ducks. Playing poker for high stakes. And the food and the booze he puts away! Yet *he* has a cardiac condition."

"Maybe Rose McTaggart doesn't care what happens to *her* husband."

"Well, if you put it that way I guess I can't argue with you. And maybe if I were married to Rose, I'd just as soon conk out in a duck blind. Maybe that's what Hap's doing, I don't know. But *I'm* not. I take very good care of myself. I don't overdo. And coming here weekends, just the two of us, I figure another fifteen months before I step down. These weekends and two long vacations, enough rest and relaxation from tension."

"Then hereafter don't bring two attaché cases full of business papers."

"Only one full of business papers. The other, the old one, that has other things in it."

"I can imagine what other things. The George R. Miles Foundation. The Phi Gamma Delta scholarship."

"Those things relax me. Some men like mystery stories. They bore the pants off of me . . . How many of these little birds did you cook?"

"Two."

"I could eat another. See? My appetite's fine. Elsie, I think you're the one that needs to relax."

"Only when we come here. I'm relaxed the rest of the week."

"Well, another year and a half, fifteen months, and we can both relax at the same time. I want to go to Hong Kong. I want to go to Hong Kong, and I want to spend three weeks in Scotland. I'd like to spend all fall at Ann Arbor, just watching the team develop. Get to know the individual players. Like to see more of the grandchildren. And I want to read up on the Civil War. Not just the battles. I want to decide for myself what the economic factors were. For instance, did you ever know that there was a hell of a ruckus outside of the Somerset Club? The Somerset Club, in *Boston*, because some of the members objected to a parade going by, and they pulled down the shades. That's Boston, mind you. A parade of soldiers on their way to fight the Confederates. They say it was worse than the time the old Union Club displayed a Union Jack during a St. Patrick's Day parade. I want to look into all these things, things I never had time for. You'd enjoy Hong Kong, wouldn't you?"

"Of course I would."

"And seeing more of the grandchildren. And with a name like Stewart, you'd enjoy Scotland. Maybe we ought to use your maiden name while we're there. If we were

Spanish, you know, our kids would be called Miles y Stewart. Not the letter *e*. The letter y, Spanish for *and*. Miles and Stewart."

"I know," she said.

"Do you want help with the dishes?"

"No thanks, not tonight."

"You sure?"

"Positive," she said. She stood up and looked at him. "Do you know what I wish you *would* do for me?"

"What?"

She looked at him again, and knew she could not say what she had intended to say. "Buy me something."

"You mean something in particular?"

"Yes."

"What?"

"A nice pin, with a ruby in it."

He laughed. "Got it all picked out, eh?"

"Yes," she said.

"All right," he said. "I don't see why not. There aren't many things you really want, are there?"

"Not many," she said.

TWO TURTLEDOVES

O'Brien rose from his chair, folded his newspaper, took off his glasses and reached for a bottle of rye, saying, "The same?"

"The same it'll be," said Kane. "Don't hardly seem worth staying open."

"Oh, we'd a good crowd earlier," said O'Brien, filling a shot glass. "A lot of them went home to watch the midnight Mass on TV."

Kane grinned. "Why don't you have your own set on? You'd of kept them here."

"That I won't have. One or two suggested it, but a saloon is no place to be watching Mass."

"I was only joking," said Kane.

"Why's it you're not home watching?" said O'Brien.

"Christmas Eve's no different to any other in my line of work," said Kane. "I just come from a lady's apartment over on the Boulevard. One of her kids dropped a whole wad of wrapping paper, thick heavy stuff, down the bowl. There was water half an inch deep all over the bathroom floor."

"How would she know your home phone number?"

"I got an answering service."

"Oh, sure. I never thought of that."

"Wait'll she sees her bill," said Kane.

"You're gonna give it to her good?"

"She can afford it. One of them apartments with three bathrooms, over on the Boulevard."

"I can remember when there was only private houses there. The Park Avenue of Jersey City."

"Not that I minded going out. The wife has her two sisters and their husbands to our place. Trimming the tree. Trimming the *tree*! You should see the size of the tree. It's no more than thirty inches high and it ain't even wood. Some kind of a plastic proposition. You could trim it in ten minutes' work. But you've a nice tree, Bob."

"Not as big as some I had in years past, but it's a nice spruce."

"Who trimmed it for you?"

"The day fellows. It's been up over a week."

"It's over a week since I was in."

"Drink up and have one," said O'Brien, with the rye bottle poised.

"Well, bein's it's Christmas. Merry Christmas, Bob."

"The same to you and many of them, John. I think I'll have one myself," said O'Brien.

"This is an occasion."

"I think I'll close up early. I was expecting some of the lads from the post office, but it don't look like they're coming after all."

"It don't always pay to be accommodating."

"Oh, I wasn't only waiting for them," said O'Brien. He lowered his voice. "I got a man and a woman in the back room in one of the booths. They been there since before ten o'clock."

(*386*)

"You'd think they'd go to a hotel."

"Oh, there's none of that. I won't have that in my place. These are just a man and woman in their forties, sitting there and talking and looking at one another."

"Do you know them?"

"I seen him come in once in a while. She's a stranger to me. He come in a little before ten and went straight back to the back room, and then a few minutes later she drove up in a taxi. Nobody here knew her or him. And now they been sitting and talking for over three hours. Well, just about three hours. There's nothing going on. They ain't even sitting on the same side of the table, and a couple times I went in and they weren't even talking."

"Well, you're accommodating *them*. Does it pay?"

"You mean are they spending? Well, they got a bottle of good Scotch on the table, and they bit quite a hole out of it, and take a look at this." O'Brien reached in his vest pocket and held up a neatly folded fifty-dollar bill. "For Christmas, he says, but it ain't for Christmas. It's for leaving them be."

"Nobody around here gives fifty-dollar bills to saloon-keepers," said Kane. "You don't know what he does for a living?"

"He looks like some kind of a professional man. A lawyer, maybe, or a doctor. A professional man, though."

"A politician?"

O'Brien grinned. "Oho, no. Is there a politician I don't know?"

"Maybe mixed up in one of the rackets?"

"I thought of that, but other times when he come in he didn't seem to be acquainted with the racket guys. He never spoke to them and they never had anything to say to him."

"A man of mystery."

"Not even that. I size him up for a professional man, and him and her wanted to be together on Christmas Eve."

"Where was the taxi from?" said Kane. "From around here?"

"I didn't take notice to that, I was too busy. I just happened to see her get out and come right in. I guess she paid the driver before she got out."

"Very likely gave him a bill and told him to keep the change," said Kane.

"Very likely."

"You aroused my curiosity. Is it all right if I go back and have a look at them?"

"If you want to. But now don't interfere with them or anything like that. He gave me the fifty bucks."

"Listen, I won't bother them. I just want to have a look."

Kane sauntered to the back room and returned in a minute or so, shaking his head. "Never saw him or her before in me whole life. But I think she's getting a crying jag on."

"No," said O'Brien. "She looked that way two hours ago. It's no jag."

"A married woman and he wants her to leave her husband," said Kane.

"Maybe."

"Two people that promised to meet each other every Christmas Eve."

"Maybe that. I don't know."

"Or maybe they never seen one another before this afternoon and he's on the make."

"That I don't believe."

"Me either, but anything's possible. Maybe they used to be husband and wife."

"Yes, that I thought of. One of them married again but one not."

"I got a brother a detective in Paterson, but my wife says I should of been the detective and him the plumber . . . She's no hooker."

"No, I can spot them. This woman's no hooker."

"I didn't think so, either. Anyway, a hooker'd have a room to take him to."

"One look'd tell you she was no hooker."

"Does he have a car? You could tell something from that if he had a car."

"I never seen him get out of a car. He only come in here about a half dozen times before."

"She looks as if a Cadillac wouldn't be too much for her."

"A Cadillac or one of them," said O'Brien.

"The funny thing to me is a woman like her coming here on Christmas Eve. Not that I'm knockin' the place, Bob."

"You don't have to apologize. I got no illusions."

"I'm pretty convinced that she's the married one, but how did she get away from her family for all Christmas Eve?"

"Well, you had to fix somebody's toilet on Christmas Eve."

"How do you mean that, Bob?"

"Oh, hell, I don't know. You know what let's do? Let's just leave them be."

"All right," said Kane. He studied O'Brien. "You taking umbrage, Bob?"

"I'm not taking anything, but they're not bothering nobody, so you and me have a drink and then I think I'll close up."

"Close up, then," said Kane. "I can pay for me own drinks." He pulled his leather cap down squarely on his head and went out.

O'Brien put on his glasses, picked up his newspaper, and returned to his chair at the end of the bar.

WINTER DANCE

When the big Packard Twin-Six came rumbling into view
it was an exciting sight to the boy. The radiator and hood
had a leather cover that was streaked with ice. Strapped to
the spare tires at the rear of the car was a long-handled
shovel, crusted with snow. Icicles hung from the fenders,
and the running-boards carried an extra thickness of frozen
slush. All the side curtains were securely in place. The windshield was solid ice except for an arc, directly in front of
the chauffeur, which the manually operated wiper had kept
partially clear. The heavy car moved slowly as the tire
chains bit into the snow. You could not see the spokes of
the artillery wheels; they were hidden by a disc of ice and
snow. But the big car had made it, as it nearly always made
it in spite of the winter in the mountains. Now, moving
slowly along South Main Street, the car made the boy think
of those trains in the far West that were drawn by two and
three locomotives up and through the mountain passes.
There was something triumphant and majestic now in the
way the big Packard eased its way along South Main. Here
it was safe and sound, the dignified winner over fifteen miles
of narrow, winding mountain roads and the hazards that
winter could put in its way.

The boy watched the Packard until it came to a stop

ten feet from the curb but as close as it could get to Winkleman, the furrier's.

"There goes your girl, Ted."

"Aw, shut up," said the boy.

"She's stopping at Winkleman's. Why don't you go in and price his coonskins? He has a coonskin in the window."

"And a card on it saying three hundred dollars," said the boy.

"Well, ask him if he's got any for less."

"In front of her?" said the boy.

"Okay. I was only trying to be helpful."

"We could take a walk down and have a *look* at the coat," said the boy.

"And wait till she comes out? She may be all day. Go on in and try it on."

"Winkleman knows I'm not in the market for a coonskin," said the boy.

"Listen, for Christ's sake, Ted. This is your best chance to talk to her. You know where she's probably going from there."

"I know."

"You want to talk to her, don't you?"

"Sure," said the boy.

"And not with the older crowd."

"Yes," said the boy.

"Well, you won't be able to get her away from the older crowd. Even if you cut in on her, they won't let you get two steps with her."

"Shall we take a walk down to Winkleman's?" said the boy.

"Give her a few seconds to get out of the car and inside of the store."

"That's a good idea. We'll wait till she gets inside,"

said the boy. "But then I don't know what to say."

"Just strike up a conversation."

"That's easier said than done," said the boy. "Think of something."

"Well, just casually sidle up to her and say, 'Oh, hello, Natalie. Going to the tea dance?' And she'll say, 'Yes, are you?' "

"End of conversation," said the boy.

"Not necessarily. Ask her where she's staying tonight."

"I know where she's staying, and anyway, she'll think it's kind of fresh. It's none of my business where she's staying," said the boy.

"Well, have you got some money with you?"

"Dollar and forty, forty-five cents."

"That's enough. Ask her if she wants a hot chocolate. She just had a cold ride, and I'll bet she'd welcome a hot chocolate."

"*I've* never asked her to have a hot chocolate."

"What if you haven't? You have to start sometime, you dumb bastard. I'll bet she'd give anything for a hot chocolate. That's a cold ride, believe you me. And even if she says no, at least she'll give you credit for being considerate. My sister Kit, I've heard her say a hundred times, next to a good dancer, if a boy's considerate."

"She's liable to think I'm too young to buy her a hot chocolate. She's at least twenty."

"You have a dollar and forty cents. A hot chocolate will set you back fifteen cents. She knows fifteen cents won't break you. Maybe she won't even think of that, if she *wants* a hot chocolate. She's probably half frozen."

"No. They have one of those charcoal heaters, and sixty-five robes. It's as warm in her car as Mrs. Hofman's limousine."

"How do you know?"

"Because last year she gave us all a ride home from tobogganing."

"Natalie?"

"Well, not Mrs. *Hofman*. Huh. Fancy that, Mrs. Hofman giving us a ride in her limousine. I'd like to see *that*."

"Well, she's inside. Now's your chance."

"I wish it was some other store," said the boy. "I don't like to go barging in Winkleman's. That's a woman's store."

"He has a man's raccoon coat in the window. And who else is going to buy a raccoon if we don't? Not my *father*. Not *your* father. Maybe Winkleman will think you're getting one for a Christmas present. *I* am, but not this year."

"Oh, I'm getting one, next year or the year after," said the boy.

"Well, then you have a good excuse."

"The only trouble is, Winkleman will start waiting on us, and then how do I get to strike up a conversation with *her*? 'What can I do for you, boys?' And then I barge over and ask her if she wants a hot chocolate. Boy, will she see through that. She'll know we followed her in, and she'll be sore as hell."

"She'll be so busy she won't pay any attention till you speak to her. Didn't you ever go shopping with a woman?"

"Oh, you know so much about everything, you make me sick."

"You're the one that makes me sick. What's the worst she can do? Chop off your head and put it on a pikestaff? The positively worst she can do is say, 'No thank you, Ted. I do not wish a hot chocolate.' "

"If I thought for sure she wanted a hot chocolate," said the boy. "Maybe she's not going to stay in there very long. By the time we get there maybe she'll be just leaving.

Nobody gets to the tea dance before six. She's spending the night at Margery Hill's. If they all left at half past five, they'll be at the club around six. If she has to change her dress, that'll take her at least a half an hour. Five o'clock. I'm trying to dope out whether she's going to be in Winkleman's long enough. And anyway, maybe she's going some place else besides Winkleman's. I don't think Winkleman's is such a good idea. I'll bet she has other places to go. No, she wouldn't have time for a hot chocolate."

"Well, you're right. She's leaving Winkleman's. Let's see where she goes."

The girl in her six-buckle arctics came out of the fur shop, stepped into the snowbank and got in her car. The boy and his friend watched the big Packard moving slowly southward and turning west into Lantenengo Street. They did not speak until the car was out of sight.

"Well, you're fifteen cents ahead. Buy *me* a hot chocolate."

"You just had one," said the boy.

"I could polish off another."

"Oh, all right. Then what? Shall we start for the club?"

"Christ, it's only twenty after four."

"I have to pick up the kid sister. The old man wouldn't let me have the car unless I dragged her. *They* want to get there *early*. They *always* want to get there early."

"Yeah, they don't want to miss anything. What's there to miss before six o'clock? But what do *you* want to get there early for?"

"Because my damn kid sister wants to, and my old man said I had to," said the boy. "And I have to dance the first dance with her, and if she's left in the lurch I have to dance with her, and when she's ready to go home *we* have to go home. God damn it I wish I had my own car."

(395)

"I'm getting one when I graduate. I don't know whether
I want a Ford or a Dodge."

"New or second-hand?"

"Brand-new."

"The Dodge costs more, but around here you need a
Ford for the hills," said the boy.

"Yeah, but I wouldn't use it much around here. I'd use
it mostly in the summer, and the Vineyard's practically all
flat."

"I never thought of that," said the boy. "Well, I guess
we ought to get started."

"Where's your car?"

"Henderson's Garage. The old man left it there to get
new chains put on. Finish your hot chocolate. You'll get
plenty at the club, free."

"It'll have skin on it. Christ, I hate skin on hot chocolate. It makes me puke."

"You're so delicate," said the boy.

"Well, do you like it?"

"No," said the boy. "But I have sense enough to drink
tea."

The orchestra was playing "Rose of the Rio Grande,"
a fine fox trot with a melody that could just as easily have
had a lyric about China, and the next tune *was* about Chinese—"Limehouse Blues." The band was just getting started,
and trying to fill the dance floor.

"Stop trying to lead," said the boy.

"Oh, you stop being so bossy," said his sister. "Why
are you so grouchy? Because your girl isn't here? Well, here
she comes."

"Where?"

"In the vestibule. All the older crowd. Margery Hill
has a new hat. Oh, isn't that becoming?"

" 'Oh, isn't that becoming?' You sound like Mother."

"And you sound like the Terrible-Tempered Mr. Bangs. Oh, hello, Ralph. Are you cutting in on my adorable brother? Teddy, dear, will you relinquish me?"

"Thanks for the dance," said the boy. He joined the stag line and lit a cigarette.

"Got a butt?"

"Hello, Jonesy. Sure," said the boy, offering a pack.

"Your girl's here. Just got here a minute ago."

"Oh, crack wise," said the boy, and turned away. Presently the fellows from the older crowd gathered in the vestibule, waiting for the girls to come downstairs from the ladies' dressing-room.

"Hello, Teddy," said Ross Dreiber.

"Hello, Ross," said the boy.

"Why aren't you out there tripping the light fantastic? Looking them over?"

"Just looking them over."

"Any new talent? I see your sister. She fourteen?"

"Fifteen."

"Fifteen. Well, I'll be out of college by the time she's allowed to go to proms. But she certainly has sprung up since last summer."

"Sure has."

"What have you got? Two more years?"

"One more after this," said the boy.

"Then where?"

"Lafayette, I guess. Maybe Princeton."

"Well, when you get ready to go, if you decide on Lafayette, I'd be glad to write a letter to our chapter there. You know you can't go wrong with Deke, anywhere. What was your father?"

"Theta Delt."

(397)

"Well, I have nothing to say against Theta Delt. They're a keen organization. But take a look at Deke before you shake hands. And think twice about Princeton, boy. I know a lot of good eggs were awfully disappointed they went to Princeton. Take my word for it. But of course it all depends on the man."

"Yeah. Sure."

"Have you got another butt on you? . . . Omars! My brand! Deke for you, boy. You even smoke the right cigarettes."

The boy held a match to Dreiber's cigarette.

"*Hello, Teddy.*"

He turned. "Hello, Nat," he said.

"Finish your cigarette, Ross. I'll dance with Teddy. Or are you waiting for somebody?"

"No, I'm not waiting for anybody. But do you mean it?"

"Of course I do. Come on," she said.

"Probably get about two steps," said the boy.

"Well, then let's walk down to the other end of the room and start from there. Shall we?"

"Fine," said the boy.

She took his arm and they marched to the far end of the room. She greeted friends along the way, but said nothing to the boy. Then she held up her arms and said, "All right?" and they began to dance. He was good, and he had self-confidence because he was good. She was good, and she liked dancing with him. There was no need to talk, and at this end of the room people got out of their way. They got all through two choruses of "Stumbling" before the music stopped. "Oh, that was grand," she said. She applauded with him.

"Shall we sit down?" said the boy.

(398)

THE WOMEN OF
MADISON AVENUE

Mrs. Dabner walked boldly if not bravely up Madison Avenue, thinking of how she would look to someone in a bus. How often, when she came to New York, she would be in a Madison Avenue bus and see a woman like herself—nice-looking, well-dressed, late-thirtyish, early-fortyish—and wonder what the woman was doing, where she was bound, what she was thinking. "I'll bet I know a lot of people you know," she would say to that woman. "I'll bet we could sit down together and inside of five minutes—why, we might even be related."

There were always so many attractive women on Madison Avenue after lunch. They would come in pairs from the restaurants in the upper Fifties and the Sixties, say a few words of farewell at the Madison Avenue corner, and go their separate ways, the one on her way to the hairdresser or to finish her shopping, the other deciding to walk home. So many of them were so attractive, and Ethel Dabner liked to look at them from her seat in the bus. But today she was walking, and inside one of those buses, looking at her, possibly thinking how attractive *she* was, might be the one woman in New York who had good reason to hate her. Ethel Dabner did not like people to hate her, and if she could ever sit down and have a sensible talk with Laura

"Well, I think I'd better find our crowd."

"Don't do that, Nat. Please?" said the boy.

"No, Teddy. I must, really," she said. "Cut in later."

"Couldn't we just sit down a minute?"

She shook her head. "You know they'll only kid you."

"Oh, you know that?"

"Uh-huh. They kid me too, don't forget."

"They do? Who does?"

"Oh, my crowd. Same as your crowd kids you."

"You're not sore at me because they kid you?"

"Of course not. And don't you be embarrassed, either."

"You know it's all my fault, Nat," said the boy.

She hesitated. "You mean on account of the postcard?"

"I showed it to everybody. I shouldn't have."

"Well, if I felt like sending a friend of mine a post-card," she said.

"But I went around bragging about it, and showing it to everybody."

"Well, if you wanted to. I don't even remember what I said on the card."

" 'You would love it here. Lots of good trout fishing. Have gone on two pack trips. See you at Christmas. Natalie.' And a picture of the ranch."

"I remember," she said. "Not very incriminating, was it? Will you take me over to their table now, Teddy?"

"And your word of honor you're not annoyed with me."

"Only if you let them embarrass you," she said.

"Nat?"

"What?"

"I don't have to say it, do I? You know, don't you? You do know?"

She nodded. "Give me your arm," she said.

(*399*)

Howell she could make Laura realize that she really had no reason to hate her. But how long since anyone had been able to sit down and have a sensible talk with Laura Howell?

Ethel Dabner turned her head to look at a crowded bus, but what was the use of looking for a woman she had never seen?

At Sixty-fourth Street she left Madison Avenue and was glad to leave it, with its crowded buses and all those women, one of whom could have been Laura Howell. She let herself in the ground-floor apartment and was relieved, though not surprised, to find that she was alone. Half past three, he had said, and that was half an hour away, but sometimes he was early and invariably he was punctual. "I may even be a little late today," he had said. "I don't know how long this meeting'll last, but if I'm still in there at ha' past three I'll get word to you."

"You'll get word to me? How will you get word to me? You can't tell your secretary to call me and say you'll be late."

"No, but . . ."

"But what?"

"Well, I was thinking," he said. "I can tell Miss Bowen to call this number and have her say that Mr. Howell would be late for his appointment with Mr. Jenkins."

"Who's Mr. Jenkins?"

"There is no Mr. Jenkins, but you're Mr. Jenkins's secretary. Do you see? You'll answer, and Miss Bowen will think you're Mr. Jenkins's secretary."

" 'Tisn't worth the bother. You just get here when you can."

"Well, just so you understand I may be a little late."

"Honey, I understand. All you have to do is tell me you'll be a little late."

He was so careful, so elaborate, so—as he put it—
ready for any and all contingencies. The simple thing, to
meet her in her hotel, was too simple for him. "I could
run into sixty-five thousand people in your hotel," he had
said. "I could just be *seen* there, without knowing who saw
me." And so there was this apartment, rented by his bachelor son who was now in the army. "I told Robbie I'd
keep it for him while he was away, for when he got leave."

"Who do you think you're kidding? Doesn't he know
you want it for yourself?"

"If he wants to guess, but he's on my side."

"One of these days we'll be there and the door'll fly
open and there'll be your son and a half dozen of his G.I.
buddies."

"No. He'll have a little problem of getting the key. I
took care of *that* contingency."

"What's to prevent someone seeing me leave the apartment? Did you take care of that contingency?"

"How many people do you know in New York?"

"Half the girls I went to school with and a lot of their
husbands. First *and* second husbands, if it comes to that."

"All right. You're in town for a visit. Couldn't you be
calling on someone on East Sixty-fourth Street? Someone
they don't know?"

"I guess I could. I guess so."

It was a strange apartment for such goings-on. From
the beginning she had felt as though they had invaded the
dormitory rooms of a sophisticated undergraduate. There
were a few college souvenirs: an initiation paddle marked
D.K.E., some group photographs, some pewter mugs and
silver trophies; but the pictures on the walls were esoteric
moderns, the statuettes unidentifiable forms in ebony and
aluminum, and hanging above the fireplace a small collec-

tion of Polynesian stringed instruments. In the bathroom there was an explicit drawing of a nude, that seemed to have been cut rather than drawn, the lines were so sharp, and the nakedness of the woman offended Ethel Dabner. It was a *map* of a woman, without mystery, without charm, without warmth or even sensuality, and she hated the drawing and the German who had made it, so much so that she based her dislike of her lover's son on the fact that he would own such a picture.

She hung her street clothes in Robbie's closet, in among the plastic-covered civilian suits and the treed shoes. She put on his kimono and went to the kitchen and filled a bucket with ice cubes from the nearly empty refrigerator. Burt would want a Scotch and soda when he arrived, and now she had nothing to do but wait.

If he had been his usual punctual self he would be here now; it was half past three. But in spite of having been forewarned, she was annoyed to find that at three-thirty-two he had not arrived. He was two minutes late, and she had had to fish in her purse for glasses in order to read the time on her wristwatch. Her watch, her rings, her bracelet, her necklace lay on the coffee table, and she thought of taking them to the bathroom and leaving them on the glass shelf, where they would be all together in one place when she was ready to put them on again. But she had no desire to go back to the bathroom; she had a desire *not* to go back to the bathroom and that nasty drawing.

Every little sound she made was distinct in the silence of the apartment, but in a little while the outside street noise began to break up into individual sounds, notably the sounds of the buses starting and stopping. There were the other sounds, too, but her ear kept going back to the special sounds of the buses, and she thought of the women on the buses, looking out at the women who walked, the attractive, well-dressed women who had decided to walk home after a pleasant, happy lunch with a woman friend. What would she be thinking about, the attractive woman who was walking home? How nice it was to have Jane Jones for a friend? How well Jane looked? She would walk up Madison Avenue, this woman, with a little smile on her face because she was thinking of her friend Jane Jones, and that was one of the things that would make her attractive, that smile of appreciation for her friend. People in the buses would look out at her and think what an attractive woman she was, a woman other women could trust.

Fourteen minutes to four, and the telephone rang. "Hello," she said, then, remembering: "Mr. Jenkins' office."

There was a loud laugh at the other end. "It's me," he said. "I just broke up the meeting. I told those bastards we had to wind it up by quarter to four, so I'll be right there, honey."

"Well, you just hurry, d'you hear?" she said.

"Listen, I'm just as eager as you are," he said.

"I didn't mean that," she said. "I'm just tired of sitting here all by myself in this apartment."

"Shouldn't take me but twenty minutes," he said.

"All right," she said, and hung up.

So sure of himself, so sure of her, whichever it was, she hated it. She hated what he took for granted, that she wanted and needed him, was as eager as he was. And now she found that a decision had been made for her; he had not made it, she had not made it, but it was there and only needed to be acted upon. She got all dressed again and satisfied herself that anyone seeing her from the bus would consider her very attractive and nice. She took the nasty picture down from the bathroom wall and put it face down on the floor and stamped on it. She next put the apartment key on the coffee table near the ice bucket, and for the last time she left the apartment.

In the bus she got a seat next to the window and at Sixtieth or maybe it was Sixty-first Street an attractive, nice-looking woman walking up Madison happened to look in the window and catch her eye. Ethel Dabner smiled and bowed, and the nice-looking woman smiled back.

YOU DON'T REMEMBER ME

The question was sometimes asked about Stan Wigmore: "Has he any money of his own?" It was a mean question, because the people who asked it were generally well aware that Stan Wigmore had some money of his own, but not very much, and nowhere near as much as Dee Wigmore. You would hear the question after Stan had been in some escapade or was more offensive than usual, and it was not so much a query for information as a criticism and a protest. The comparative financial status of Stan Wigmore and of Dee was his most vulnerable aspect, and it provided comfort for those who had been recently shocked or offended by him.

It was, therefore, highly irregular for Mary Chorpenning to have replied to Jack Spangler when he asked the usual question. The scene was the beach club; the time, about two o'clock one Sunday afternoon in the early part of the summer. Stan Wigmore, alone, wearing a Hong Kong pajama suit and Paisley scarf, no socks, and highly polished alligator loafers, had a plate of food in one hand and a tall iced coffee in the other, and he was looking around for a place to sit. After a quick and rather expert appraisal of the crowd he went to a table where there were four young people and two vacant chairs. He asked if he could sit with them, and they nodded. He did not attempt to make conversation with the young people. He ate his food and sipped his iced coffee, taking quick looks at the other tables and out at the ocean while ministering to his appetite. The young people remained silent as he hurried through his lunch, wiped his mouth with a paper napkin, lit a cigarette and departed. The moment he left the young people's table they relaxed into the frenetic weariness that is their current mode; in the minutes, fewer than ten, that he had been with them they had sat stiffly, watching him raise fork to mouth as though observing some new and alien custom.

Wigmore, cigarette in hand, walked up to the top of the dune, speaking to no one on the way, and slowly but uninterruptedly scanned the bathers on the beach who had not come up for lunch. He saw, or did not see, what or whom he was looking for, then abruptly he turned his back to the ocean and walked rapidly away in the direction of the club entrance, out and down the road to a hulking new Bentley saloon.

The group about the umbrella table watched him drive off in the big green car, and Jack Spangler was the first to speak. "Stanley M-for-Martin Wigmore," said Spangler. "Has he any money of his own?"

"Well, he has enough so he doesn't have to go on living with Dee," said Mary Chorpenning.

"He has? I didn't realize that," said Spangler. "When did that happen?"

"He always did have," said Mary Chorpenning.

"Now how the hell would you know a thing like that?"

"*You* must have known it at one time. He was never starving."

"Oh, that's different," said Spangler. "I thought you were trying to say he had some secret fortune of his own."

"Not at all. But enough to live on," said Mary Chorpenning.

"To live on. The subsistence level. But not Bentleys. No ninety-dollar shoes," said Spangler. "You're not telling us anything new, Mary, but I'm curious to know why you're defending him all of a sudden."

"I'm not defending him. Only making a statement of fact. Stan Wigmore has always had some money of his own," said Mary Chorpenning.

"And about thirty million dollars of Barlow money via Dee," said Spangler. "And he needs every cent of it to get away with what he gets away with."

"Well, now, why? What's he done now?" said Agnes Lamb.

"Who do you suppose he was looking for so casually a minute ago?" said Spangler.

"I don't know," said Agnes Lamb. "I've been away."

"I'm almost afraid to mention it in front of Mary," said Spangler. "Mary seems to be on some defensive kick about him. So you tell her, Mary."

"The Maclyn girl," said Mary Chorpenning.

"Kitty Maclyn?"

"That's what they say," said Mary.

"But she's only about seventeen, isn't she? Isn't she at Miss Curry's?" said Agnes Lamb.

"No, I think she's at college somewhere. She's eighteen or nineteen," said Mary.

"Still a lot less than half his age," said Agnes. "Well, I didn't know anything about that. Is it something new?"

"I don't know," said Mary. "Jack probably knows."

"I understand it's not new, but it's certainly out in the open now," said Spangler.

"To what extent?" said Agnes Lamb. "Does Dee know?"

"Of course she knows," said Spangler. "But she always *has* looked the other way."

"Well, let's get down to cases. Is it an *affair?*"

"Everybody seems to think so," said Spangler.

"Well, the thing I always want to know is, where do they go? But then where does anyone go? Lots of places, I suppose, or else whenever I come down here I wouldn't always seem to hear of some new pairing off."

"You're so pious, Agnes," said Spangler. "Where did *you* go when you were still married to Jim and seeing Pete?"

"That was ages ago, and I wouldn't tell you anyway. But you can be very sure Stan Wigmore and Kitty Maclyn aren't going there."

"Somebody's house," said Spangler. "Well, that's probably where Wigmore and Kitty go."

"Not your house, Jack?" said Agnes.

"No, not my house. In the first place, I wouldn't be so disloyal to Dee. And in the second place, I'm not doing any favors for Stanley Wigmore if I can help it. I've let my house be used for assignation purposes, but for friends only. Not that I haven't got a pretty good idea whose house Wigmore could borrow."

"Don't look at *me*," said Mary Chorpenning.

"I wasn't thinking of you, dear. I just happened to take that moment to study your pearls. Are those the ones that your aunt paid so much for and they turned color?"

"Yes. They're the real ones. Now worth about five hundred," said Mary.

"And what was it your aunt paid for them?"

"Oh, heavens. I think it was thirty thousand."

"Was it because she was acid?"

"That's what made them change color, but real pearls aren't worth anything anyway," said Mary.

"Let's not change the subject," said Agnes Lamb.

"What does George Maclyn say about all this? Kay—I wouldn't expect her to come up out of her highball glass. But when I used to know George years ago, when he and Kay were first married, no daughter of his would dare have anything to do with a married man. Do you remember, Mary? What was it we used to call him?"

"George? Uh—Father, wasn't it?"

"No, no. It wasn't Father. *The Vicar*. We used to call him The Vicar."

"Oh, you don't have to tell me anything about George," said Spangler. "I went to Allen-Stevenson with him for three years. I used to get him in boxing."

"You boxed?" said Mary Chorpenning.

"We had to, and he was just as nasty-mean-cruel as he could be. If Kay's gassed half the time, I can fully understand why. She's married to a mean, sadistic—"

"Then what's he doing letting his eighteen-year-old daughter play around with someone like Stan Wigmore?" said Agnes Lamb.

"I don't really think they're playing around," said Mary Chorpenning.

"Here we go again," said Spangler.

"Maybe they are, I don't know, but I just don't think so," said Mary.

"Well, of course the whole thing's all news to me, but it just isn't like Stan Wigmore to—and none of these kids have Platonic affairs, so I'm told. I was never sure about my own, but thank heaven they're both married and I *guess* settled down."

"Mary, Mary, watch this," said Spangler, nervously excited. He lowered his voice and spoke to Agnes Lamb. "Coming up the boardwalk. Kitty Maclyn. Now don't just stop talking, for heaven's sake, but watch."

The girl was quite tall, her blond hair worn almost at shoulder length and swinging as she walked. She had on a white blouse, left unbuttoned except over her middle, and her narrow blue pants were a tight fit. Her shoes were flats of leather with thongs between her bare toes. She was carrying a long cigarette in her right hand, which she held at arm's length behind her. She was fearfully self-conscious and arrogantly affected in manner and clothes, and she defied the world to deny that she was beautiful.

"Good Lord, that's Kitty Maclyn?" said Agnes Lamb.

"That's our Kitty," said Spangler.

"I never thought I'd feel sorry for Dee Barlow," said Agnes Lamb.

The girl went to the table at which Wigmore had eaten his hasty lunch. She sat in the very chair he had been sitting in.

"I wish we could hear what they're saying," said Agnes Lamb. "Who are the others?"

"The boy with the khaki pants is Mike Raymond, next to him, Amy Compton. The boy in the blazer is I don't know who, and the other girl is Carmelita Dougherty," said Spangler. "And that ought to make you feel a hundred."

The Maclyn girl and the others exchanged no greetings but immediately began a conversation, in which all but the boy in the blazer participated. The Maclyn girl sat with her legs stretched out under the table and moved her body back and forth in a rocking motion. She smoked her cigarette and looked at the top of the table rather than at her friends while talking. The Raymond boy put his arm around her shoulder, and she reached back and gently removed it and in a continuous motion smoothed her back hair, fondly, sensually. She dinched her cigarette in a glass ash tray and again in a continuous motion picked up the Raymond boy's wrist and squinted at his watch. She got up and left her friends and started back toward the entrance, but as she reached the Spangler table she halted.

"Hello, Mrs. Chorpenning. Hello, Mr. Spangler. Hello, Mrs. Lamb. You don't remember me, but I'm Kitty Maclyn." She put out her hand.

"Of course I remember you, Kitty. How are your mother and father?" said Agnes Lamb.

"Very well, thank you. Are you down for the summer?"

"No, just till the first of August."

"Mummy would love to see you, I'm sure," said the girl. Then a second's awkwardness, and she said: "Well, nice to've seen you again, Mrs. Lamb. Mrs. Chorpenning. Mr. Spangler." She went on her way.

"*She* is *gorgeous*," said Agnes Lamb.

"Isn't she?" said Mary Chorpenning.

"Perfectly lovely," said Agnes Lamb.

"Are you *crying?*" said Spangler.

"Oh—shut—up," said Agnes Lamb.

YOUR FAH NEEFAH NEEFACE

This woman, when she was about nineteen or twenty, had a stunt that she and her brother would play, usually in a railroad station or on a train or in a hotel lobby. I saw them work the stunt under the clock at the Biltmore in the days when that meeting-place was a C-shaped arrangement of benches, and I remember it so well because it was the first time I ever saw the stunt and the first time I ever saw her or her brother. It was more than thirty years ago.

She was sitting there, quite erect, her legs crossed, smoking a cigarette and obviously, like everyone else, waiting to meet someone. She was wearing a beret sort of hat that matched her suit, and it was easy to tell by the way she smoked her cigarette that she had handled many of them in her short life. I remember thinking that I would like to hear her talk; she was so self-possessed and good-humored in her study of the young men and young women who were keeping dates at the clock. The drag she took on her cigarette was a long one; the smoke kept coming from her nostrils long after you thought it was all gone. She was terribly pretty, with a straight little nose and lively light blue eyes.

Presently a young man came up the stairs in no great

hurry. He was wearing a black topcoat with a velvet collar and carrying a derby hat. He was tall, but not outstandingly so, and he had tightly curled blond hair—a 150-pound crew type, he was. He reached the meeting-place, scanned the faces of the people who were seated there, and then turned away to face the stairs. He watched the men and women coming up the stairs, but after a minute or so he turned his head and looked back at the girl, frowned as though puzzled, then again faced the incoming people. He did that several times, and I began to think that this was a young man on a blind date who had not been given a full or accurate description of his girl. She meanwhile was paying no attention to him.

Finally he went directly to the girl, and in a firm voice that everyone under the clock could hear he said, "Are you by any chance Sallie Brown?"

"I am, but what's it to you?" she said.

"Do you know who I am?" he said.

"No."

"You don't recognize me at all?"

"Never saw you in my whole life."

"Yes you did, Sallie. Look carefully," he said.

"I'm sorry, but I'm quite positive I've never seen you before."

"Asbury Park. Think a minute."

"I've been to Asbury Park, but so've a lot of people. Why should I remember you?"

"Sallie. It's Jack. I'm *Jack*."

"Jack? Jack Who? . . . No! My brother! You— you're Jack? Oh, darling, darling!" She stood up and looked at the people near her and said to them, rather helplessly, "This is my brother. My *brother*. I haven't seen him since —oh, darling. Oh, this is so wonderful." She put her arms

(*414*)

around him and kissed him. "Oh, where have you *been?* Where have they been keeping you? Are you all right?"

"I'm all right. What about you?"

"Oh, let's go somewhere. We have so much to talk about." She smiled at all the other young men and women, then took her brother's arm and they went down the stairs and out, leaving all of us with the happy experience to think about and to tell and re-tell. The girl I was meeting arrived ten or fifteen minutes after Sallie and Jack Brown departed, and when we were in the taxi on our way to a cocktail party I related what I had seen. The girl waited until I finished the story and then said, "Was this Sallie Brown blond? About my height? And was her brother a blond too, with curly hair cut short?"

"Exactly," I said. "Do you know them?"

"Sure. The only part of the story that's true is that they are brother and sister. The rest is an act. Her name is Sallie Collins and his name is Johnny Collins. They're from Chicago. They're very good."

"Good? I'll say they're good. They fooled me and everybody else."

"They always do. People cry, and sometimes they clap as if they were at the theater. Sallie and Johnny Collins, from Chicago. Did you ever hear of the Spitbacks?"

"No. Spitbacks?"

"It's a sort of a club in Chicago. You have to be kicked out of school to be a Spitback, and Johnny's been kicked out of at least two."

"And what about her?"

"She's eligible. She was two years behind me at Farmington."

"What was she kicked out for?"

"Oh, I don't know. Smoking, I think. She wasn't there

(415)

very long. Now she's going to school in Greenwich, I think. Johnny's a runner downtown."

"What other tricks do they do?"

"Whatever comes into their heads, but they're famous for the long-lost-brother-and-sister one. They have it down pat. Did she look at the other people as much as to say, 'I can't believe it, it's like a dream'?"

"Yes."

"They can't do it as much as they used to. All their friends know about it and they've told so many people. Of course it annoys some people."

"What other *kind* of thing do they do?"

"Oh—I don't know. Nothing mean. Not practical jokes, if that's what you're thinking of."

"I'd like to meet her sometime. And him. They seem like fun," I said.

I never did meet Johnny. He was drowned somewhere in Northern Michigan a year or so after I was a member of their audience at the Biltmore, and when I finally met Sallie she was married and living in New Canaan; about thirty years old, still very pretty; but instinctively I refrained from immediately recalling to her the once famous long-lost-brother stunt. I do not mean to say that she seemed to be mourning Johnny after ten years. But fun was not a word that came quickly to mind when I was introduced to her. If I had never seen her before or known about her stunts I would have said that *her* idea of fun would be the winning of the Connecticut State Women's Golf Championship. Women who like golf and play it well do seem to move more deliberately than, for instance, women who play good tennis, and my guess that golf was her game was hardly brilliant, since I knew that her husband was a 4-handicap player.

"Where are you staying?" she said, at dinner.

"At the Randalls'."

"Oh, do you sail?"

"No, Tom and I grew up together in Pennsylvania."

"Well, you're going to have a lot of time to yourself this weekend, aren't you? Tom and Rebecca will be at Rye, won't they?"

"I don't mind," I said. "I brought along some work, and Rebecca's the kind of hostess that leaves you to your own devices."

"Work? What kind of work?"

"Textiles."

"Well, that must be a very profitable business these days, isn't it? Isn't the Army ordering millions of uniforms?"

"I don't know."

"You're not in that kind of textiles?"

"Yes, I am. But I'm not allowed to answer any questions about the Army."

"I would like to be a spy."

"You'd make a good one," I said.

"Do you think so? What makes you think I would?"

"Because the first time I ever saw you . . ." I then had been in her company for more than an hour, and felt better about recalling the incident at the Biltmore.

"How nice of you to remember that," she said, and smiled. "I wonder why you did?"

"Well, you were very pretty. Still are. But the whole performance was so expert. Professional. You could probably be a very good spy."

"No. That was all Johnny. All those things we used to do, Johnny thought them up. He was the brains of the team. I was the foil. Like the girl in tights that magicians always have. Anybody could have done it with Johnny masterminding . . . Would you like to come here for lunch Sunday? I happen to know that Rebecca's without a cook, so you're going to have to go to the club, otherwise. Unless of course you have another invitation."

I said I would love to come to lunch Sunday, and she thereupon engaged in conversation with the gentleman on her left. I was surprised to find on Sunday that she and I were lunching alone. We had cold soup, then were served crab flakes and some vegetables, and when the maid was gone Sallie took a piece of paper from the pocket of her blouse. "This is the clock at the Biltmore that day. This is where I was sitting. Here is where you were sitting. If I'm not mistaken, you were wearing a grey suit and you sat with your overcoat folded over your lap. You needed a haircut."

"By God, you're absolutely right."

"You had a watch on a chain, and you kept taking it out of your pocket, and putting it back."

"I don't remember that, but probably. The girl I was meeting was pretty late. Incidentally, went to Farmington with you. Laura Pratt."

"Oh, goodness. Laura. If she'd been on time you never would have seen the long-lost-brother-and-sister act. She hated me at Farmington, but I see her once in a while now. She lives in Litchfield, as I suppose you know. But have I convinced you that I remembered you as well as you remembered me?"

"It's the greatest compliment I ever had in my life."

"No. You were good-looking and still are, but what I chiefly remembered was that I was hoping you'd try to pick me up. Then I was just a little bit annoyed that you didn't try. God, that was forever ago, wasn't it?"

"Just about," I said. "How come you didn't say anything at dinner the other night?"

"I'm not sure. Selfish, I guess. That was *my* evening. I wanted you to do all the remembering, and I guess I wanted to hear you talk about Johnny."

"He drowned," I said. "In Michigan."

"Yes, but *I* didn't tell you that. How did you know?"

"I saw it in the paper at the time."

"Rebecca told me you were getting a divorce. Does that upset you? Not her telling me, but breaking up with your wife."

"It isn't the pleasantest experience in the world," I said.

"I suppose not. It never is. I was married before I married my present husband, you know."

"No, I didn't know."

"It lasted a year. He was Johnny's best friend, but other than that we had nothing in common. Not that a married couple have to have too much in common, but they ought to have something else besides loving the same person, in this case my brother. Hugh, my first husband, was what Johnny used to call one of his stooges, just like me. But somehow it isn't very attractive for a *man* to be another man's stooge. It's all right for a sister to be a stooge, but not another man, and almost the minute Johnny died I suddenly realized that without Johnny, Hugh was nothing. As a threesome we had a lot of fun together, really a lot of fun. And with Hugh I could have sex. I don't think there was any of that in my feeling for Johnny, although there may have been. If there was, I certainly managed to keep it under control and never even thought about it. I didn't know much about those things, but once or twice I vaguely suspected that if either of us had any of that feeling for Johnny, it was Hugh. But I'm sure he didn't know it either."

"So you divorced Hugh and married Tatnall."

(*419*)

"Divorced Hugh and married Bill Tatnall. All because you were afraid to pick me up and ditch Laura Pratt."

"But I could have become one of Johnny's stooges, too," I said. "I probably would have."

"No. Johnny's stooges all had to be people he'd known all his life, like me or Hugh, or Jim Danzig."

"Who is Jim Danzig?"

"Jim Danzig was the boy in the canoe with Johnny when it overturned. I don't like to talk about poor Jim. He blamed himself for the accident and he's become a hopeless alcoholic, at thirty-two, mind you."

"Why did he blame himself? Did he have any reason to?"

"Well—he was in the canoe, and they were both a little tight. It was at night and they'd been to a party at the Danzigs' cabin and decided to row across the lake to our cabin, instead of driving eight or nine miles. A mile across the lake, eight and a half miles by car. One of those crazy ideas you get when you're tight. Johnny would have been home in fifteen minutes by car, but they started out in the canoe, heading for the lights on our landing. I guess there was some kind of horseplay and the canoe overturned, and Jim couldn't find Johnny. He kept calling him but he didn't get any answer, and he couldn't right the canoe, although Jim was almost as good a boatman as Johnny—when sober. But they'd had an awful lot to drink, and it was pitch dark. No moon. And finally Jim floated and swam ashore and then for a while was lost in the woods. It was after Labor Day and most of the cabins were boarded up for the winter, and Jim in his bare feet, all cut and bleeding by the time he got to the Danzigs' cabin, and a little out of his head in addition to all he'd had to drink. I think they had to dynamite to recover Johnny's body. I wasn't there and I'm glad I wasn't.

From the reports it must have been pretty horrible, and even now I'd rather not think about it."

"Then don't," I said.

"No, let's change the subject," she said.

"All right. Then you married Tatnall."

"Married Bill Tatnall a year and a half after Hugh and I were divorced. Two children. Betty, and Johnny, ages six and four. You haven't mentioned any children. Did you have any?"

"No."

"Children hold so many marriages together," she said.

"Yours?"

"Of course mine. I wouldn't have said that otherwise, would I? How often do you see the Randalls?"

"Oh, maybe once or twice a year."

"Did they know you were coming here for lunch?"

"No," I said. "They left very early this morning, before I was up."

"That explains it, why you don't know about Bill and me. Well, when you tell them you were here today, don't be surprised if they give you that tut-tut look. Naughty-naughty. Bill and I raise a lot of eyebrows hereabouts. Next year it'll be some other couple, but at the moment it's Bill and I."

"Who's the transgressor? You, or your husband?"

"It's the marriage, more so than Bill or I individually. In a community like this, or maybe any suburban or small-town community, they don't seem to mind adultery if they can blame one person or the other. The husband or the wife has to be the guilty party, but not both."

"I don't agree with you," I said. "I think that when a marriage is in trouble people take sides, one side or the other, and they mind a great deal."

"Yes, they want the marriage to break up and they want to be able to blame one or the other. But when the marriage doesn't break up, when people can't fix the blame on one person, they're deprived of their scandal. They feel cheated out of something, and they're outraged, horrified, that people like Bill and I go on living together. They really hate me for putting up with Bill's chasing, and they hate Bill for letting me get away with whatever I get away with. Bill and I ought to be in the divorce courts, fighting like cats and dogs. Custody fights, fights about alimony."

"But you and your husband have what is commonly called an arrangement?" I said.

"It would seem that way, although actually we haven't. At least not a spoken one. You see, we don't even care that much about each other. He just goes his way, and I go mine."

"You mean to say you never had a discussion about it? The first time he found out you were unfaithful to him, or he was unfaithful to you? You didn't have any discussion at all?"

"Why is that so incredible?" she said. "Let's have our coffee out on the porch."

I followed her out to the flagstone terrace and its iron-and-glass furniture. She poured the coffee and resumed speaking. "I guessed that Bill had another girl. It wasn't hard to guess. He left me severely alone. Then I guessed he had another, and since I hadn't made a fuss about the first one I certainly wasn't going to make a fuss about the second. Or the third."

"Then I gather you began to have gentlemen friends of your own."

"I did. And I guess Bill thought I'd been so nice about his peccadillos that he decided to be just as nice about mine."

"But without any discussion. You simply tacitly agreed not to live together as man and wife?"

"You're trying to make me say what you want me to say, that somehow we did have a discussion, a quarrel, a fight ending in an arrangement. Well, I won't say it."

"Then there's something a lot deeper that I guess I'd better not go into."

"I won't deny that, not for a minute."

"Was it sexual incompatibility?"

"You can call it that. But that isn't as deep as you seem to think it was. A lot of men and women, husbands and wives, are sexually incompatible. This was deeper, and worse. Worse because Bill is a yellow coward. He never dared come out and say what he was thinking."

"Which was?"

"He got angry with me one time and said that my brother Johnny'd been a sinister influence. That's as much as he'd actually say. That Johnny'd been a sinister influence. He didn't dare accuse me—and Johnny—of what he really meant. Why didn't he dare? Because he didn't want to admit that his wife had been guilty of incest. It wasn't really so much that incest was bad as that it had happened to his own wife. Someone, one of Bill's lady friends, had planted that little idea in his thick skull, and he believed it. Now he fully believes it, but I don't care."

"A question that naturally comes to my mind," I said, "is why are you telling me all this?"

"Because you saw us together without knowing us. You saw Johnny and me doing the long-lost-brother act. How did we seem to you?"

"I thought you were genuine. I fell for it."

"But then Laura Pratt told you it was an act. What did you think then?"

"I thought you were charming. Fun."

(423)

"That's what I hoped you thought. That's what *we* thought we were, Johnny and I. We thought we were absolutely charming—and fun. Maybe we weren't charming, but we *were* fun. And that's all we were. And now people have ruined that for us. For me, at least. Johnny never knew people thought he had a sinister influence over me. Or me over him, for that matter. But aren't people darling? Aren't they lovely? They've managed to ruin all the fun Johnny and I had together all those years. Just think, I was married twice and had two children before I began to grow up. I didn't really start to grow up till my own husband made me realize what people had been thinking, *and* saying, about Johnny and me. If that's growing up, you can have it."

"Not everybody thought that about you and Johnny."

"It's enough that anybody did. And it's foolish to think that only one or two thought it," she said. "We did so many things for fun, Johnny and I. Harmless jokes that hurt nobody and that we thought were uproariously funny. Some of them I don't ever think of any more because of the interpretation people put on them . . . We had one that was the opposite of the long-lost-brother. The newlyweds. Did you ever hear of our newlyweds?"

"No," I said.

"It came about by accident. We were driving East and had to spend the night in some little town in Pennsylvania. The car broke down and we went to the local hotel and when we went to register the clerk just took it for granted that we were husband and wife. Johnny caught on right away and he whispered to the clerk, loud enough for me to hear, that we were newlyweds but that I was shy and wanted separate rooms. So we got our separate rooms, and you should have seen the hotel people stare at us that night in the dining-room and the next morning at breakfast. We laughed for a whole day about that and then we used to do the same trick every time we had to drive anywhere overnight. Didn't hurt anybody."

"What else did you do?"

"Oh, lots of things. And not only tricks. We both adored Fred and Adele Astaire, and we copied their dancing. Not as good, of course, but everybody always guessed who we were imitating. We won a couple of prizes at parties. Johnny was really quite good. 'I lahv, yourfah, neeface. Your fah, neefah, neeface.' " She suddenly began to cry and I sat still.

That was twenty years ago. I don't believe that anything that happened to her since then made much difference to Sallie, but even if it did, that's the way I remember her and always will.